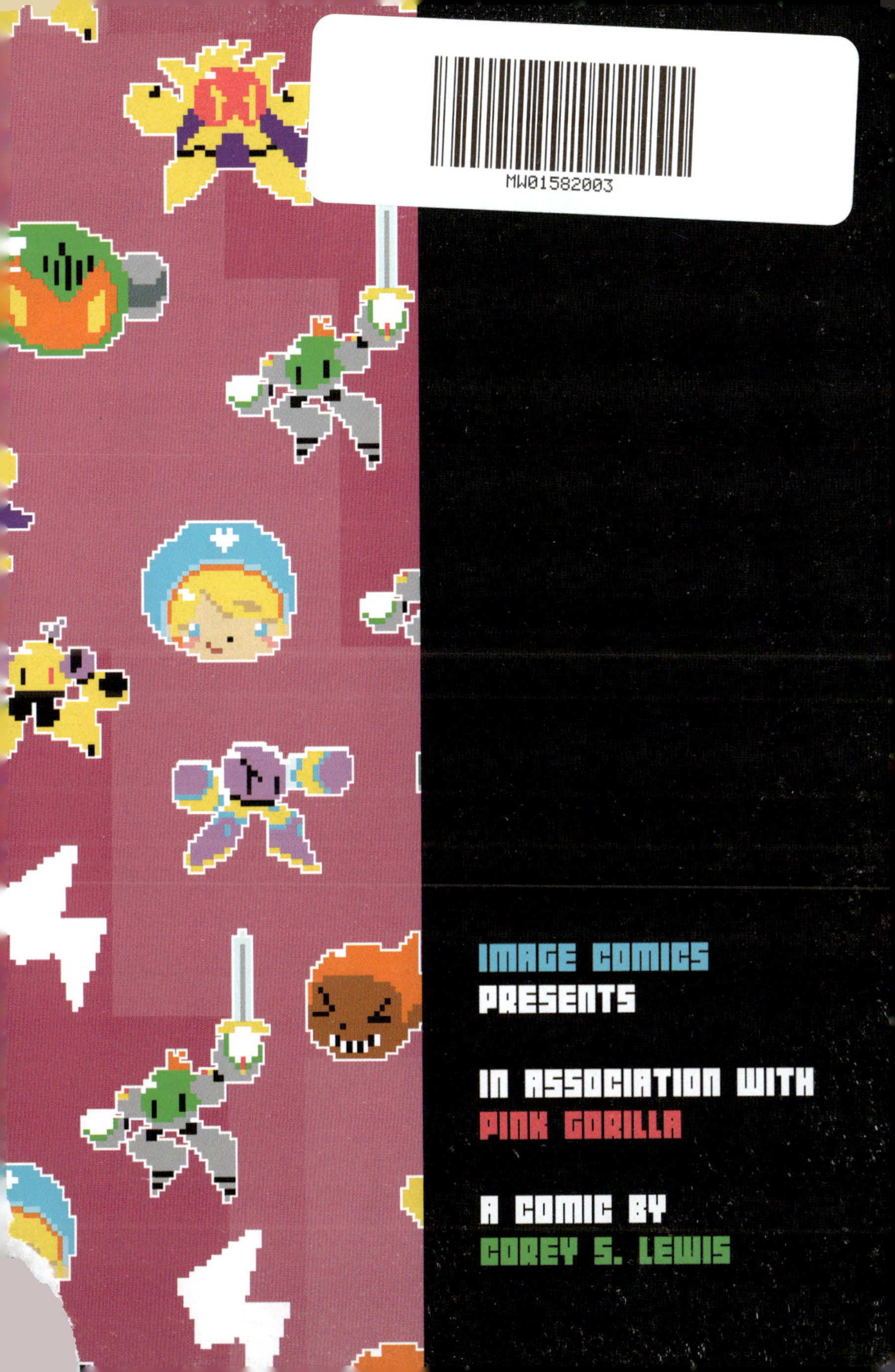

IMAGE COMICS
PRESENTS

IN ASSOCIATION WITH
PINK GORILLA

A COMIC BY
COREY S. LEWIS

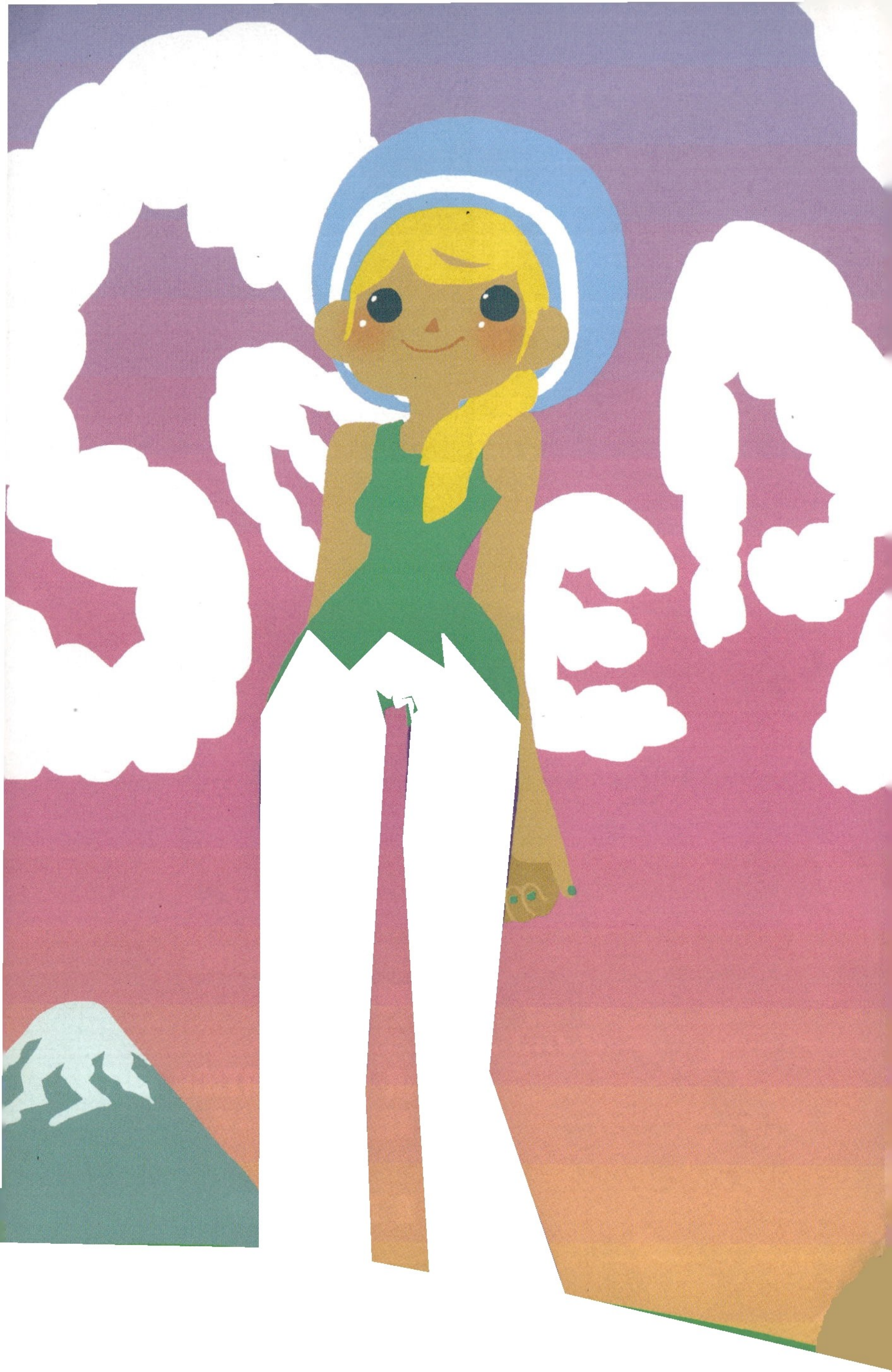

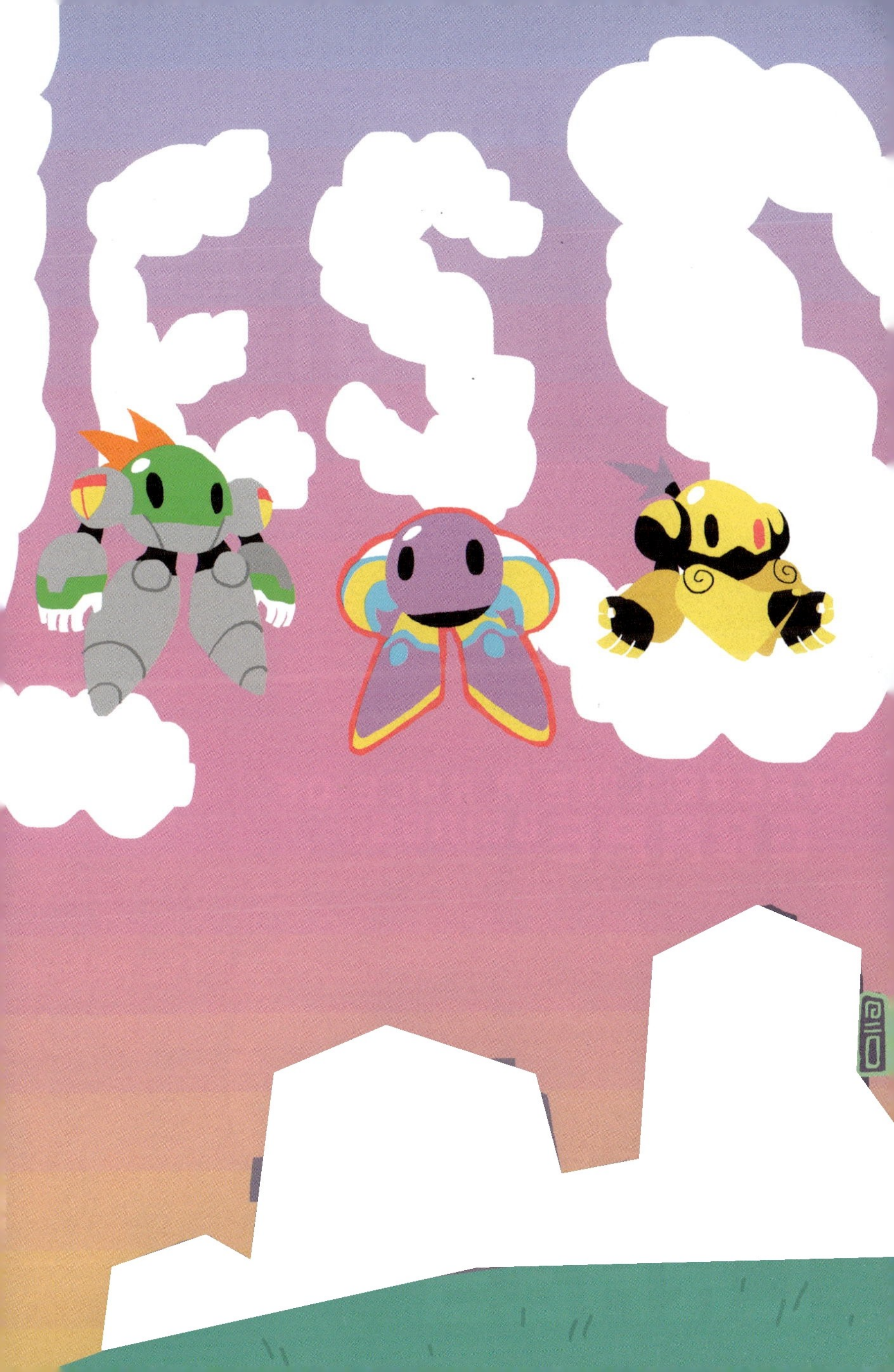

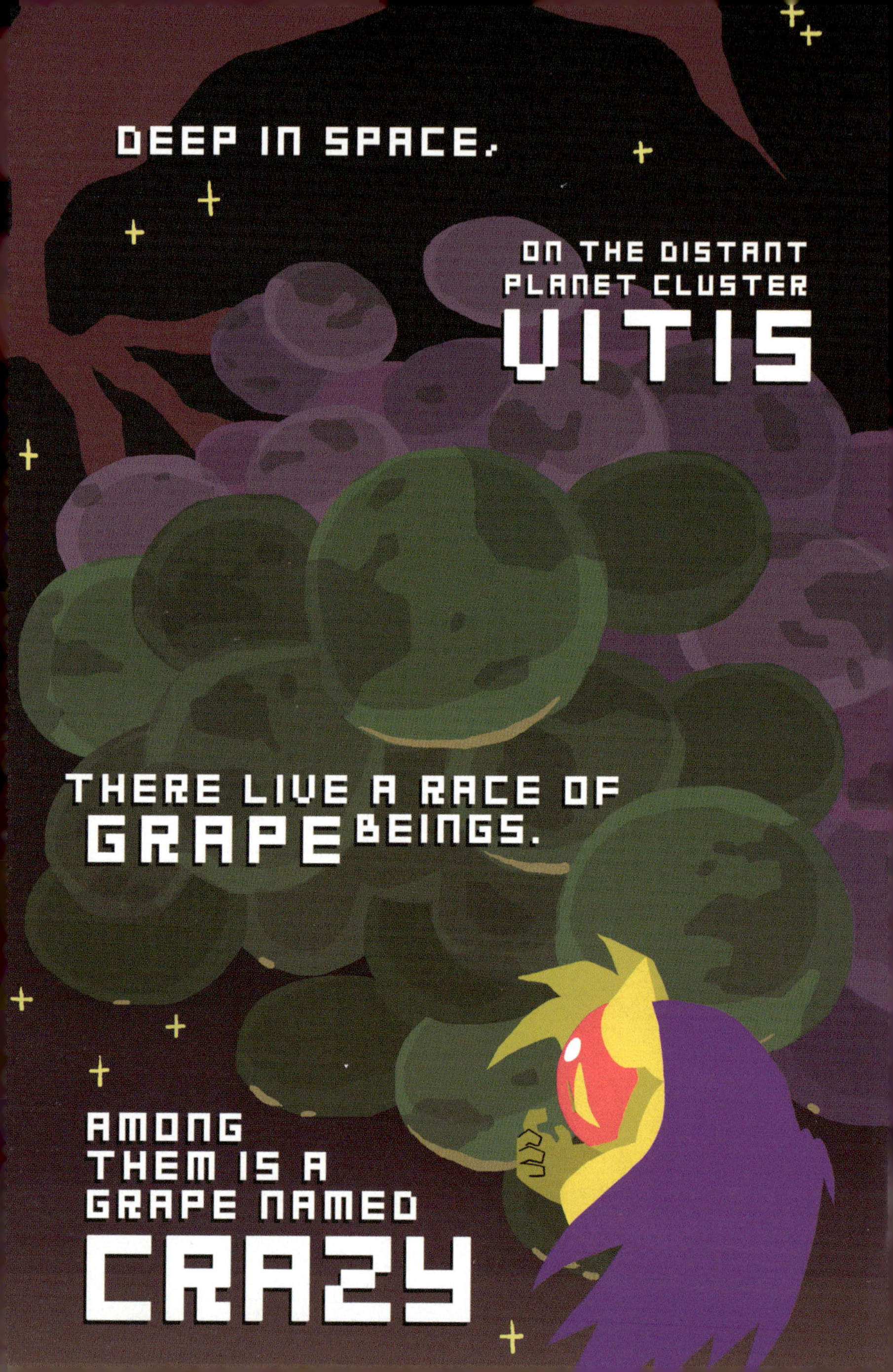
DEEP IN SPACE,
ON THE DISTANT PLANET CLUSTER
VITIS
THERE LIVE A RACE OF
GRAPE BEINGS.
AMONG THEM IS A GRAPE NAMED
CRAZY

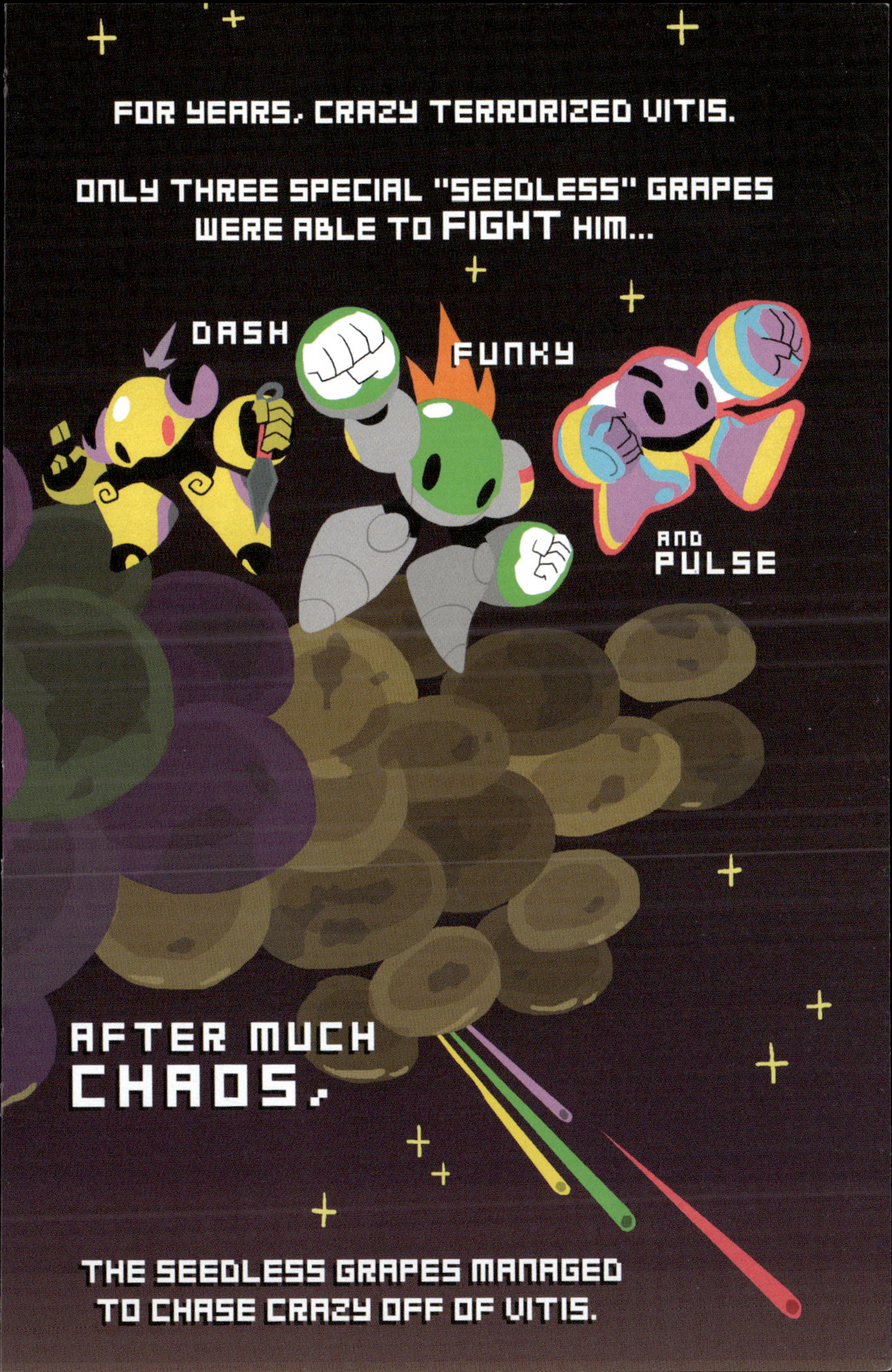
FOR YEARS, CRAZY TERRORIZED VITIS.
ONLY THREE SPECIAL "SEEDLESS" GRAPES WERE ABLE TO FIGHT HIM...
DASH
FUNKY
AND PULSE
AFTER MUCH CHAOS,
THE SEEDLESS GRAPES MANAGED TO CHASE CRAZY OFF OF VITIS.

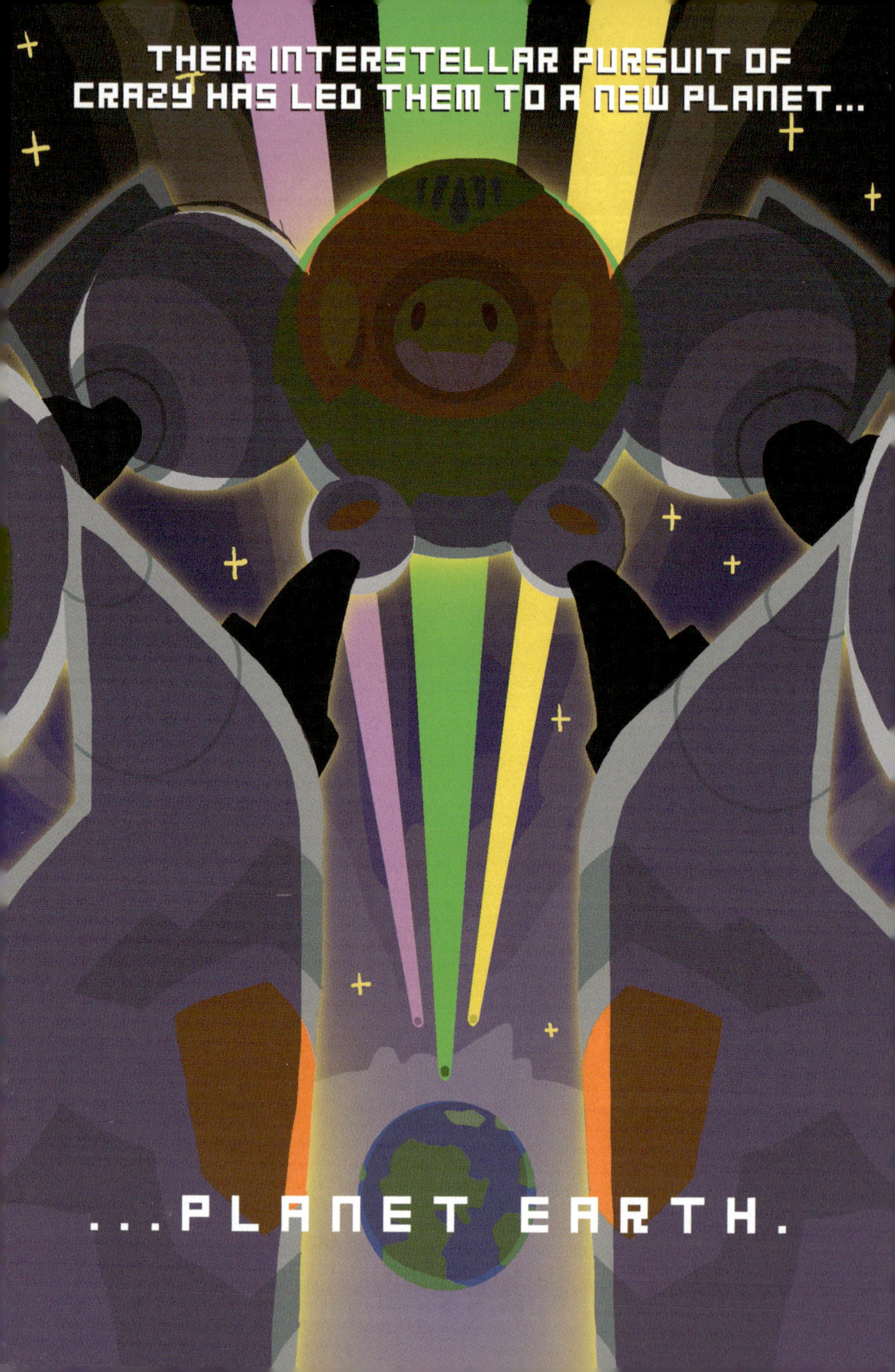
THEIR INTERSTELLAR PURSUIT OF CRAZY HAS LED THEM TO A NEW PLANET...
...PLANET EARTH.

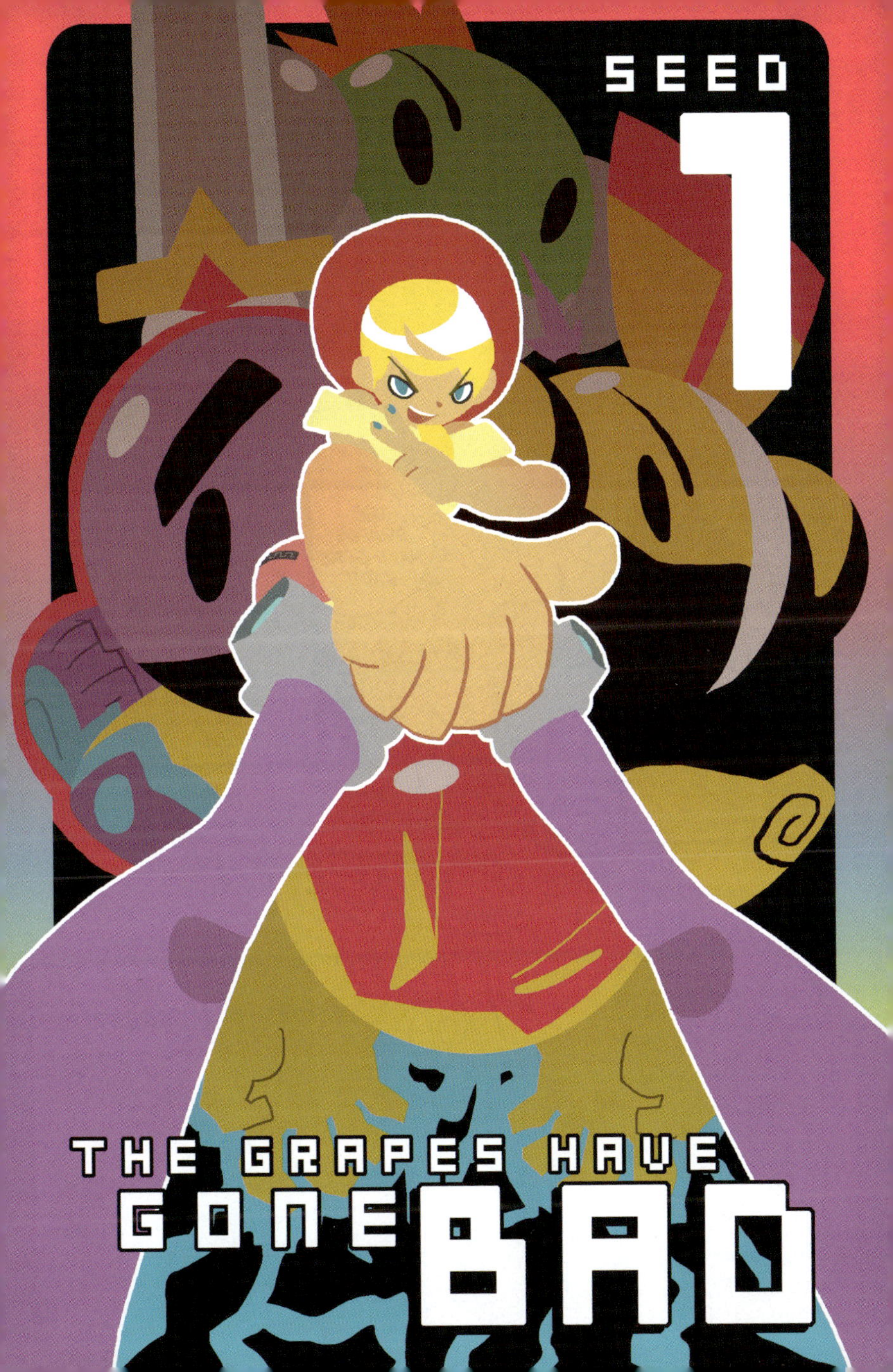
SEED
1
THE GRAPES HAVE
GONE BAD

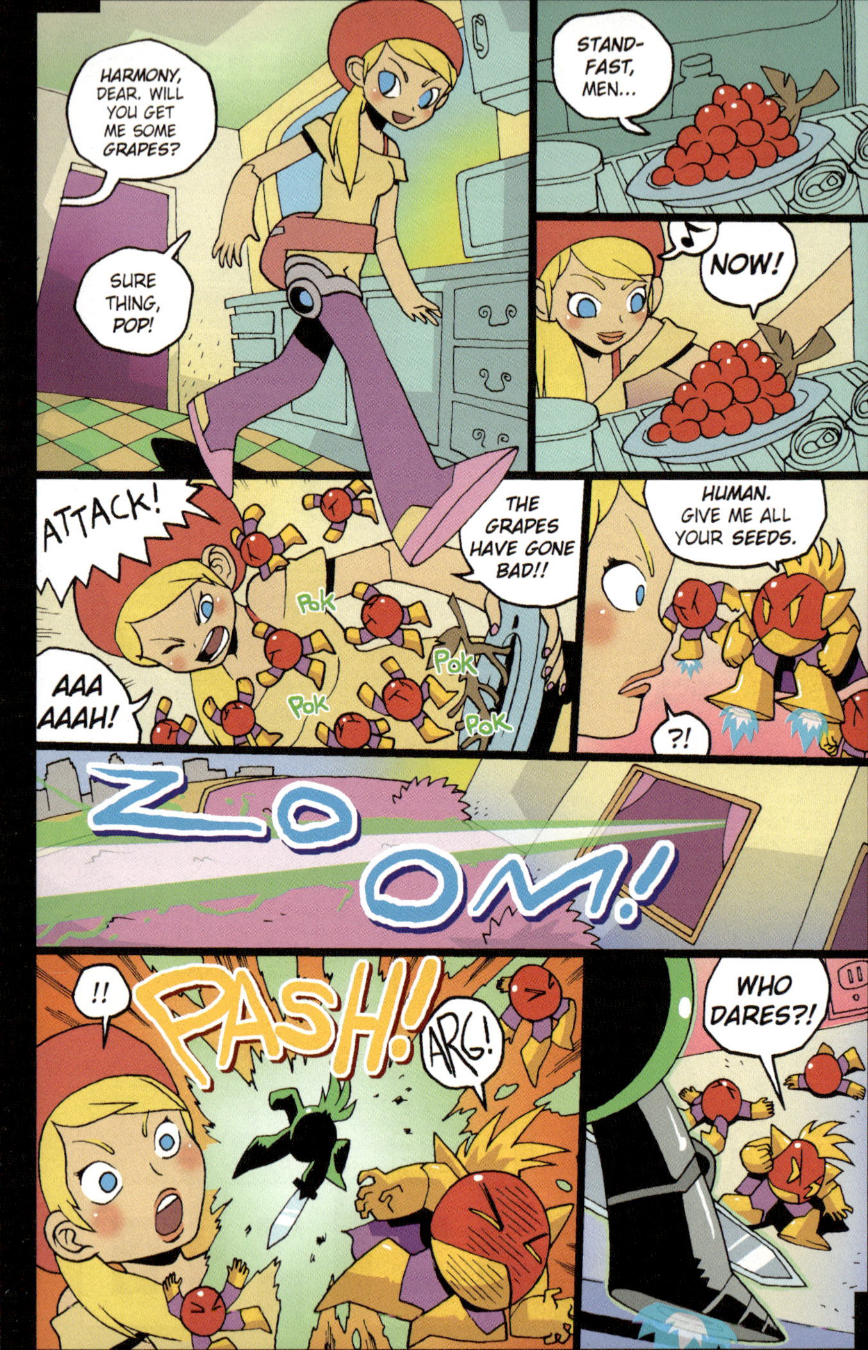
HARMONY, DEAR. WILL YOU GET ME SOME GRAPES?
SURE THING, POP!
STAND-FAST, MEN...
NOW!
ATTACK!
AAA AAAH!
POK
POK
POK
POK
THE GRAPES HAVE GONE BAD!!
HUMAN. GIVE ME ALL YOUR SEEDS.
?!
ZOOM!
!!
PASH!
ARG!
WHO DARES?!

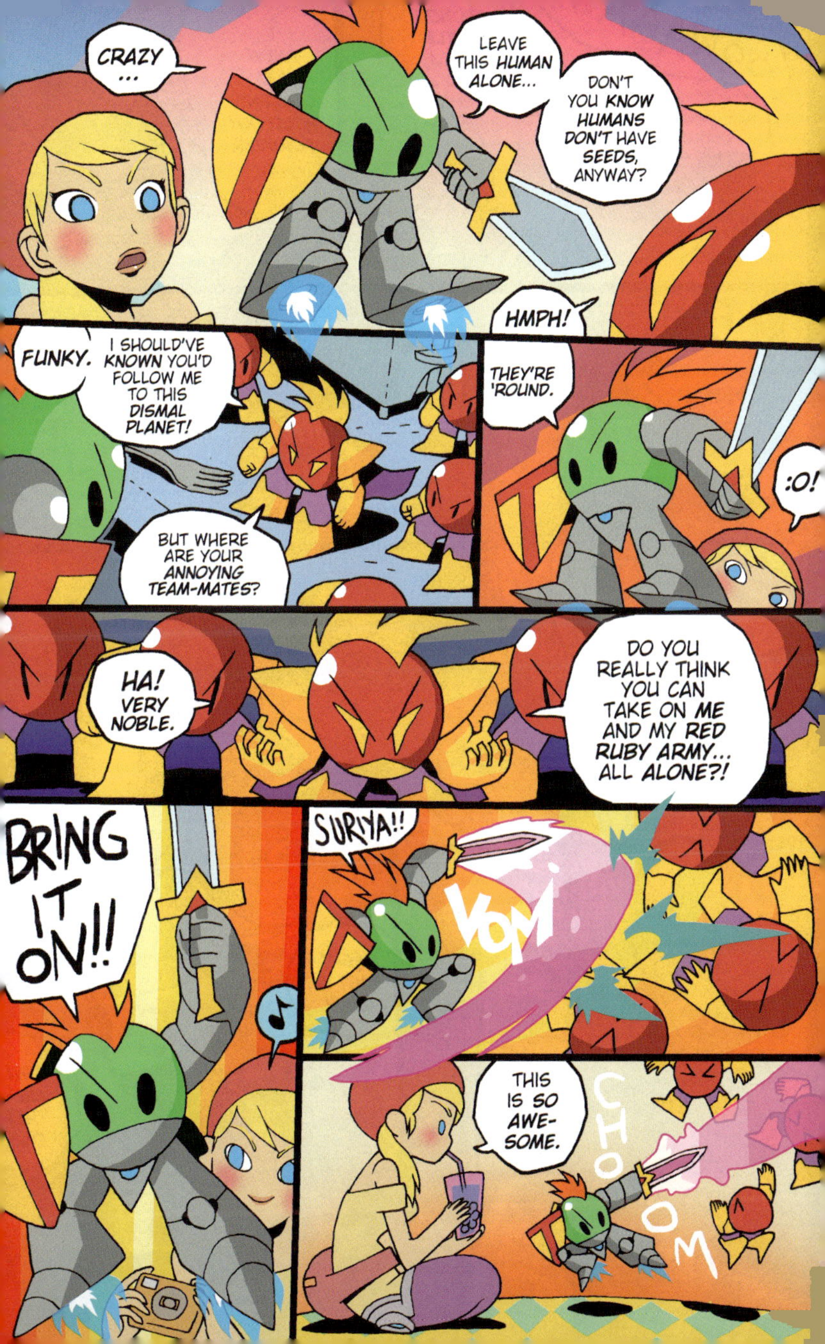
CRAZY ...
LEAVE THIS HUMAN ALONE...
DON'T YOU KNOW HUMANS DON'T HAVE SEEDS, ANYWAY?
HMPH!
FUNKY.
I SHOULD'VE KNOWN YOU'D FOLLOW ME TO THIS DISMAL PLANET!
BUT WHERE ARE YOUR ANNOYING TEAM-MATES?
THEY'RE 'ROUND.
:O!
HA! VERY NOBLE.
DO YOU REALLY THINK YOU CAN TAKE ON ME AND MY RED RUBY ARMY... ALL ALONE?!
BRING IT ON!!
SURIYA!!
VOM
THIS IS SO AWE-SOME.
CHOOM

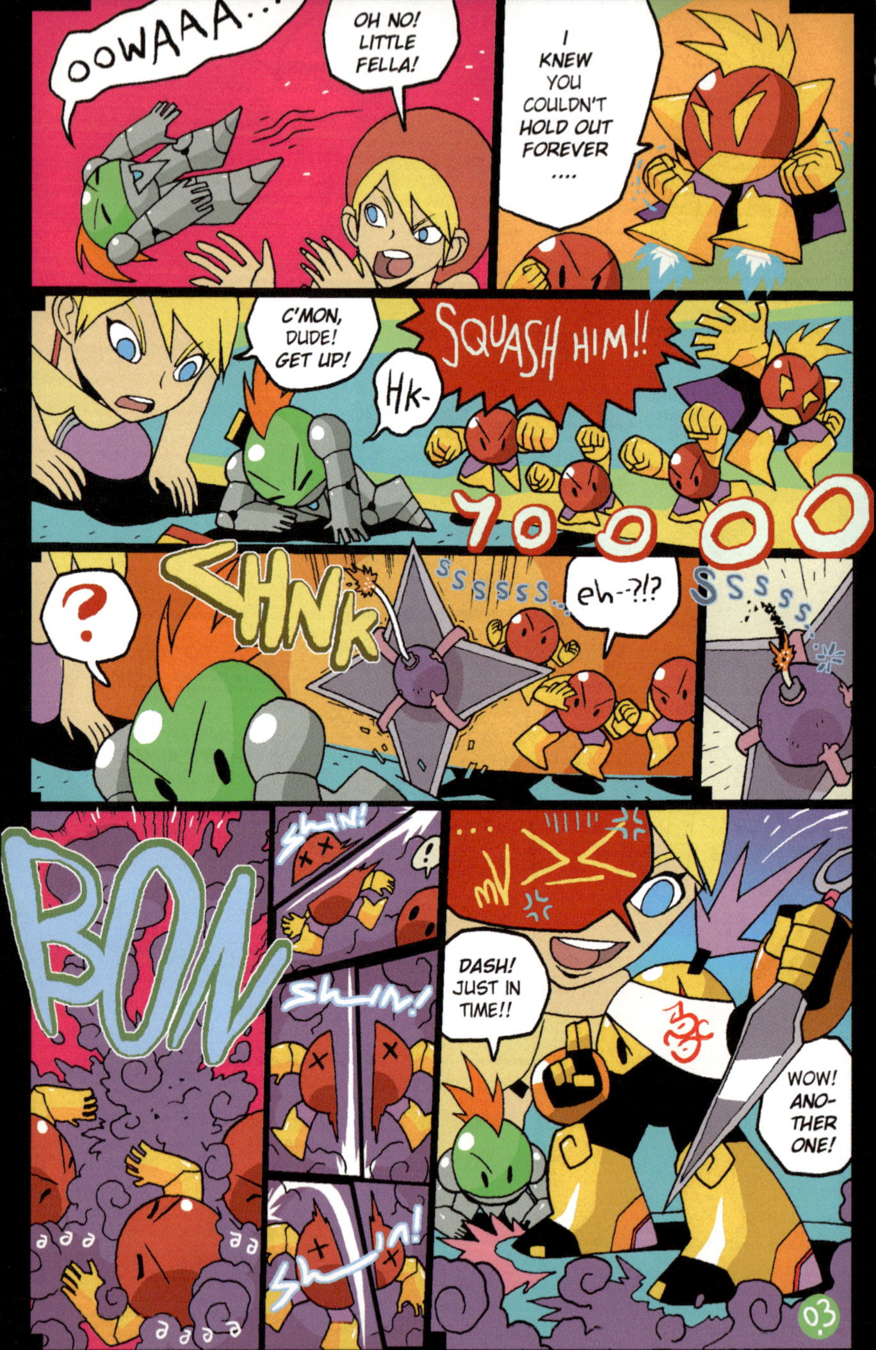
OOWAAA...
OH NO! LITTLE FELLA!
I KNEW YOU COULDN'T HOLD OUT FOREVER ....
C'MON, DUDE! GET UP!
Hk-
SQUASH HIM!!
?
CHNK
SSSSSS...
eh--?!?
SSSSS..
BON
SHIN!
SHIN!
SHIN!
DASH! JUST IN TIME!!
WOW! ANO-THER ONE!

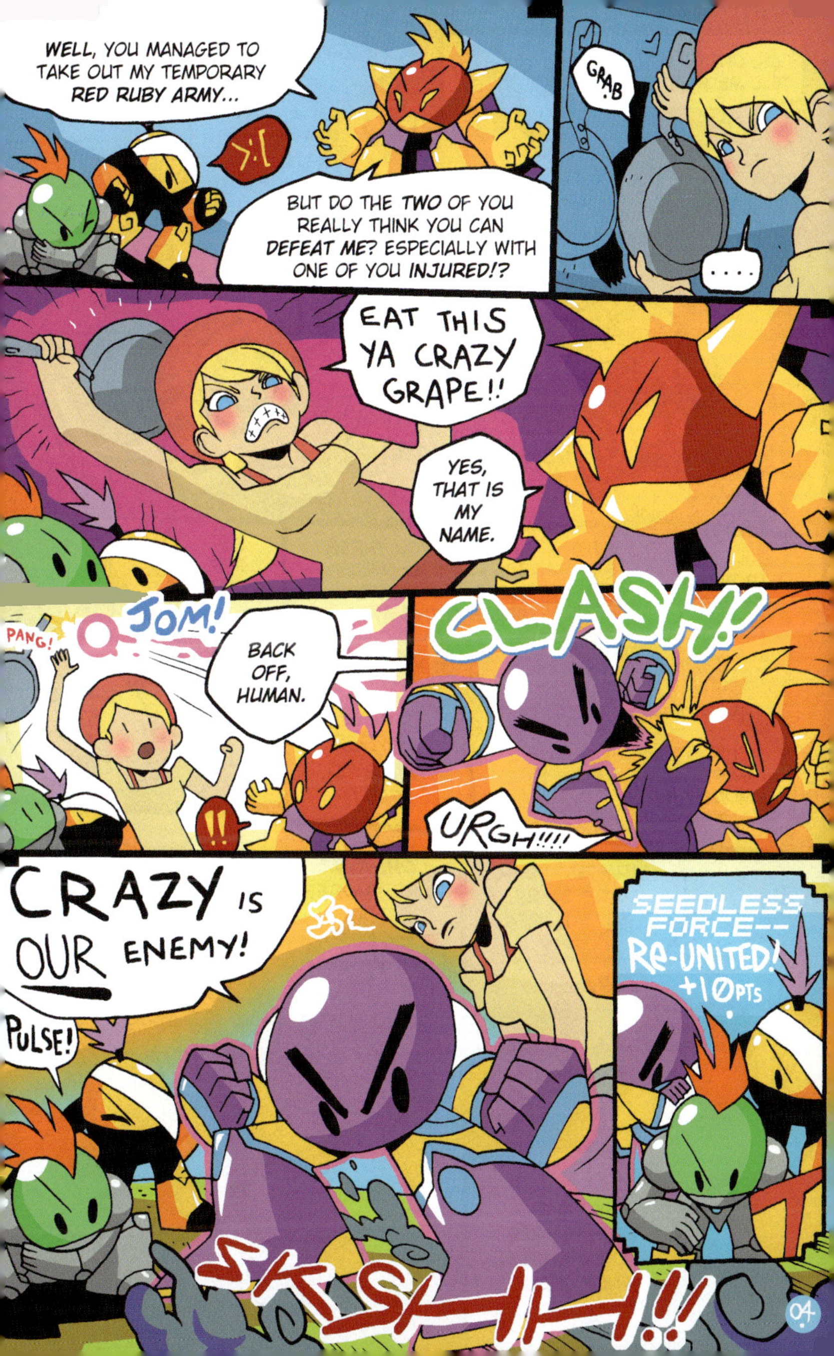
WELL, YOU MANAGED TO TAKE OUT MY TEMPORARY RED RUBY ARMY...
>:[
BUT DO THE TWO OF YOU REALLY THINK YOU CAN DEFEAT ME? ESPECIALLY WITH ONE OF YOU INJURED!?
GRAB
....
EAT THIS YA CRAZY GRAPE!!
YES, THAT IS MY NAME.
PANG!
JOM!
BACK OFF, HUMAN.
!!
CLASH!
URGH!!!!
CRAZY IS OUR ENEMY!
PULSE!
SEEDLESS FORCE-- RE-UNITED! +10PTS
SKSHH!!

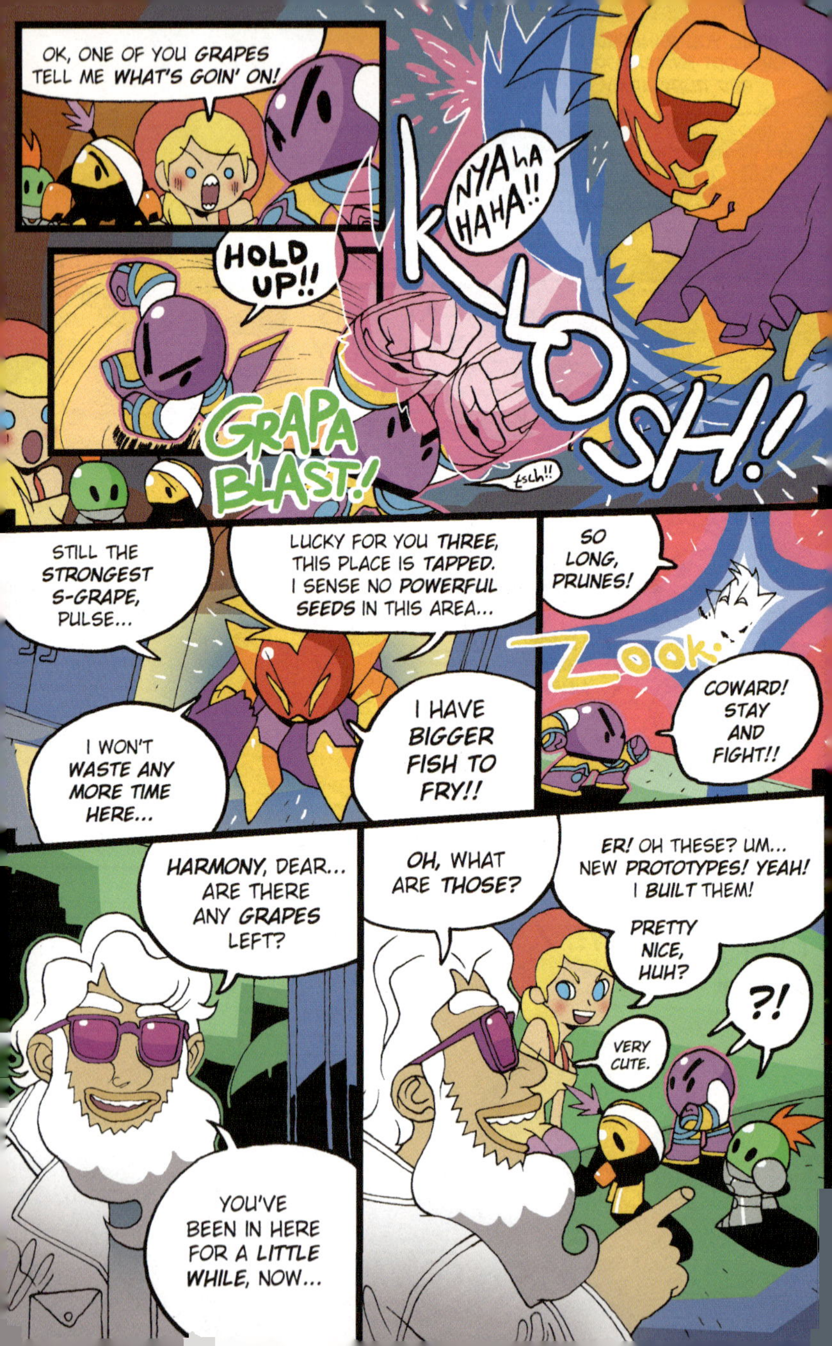
OK, ONE OF YOU GRAPES TELL ME WHAT'S GOIN' ON!
KLOOSH!
NYAHAHAHA!!
HOLD UP!!
GRAPA BLAST!
tsch!!
STILL THE STRONGEST S-GRAPE, PULSE...
LUCKY FOR YOU THREE, THIS PLACE IS TAPPED. I SENSE NO POWERFUL SEEDS IN THIS AREA...
I WON'T WASTE ANY MORE TIME HERE...
I HAVE BIGGER FISH TO FRY!!
SO LONG, PRUNES!
ZOOK
COWARD! STAY AND FIGHT!!
HARMONY, DEAR... ARE THERE ANY GRAPES LEFT?
YOU'VE BEEN IN HERE FOR A LITTLE WHILE, NOW...
OH, WHAT ARE THOSE?
ER! OH THESE? UM... NEW PROTOTYPES! YEAH! I BUILT THEM!
PRETTY NICE, HUH?
VERY CUTE.
?!

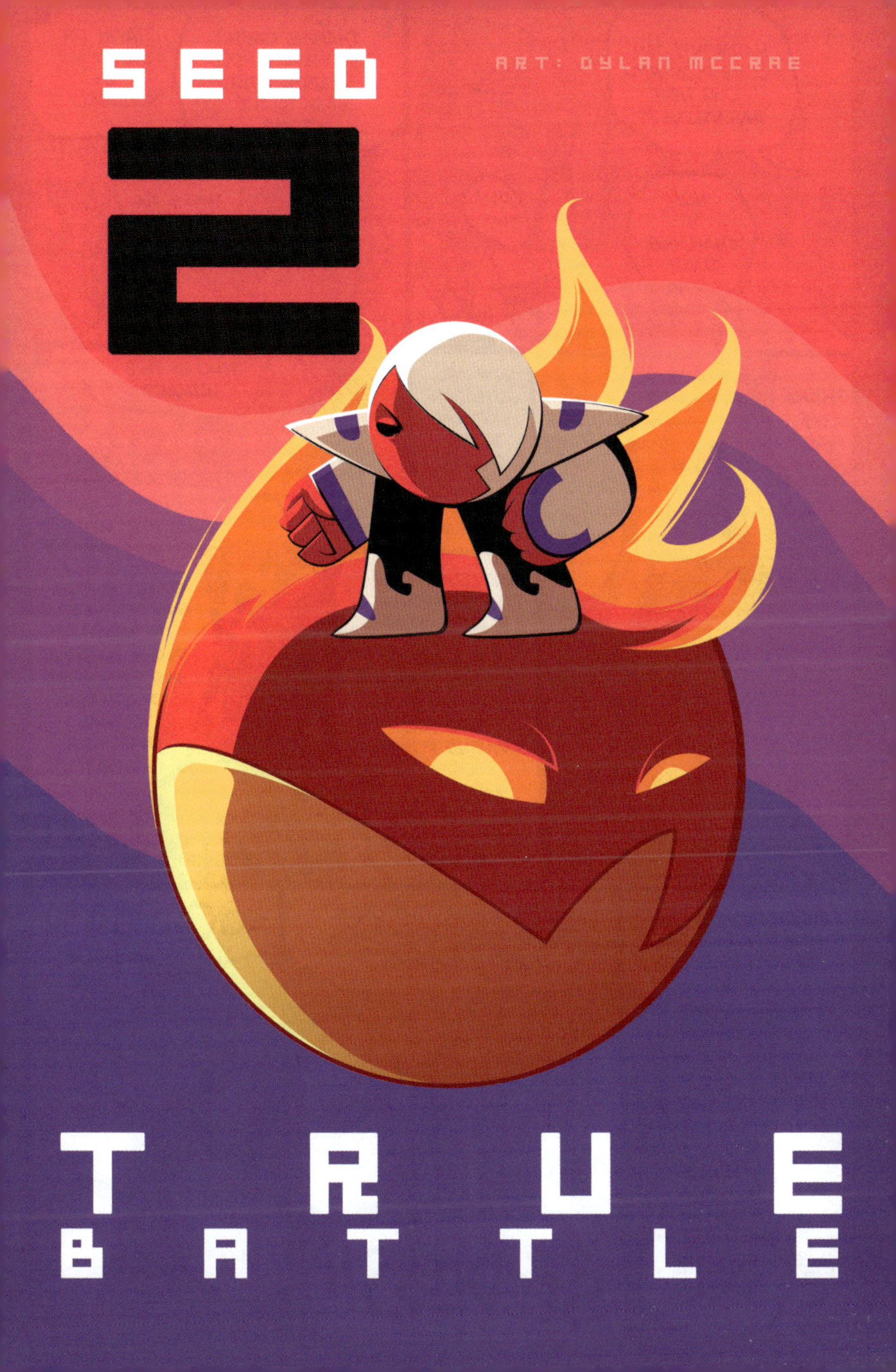
SEED
ART: DYLAN MCCRAE
2
TRUE
BATTLE

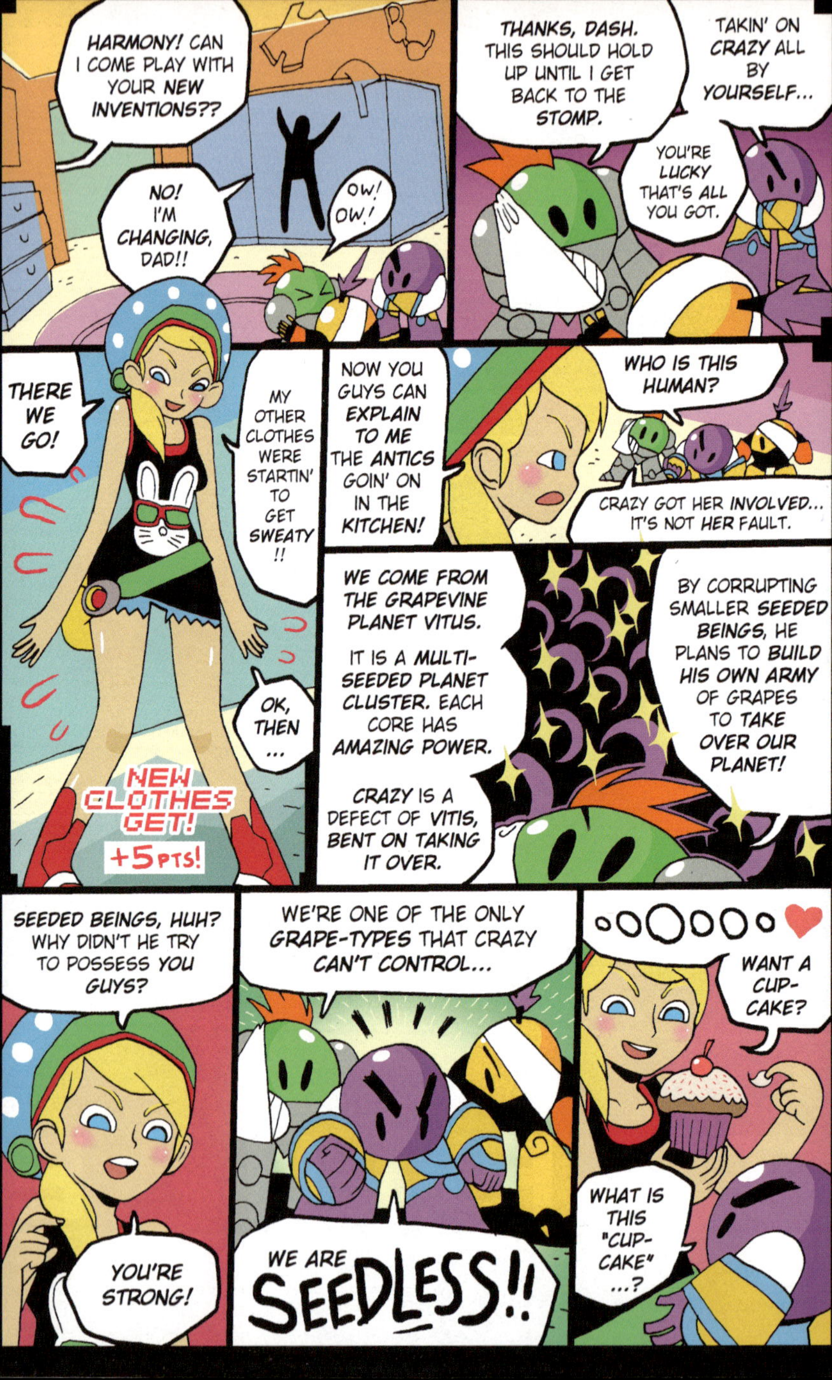
HARMONY! CAN I COME PLAY WITH YOUR NEW INVENTIONS??
NO! I'M CHANGING, DAD!!
OW! OW!
THANKS, DASH. THIS SHOULD HOLD UP UNTIL I GET BACK TO THE STOMP.
TAKIN' ON CRAZY ALL BY YOURSELF...
YOU'RE LUCKY THAT'S ALL YOU GOT.
THERE WE GO!
MY OTHER CLOTHES WERE STARTIN' TO GET SWEATY !!
OK, THEN ...
NEW CLOTHES GET!
+5 PTS!
NOW YOU GUYS CAN EXPLAIN TO ME THE ANTICS GOIN' ON IN THE KITCHEN!
WHO IS THIS HUMAN?
CRAZY GOT HER INVOLVED... IT'S NOT HER FAULT.
WE COME FROM THE GRAPEVINE PLANET VITUS.
IT IS A MULTI-SEEDED PLANET CLUSTER. EACH CORE HAS AMAZING POWER.
CRAZY IS A DEFECT OF VITIS, BENT ON TAKING IT OVER.
BY CORRUPTING SMALLER SEEDED BEINGS, HE PLANS TO BUILD HIS OWN ARMY OF GRAPES TO TAKE OVER OUR PLANET!
SEEDED BEINGS, HUH? WHY DIDN'T HE TRY TO POSSESS YOU GUYS?
YOU'RE STRONG!
WE'RE ONE OF THE ONLY GRAPE-TYPES THAT CRAZY CAN'T CONTROL...
WE ARE SEEDLESS!!
WANT A CUP-CAKE?
WHAT IS THIS "CUP-CAKE" ...?

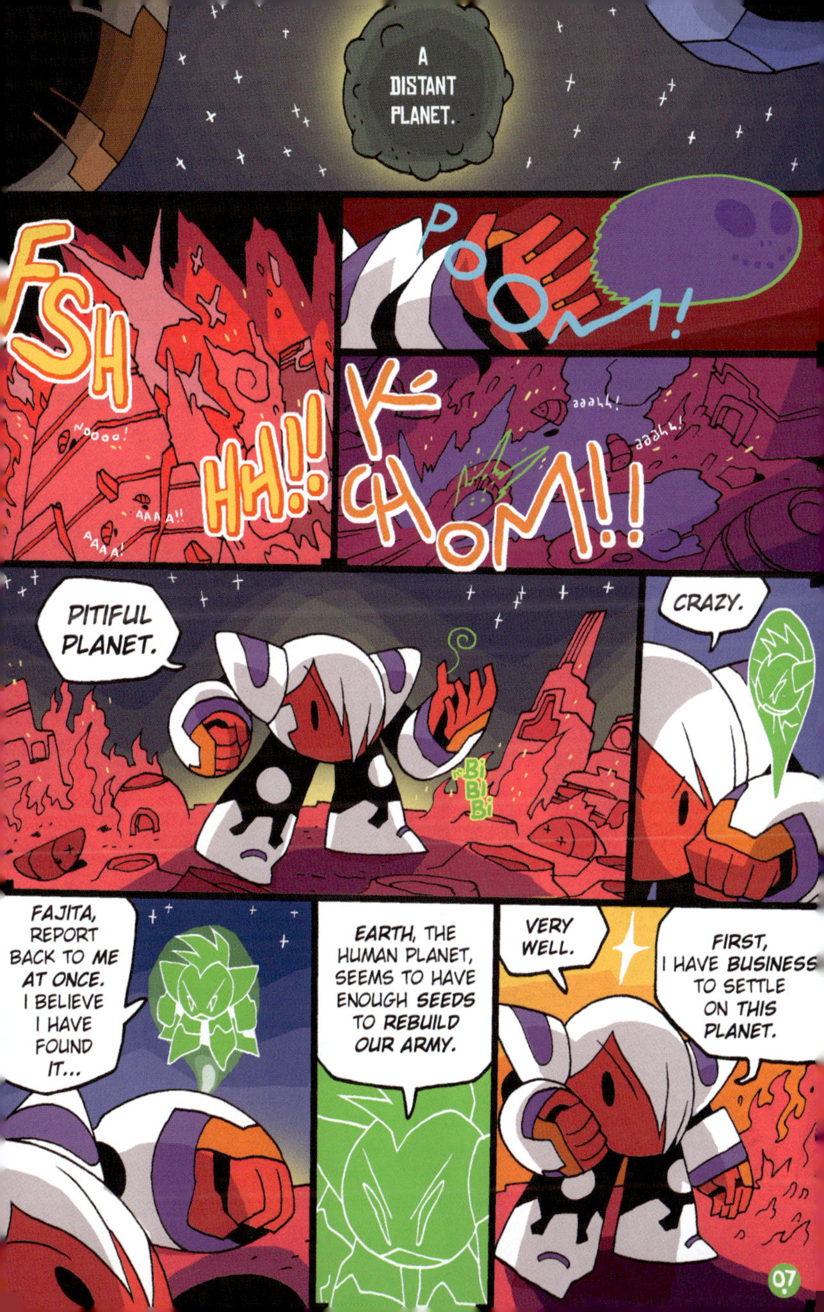

A DISTANT PLANET.
FSHHH!!
NOOOO!
AAAA!!
AAAA!
POOM!
K-CHOM!!
AAAHH!
AAAHH!
PITIFUL PLANET.
BI BI BI
CRAZY.
FAJITA, REPORT BACK TO ME AT ONCE. I BELIEVE I HAVE FOUND IT...
EARTH, THE HUMAN PLANET, SEEMS TO HAVE ENOUGH SEEDS TO REBUILD OUR ARMY.
VERY WELL.
FIRST, I HAVE BUSINESS TO SETTLE ON THIS PLANET.

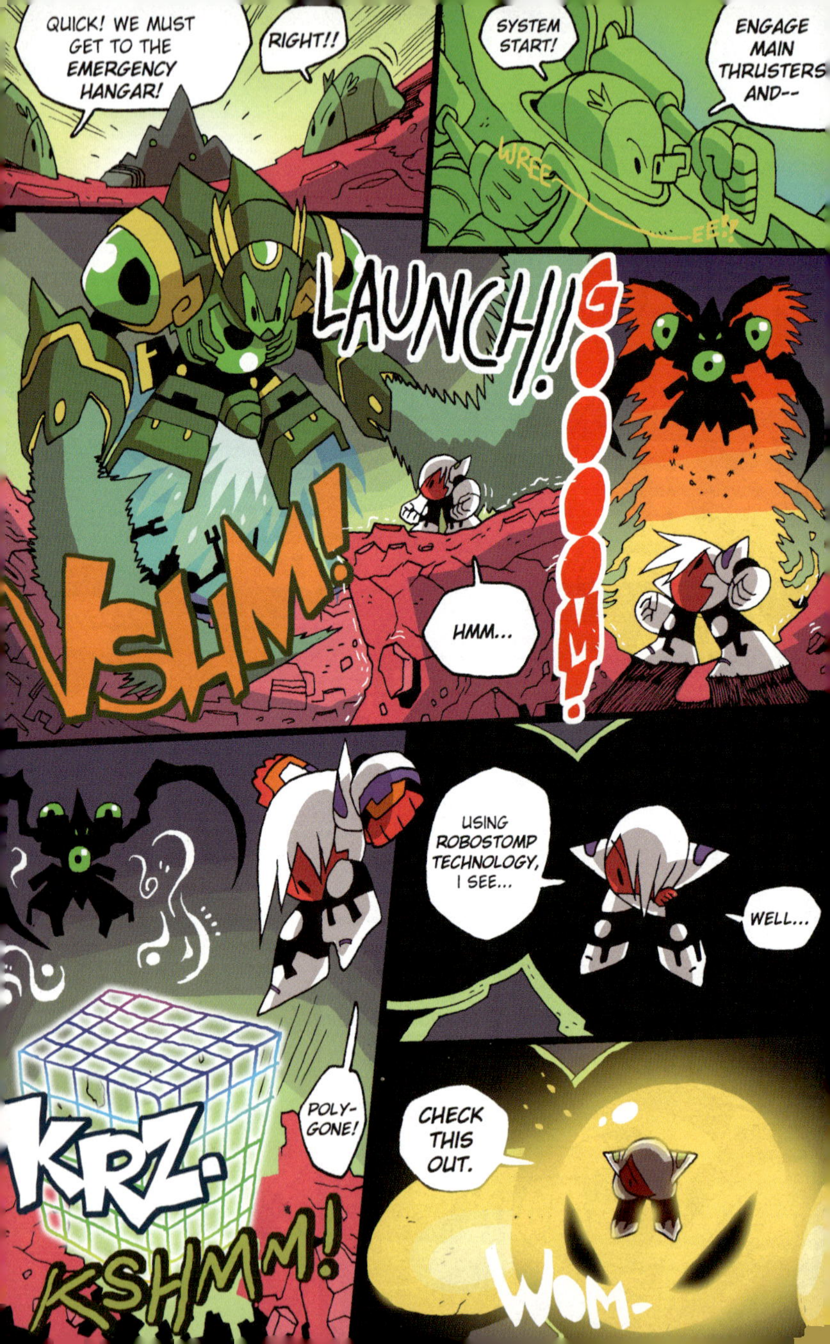
QUICK! WE MUST GET TO THE EMERGENCY HANGAR!
RIGHT!!
SYSTEM START!
ENGAGE MAIN THRUSTERS AND--
WREE--EE!
LAUNCH!
GOOOOOOM!
VSHM!
HMM...
USING ROBOSTOMP TECHNOLOGY, I SEE...
WELL...
POLY-GONE!
KRZ.
KSHMM!
CHECK THIS OUT.
WOM-

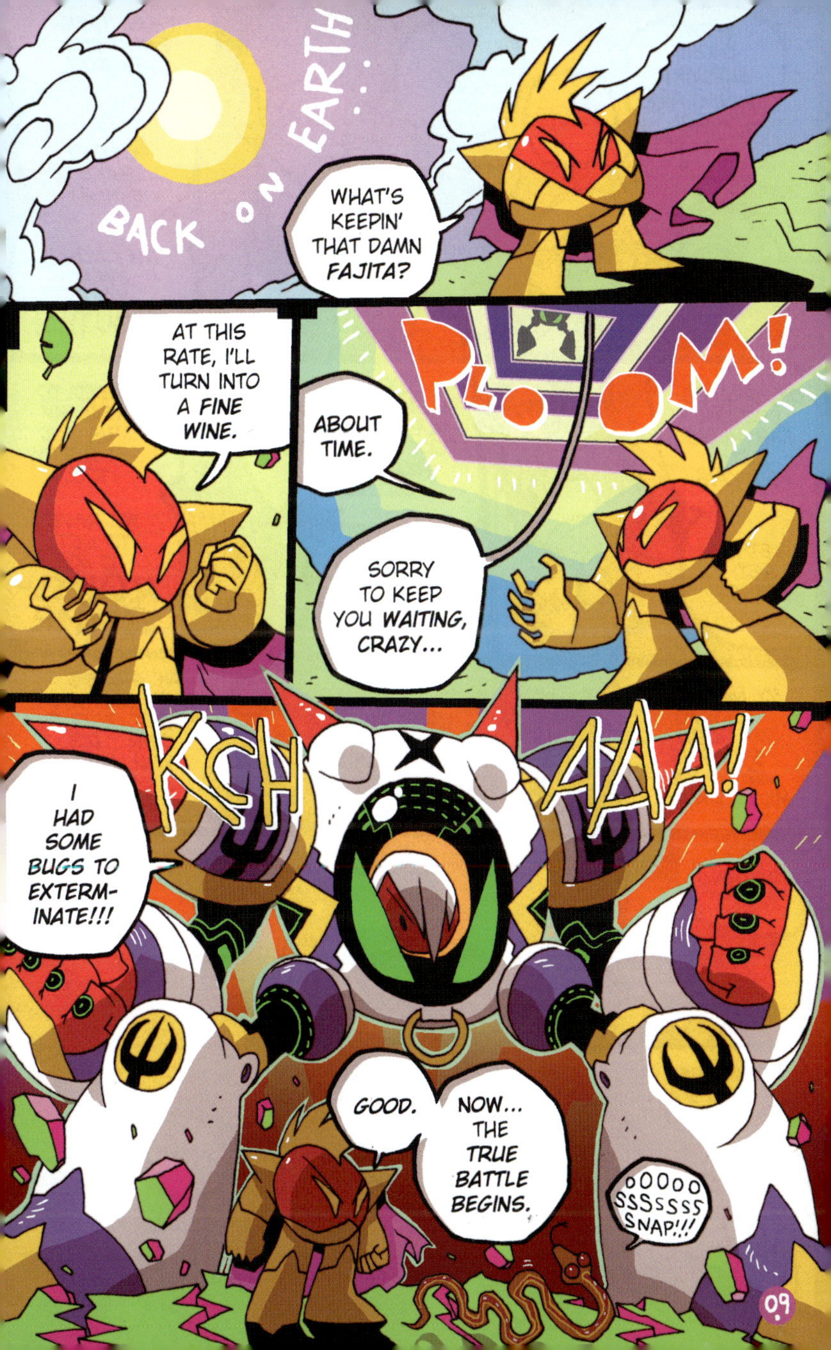
BACK ON EARTH...
WHAT'S KEEPIN' THAT DAMN FAJITA?
AT THIS RATE, I'LL TURN INTO A FINE WINE.
PLOOM!
ABOUT TIME.
SORRY TO KEEP YOU WAITING, CRAZY...
KCHAAAA!
I HAD SOME BUGS TO EXTERMINATE!!!
GOOD.
NOW... THE TRUE BATTLE BEGINS.
OOOOOSSSSSSSSNAP!!!

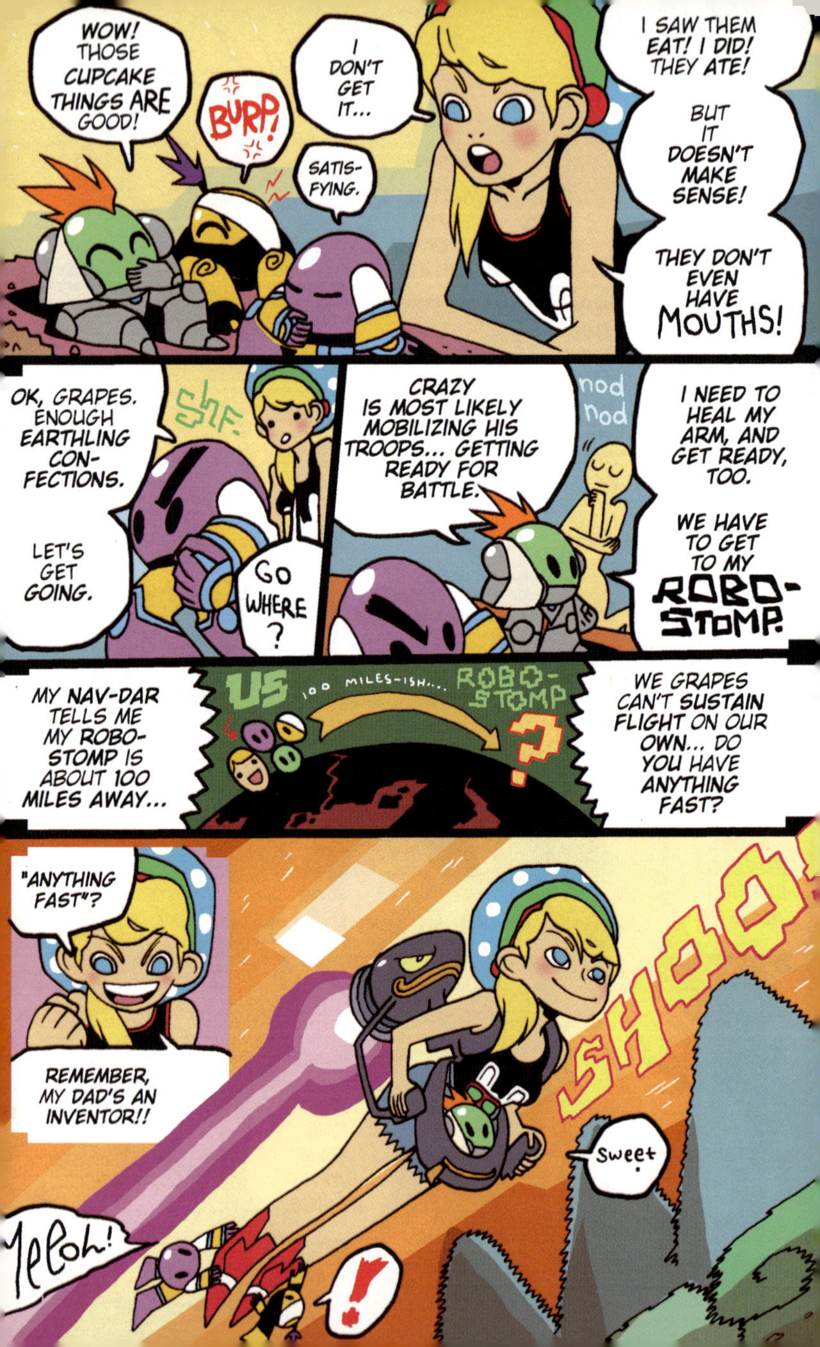

WOW! THOSE CUPCAKE THINGS ARE GOOD!
BURP!
I DON'T GET IT...
SATIS-FYING.
I SAW THEM EAT! I DID! THEY ATE!
BUT IT DOESN'T MAKE SENSE!
THEY DON'T EVEN HAVE MOUTHS!
OK, GRAPES. ENOUGH EARTHLING CON-FECTIONS.
SHF.
LET'S GET GOING.
GO WHERE ?
CRAZY IS MOST LIKELY MOBILIZING HIS TROOPS... GETTING READY FOR BATTLE.
nod nod
I NEED TO HEAL MY ARM, AND GET READY, TOO.
WE HAVE TO GET TO MY ROBO-STOMP.
MY NAV-DAR TELLS ME MY ROBO-STOMP IS ABOUT 100 MILES AWAY...
US
100 MILES-ISH...
ROBO-STOMP
?
WE GRAPES CAN'T SUSTAIN FLIGHT ON OUR OWN... DO YOU HAVE ANYTHING FAST?
"ANYTHING FAST"?
REMEMBER, MY DAD'S AN INVENTOR!!
SHOO
Sweet.
Yeooh!
!

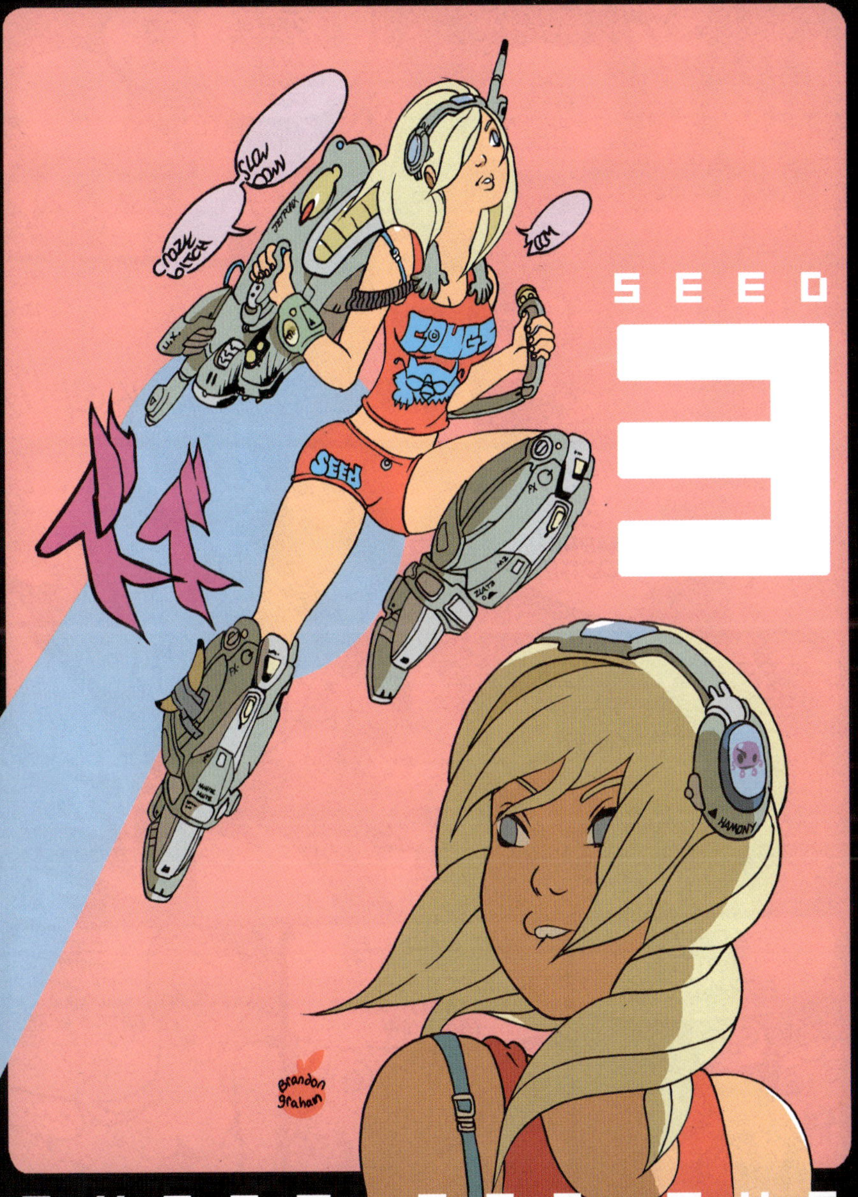
SEED
3
SLOW DOWN
CRAZY BITCH
ZOOM
COUGS
SEED
HAMONY
Brandon graham

QUEST FOR THE ROBOSTOMP!

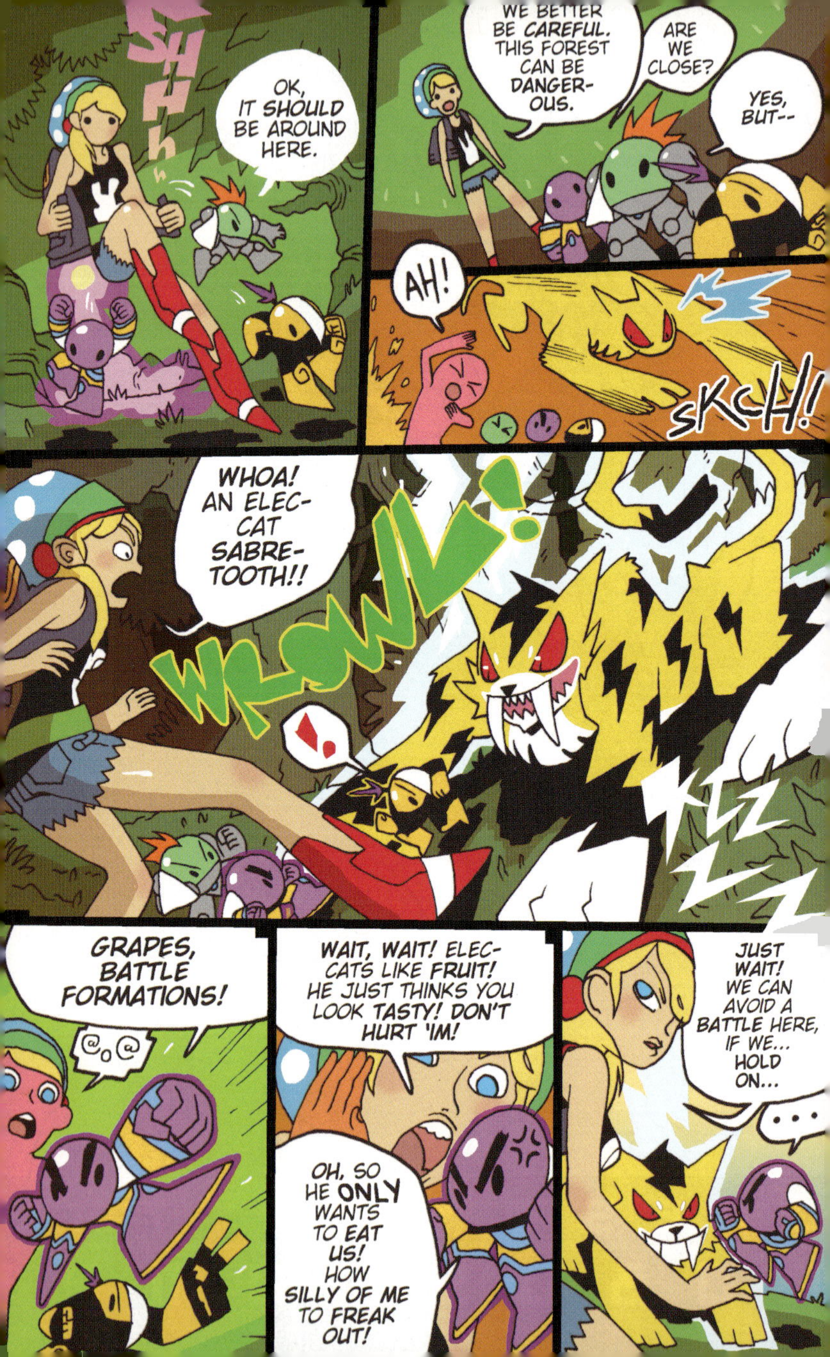
SHHh
OK, IT SHOULD BE AROUND HERE.
WE BETTER BE CAREFUL. THIS FOREST CAN BE DANGER-OUS.
ARE WE CLOSE?
YES, BUT--
AH!
SKCH!
WHOA! AN ELEC-CAT SABRE-TOOTH!!
WROWL!
!
KZZ
GRAPES, BATTLE FORMATIONS!
@o@
WAIT, WAIT! ELEC-CATS LIKE FRUIT! HE JUST THINKS YOU LOOK TASTY! DON'T HURT 'IM!
OH, SO HE ONLY WANTS TO EAT US! HOW SILLY OF ME TO FREAK OUT!
JUST WAIT! WE CAN AVOID A BATTLE HERE, IF WE... HOLD ON...
...

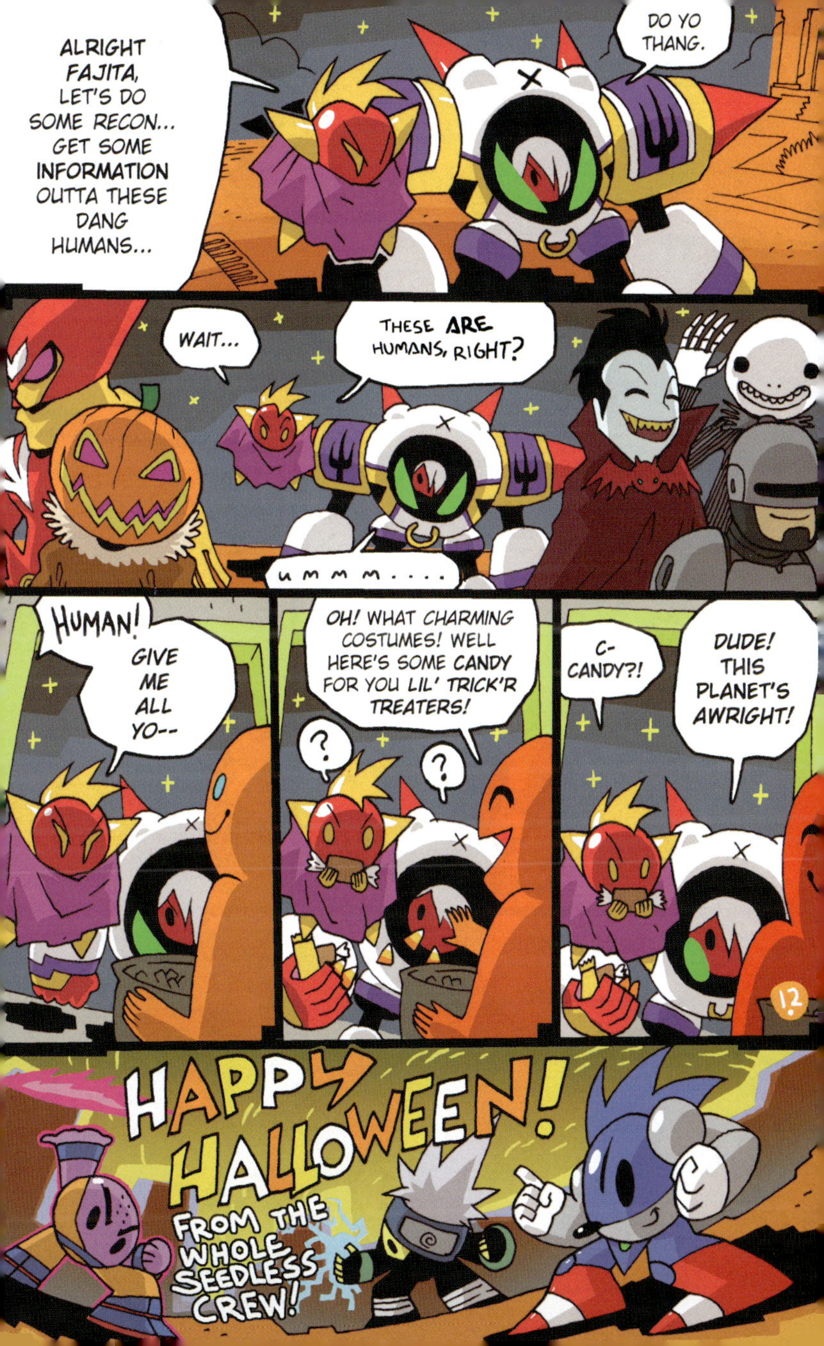
ALRIGHT FAJITA, LET'S DO SOME RECON... GET SOME INFORMATION OUTTA THESE DANG HUMANS...
DO YO THANG.
WAIT...
THESE ARE HUMANS, RIGHT?
UMMM....
HUMAN!
GIVE ME ALL YO--
OH! WHAT CHARMING COSTUMES! WELL HERE'S SOME CANDY FOR YOU LIL' TRICK'R TREATERS!
?
?
C-CANDY?!
DUDE! THIS PLANET'S AWRIGHT!
12
HAPPY HALLOWEEN!
FROM THE WHOLE SEEDLESS CREW!

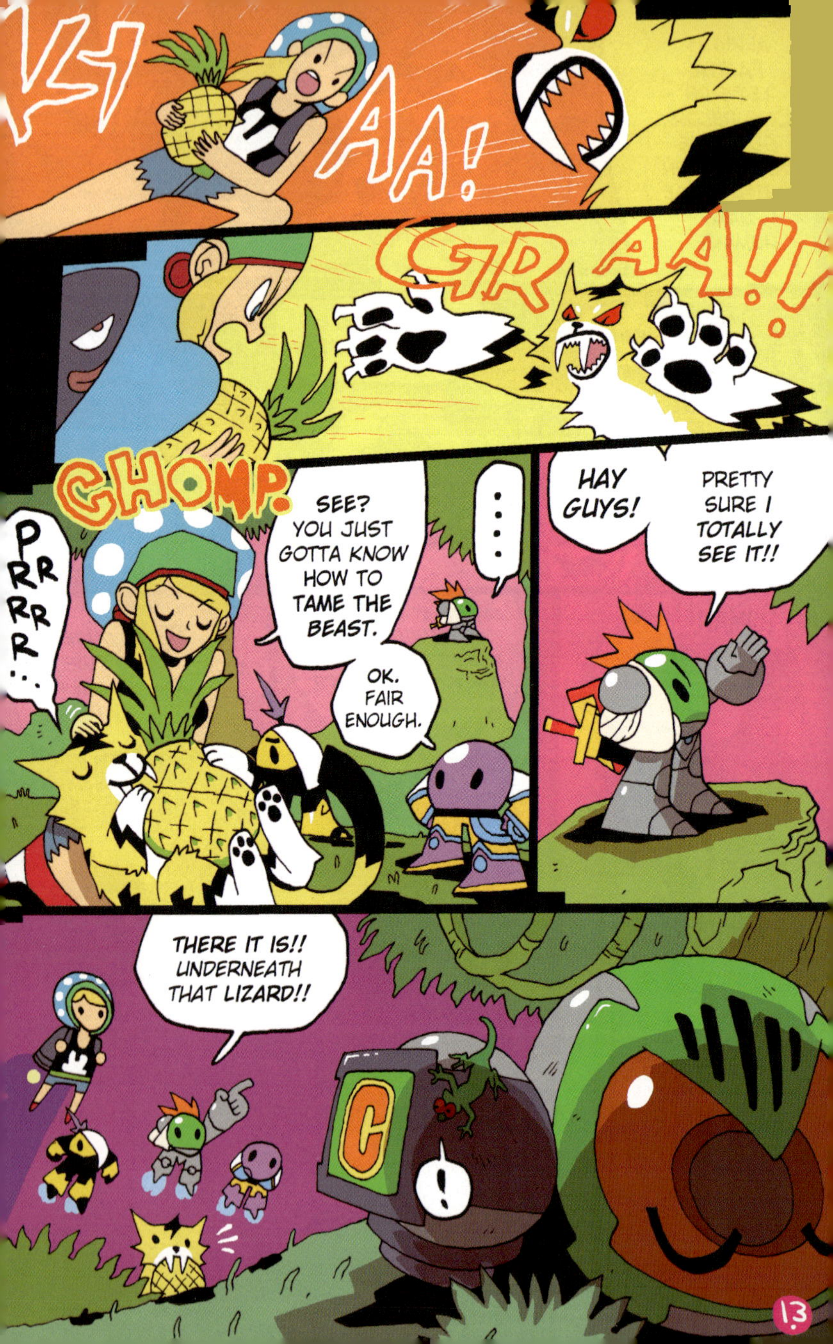

KYAA!
GRAA!!
CHOMP
PRRRRR..
SEE? YOU JUST GOTTA KNOW HOW TO TAME THE BEAST.
....
OK. FAIR ENOUGH.
HAY GUYS!
PRETTY SURE I TOTALLY SEE IT!!
THERE IT IS!! UNDERNEATH THAT LIZARD!!
C
!

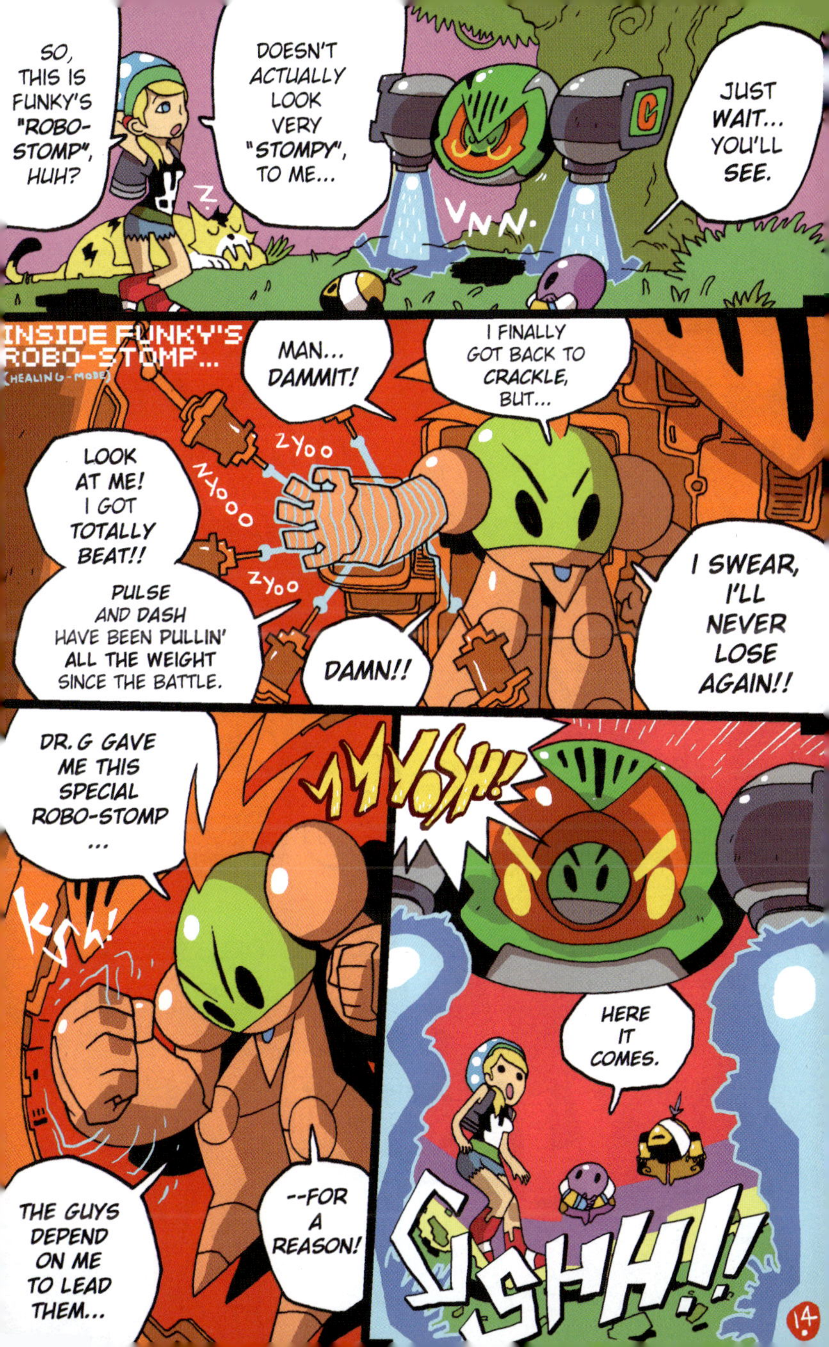
SO, THIS IS FUNKY'S "ROBO-STOMP", HUH?
DOESN'T ACTUALLY LOOK VERY "STOMPY", TO ME...
Z
VNN.
JUST WAIT... YOU'LL SEE.
INSIDE FUNKY'S ROBO-STOMP...
(HEALING-MODE)
MAN... DAMMIT!
I FINALLY GOT BACK TO CRACKLE, BUT...
LOOK AT ME! I GOT TOTALLY BEAT!!
ZYOO
ZYOOO
ZYOO
PULSE AND DASH HAVE BEEN PULLIN' ALL THE WEIGHT SINCE THE BATTLE.
DAMN!!
I SWEAR, I'LL NEVER LOSE AGAIN!!
DR. G GAVE ME THIS SPECIAL ROBO-STOMP ...
KSH!
THE GUYS DEPEND ON ME TO LEAD THEM...
--FOR A REASON!
VYYYOSH!
HERE IT COMES.
GSHH!!

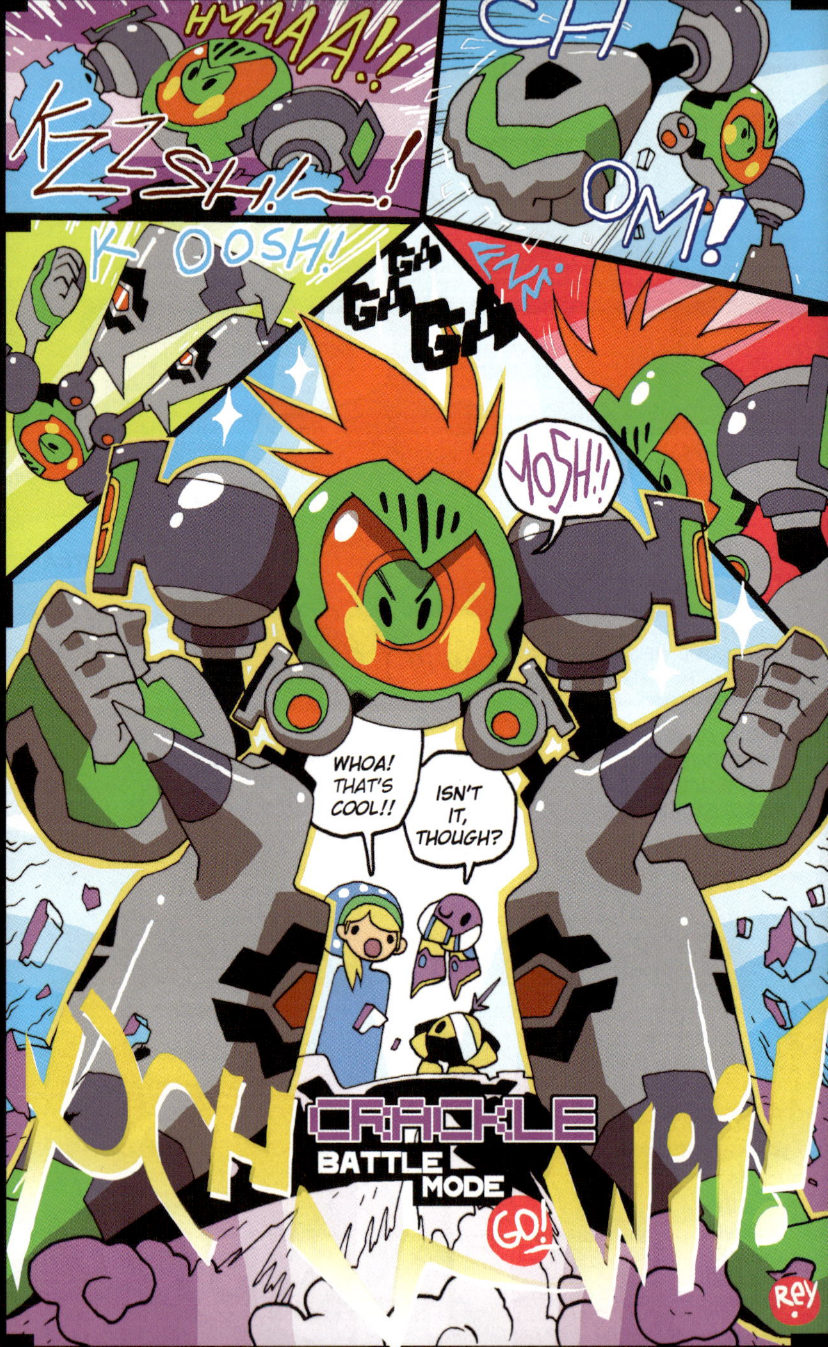
HYAAAA!!
KZZSH!~!
CH
OM!
KOOSH!
GA GA GA GA
FNN
YOSH!!
WHOA! THAT'S COOL!!
ISN'T IT, THOUGH?
CRACKLE
BATTLE MODE
GO!
REY

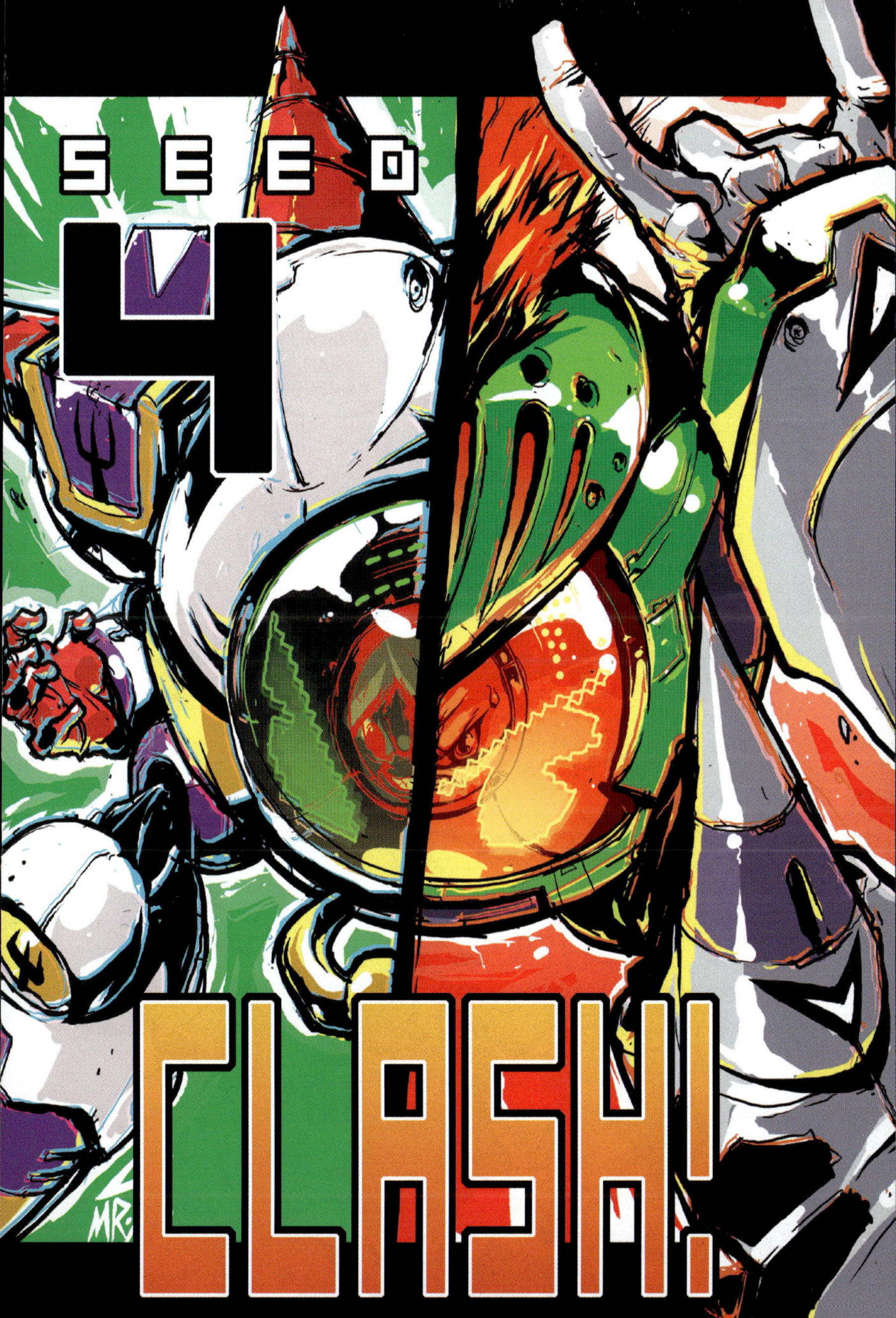
SEED
4
CLASH!

ART: SHELDON VELLA

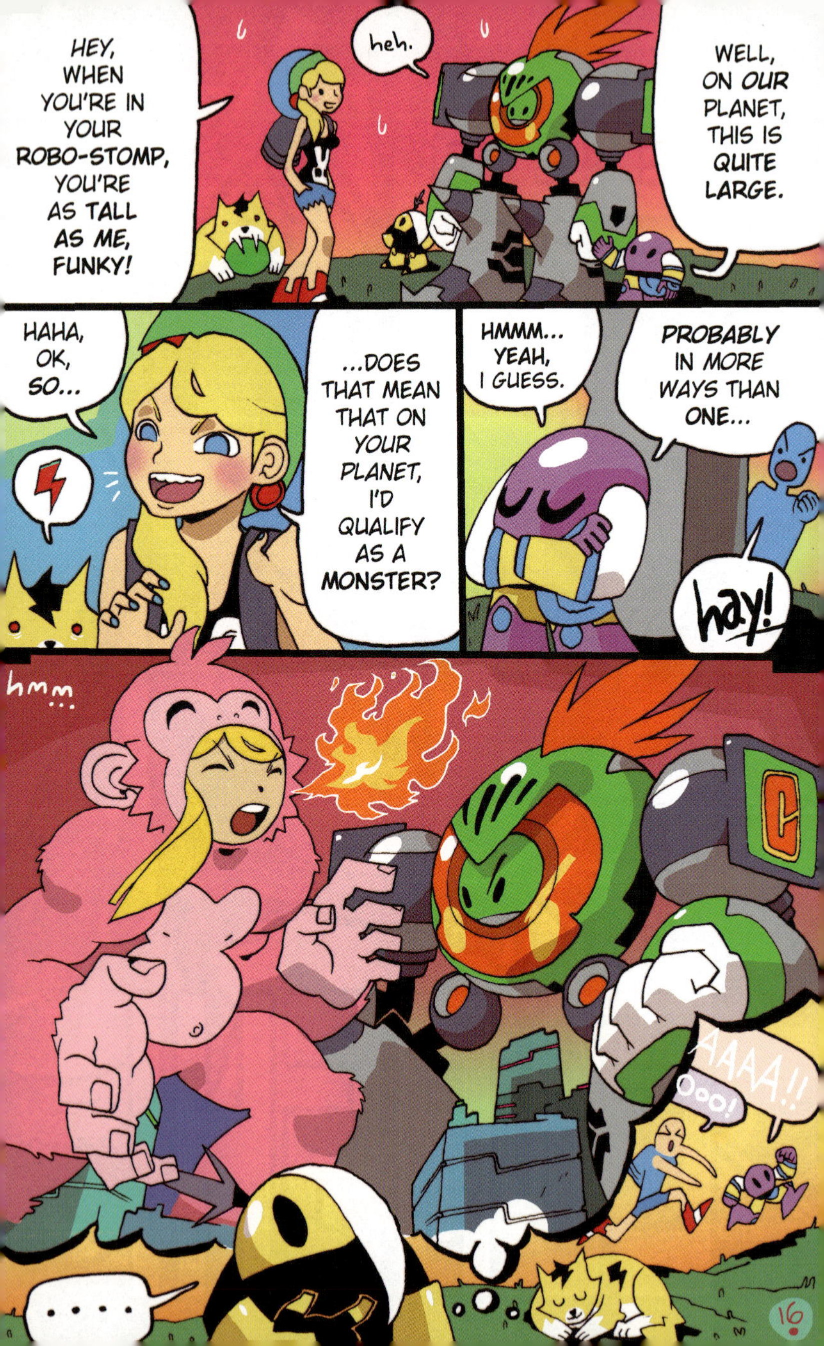
HEY, WHEN YOU'RE IN YOUR ROBO-STOMP, YOU'RE AS TALL AS ME, FUNKY!
heh.
WELL, ON OUR PLANET, THIS IS QUITE LARGE.
HAHA, OK, SO...
...DOES THAT MEAN THAT ON YOUR PLANET, I'D QUALIFY AS A MONSTER?
HMMM... YEAH, I GUESS.
PROBABLY IN MORE WAYS THAN ONE...
hay!
hmm...
AAAA!!
Ooo!
....

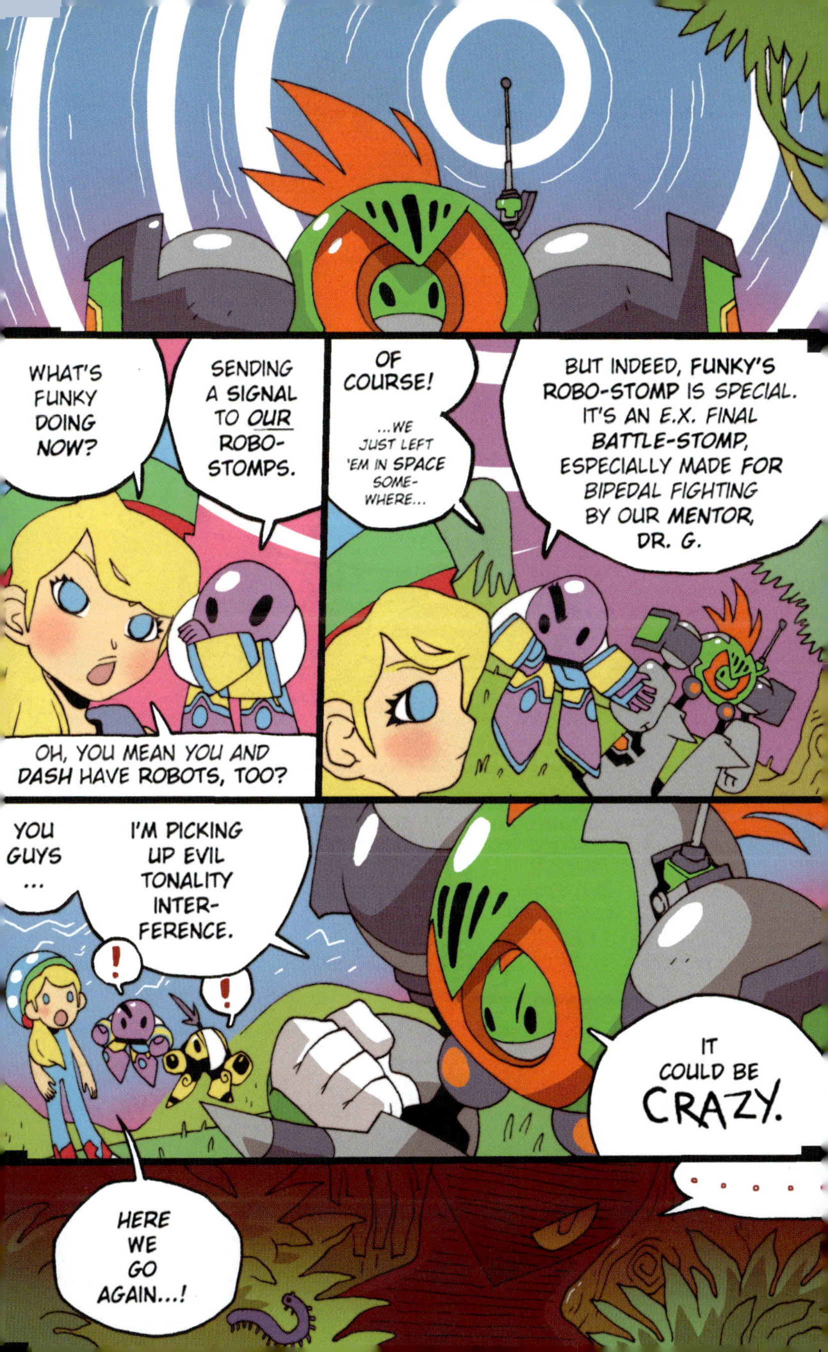
WHAT'S FUNKY DOING NOW?
SENDING A SIGNAL TO OUR ROBO-STOMPS.
OH, YOU MEAN YOU AND DASH HAVE ROBOTS, TOO?
OF COURSE!
...WE JUST LEFT 'EM IN SPACE SOMEWHERE...
BUT INDEED, FUNKY'S ROBO-STOMP IS SPECIAL. IT'S AN E.X. FINAL BATTLE-STOMP, ESPECIALLY MADE FOR BIPEDAL FIGHTING BY OUR MENTOR, DR. G.
YOU GUYS ...
I'M PICKING UP EVIL TONALITY INTER-FERENCE.
!
!
IT COULD BE CRAZY.
HERE WE GO AGAIN...!
.....

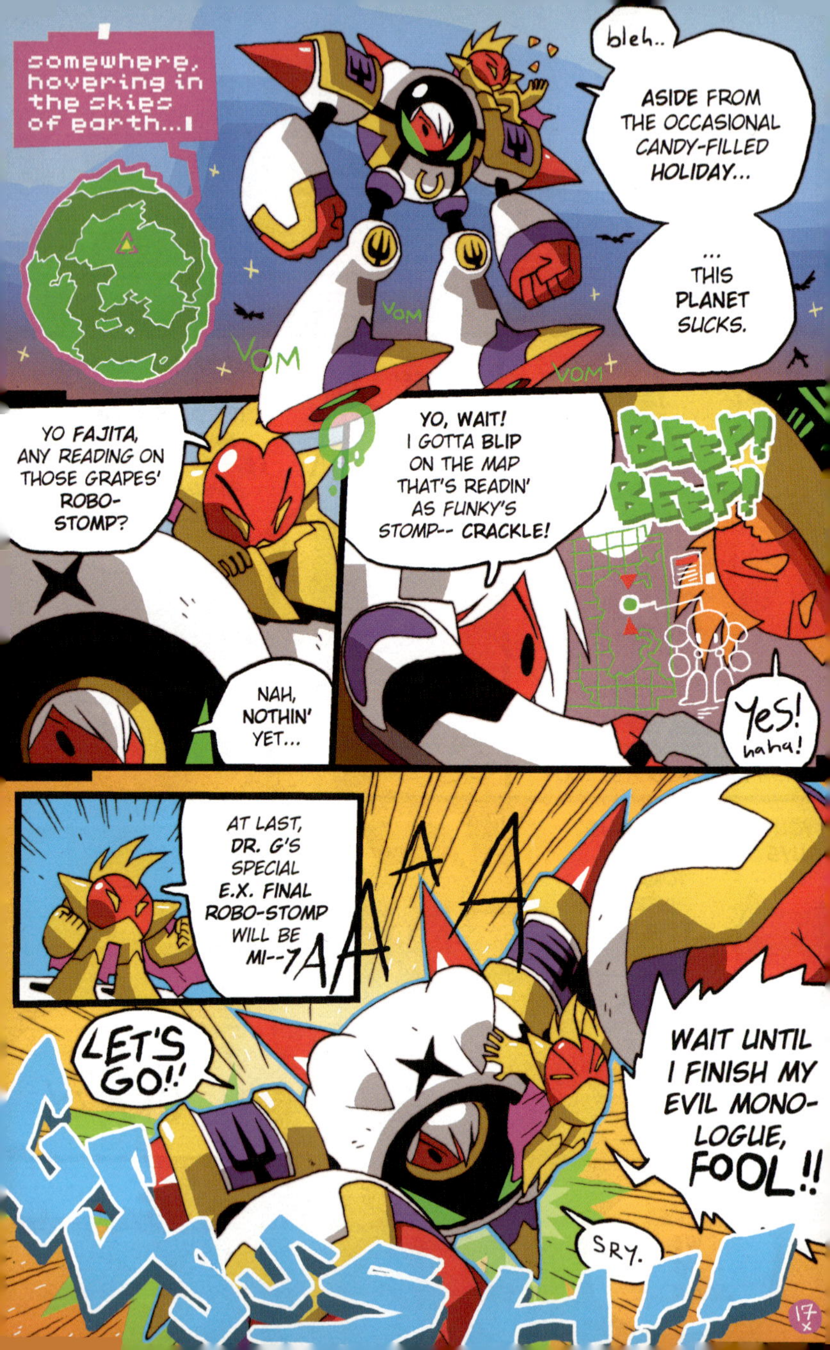
somewhere, hovering in the skies of earth...
bleh..
ASIDE FROM THE OCCASIONAL CANDY-FILLED HOLIDAY...
... THIS PLANET SUCKS.
VOM
VOM
VOM
YO FAJITA, ANY READING ON THOSE GRAPES' ROBO-STOMP?
NAH, NOTHIN' YET...
YO, WAIT! I GOTTA BLIP ON THE MAP THAT'S READIN' AS FUNKY'S STOMP-- CRACKLE!
BEEP! BEEP!
Yes! haha!
AT LAST, DR. G'S SPECIAL E.X. FINAL ROBO-STOMP WILL BE MI--
AAAAA
LET'S GO!!
WAIT UNTIL I FINISH MY EVIL MONO-LOGUE, FOOL!!
SRY.
GOOSSH!!

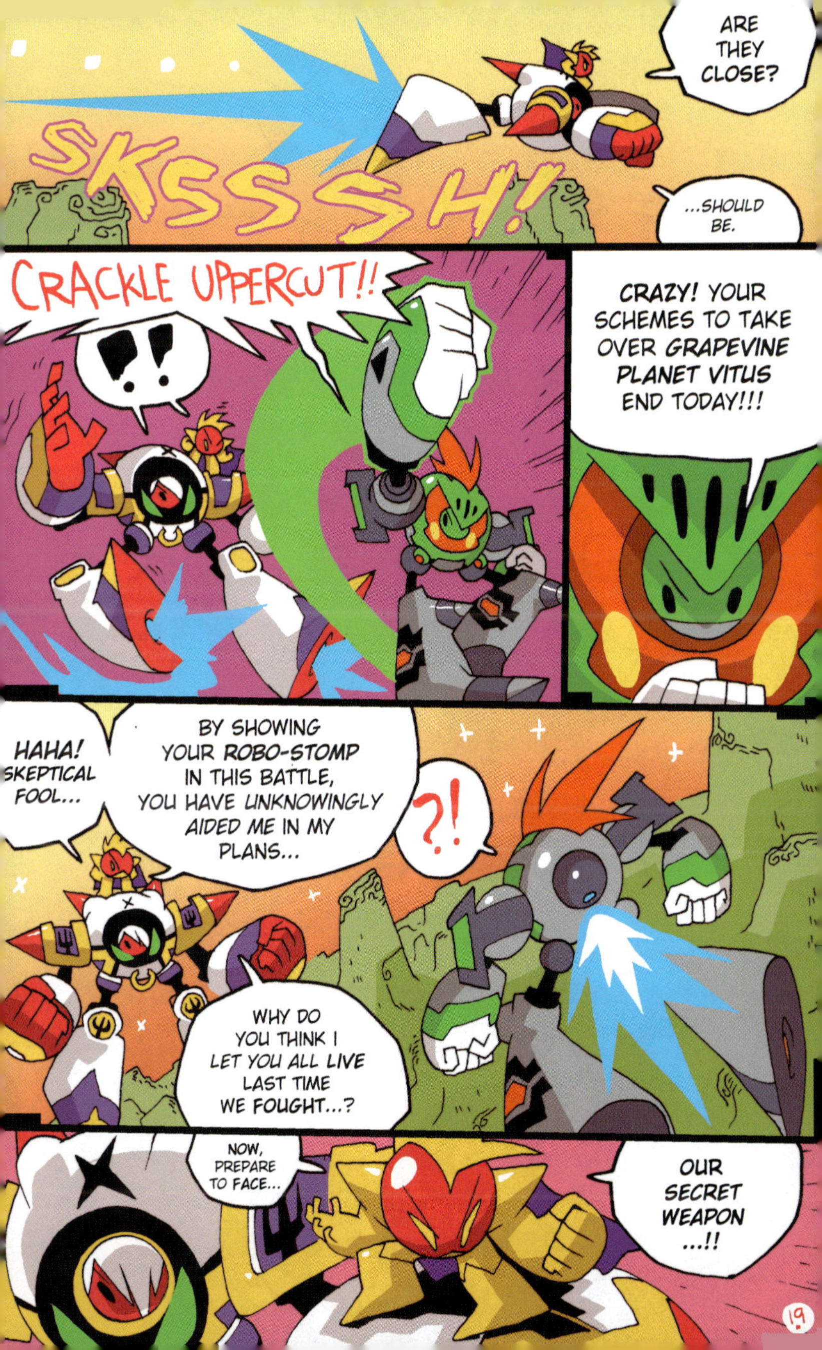
SKSSSH!
ARE THEY CLOSE?
...SHOULD BE.
CRACKLE UPPERCUT!!
!!
CRAZY! YOUR SCHEMES TO TAKE OVER GRAPEVINE PLANET VITUS END TODAY!!!
HAHA! SKEPTICAL FOOL...
BY SHOWING YOUR ROBO-STOMP IN THIS BATTLE, YOU HAVE UNKNOWINGLY AIDED ME IN MY PLANS...
?!
WHY DO YOU THINK I LET YOU ALL LIVE LAST TIME WE FOUGHT...?
NOW, PREPARE TO FACE...
OUR SECRET WEAPON ...!!

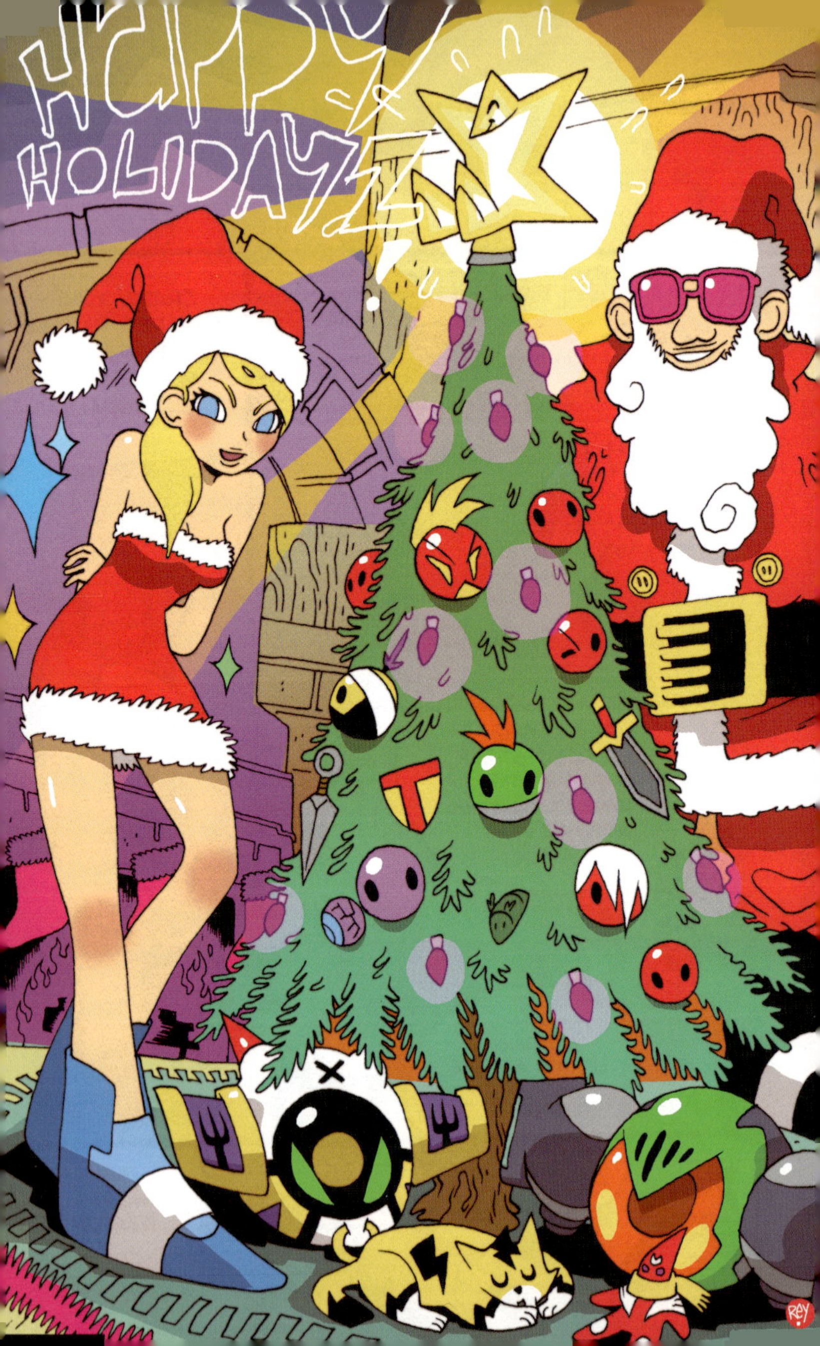
HAPPY
HOLIDAYZZZ
REY

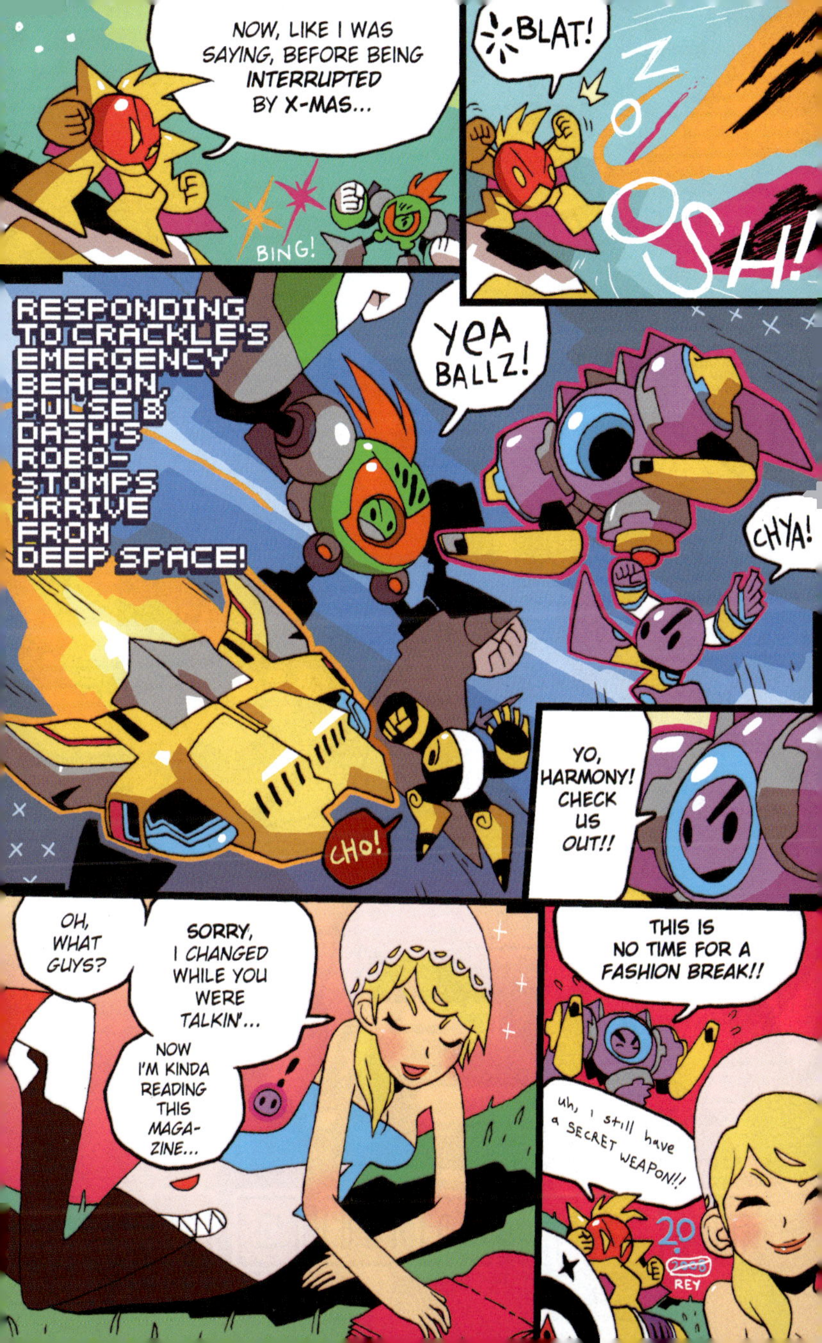
NOW, LIKE I WAS SAYING, BEFORE BEING INTERRUPTED BY X-MAS...
BING!
BLAT!
ZOOOSH!
RESPONDING TO CRACKLE'S EMERGENCY BEACON, PULSE & DASH'S ROBO-STOMPS ARRIVE FROM DEEP SPACE!
yea BALLZ!
CHYA!
CHO!
YO, HARMONY! CHECK US OUT!!
OH, WHAT GUYS?
SORRY, I CHANGED WHILE YOU WERE TALKIN'...
NOW I'M KINDA READING THIS MAGA-ZINE...
THIS IS NO TIME FOR A FASHION BREAK!!
uh, i still have a SECRET WEAPON!!
20
REY

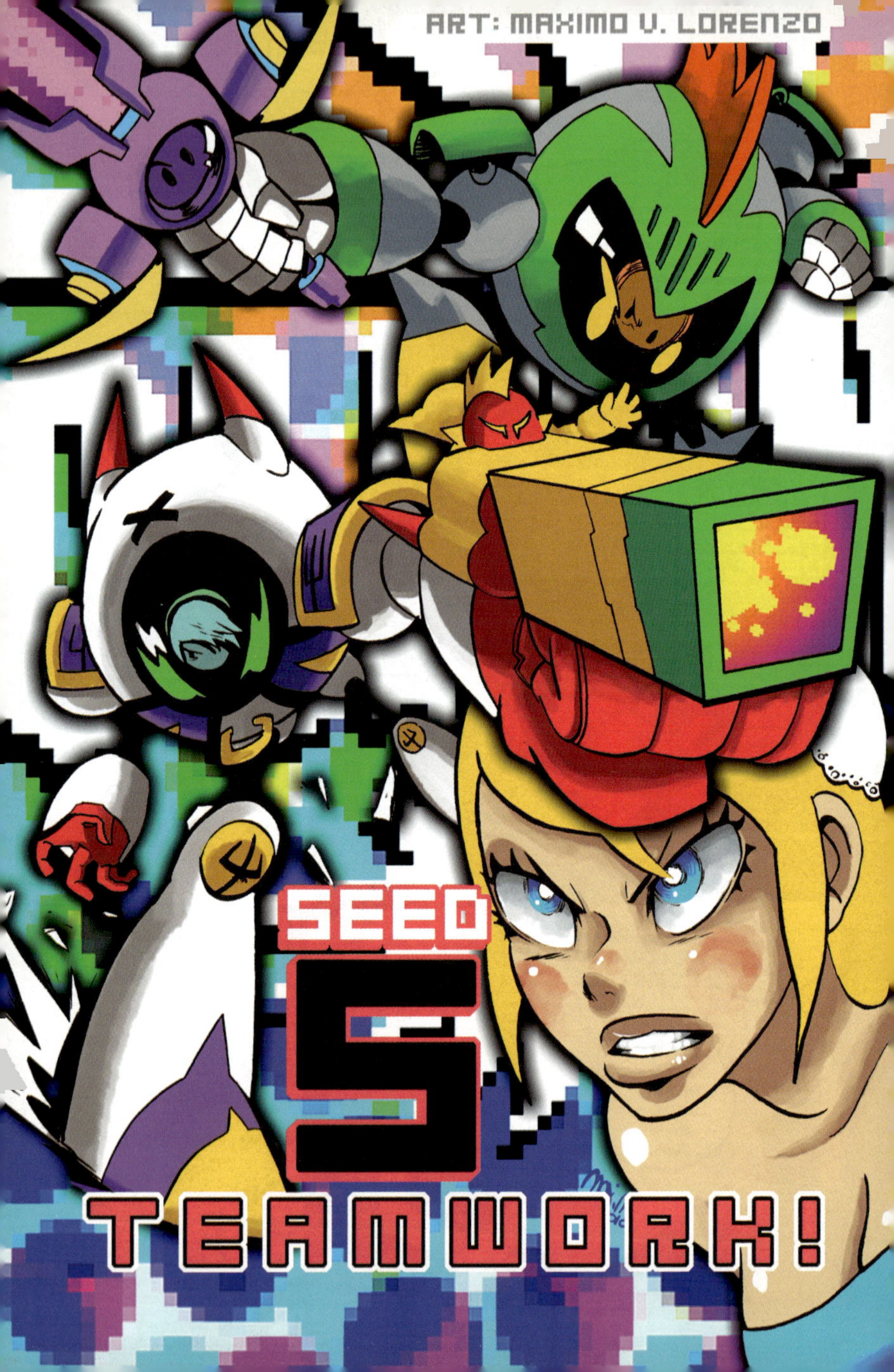
ART: MAXIMO V. LORENZO
SEED
5
TEAMWORK!

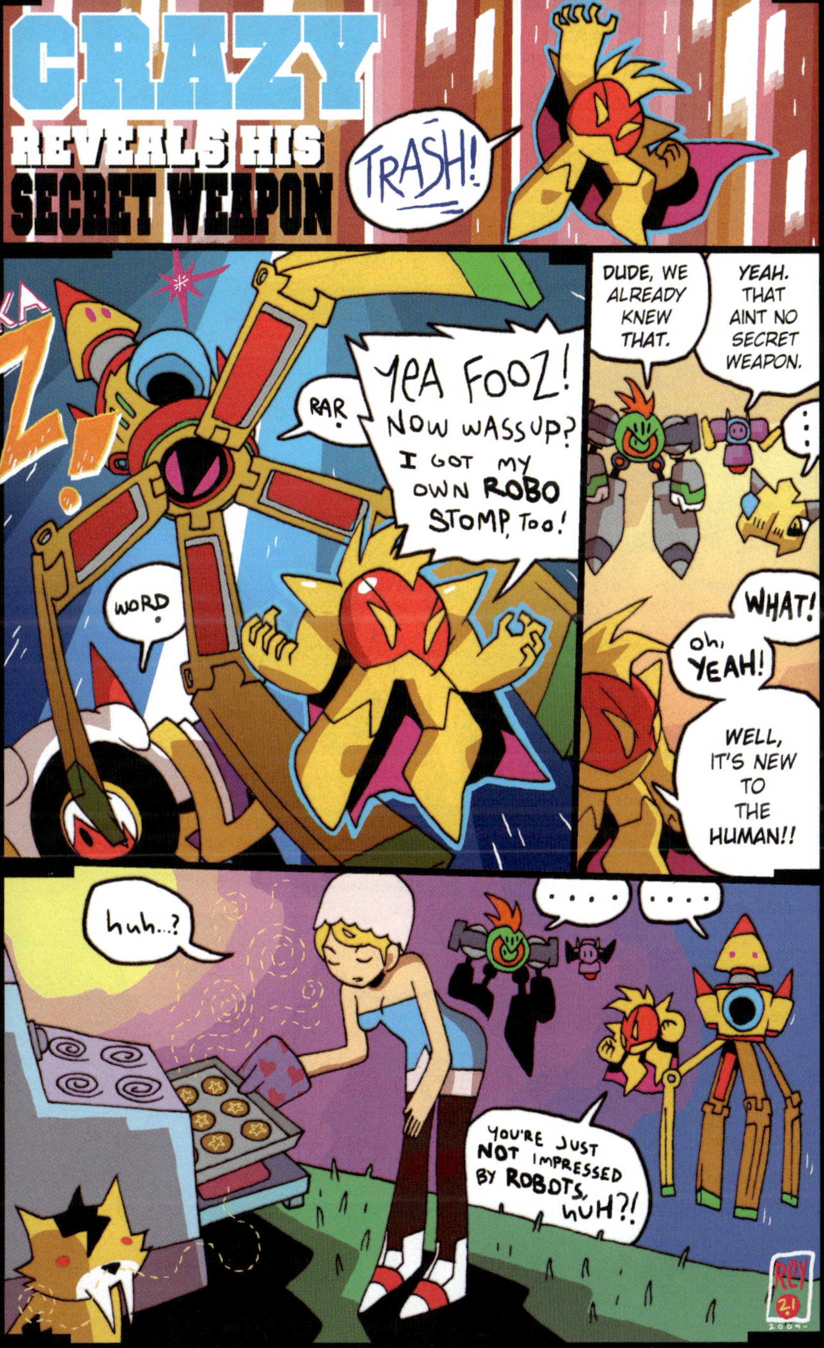
CRAZY
REVEALS HIS
SECRET WEAPON
TRASH!
KA
Z!
RAR.
YEA FOOZ! NOW WASSUP? I GOT MY OWN ROBO STOMP, TOO!
WORD.
DUDE, WE ALREADY KNEW THAT.
YEAH. THAT AINT NO SECRET WEAPON.
...
WHAT!
Oh, YEAH!
WELL, IT'S NEW TO THE HUMAN!!
huh...?
....
....
YOU'RE JUST NOT IMPRESSED BY ROBOTS, HUH?!
REY 21

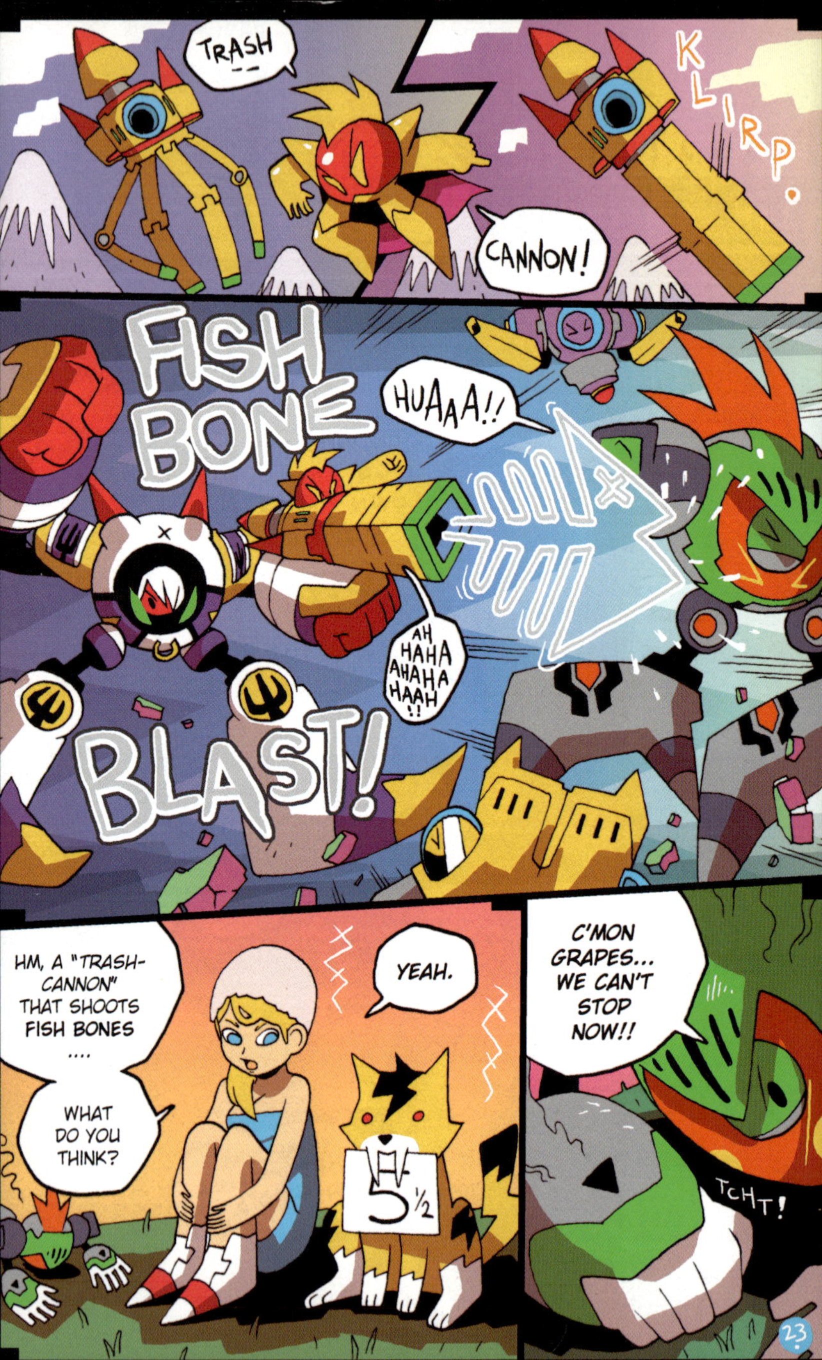
TRASH
CANNON!
KLIRP.
FISH BONE
HUAAA!!
AH HAHA AHAHA HAAH!!
BLAST!
HM, A "TRASH-CANNON" THAT SHOOTS FISH BONES ....
WHAT DO YOU THINK?
YEAH.
5 1/2
C'MON GRAPES... WE CAN'T STOP NOW!!
TCHT!

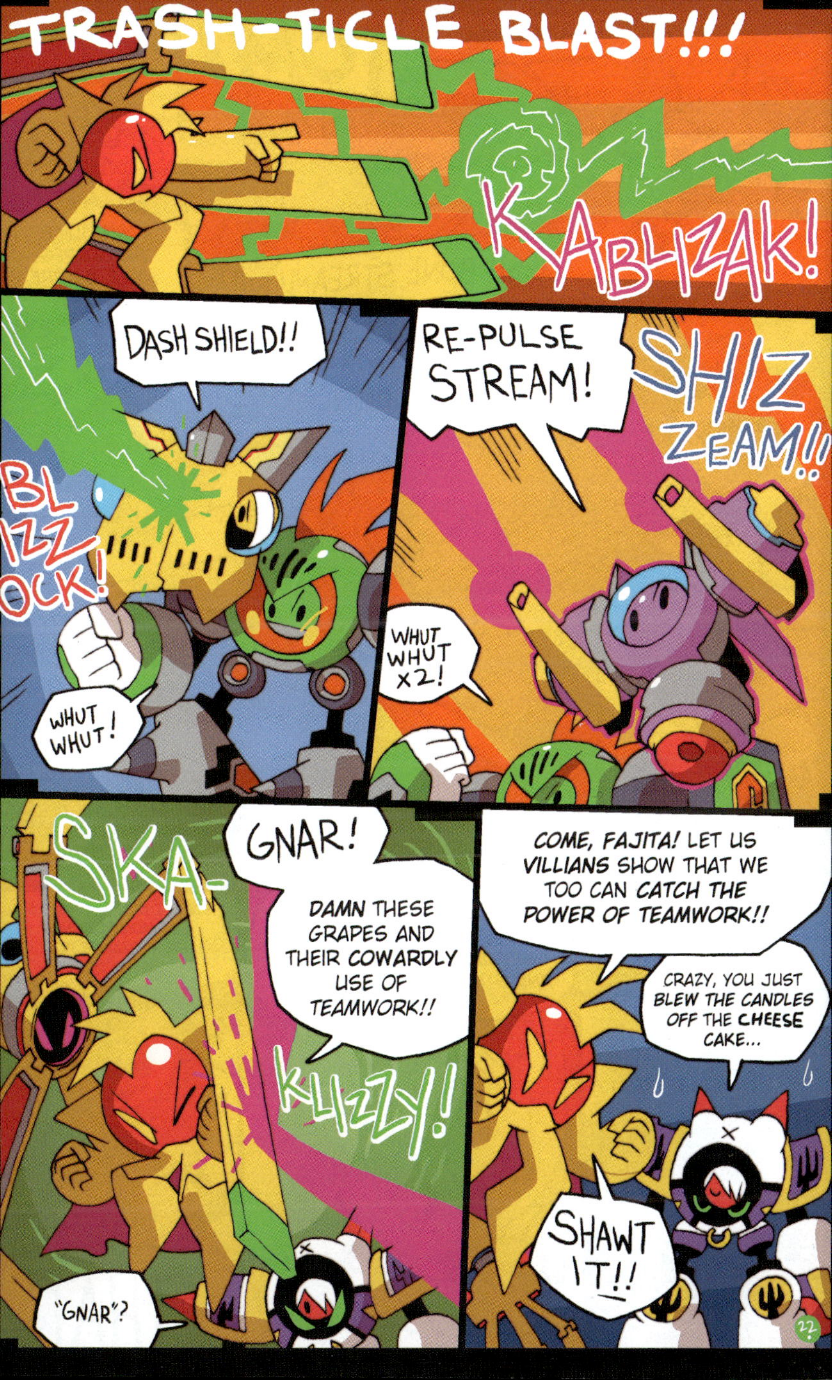

TRASH-TICLE BLAST!!!
KABLIZAK!
DASH SHIELD!!
BL IZZ OCK!
WHUT WHUT!
RE-PULSE STREAM!
SHIZ ZEAM!!
WHUT WHUT x2!
SKA-
GNAR!
DAMN THESE GRAPES AND THEIR COWARDLY USE OF TEAMWORK!!
KLIZZY!
"GNAR"?
COME, FAJITA! LET US VILLIANS SHOW THAT WE TOO CAN CATCH THE POWER OF TEAMWORK!!
CRAZY, YOU JUST BLEW THE CANDLES OFF THE CHEESE CAKE...
SHAWT IT!!
22

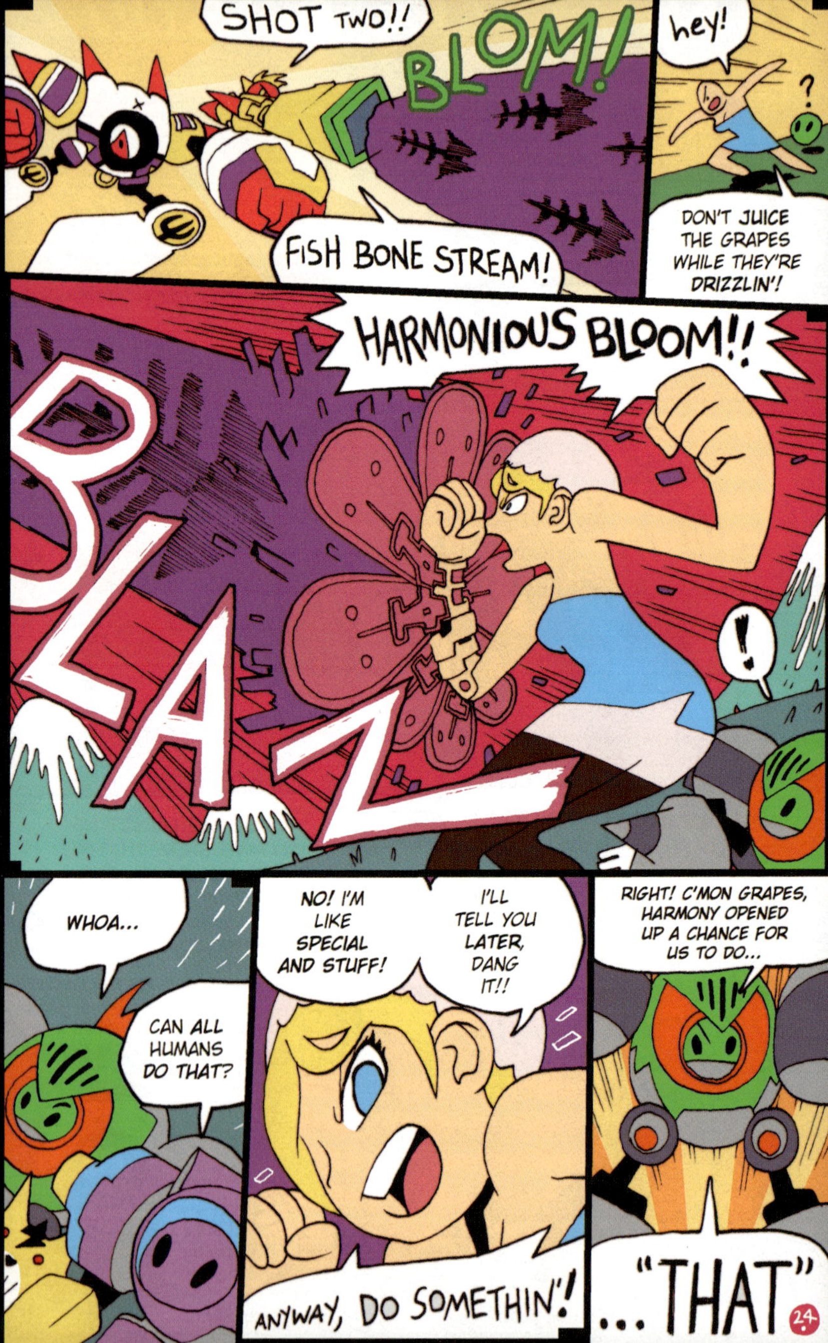
SHOT TWO!!
BLOOM!
hey!
FISH BONE STREAM!
DON'T JUICE THE GRAPES WHILE THEY'RE DRIZZLIN'!
HARMONIOUS BLOOM!!
BLAZ
!
WHOA...
CAN ALL HUMANS DO THAT?
NO! I'M LIKE SPECIAL AND STUFF!
I'LL TELL YOU LATER, DANG IT!!
ANYWAY, DO SOMETHIN'!
RIGHT! C'MON GRAPES, HARMONY OPENED UP A CHANCE FOR US TO DO...
..."THAT"

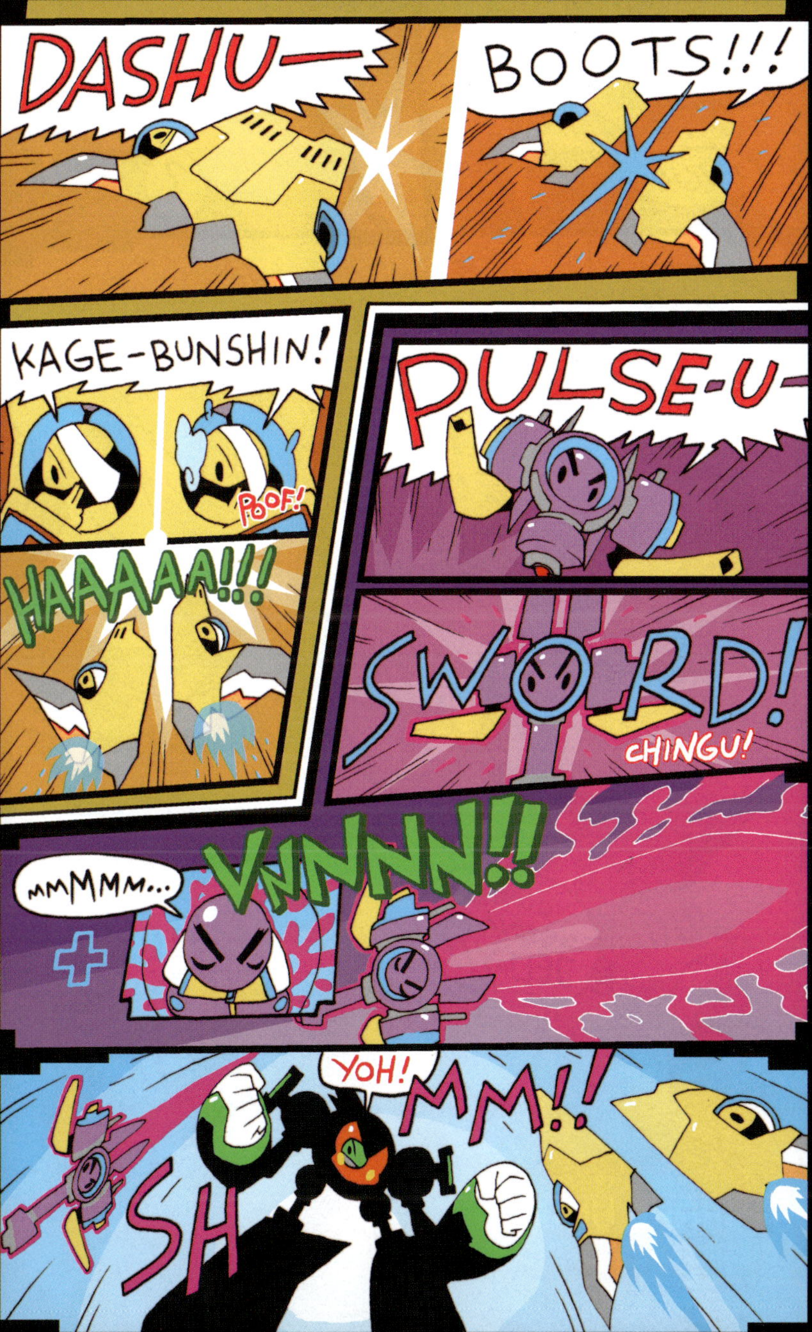
DASHU—
BOOTS!!!
KAGE-BUNSHIN!
POOF!
HAAAAAA!!!
PULSE-U-
SWORD!
CHINGU!
MMMMM...
VNNNN!!
YOH!
SHMM!!

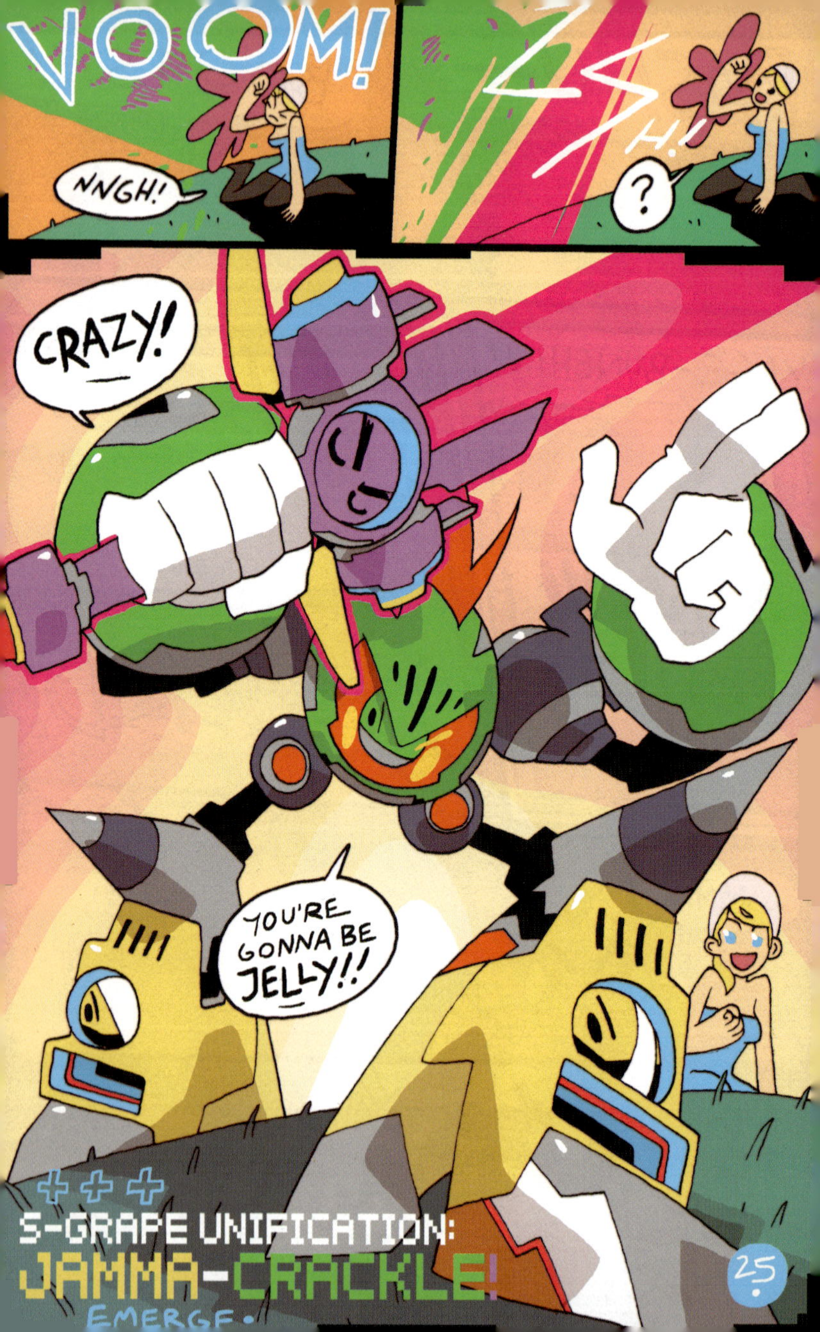
VOOM!
NNGH!
ZZSH!
?
CRAZY!
YOU'RE GONNA BE JELLY!!
S-GRAPE UNIFICATION:
JAMMA-CRACKLE!
EMERGE.
25

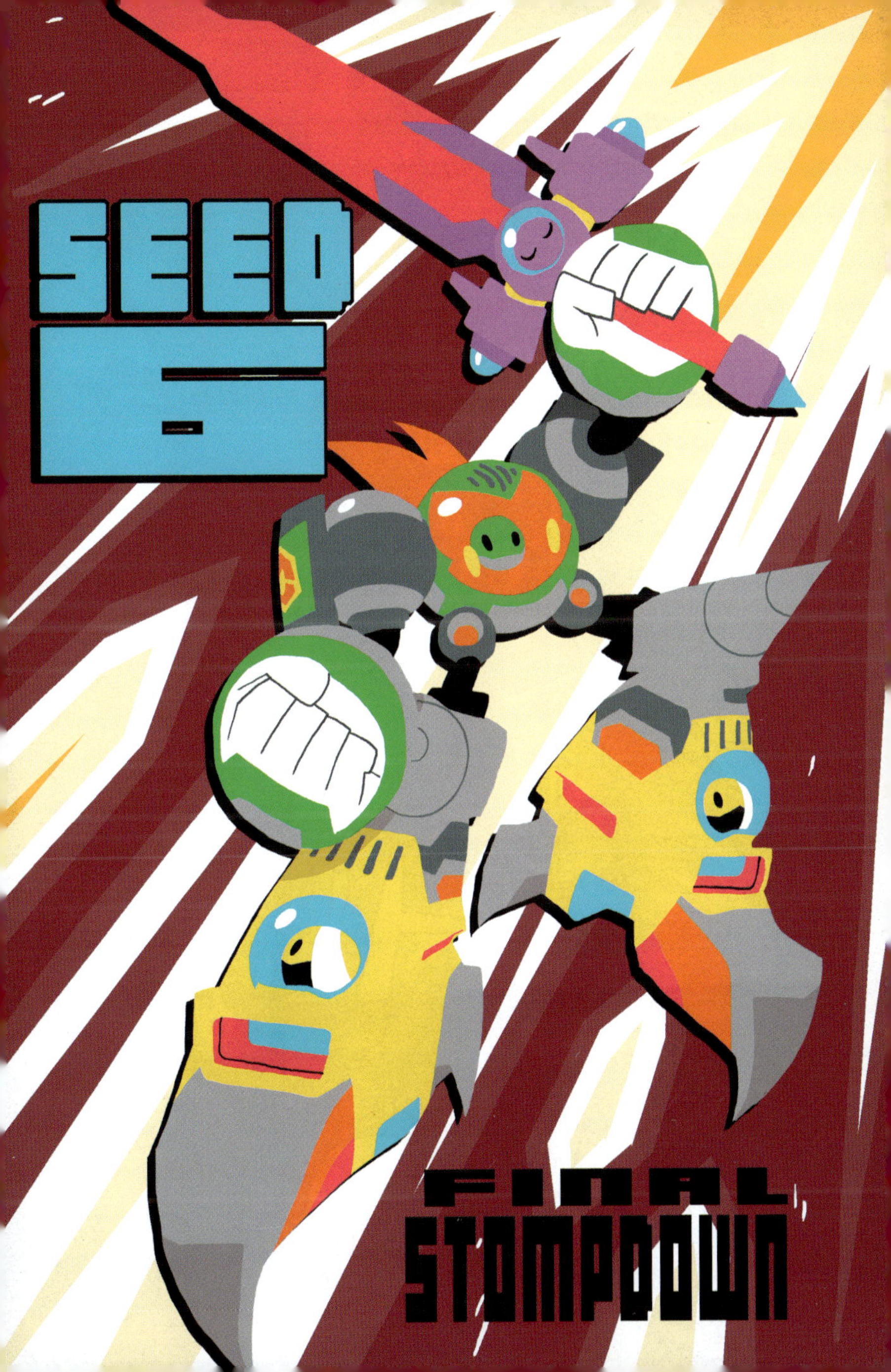
SEED 6
FINAL STOMPDOWN

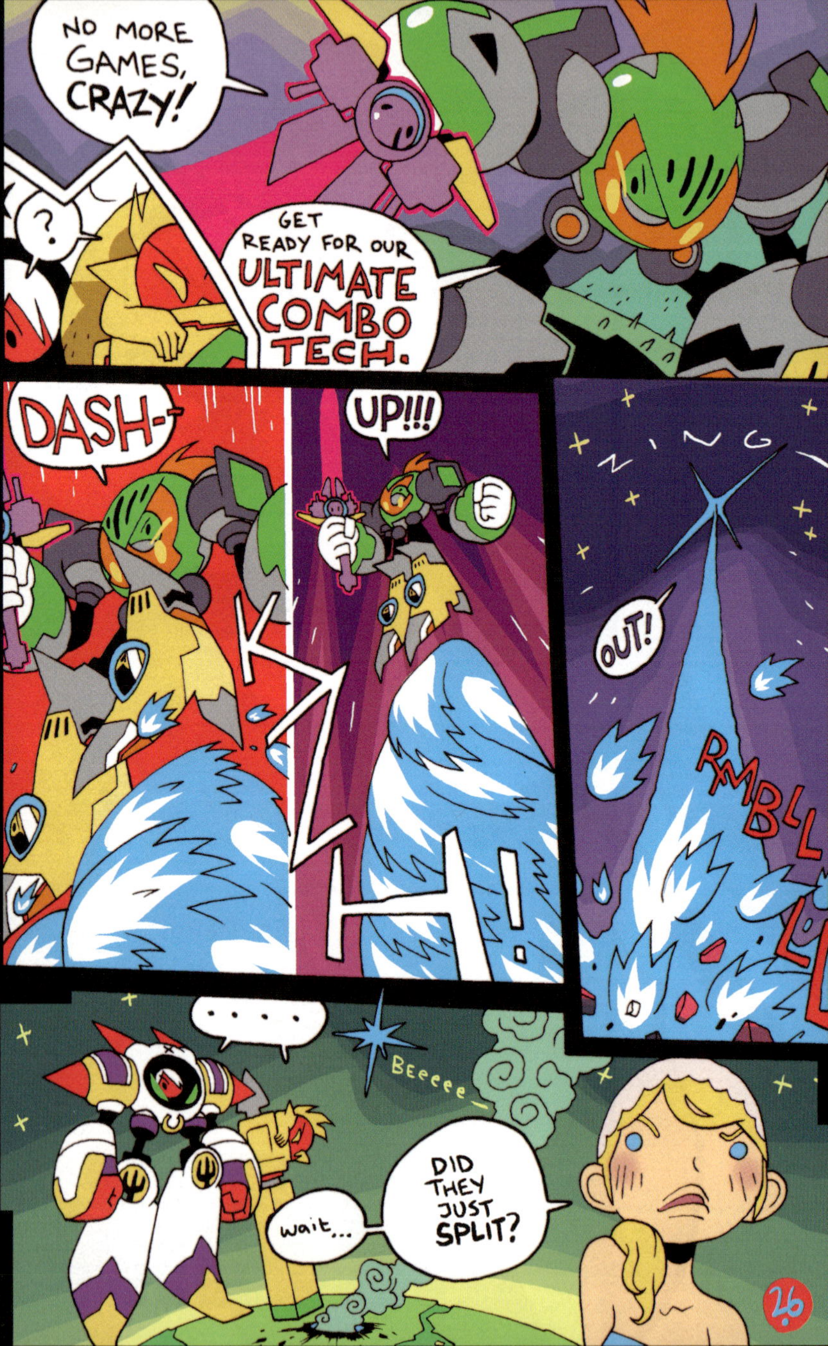
NO MORE GAMES, CRAZY!
?
GET READY FOR OUR ULTIMATE COMBO TECH.
DASH-
UP!!!
KZZH!
ZING
OUT!
RMBLLLL
....
Beeeee—
wait...
DID THEY JUST SPLIT?
26

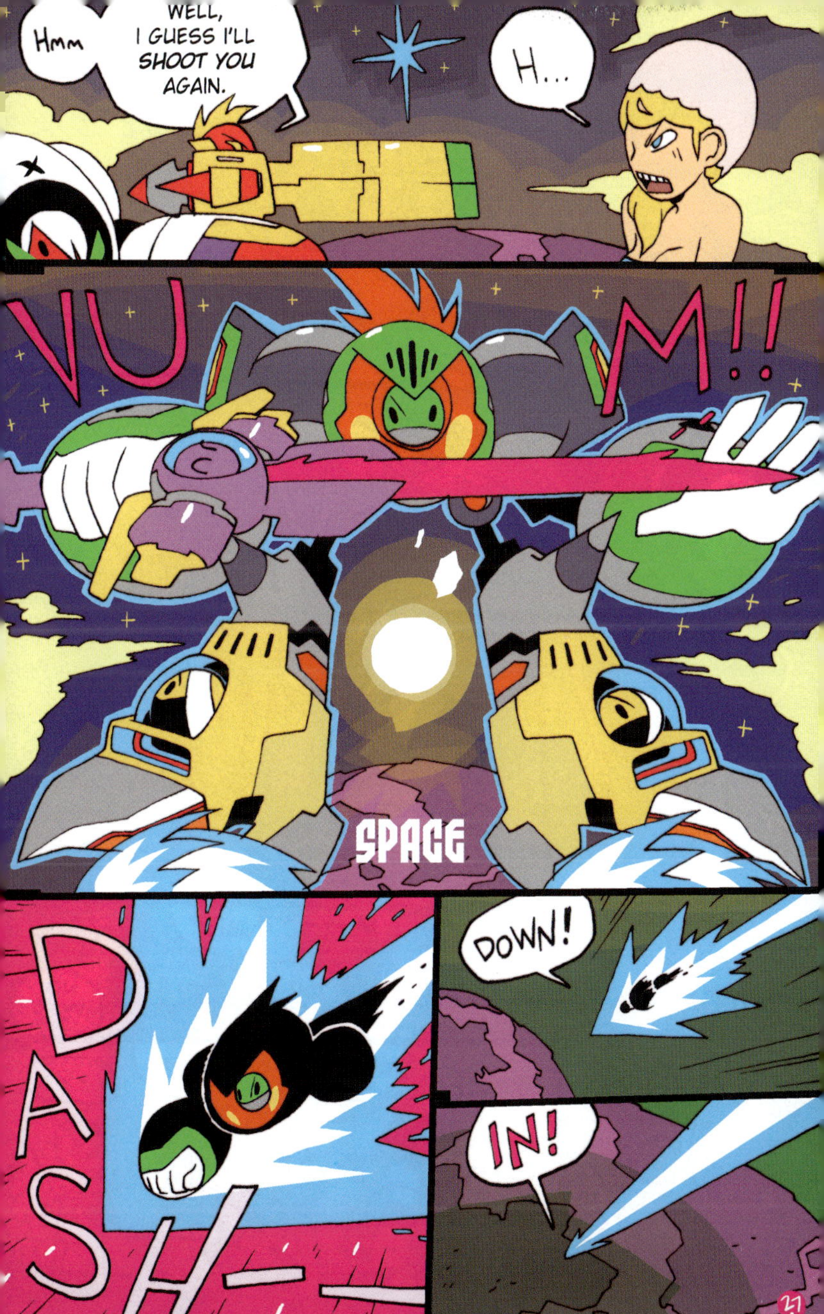
Hmm
WELL, I GUESS I'LL SHOOT YOU AGAIN.
H...
VU
M!!
SPACE
DASH-
DOWN!
IN!

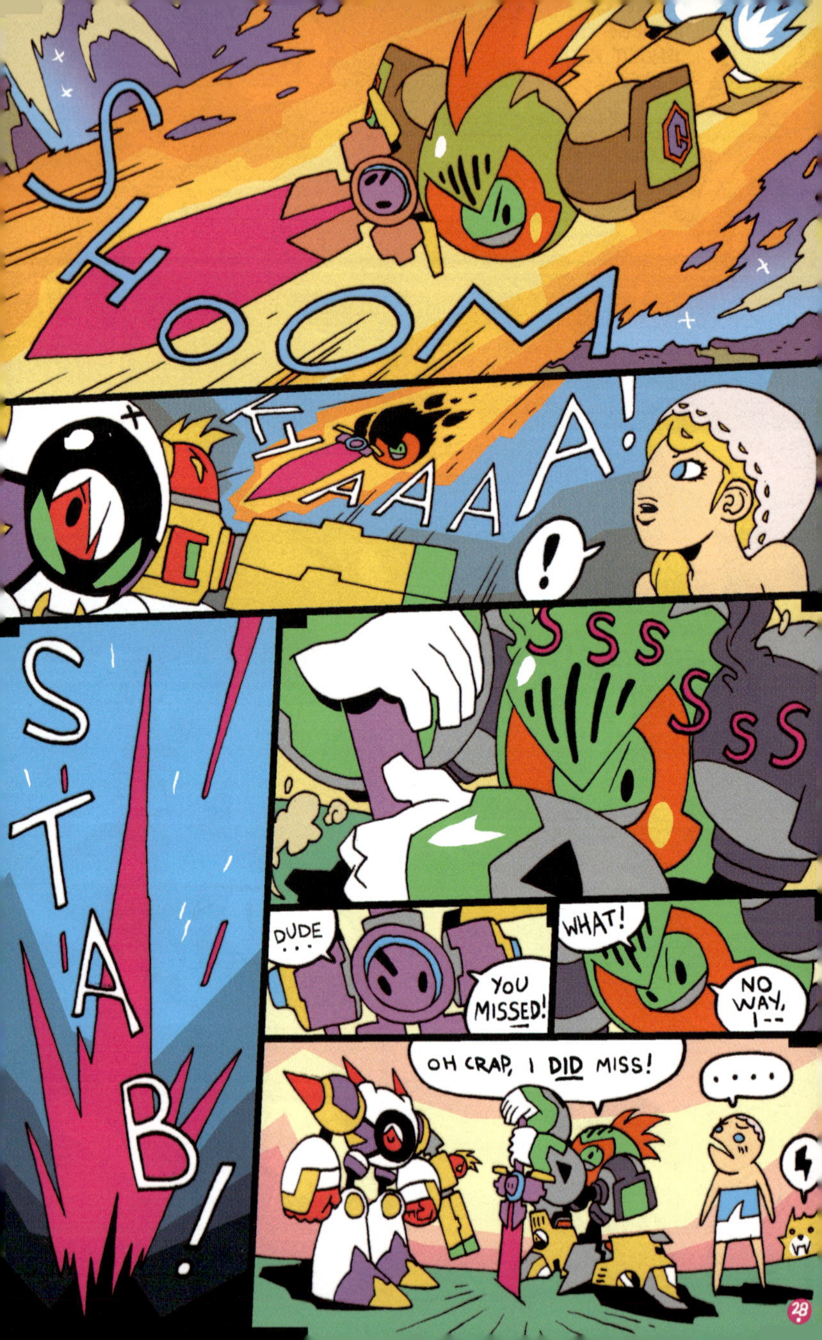
SHOOM
KIIAAAAA!
!
SSSSSSSS
STAB!
DUDE...
YOU MISSED!
WHAT!
NO WAY, I--
OH CRAP, I DID MISS!
....

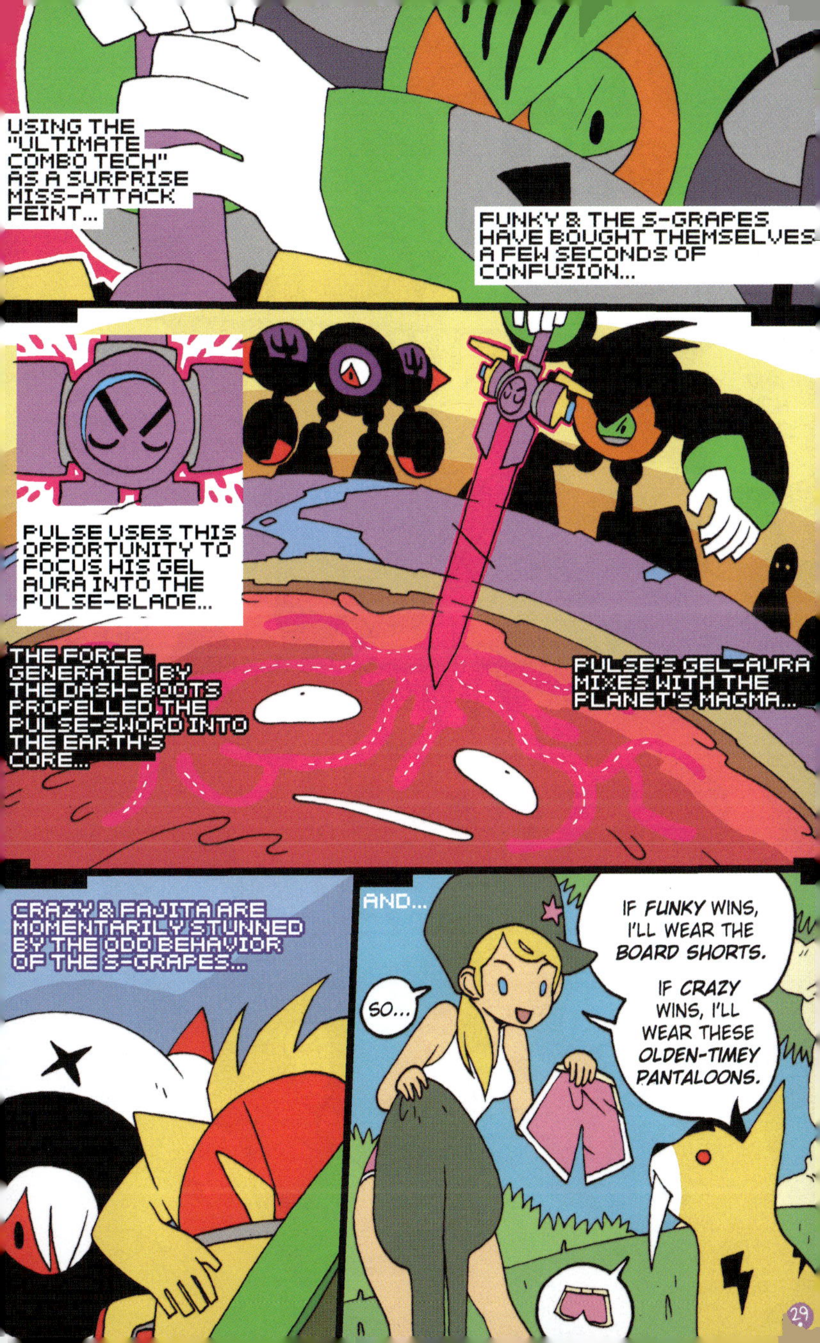
USING THE "ULTIMATE COMBO TECH" AS A SURPRISE MISS-ATTACK FEINT...
FUNKY & THE S-GRAPES HAVE BOUGHT THEMSELVES A FEW SECONDS OF CONFUSION...
PULSE USES THIS OPPORTUNITY TO FOCUS HIS GEL AURA INTO THE PULSE-BLADE...
THE FORCE GENERATED BY THE DASH-BOOTS PROPELLED THE PULSE-SWORD INTO THE EARTH'S CORE...
PULSE'S GEL-AURA MIXES WITH THE PLANET'S MAGMA...
CRAZY & FAJITA ARE MOMENTARILY STUNNED BY THE ODD BEHAVIOR OF THE S-GRAPES...
AND...
SO...
IF FUNKY WINS, I'LL WEAR THE BOARD SHORTS.
IF CRAZY WINS, I'LL WEAR THESE OLDEN-TIMEY PANTALOONS.

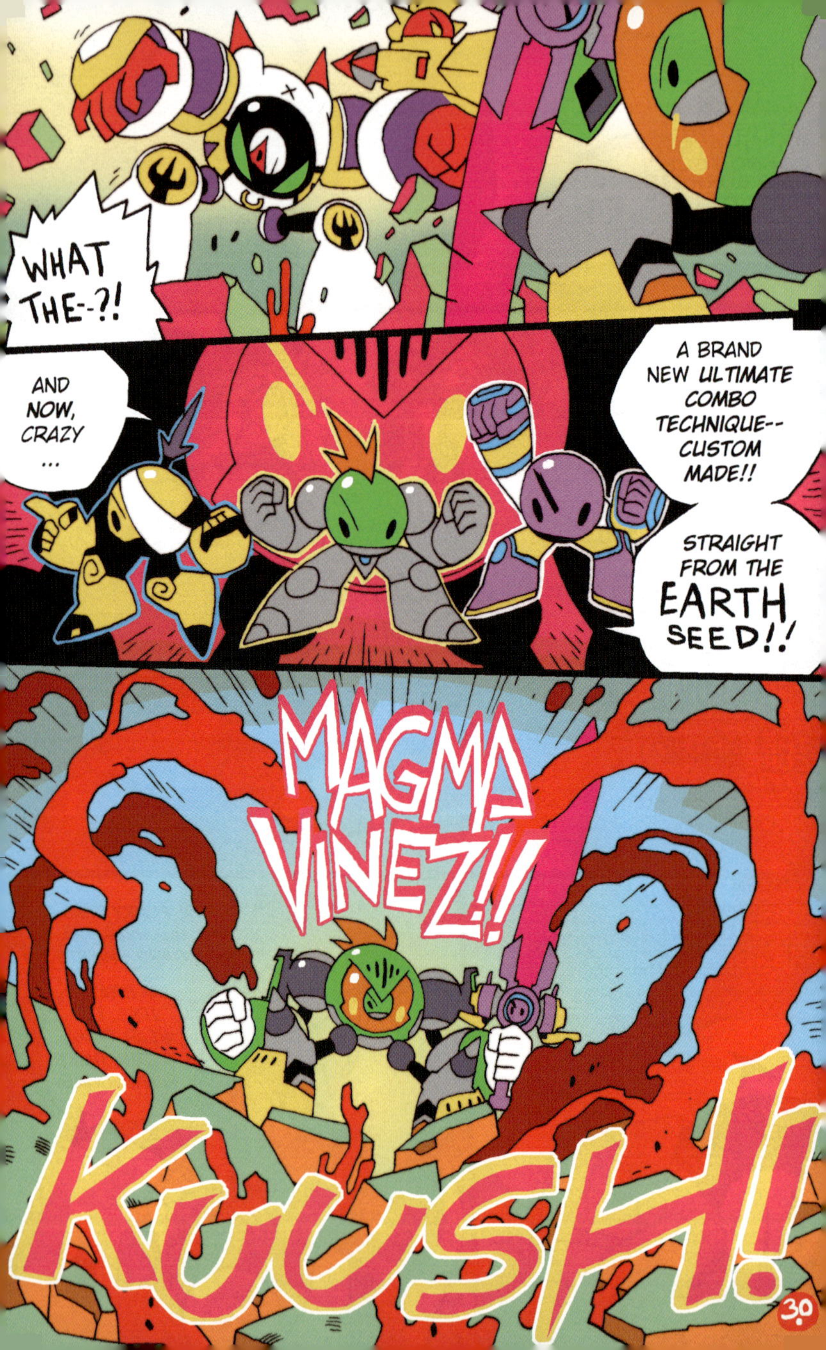
WHAT THE--?!
AND NOW, CRAZY ...
A BRAND NEW ULTIMATE COMBO TECHNIQUE-- CUSTOM MADE!!
STRAIGHT FROM THE EARTH SEED!!
MAGMA VINEZ!!
KUUSH!
30

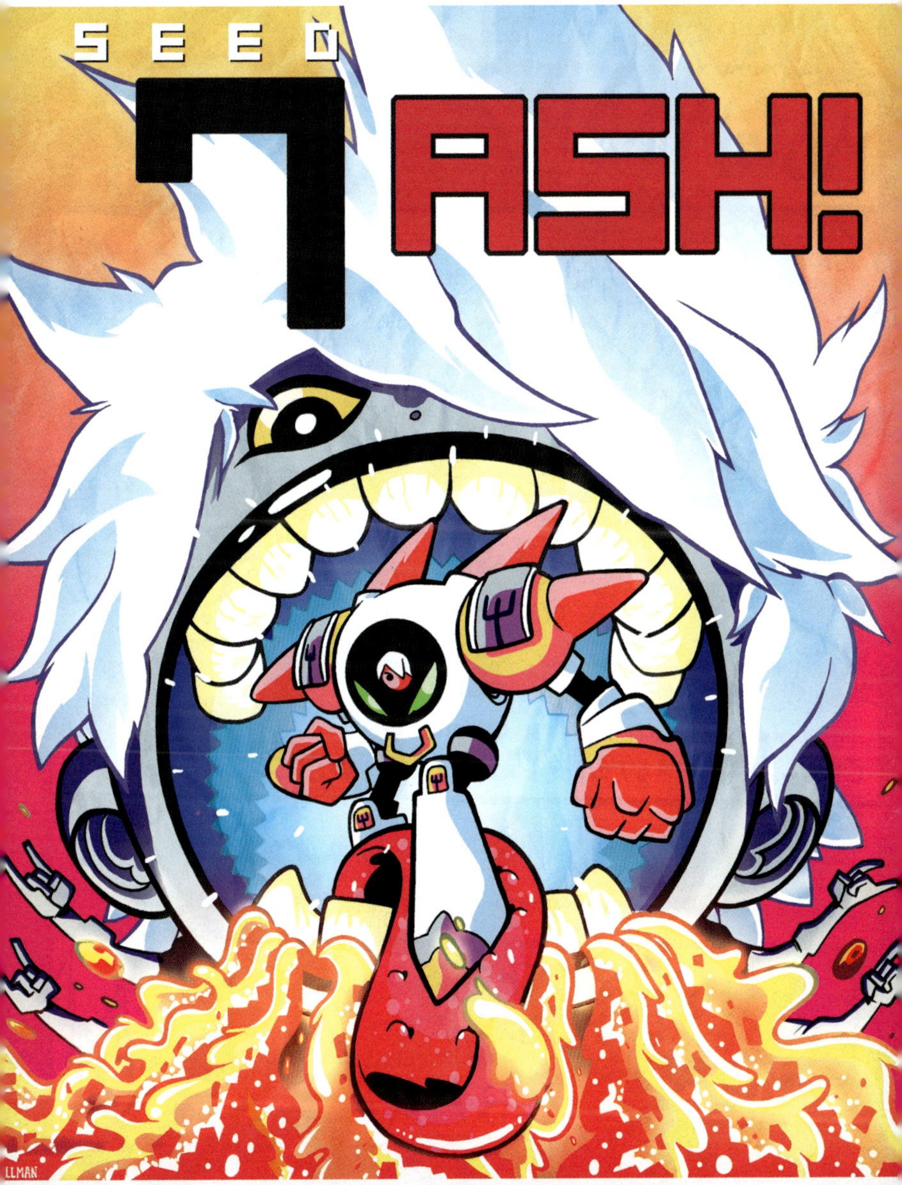
SEED
7
ASH!
LLMAN

ART: SHANE HILLMAN

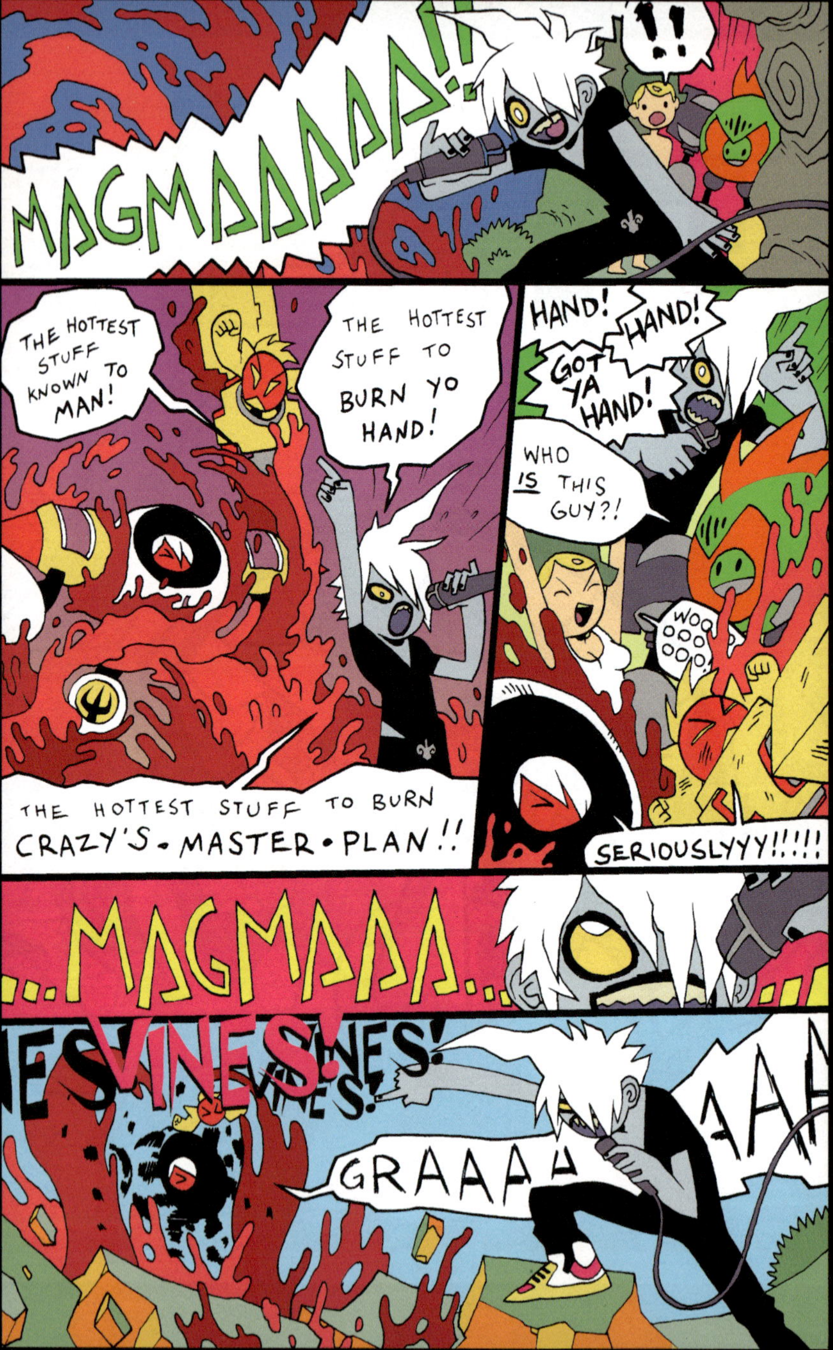
MAGMAAAAA!!
!!
THE HOTTEST STUFF KNOWN TO MAN!
THE HOTTEST STUFF TO BURN YO HAND!
THE HOTTEST STUFF TO BURN CRAZY'S • MASTER • PLAN!!
HAND!
HAND!
GOT YA HAND!
WHO IS THIS GUY?!
WOOOOOOOO
SERIOUSLYYY!!!!!
...MAGMAAA...
VINES!
GRAAAA

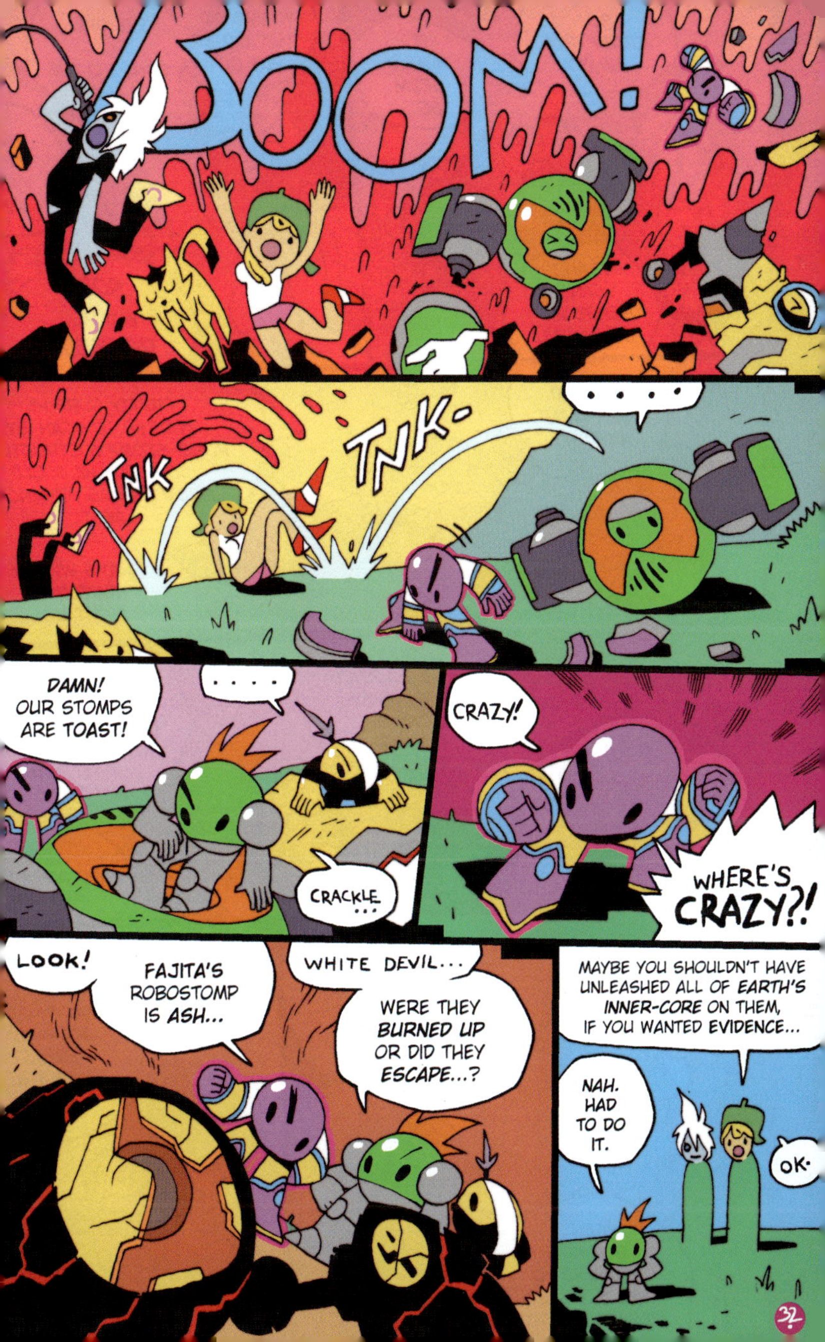
BOOM!
TNK
TNK-
....
DAMN! OUR STOMPS ARE TOAST!
....
CRACKLE...
CRAZY!
WHERE'S CRAZY?!
LOOK!
FAJITA'S ROBOSTOMP IS ASH...
WHITE DEVIL...
WERE THEY BURNED UP OR DID THEY ESCAPE...?
MAYBE YOU SHOULDN'T HAVE UNLEASHED ALL OF EARTH'S INNER-CORE ON THEM, IF YOU WANTED EVIDENCE...
NAH. HAD TO DO IT.
OK.

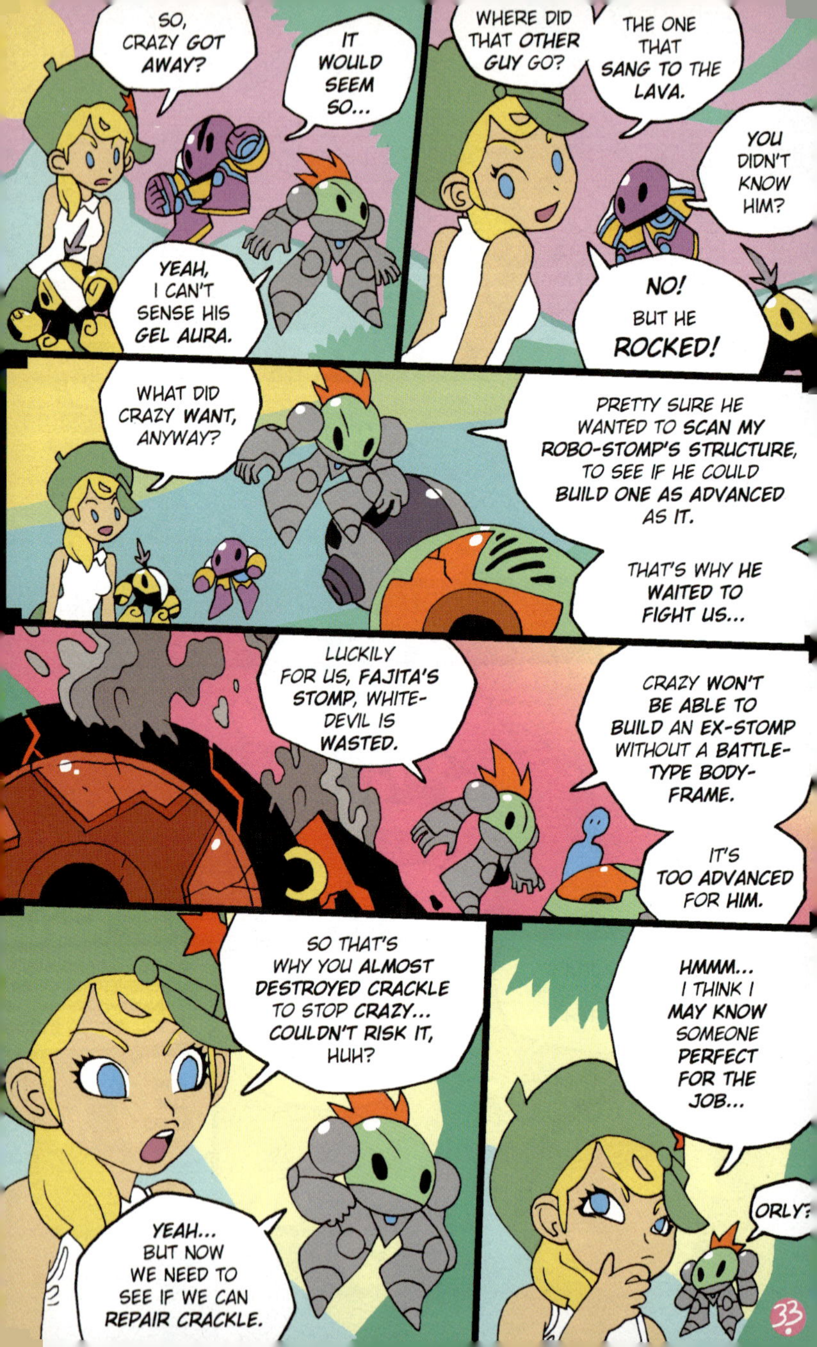
SO, CRAZY GOT AWAY?
IT WOULD SEEM SO...
YEAH, I CAN'T SENSE HIS GEL AURA.
WHERE DID THAT OTHER GUY GO?
THE ONE THAT SANG TO THE LAVA.
YOU DIDN'T KNOW HIM?
NO! BUT HE ROCKED!
WHAT DID CRAZY WANT, ANYWAY?
PRETTY SURE HE WANTED TO SCAN MY ROBO-STOMP'S STRUCTURE, TO SEE IF HE COULD BUILD ONE AS ADVANCED AS IT.
THAT'S WHY HE WAITED TO FIGHT US...
LUCKILY FOR US, FAJITA'S STOMP, WHITE-DEVIL IS WASTED.
CRAZY WON'T BE ABLE TO BUILD AN EX-STOMP WITHOUT A BATTLE-TYPE BODY-FRAME.
IT'S TOO ADVANCED FOR HIM.
SO THAT'S WHY YOU ALMOST DESTROYED CRACKLE TO STOP CRAZY... COULDN'T RISK IT, HUH?
YEAH... BUT NOW WE NEED TO SEE IF WE CAN REPAIR CRACKLE.
HMMM... I THINK I MAY KNOW SOMEONE PERFECT FOR THE JOB...
ORLY?

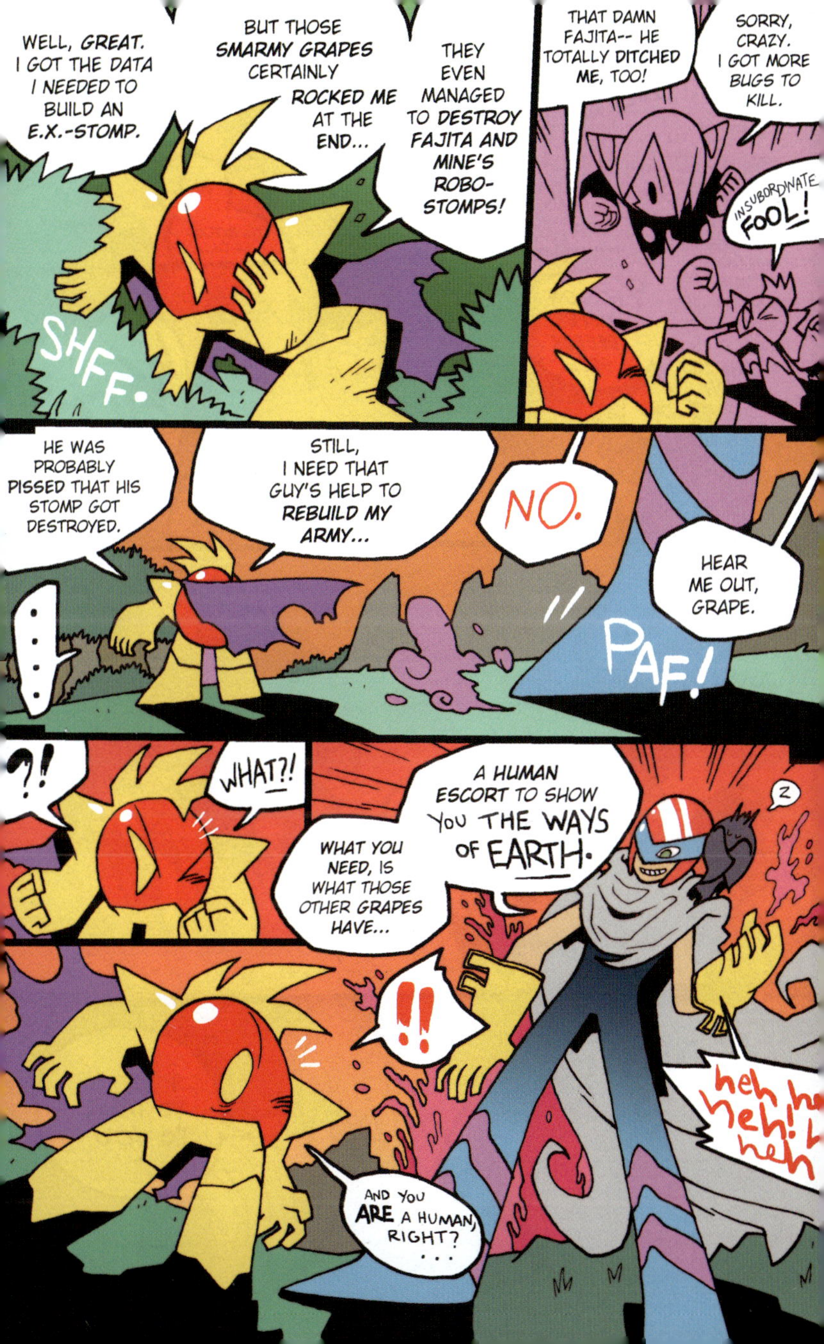
WELL, GREAT. I GOT THE DATA I NEEDED TO BUILD AN E.X.-STOMP.
BUT THOSE SMARMY GRAPES CERTAINLY ROCKED ME AT THE END...
THEY EVEN MANAGED TO DESTROY FAJITA AND MINE'S ROBO-STOMPS!
SHFF.
THAT DAMN FAJITA-- HE TOTALLY DITCHED ME, TOO!
SORRY, CRAZY. I GOT MORE BUGS TO KILL.
INSUBORDINATE FOOL!
HE WAS PROBABLY PISSED THAT HIS STOMP GOT DESTROYED.
STILL, I NEED THAT GUY'S HELP TO REBUILD MY ARMY...
NO.
HEAR ME OUT, GRAPE.
PAF!
...
?!
WHAT?!
WHAT YOU NEED, IS WHAT THOSE OTHER GRAPES HAVE...
A HUMAN ESCORT TO SHOW YOU THE WAYS OF EARTH.
!!
heh heh! heh
AND YOU ARE A HUMAN, RIGHT? ...

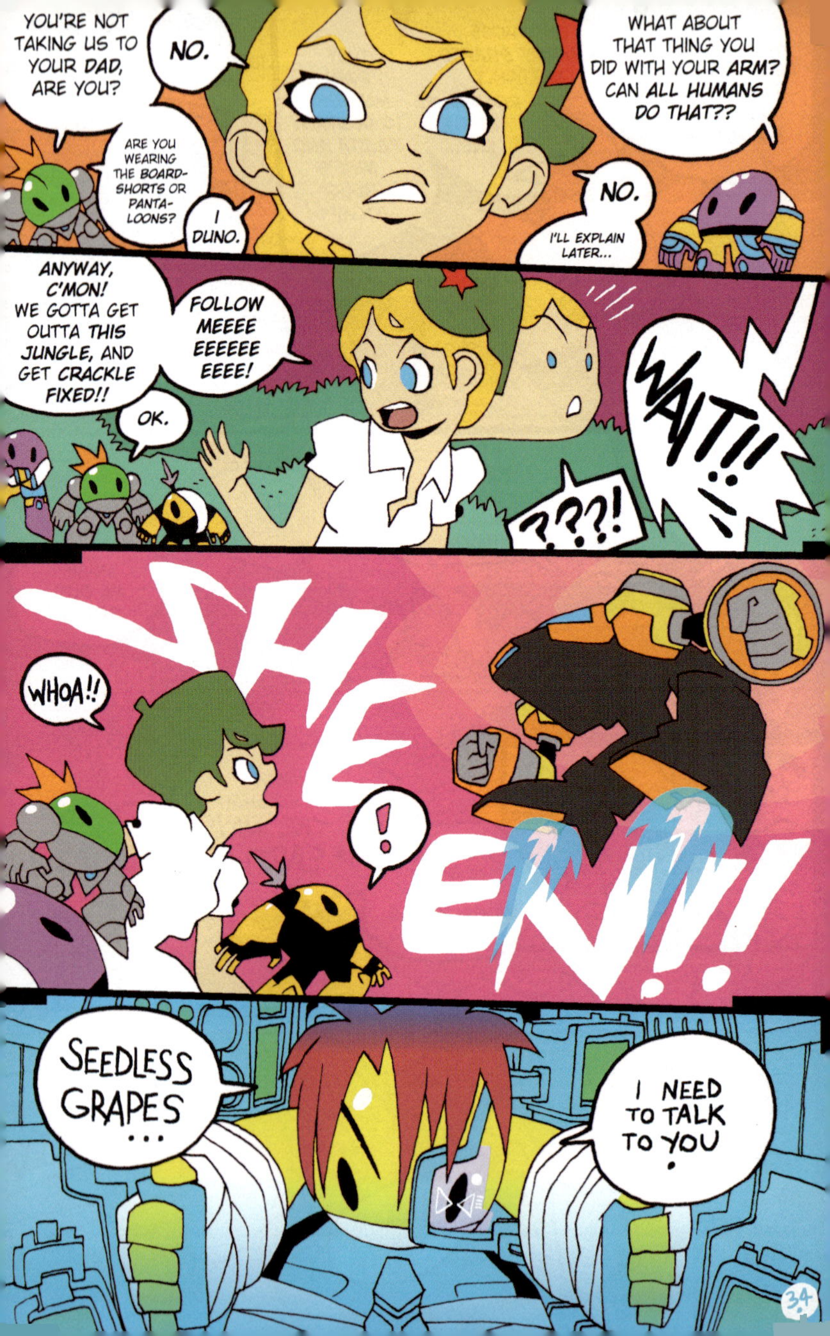
YOU'RE NOT TAKING US TO YOUR DAD, ARE YOU?
NO.
WHAT ABOUT THAT THING YOU DID WITH YOUR ARM? CAN ALL HUMANS DO THAT??
ARE YOU WEARING THE BOARD-SHORTS OR PANTA-LOONS?
I DUNO.
NO.
I'LL EXPLAIN LATER...
ANYWAY, C'MON! WE GOTTA GET OUTTA THIS JUNGLE, AND GET CRACKLE FIXED!!
FOLLOW MEEEE EEEEEE EEEE!
OK.
WAIT!!
???!
SHEEN!!
WHOA!!
!
SEEDLESS GRAPES...
I NEED TO TALK TO YOU.

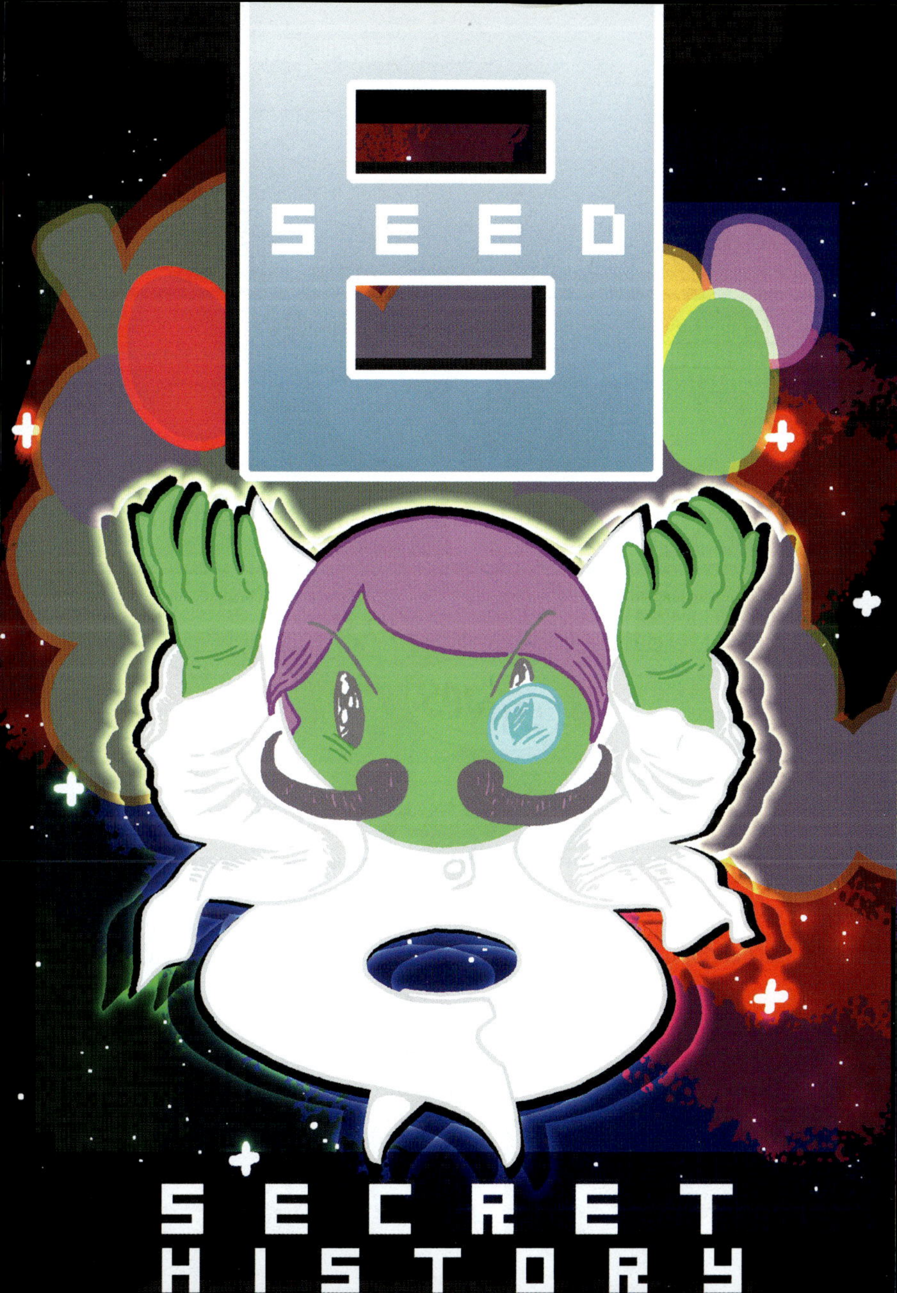
SEED
SECRET
HISTORY

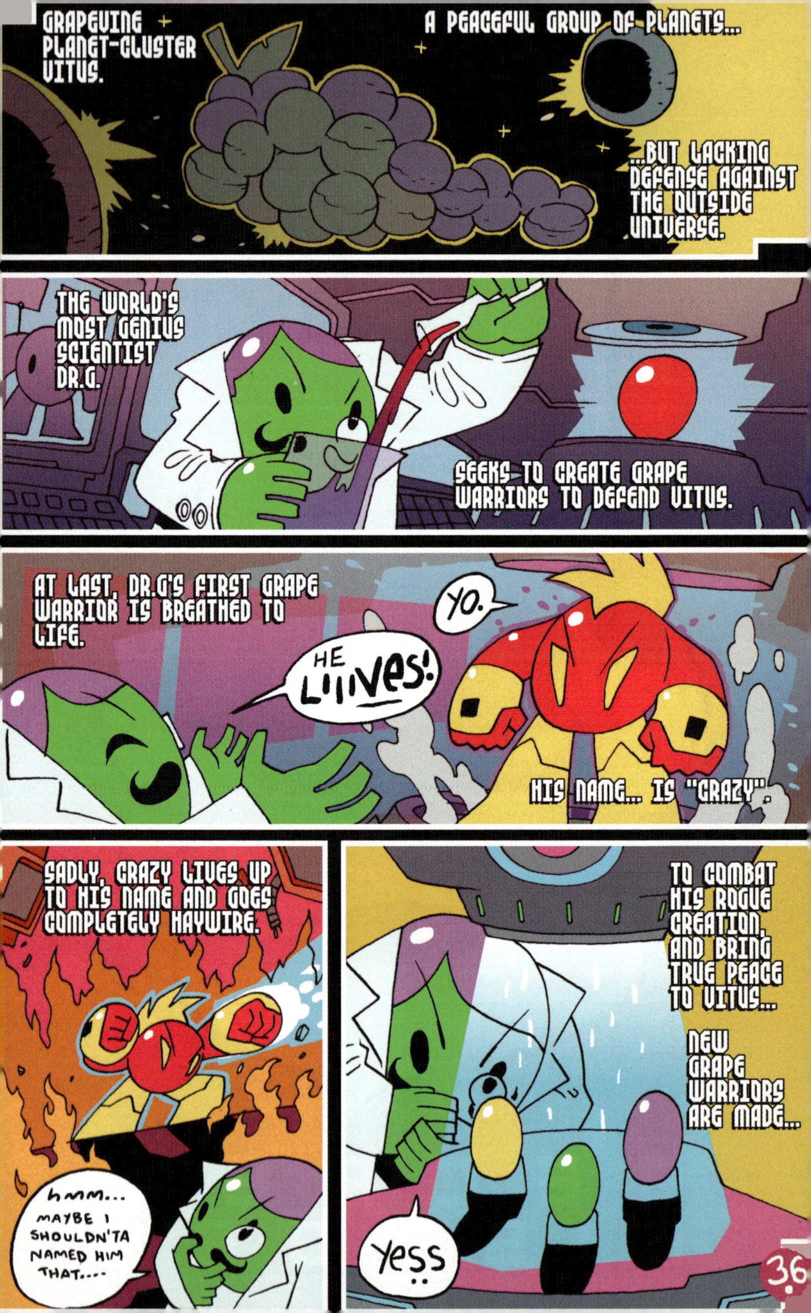
GRAPEVINE PLANET-CLUSTER VITUS.
A PEACEFUL GROUP OF PLANETS...
...BUT LACKING DEFENSE AGAINST THE OUTSIDE UNIVERSE.
THE WORLD'S MOST GENIUS SCIENTIST DR.G.
SEEKS TO CREATE GRAPE WARRIORS TO DEFEND VITUS.
AT LAST, DR.G'S FIRST GRAPE WARRIOR IS BREATHED TO LIFE.
YO.
HE LIIIVES!
HIS NAME... IS "CRAZY".
SADLY, CRAZY LIVES UP TO HIS NAME AND GOES COMPLETELY HAYWIRE.
HMM... MAYBE I SHOULDN'TA NAMED HIM THAT....
TO COMBAT HIS ROGUE CREATION, AND BRING TRUE PEACE TO VITUS...
NEW GRAPE WARRIORS ARE MADE...
YESS

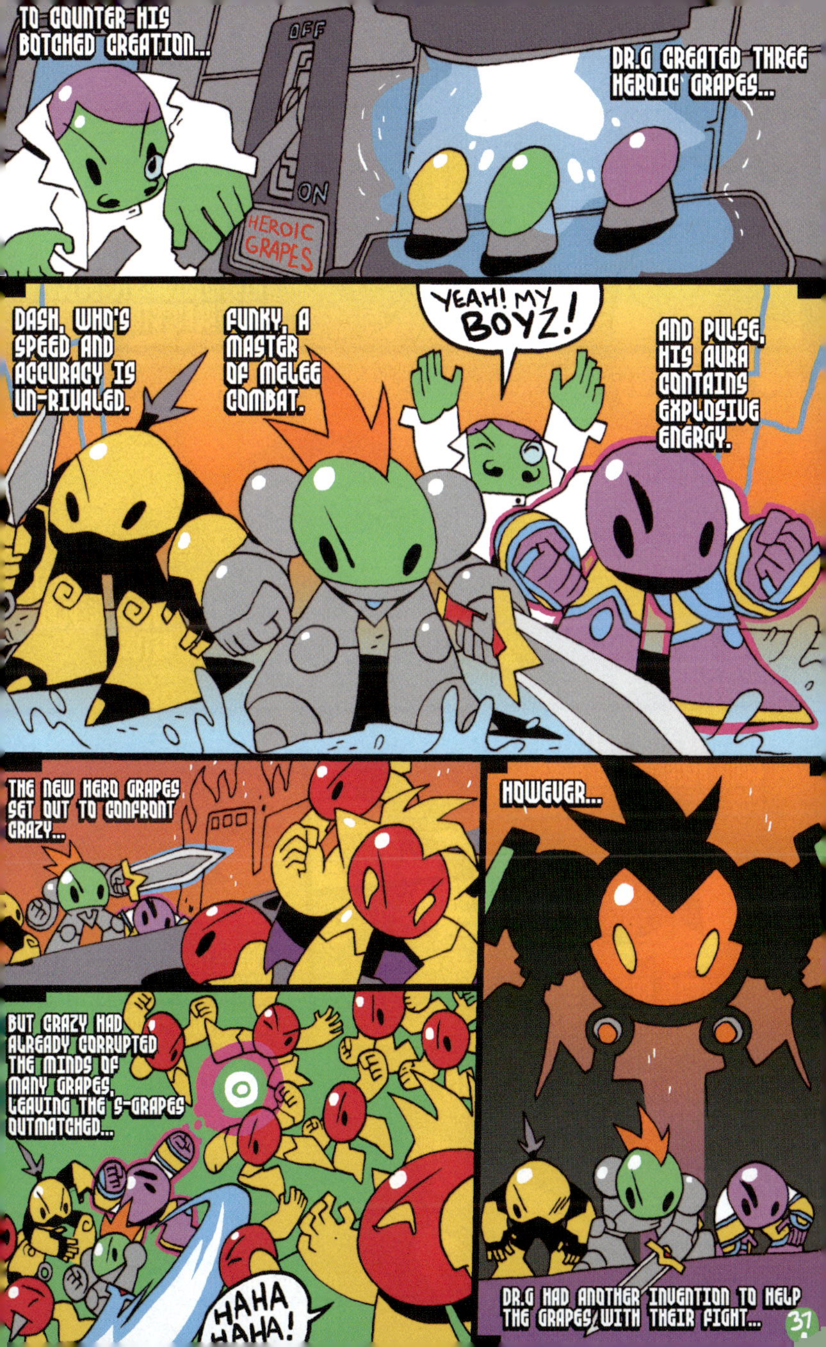
TO COUNTER HIS BOTCHED CREATION...
OFF
ON
HEROIC GRAPES
DR.G CREATED THREE HEROIC GRAPES...
DASH, WHO'S SPEED AND ACCURACY IS UN-RIVALED.
FUNKY, A MASTER OF MELEE COMBAT.
YEAH! MY BOYZ!
AND PULSE, HIS AURA CONTAINS EXPLOSIVE ENERGY.
THE NEW HERO GRAPES SET OUT TO CONFRONT CRAZY...
HOWEVER...
BUT CRAZY HAD ALREADY CORRUPTED THE MINDS OF MANY GRAPES, LEAVING THE S-GRAPES OUTMATCHED...
HAHA HAHA!
DR.G HAD ANOTHER INVENTION TO HELP THE GRAPES WITH THEIR FIGHT...

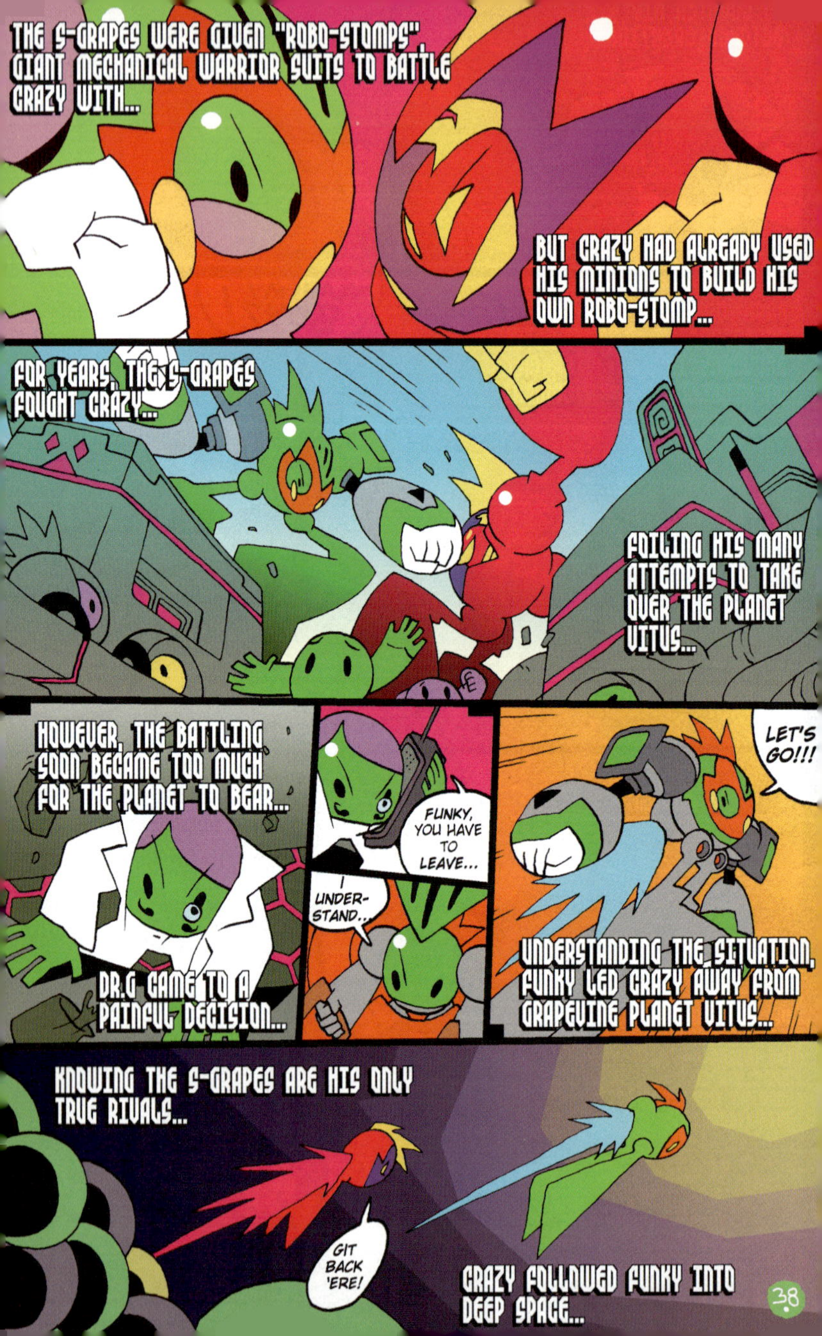
THE S-GRAPES WERE GIVEN "ROBO-STOMPS", GIANT MECHANICAL WARRIOR SUITS TO BATTLE CRAZY WITH...
BUT CRAZY HAD ALREADY USED HIS MINIONS TO BUILD HIS OWN ROBO-STOMP...
FOR YEARS, THE S-GRAPES FOUGHT CRAZY...
FOILING HIS MANY ATTEMPTS TO TAKE OVER THE PLANET VITUS...
HOWEVER, THE BATTLING SOON BECAME TOO MUCH FOR THE PLANET TO BEAR...
DR.G CAME TO A PAINFUL DECISION...
FUNKY, YOU HAVE TO LEAVE...
I UNDER-STAND...
LET'S GO!!!
UNDERSTANDING THE SITUATION, FUNKY LED CRAZY AWAY FROM GRAPEVINE PLANET VITUS...
KNOWING THE S-GRAPES ARE HIS ONLY TRUE RIVALS...
GIT BACK 'ERE!
CRAZY FOLLOWED FUNKY INTO DEEP SPACE...

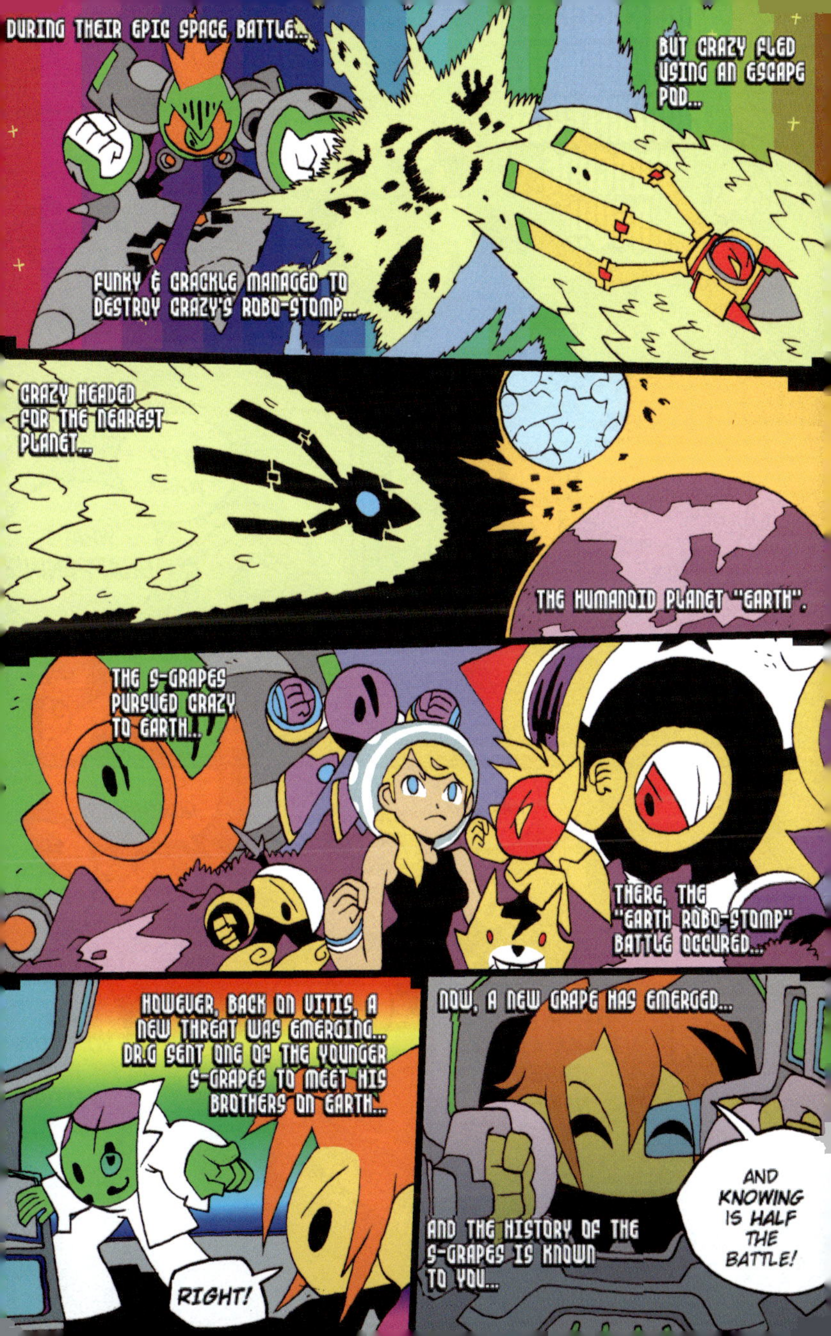
DURING THEIR EPIC SPACE BATTLE...
BUT CRAZY FLED USING AN ESCAPE POD...
FUNKY & CRACKLE MANAGED TO DESTROY CRAZY'S ROBO-STOMP...
CRAZY HEADED FOR THE NEAREST PLANET...
THE HUMANOID PLANET "EARTH".
THE S-GRAPES PURSUED CRAZY TO EARTH...
THERE, THE "EARTH ROBO-STOMP" BATTLE OCCURED...
HOWEVER, BACK ON VITIS, A NEW THREAT WAS EMERGING... DR.G SENT ONE OF THE YOUNGER S-GRAPES TO MEET HIS BROTHERS ON EARTH...
RIGHT!
NOW, A NEW GRAPE HAS EMERGED...
AND THE HISTORY OF THE S-GRAPES IS KNOWN TO YOU...
AND KNOWING IS HALF THE BATTLE!

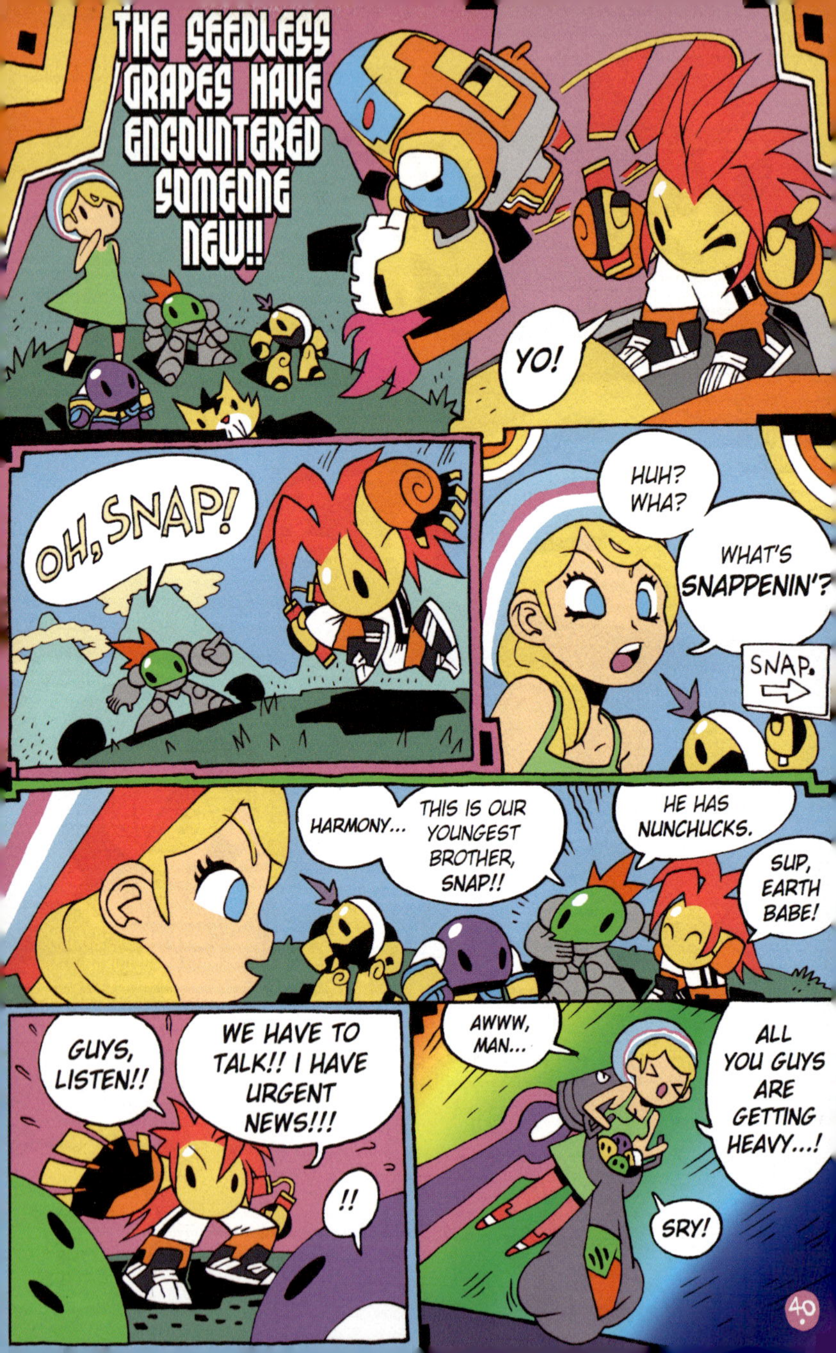
THE SEEDLESS GRAPES HAVE ENCOUNTERED SOMEONE NEW!!
YO!
OH, SNAP!
HUH? WHA?
WHAT'S SNAPPENIN'?
SNAP.
HARMONY...
THIS IS OUR YOUNGEST BROTHER, SNAP!!
HE HAS NUNCHUCKS.
SUP, EARTH BABE!
GUYS, LISTEN!!
WE HAVE TO TALK!! I HAVE URGENT NEWS!!!
!!
AWWW, MAN...
ALL YOU GUYS ARE GETTING HEAVY...!
SRY!

SEED 9

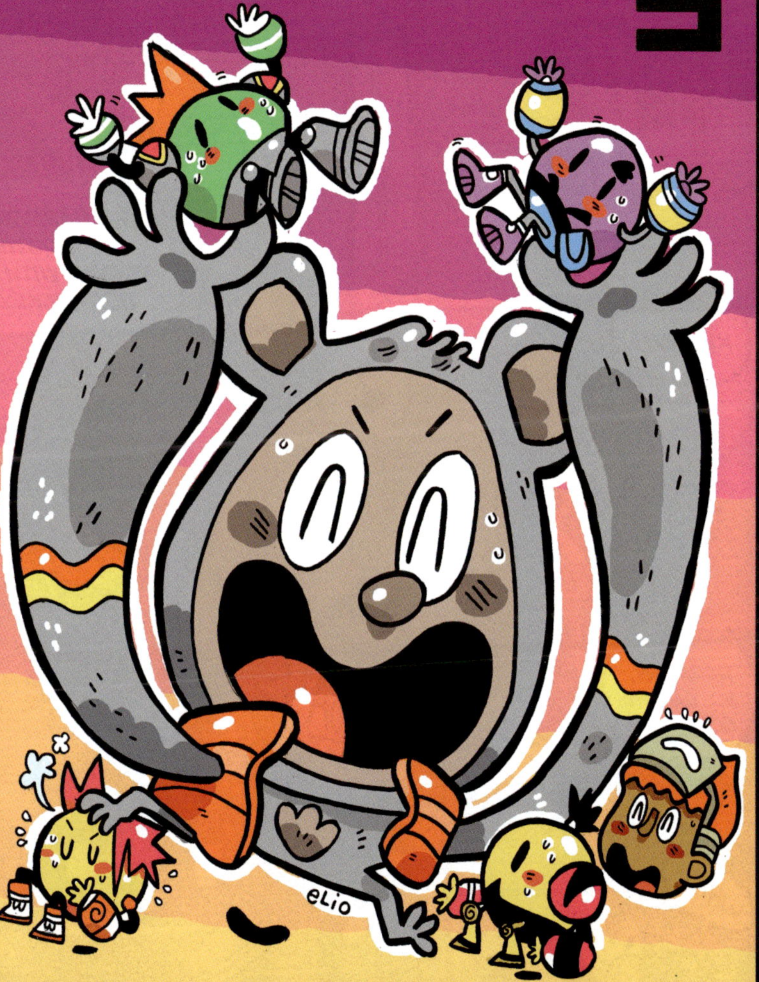
eLIO

UP-GRAPES!

ART: ELIO

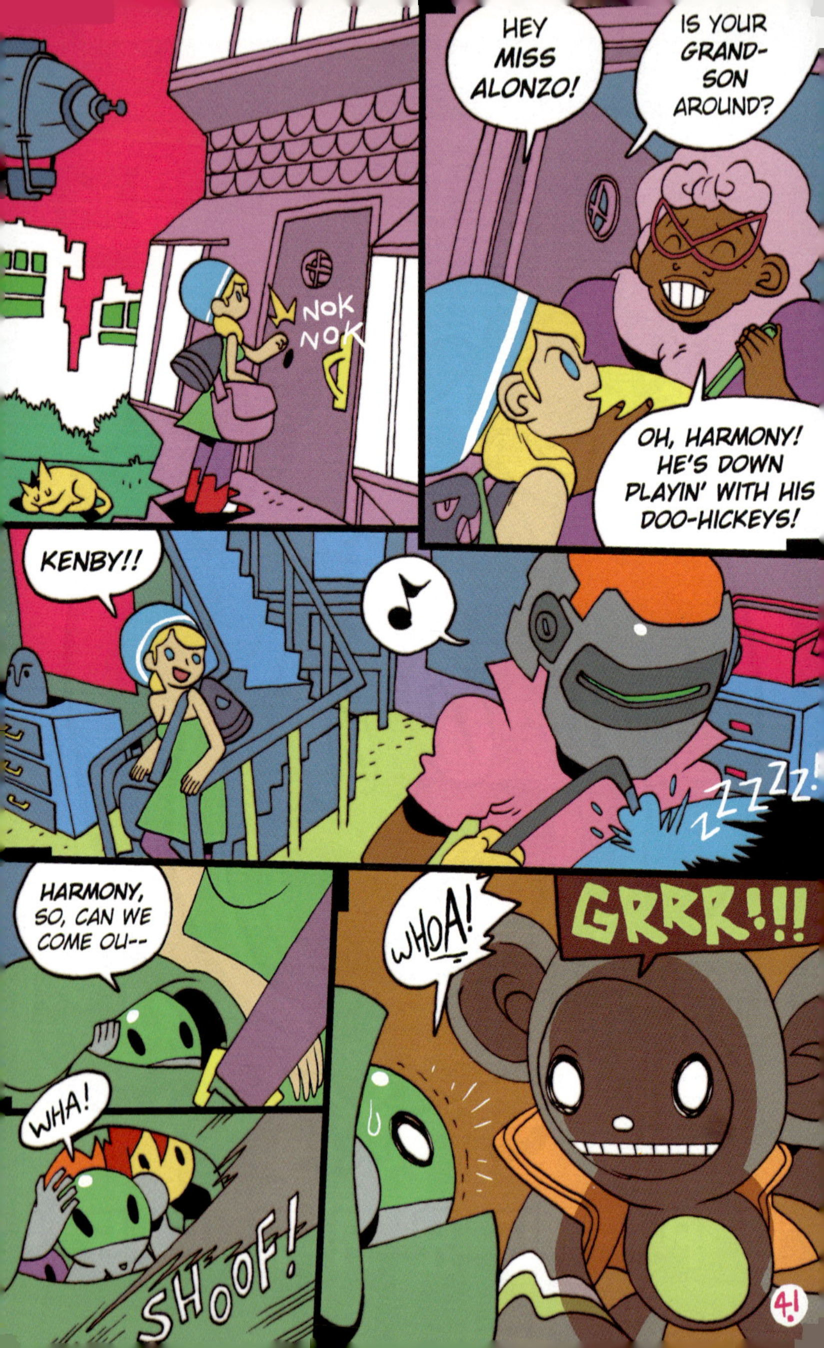
NOK NOK
HEY MISS ALONZO!
IS YOUR GRAND-SON AROUND?
OH, HARMONY! HE'S DOWN PLAYIN' WITH HIS DOO-HICKEYS!
KENBY!!
ZZZZZ!
HARMONY, SO, CAN WE COME OU--
WHA!
SHOOF!
WHOA!
GRRR!!!

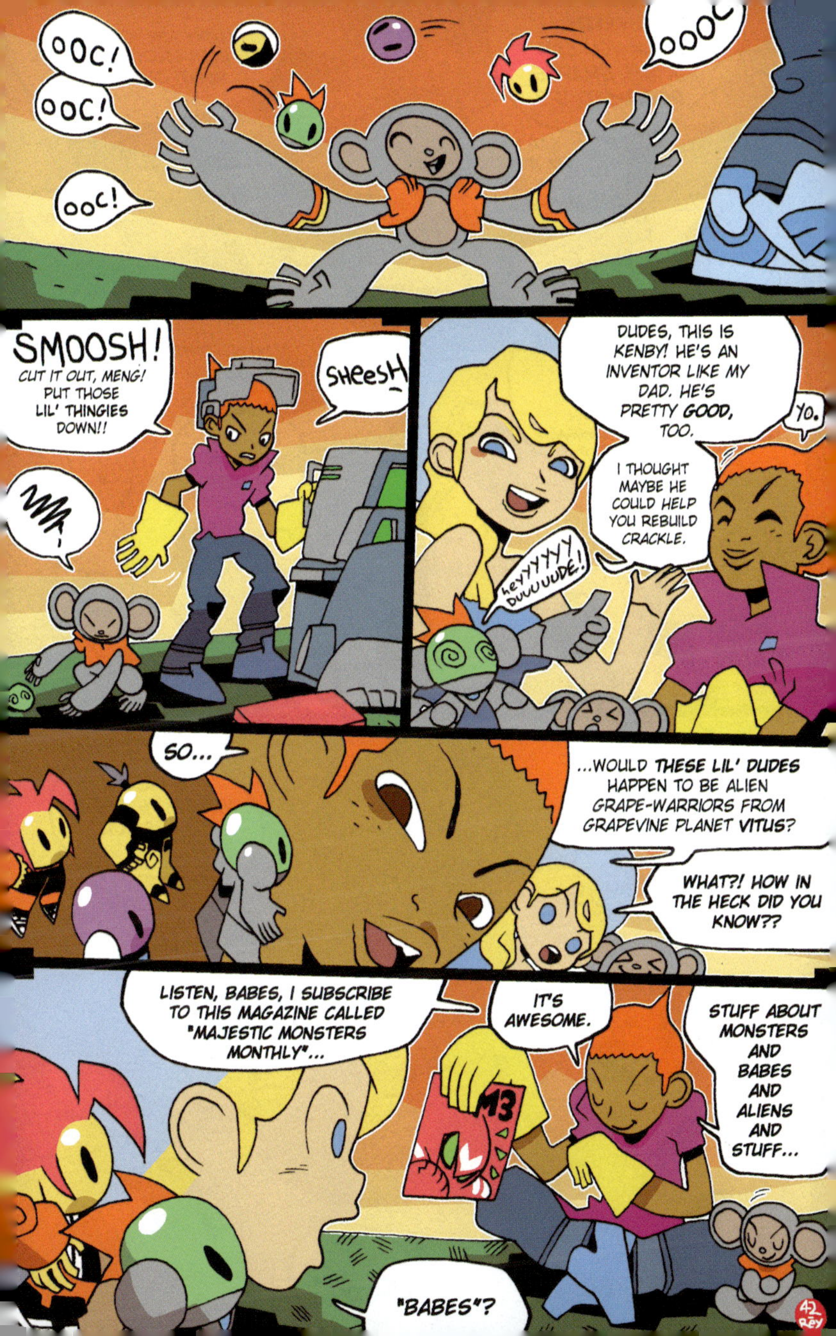
OOC!
OOC!
OOC!
OOOC
SMOOSH! CUT IT OUT, MENG! PUT THOSE LIL' THINGIES DOWN!!
SHEESH
DUDES, THIS IS KENBY! HE'S AN INVENTOR LIKE MY DAD. HE'S PRETTY GOOD, TOO.
YO.
I THOUGHT MAYBE HE COULD HELP YOU REBUILD CRACKLE.
HEYYYYYY DUUUUUDE!
SO...
...WOULD THESE LIL' DUDES HAPPEN TO BE ALIEN GRAPE-WARRIORS FROM GRAPEVINE PLANET VITUS?
WHAT?! HOW IN THE HECK DID YOU KNOW??
LISTEN, BABES, I SUBSCRIBE TO THIS MAGAZINE CALLED "MAJESTIC MONSTERS MONTHLY"...
IT'S AWESOME.
STUFF ABOUT MONSTERS AND BABES AND ALIENS AND STUFF...
M3
"BABES"?
42 Rey

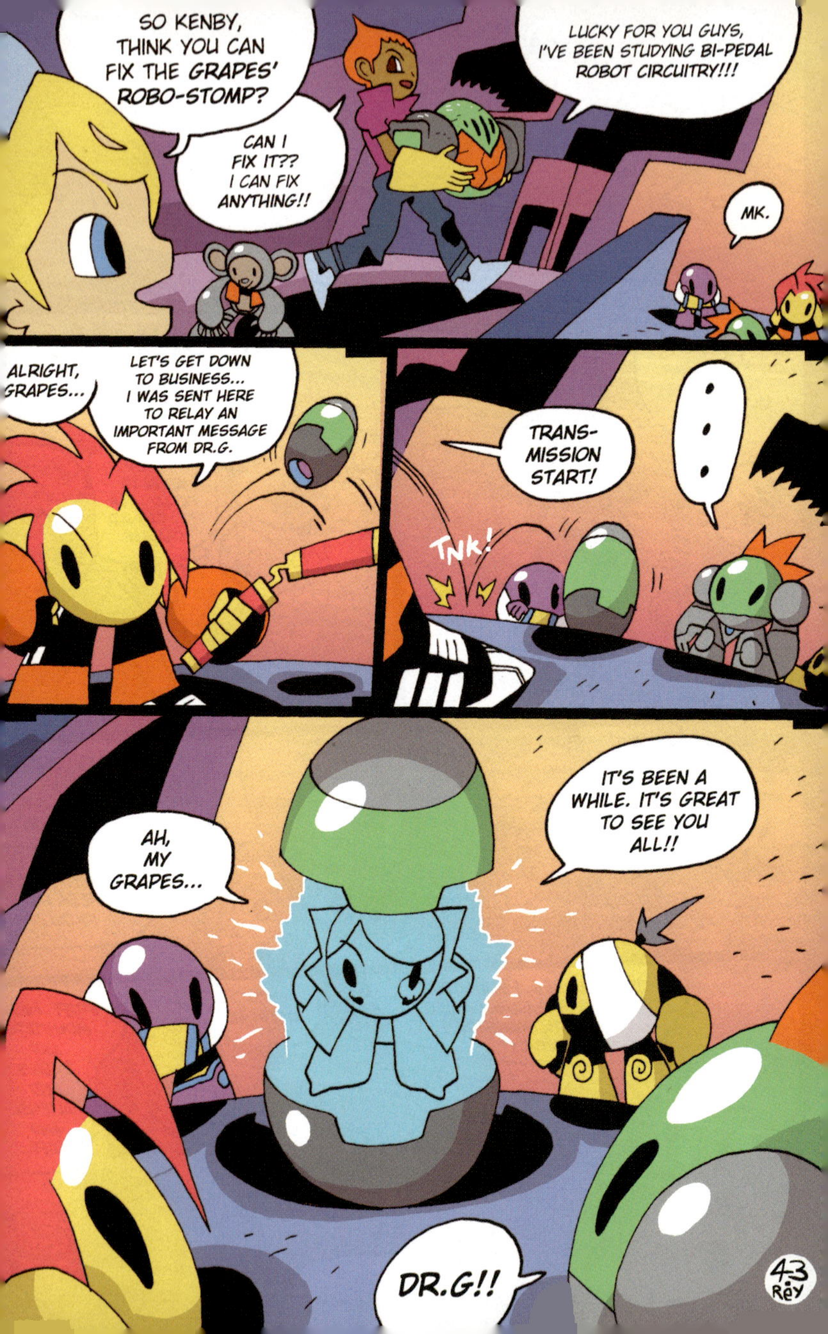
SO KENBY, THINK YOU CAN FIX THE GRAPES' ROBO-STOMP?
CAN I FIX IT?? I CAN FIX ANYTHING!!
LUCKY FOR YOU GUYS, I'VE BEEN STUDYING BI-PEDAL ROBOT CIRCUITRY!!!
MK.
ALRIGHT, GRAPES...
LET'S GET DOWN TO BUSINESS... I WAS SENT HERE TO RELAY AN IMPORTANT MESSAGE FROM DR.G.
TRANS-MISSION START!
...
TNK!
AH, MY GRAPES...
IT'S BEEN A WHILE. IT'S GREAT TO SEE YOU ALL!!
DR.G!!
43
Rey

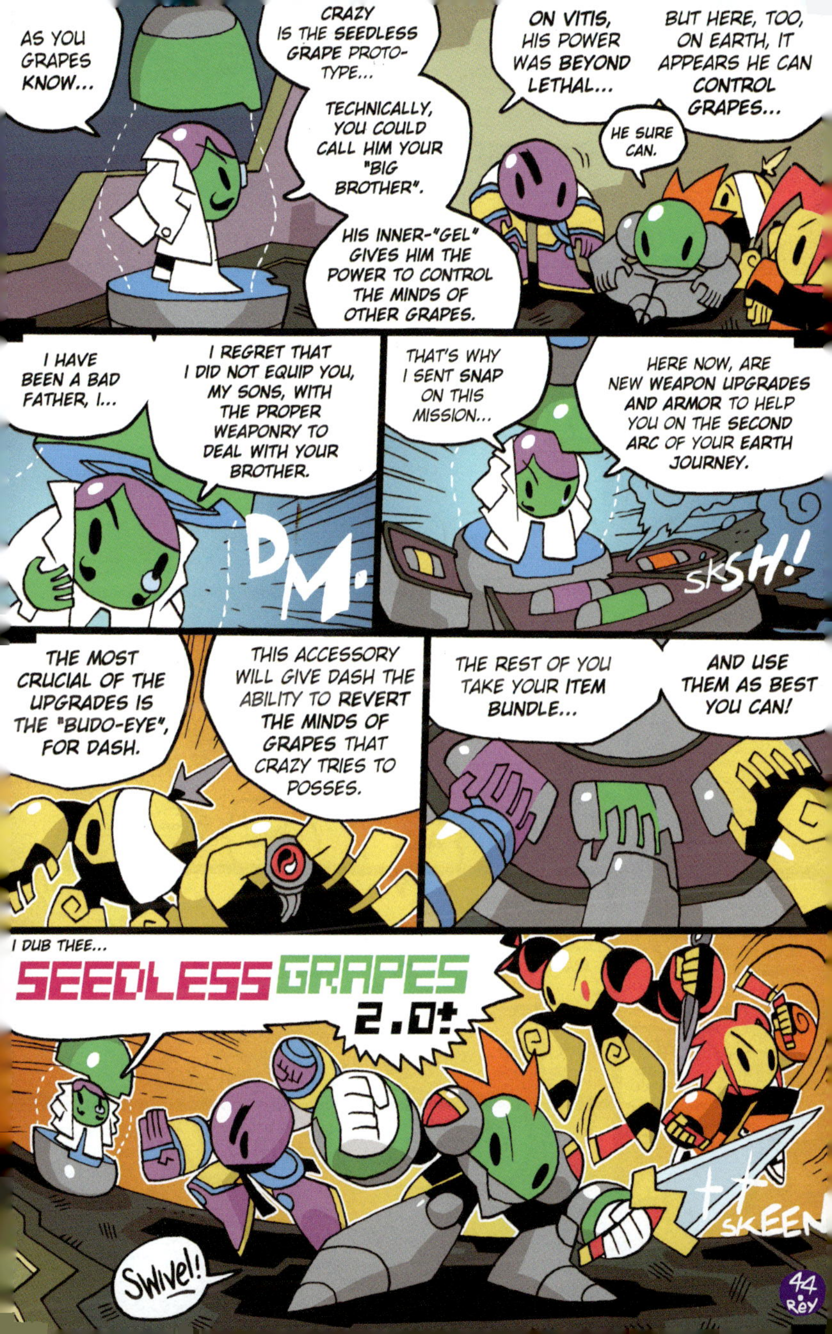
AS YOU GRAPES KNOW...
CRAZY IS THE SEEDLESS GRAPE PROTO-TYPE...
TECHNICALLY, YOU COULD CALL HIM YOUR "BIG BROTHER".
HIS INNER-"GEL" GIVES HIM THE POWER TO CONTROL THE MINDS OF OTHER GRAPES.
ON VITIS, HIS POWER WAS BEYOND LETHAL...
BUT HERE, TOO, ON EARTH, IT APPEARS HE CAN CONTROL GRAPES...
HE SURE CAN.
I HAVE BEEN A BAD FATHER, I...
I REGRET THAT I DID NOT EQUIP YOU, MY SONS, WITH THE PROPER WEAPONRY TO DEAL WITH YOUR BROTHER.
DM.
THAT'S WHY I SENT SNAP ON THIS MISSION...
HERE NOW, ARE NEW WEAPON UPGRADES AND ARMOR TO HELP YOU ON THE SECOND ARC OF YOUR EARTH JOURNEY.
SKSH!
THE MOST CRUCIAL OF THE UPGRADES IS THE "BUDO-EYE", FOR DASH.
THIS ACCESSORY WILL GIVE DASH THE ABILITY TO REVERT THE MINDS OF GRAPES THAT CRAZY TRIES TO POSSES.
THE REST OF YOU TAKE YOUR ITEM BUNDLE...
AND USE THEM AS BEST YOU CAN!
I DUB THEE... SEEDLESS GRAPES 2.0+
SKEEN
Swivel!

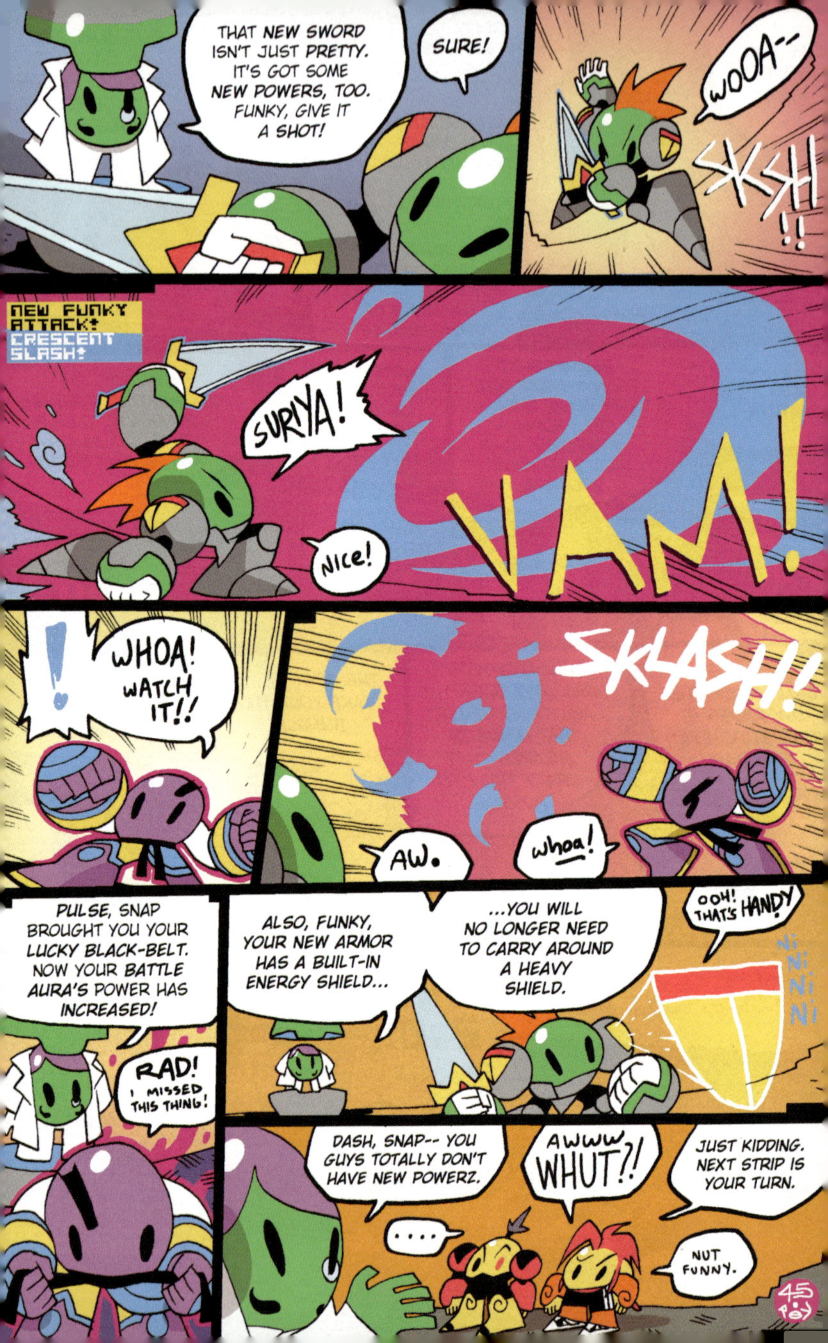
THAT NEW SWORD ISN'T JUST PRETTY. IT'S GOT SOME NEW POWERS, TOO. FUNKY, GIVE IT A SHOT!
SURE!
WOOA--
SKSH!!
NEW FUNKY ATTACK: CRESCENT SLASH!
SURIYA!
NICE!
VAM!
WHOA! WATCH IT!!
SKLASH!
AW.
whoa!
PULSE, SNAP BROUGHT YOU YOUR LUCKY BLACK-BELT. NOW YOUR BATTLE AURA'S POWER HAS INCREASED!
RAD! I MISSED THIS THING!
ALSO, FUNKY, YOUR NEW ARMOR HAS A BUILT-IN ENERGY SHIELD...
...YOU WILL NO LONGER NEED TO CARRY AROUND A HEAVY SHIELD.
OOH! THAT'S HANDY
NI NI NI NI
DASH, SNAP-- YOU GUYS TOTALLY DON'T HAVE NEW POWERZ.
AWWW WHUT?!
JUST KIDDING. NEXT STRIP IS YOUR TURN.
....
NUT FUNNY.
45

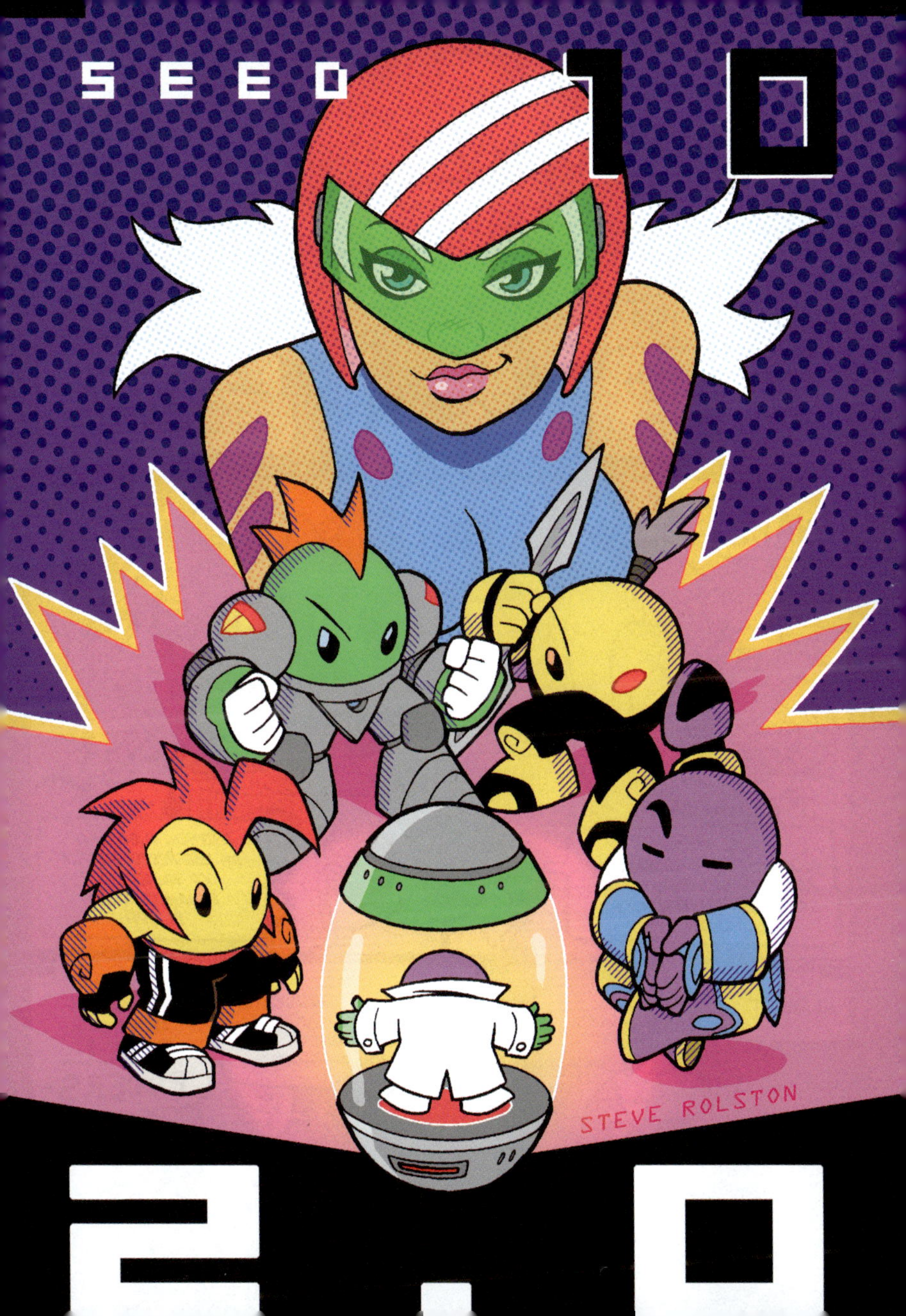
SEED 10
STEVE ROLSTON
2.0

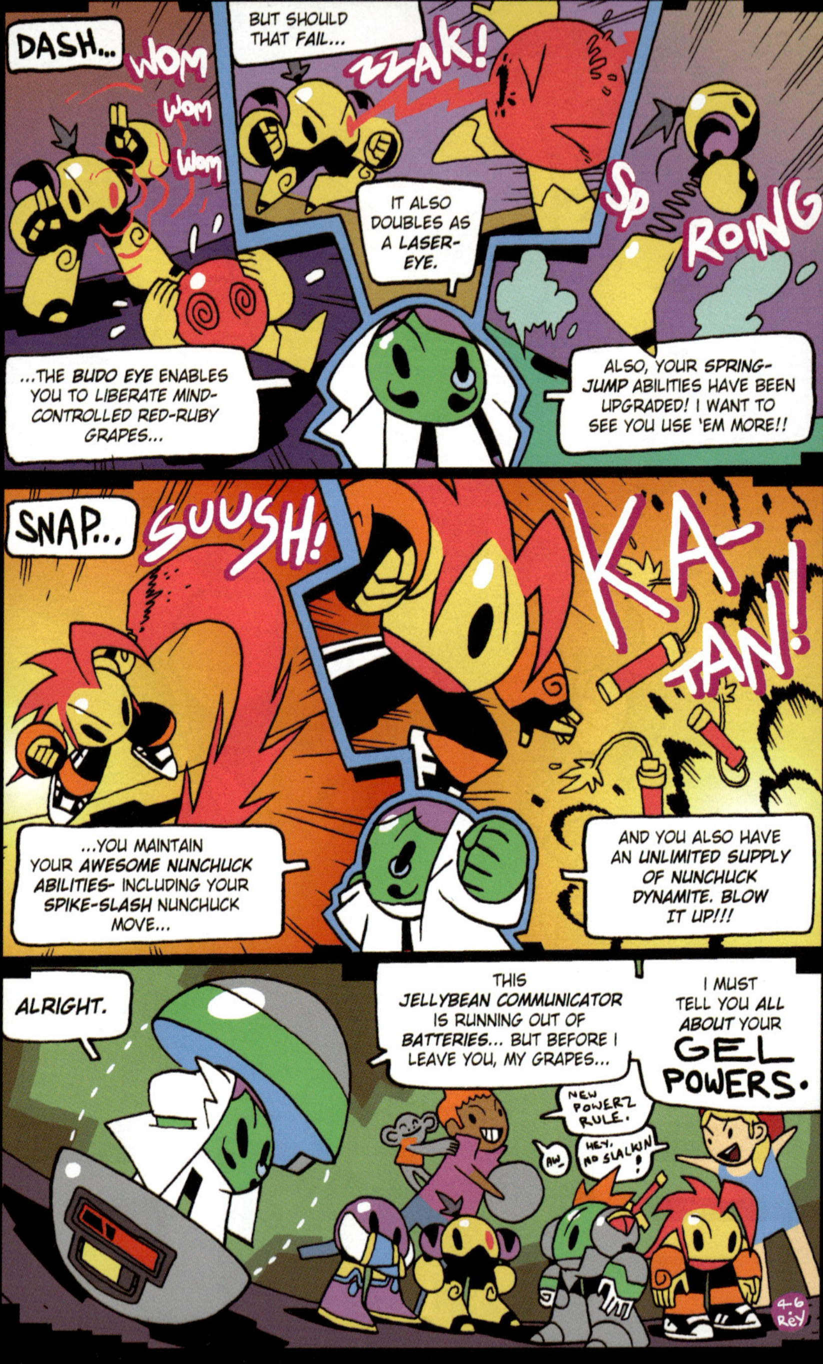
DASH...
WOM WOM WOM
BUT SHOULD THAT FAIL...
ZZAK!
IT ALSO DOUBLES AS A LASER-EYE.
SP ROING
...THE BUDO EYE ENABLES YOU TO LIBERATE MIND-CONTROLLED RED-RUBY GRAPES...
ALSO, YOUR SPRING-JUMP ABILITIES HAVE BEEN UPGRADED! I WANT TO SEE YOU USE 'EM MORE!!
SNAP...
SUUSH!
KA-TAN!
...YOU MAINTAIN YOUR AWESOME NUNCHUCK ABILITIES- INCLUDING YOUR SPIKE-SLASH NUNCHUCK MOVE...
AND YOU ALSO HAVE AN UNLIMITED SUPPLY OF NUNCHUCK DYNAMITE. BLOW IT UP!!!
ALRIGHT.
THIS JELLYBEAN COMMUNICATOR IS RUNNING OUT OF BATTERIES... BUT BEFORE I LEAVE YOU, MY GRAPES...
I MUST TELL YOU ALL ABOUT YOUR GEL POWERS.
NEW POWERZ RULE.
AW.
HEY, NO SLALKIN!
46 Rey

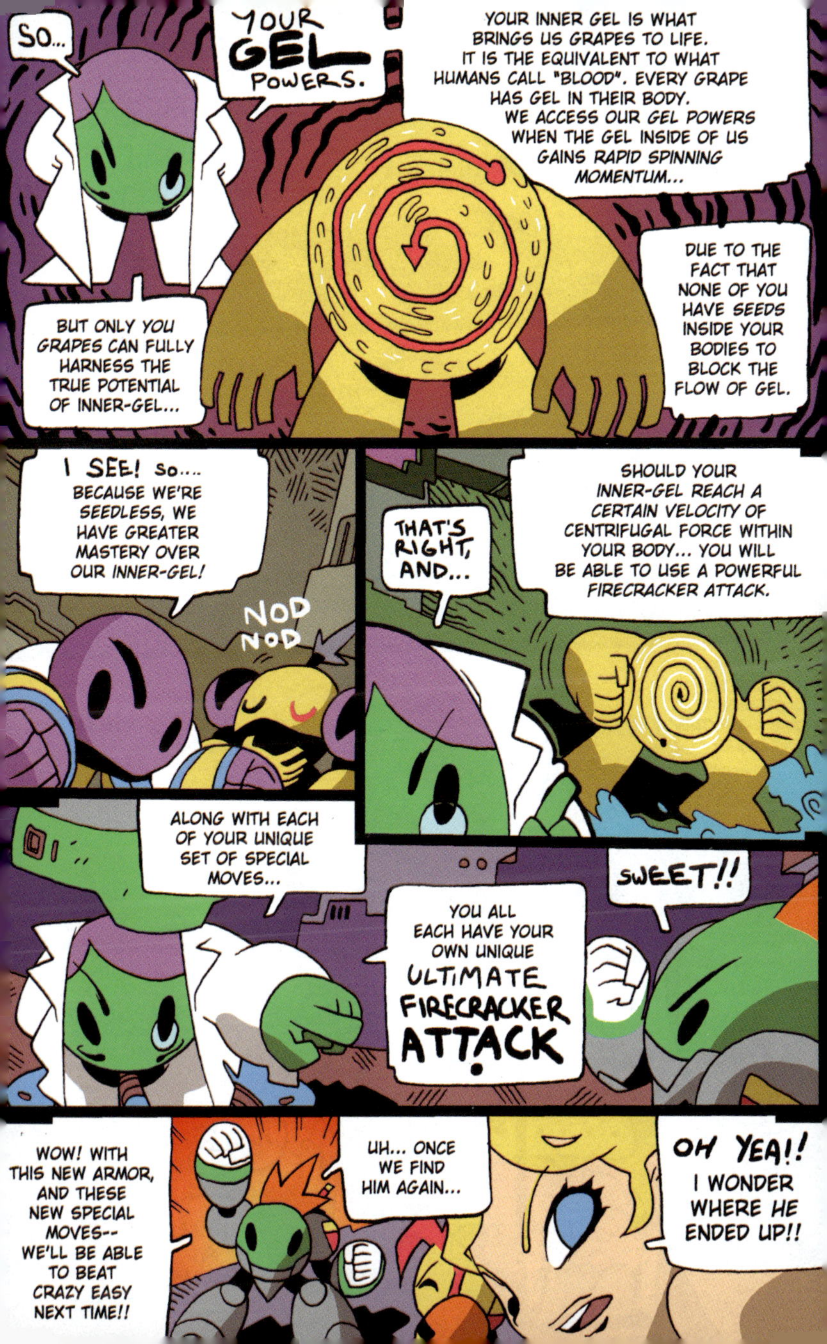
SO...
YOUR GEL POWERS.
YOUR INNER GEL IS WHAT BRINGS US GRAPES TO LIFE. IT IS THE EQUIVALENT TO WHAT HUMANS CALL "BLOOD". EVERY GRAPE HAS GEL IN THEIR BODY. WE ACCESS OUR GEL POWERS WHEN THE GEL INSIDE OF US GAINS RAPID SPINNING MOMENTUM...
BUT ONLY YOU GRAPES CAN FULLY HARNESS THE TRUE POTENTIAL OF INNER-GEL...
DUE TO THE FACT THAT NONE OF YOU HAVE SEEDS INSIDE YOUR BODIES TO BLOCK THE FLOW OF GEL.
I SEE! SO.... BECAUSE WE'RE SEEDLESS, WE HAVE GREATER MASTERY OVER OUR INNER-GEL!
NOD NOD
THAT'S RIGHT, AND...
SHOULD YOUR INNER-GEL REACH A CERTAIN VELOCITY OF CENTRIFUGAL FORCE WITHIN YOUR BODY... YOU WILL BE ABLE TO USE A POWERFUL FIRECRACKER ATTACK.
ALONG WITH EACH OF YOUR UNIQUE SET OF SPECIAL MOVES...
YOU ALL EACH HAVE YOUR OWN UNIQUE ULTIMATE FIRECRACKER ATTACK.
SWEET!!
WOW! WITH THIS NEW ARMOR, AND THESE NEW SPECIAL MOVES-- WE'LL BE ABLE TO BEAT CRAZY EASY NEXT TIME!!
UH... ONCE WE FIND HIM AGAIN...
OH YEA!! I WONDER WHERE HE ENDED UP!!

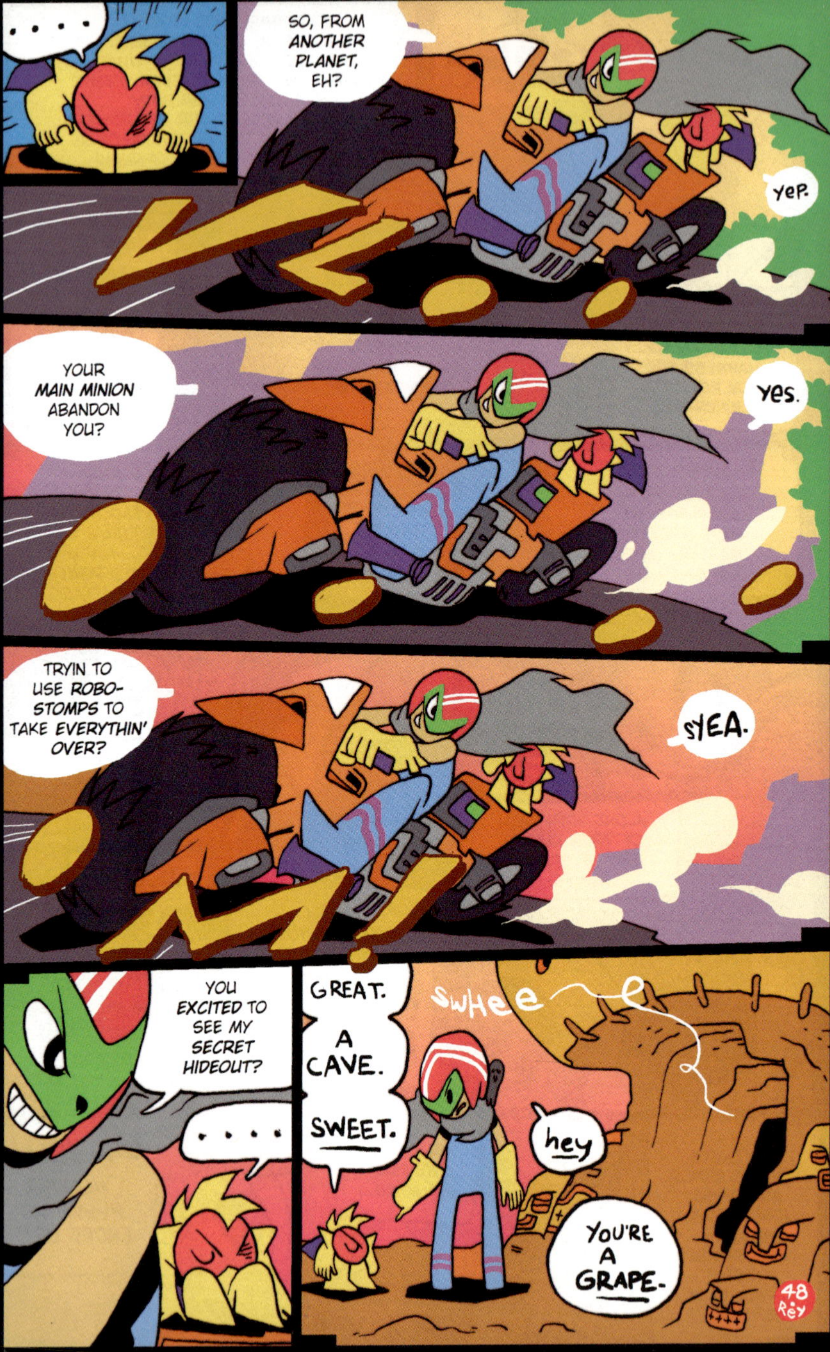
....
SO, FROM ANOTHER PLANET, EH?
yep.
YOUR MAIN MINION ABANDON YOU?
yes.
TRYIN TO USE ROBO-STOMPS TO TAKE EVERYTHIN' OVER?
SYEA.
YOU EXCITED TO SEE MY SECRET HIDEOUT?
.....
GREAT.
A CAVE.
SWEET.
SWHEE~E
hey
YOU'RE A GRAPE.

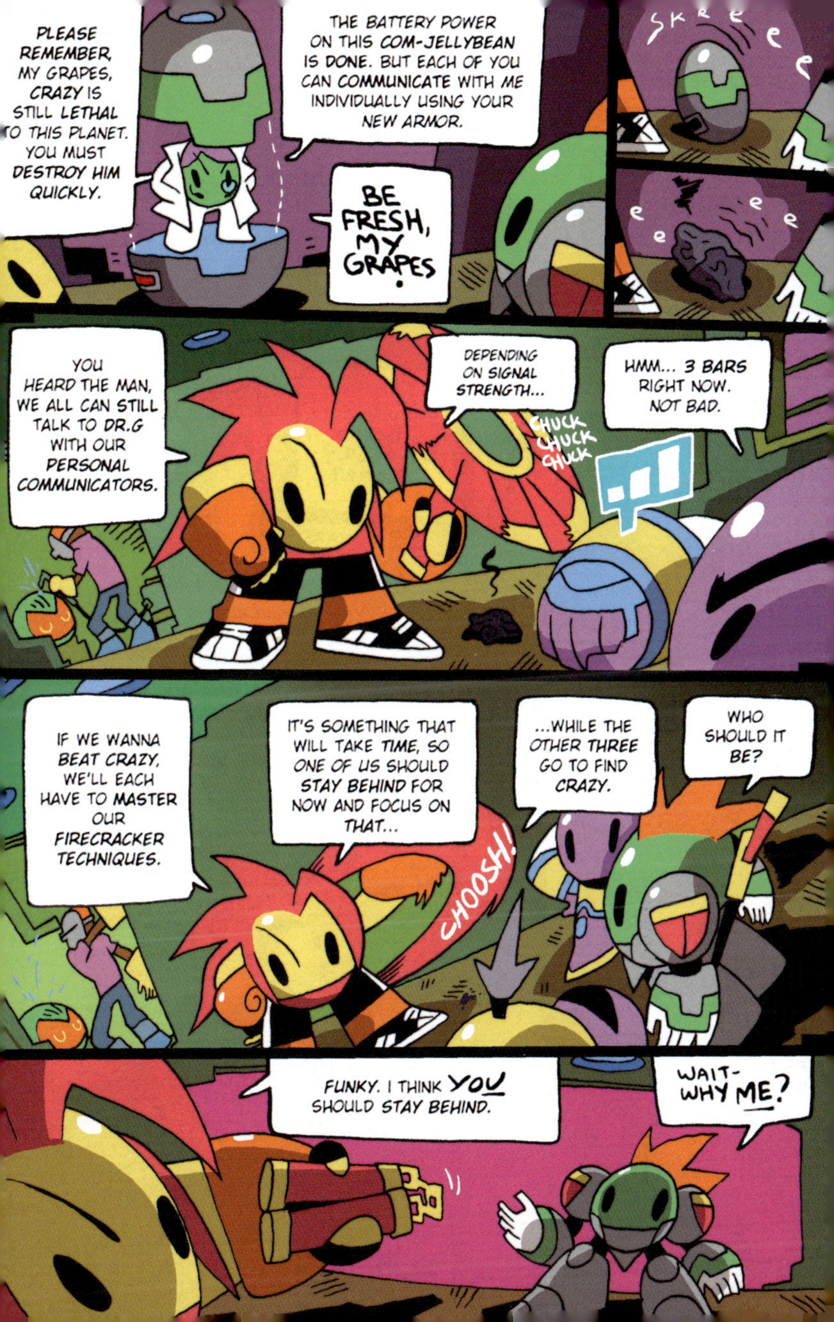
PLEASE REMEMBER, MY GRAPES, CRAZY IS STILL LETHAL TO THIS PLANET. YOU MUST DESTROY HIM QUICKLY.
THE BATTERY POWER ON THIS COM-JELLYBEAN IS DONE. BUT EACH OF YOU CAN COMMUNICATE WITH ME INDIVIDUALLY USING YOUR NEW ARMOR.
BE FRESH, MY GRAPES.
SKREEEE
EEEEE
YOU HEARD THE MAN, WE ALL CAN STILL TALK TO DR.G WITH OUR PERSONAL COMMUNICATORS.
DEPENDING ON SIGNAL STRENGTH...
CHUCK CHUCK CHUCK
HMM... 3 BARS RIGHT NOW. NOT BAD.
IF WE WANNA BEAT CRAZY, WE'LL EACH HAVE TO MASTER OUR FIRECRACKER TECHNIQUES.
IT'S SOMETHING THAT WILL TAKE TIME, SO ONE OF US SHOULD STAY BEHIND FOR NOW AND FOCUS ON THAT...
CHOOSH!
...WHILE THE OTHER THREE GO TO FIND CRAZY.
WHO SHOULD IT BE?
FUNKY. I THINK YOU SHOULD STAY BEHIND.
WAIT- WHY ME?

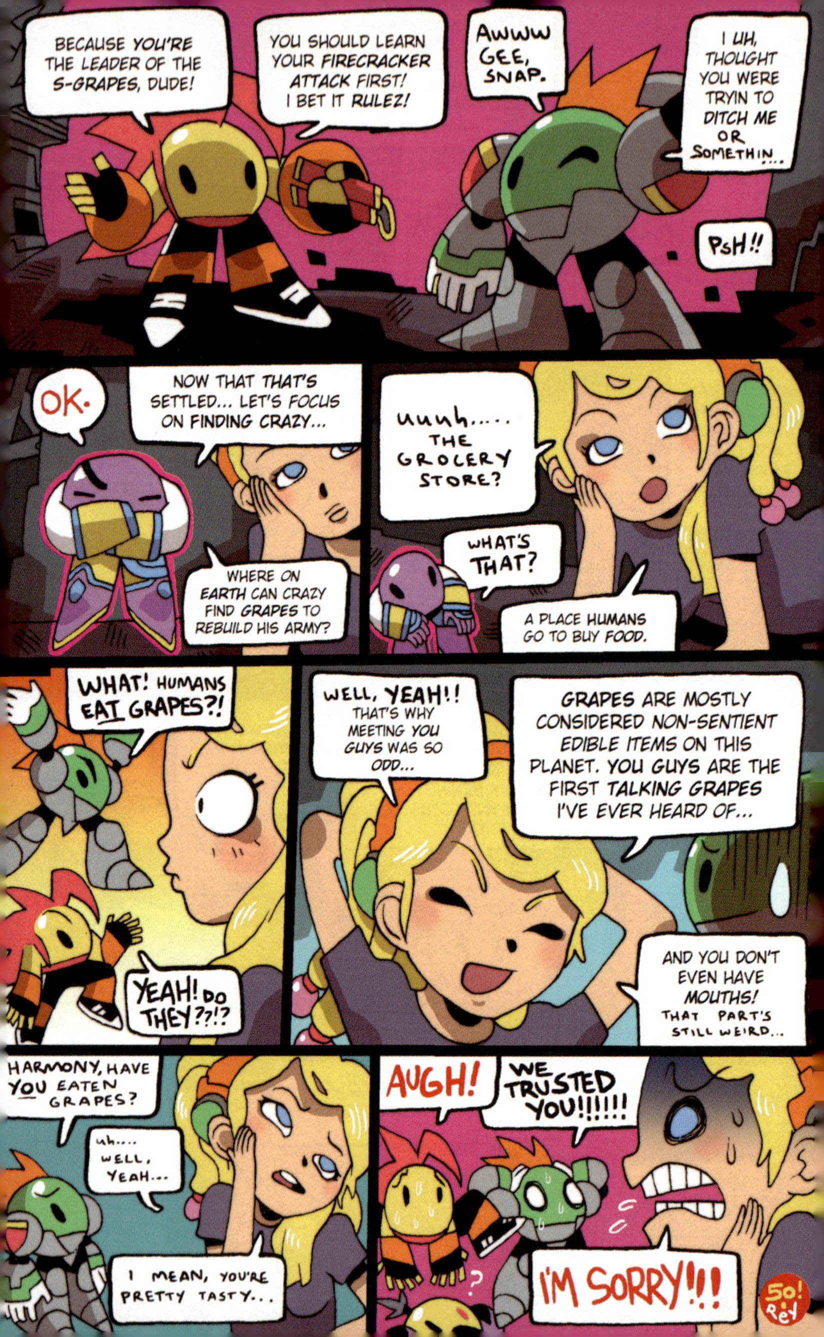
BECAUSE YOU'RE THE LEADER OF THE S-GRAPES, DUDE!
YOU SHOULD LEARN YOUR FIRECRACKER ATTACK FIRST! I BET IT RULEZ!
AWWW GEE, SNAP.
I UH, THOUGHT YOU WERE TRYIN TO DITCH ME OR SOMETHIN...
PSH!!
OK.
NOW THAT THAT'S SETTLED... LET'S FOCUS ON FINDING CRAZY...
WHERE ON EARTH CAN CRAZY FIND GRAPES TO REBUILD HIS ARMY?
uuuh..... THE GROCERY STORE?
WHAT'S THAT?
A PLACE HUMANS GO TO BUY FOOD.
WHAT! HUMANS EAT GRAPES?!
YEAH! DO THEY??!?
WELL, YEAH!! THAT'S WHY MEETING YOU GUYS WAS SO ODD...
GRAPES ARE MOSTLY CONSIDERED NON-SENTIENT EDIBLE ITEMS ON THIS PLANET. YOU GUYS ARE THE FIRST TALKING GRAPES I'VE EVER HEARD OF...
AND YOU DON'T EVEN HAVE MOUTHS! THAT PART'S STILL WEIRD...
HARMONY, HAVE YOU EATEN GRAPES?
uh.... WELL, YEAH...
I MEAN, YOU'RE PRETTY TASTY...
AUGH!
WE TRUSTED YOU!!!!!!
?
I'M SORRY!!!
50! REY

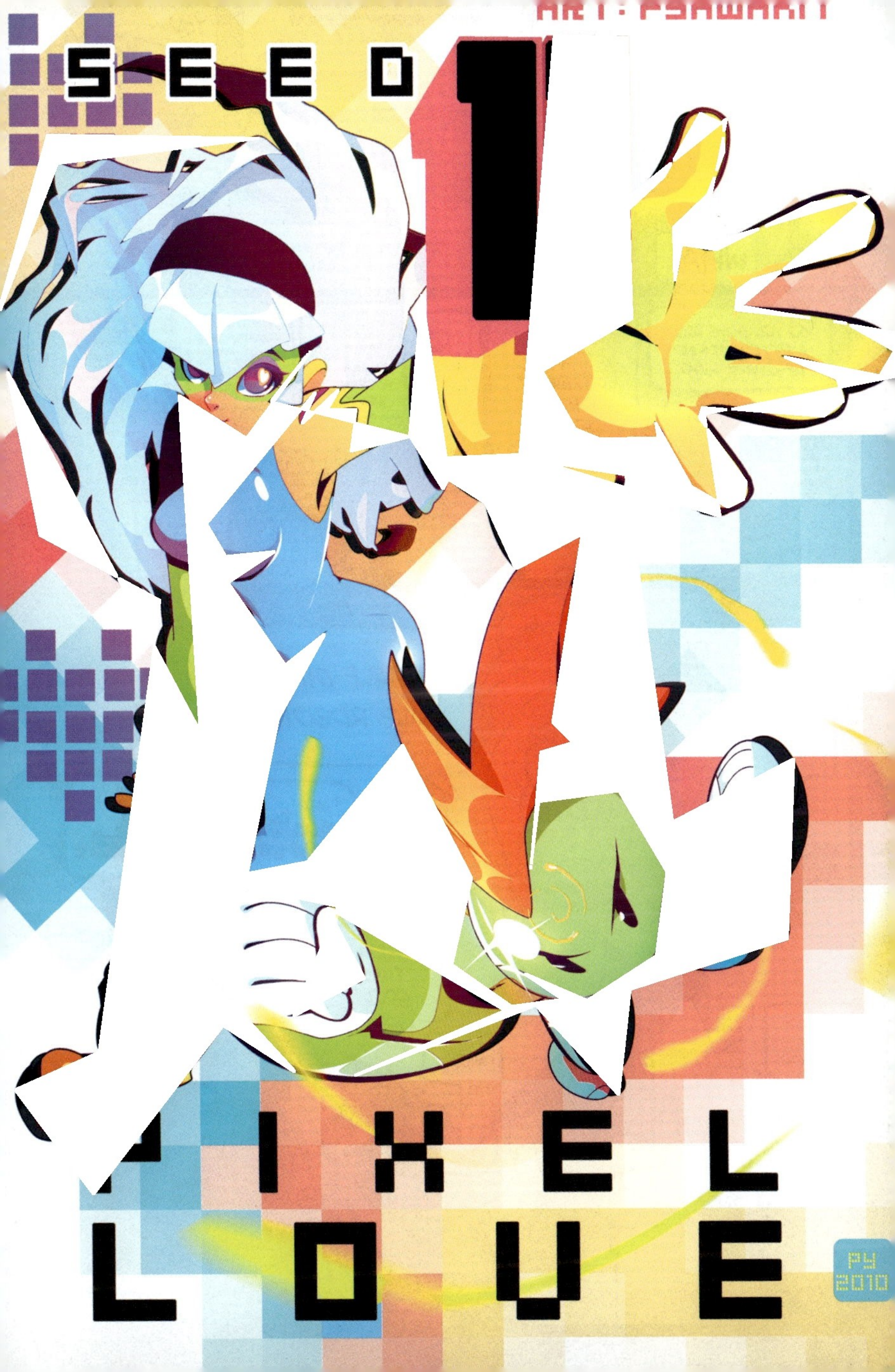

SEED 1
PIXEL
LOVE
py
2010

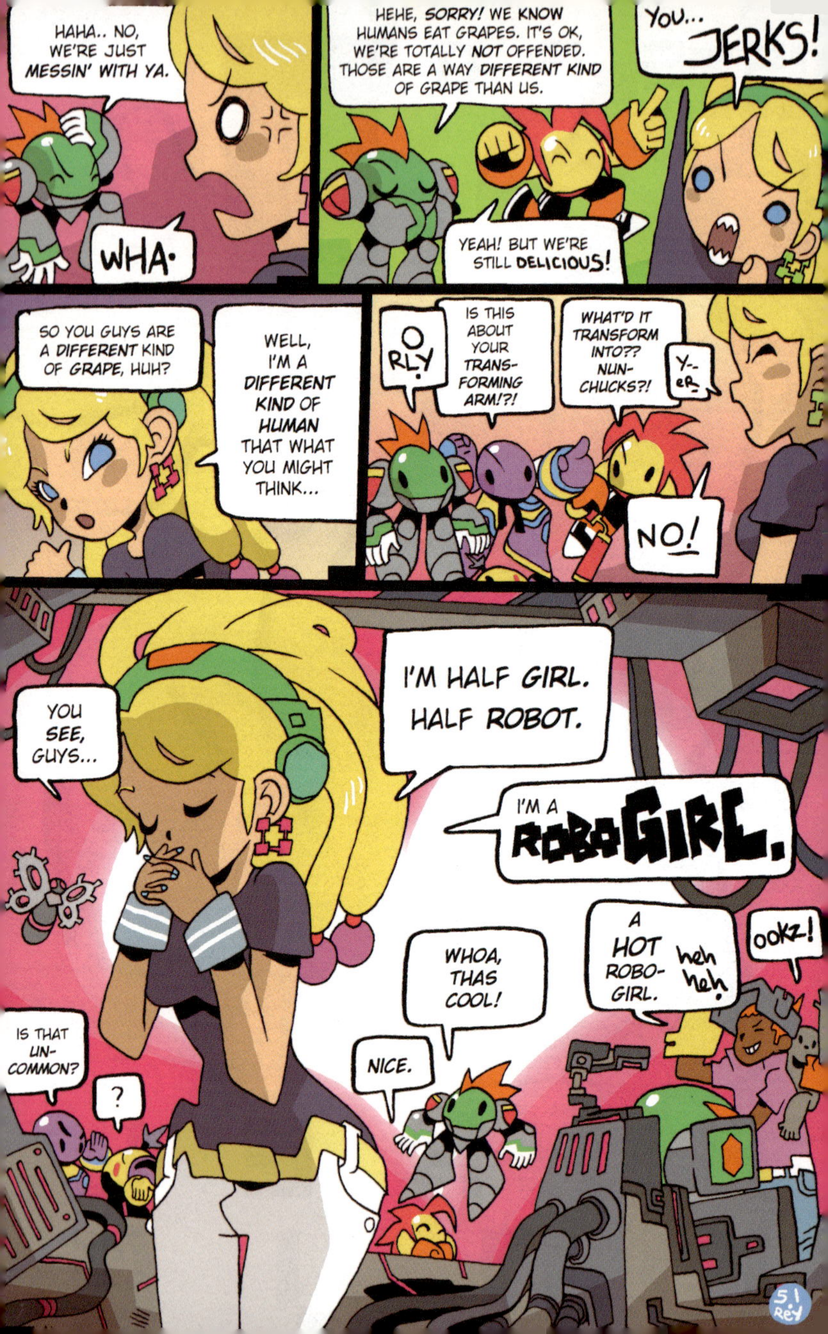
HAHA.. NO, WE'RE JUST MESSIN' WITH YA.
WHA·
HEHE, SORRY! WE KNOW HUMANS EAT GRAPES. IT'S OK, WE'RE TOTALLY NOT OFFENDED. THOSE ARE A WAY DIFFERENT KIND OF GRAPE THAN US.
YEAH! BUT WE'RE STILL DELICIOUS!
YOU... JERKS!
SO YOU GUYS ARE A DIFFERENT KIND OF GRAPE, HUH?
WELL, I'M A DIFFERENT KIND OF HUMAN THAT WHAT YOU MIGHT THINK...
O RLY
IS THIS ABOUT YOUR TRANS-FORMING ARM!?!
WHAT'D IT TRANSFORM INTO?? NUN-CHUCKS?!
Y-- eR-
NO!
YOU SEE, GUYS...
I'M HALF GIRL. HALF ROBOT.
I'M A ROBOGIRL.
WHOA, THAS COOL!
A HOT ROBO-GIRL.
heh heh!
OOKZ!
IS THAT UN-COMMON?
?
NICE.
51 Rey

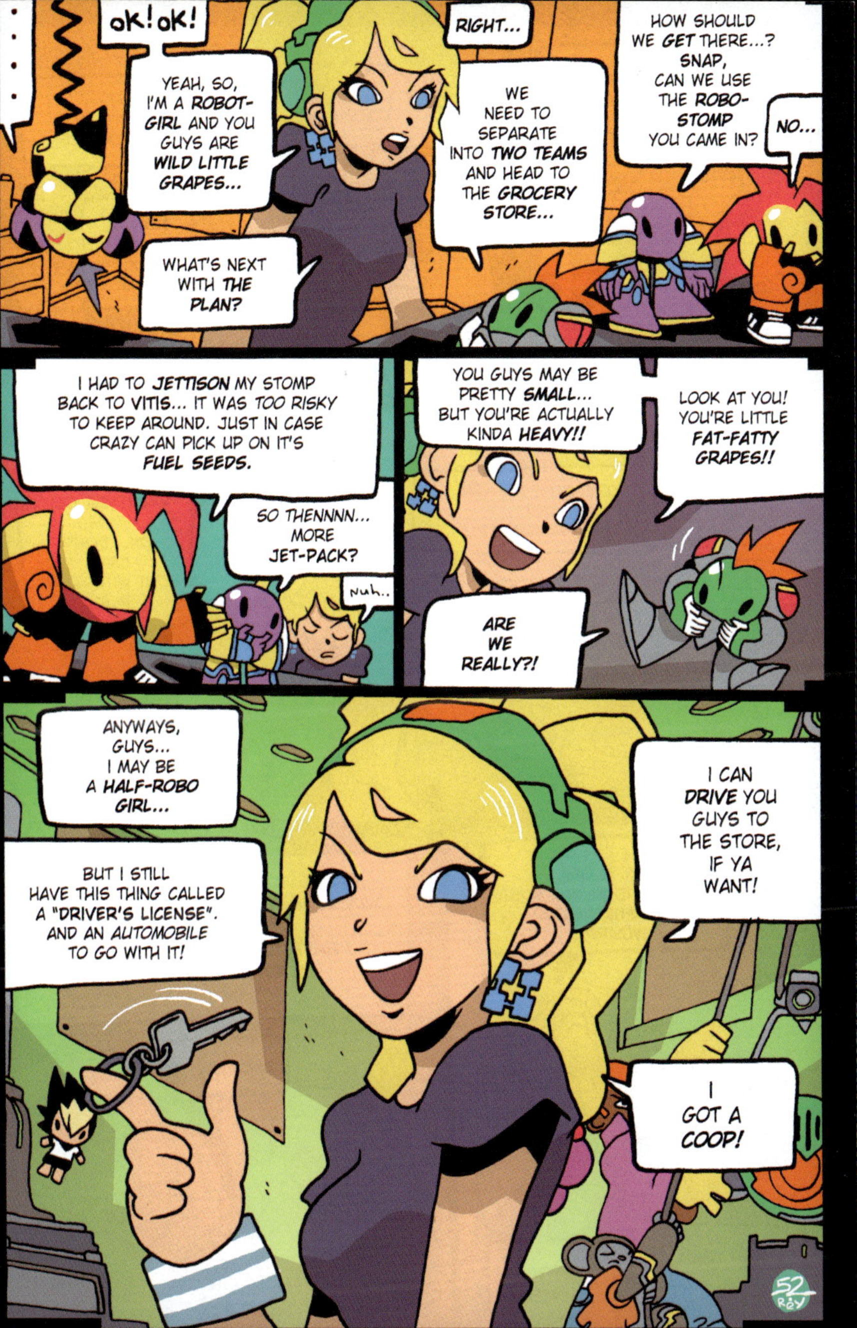

OK! OK!
YEAH, SO, I'M A ROBOT-GIRL AND YOU GUYS ARE WILD LITTLE GRAPES...
WHAT'S NEXT WITH THE PLAN?
RIGHT...
WE NEED TO SEPARATE INTO TWO TEAMS AND HEAD TO THE GROCERY STORE...
HOW SHOULD WE GET THERE...? SNAP, CAN WE USE THE ROBO-STOMP YOU CAME IN?
NO...
I HAD TO JETTISON MY STOMP BACK TO VITIS... IT WAS TOO RISKY TO KEEP AROUND. JUST IN CASE CRAZY CAN PICK UP ON IT'S FUEL SEEDS.
SO THENNNN... MORE JET-PACK?
Nuh..
YOU GUYS MAY BE PRETTY SMALL... BUT YOU'RE ACTUALLY KINDA HEAVY!!
LOOK AT YOU! YOU'RE LITTLE FAT-FATTY GRAPES!!
ARE WE REALLY?!
ANYWAYS, GUYS... I MAY BE A HALF-ROBO GIRL...
BUT I STILL HAVE THIS THING CALLED A "DRIVER'S LICENSE". AND AN AUTOMOBILE TO GO WITH IT!
I CAN DRIVE YOU GUYS TO THE STORE, IF YA WANT!
I GOT A COOP!

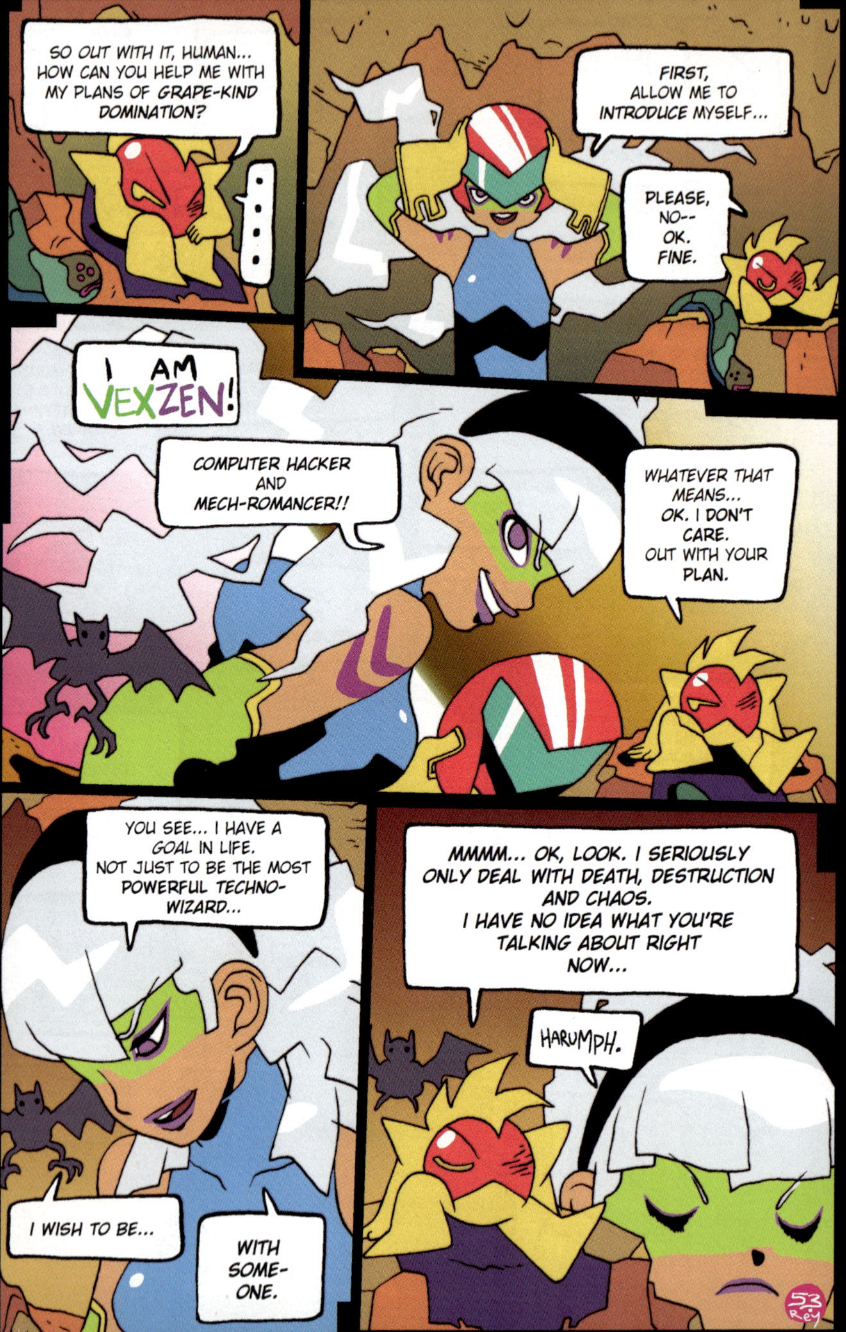
SO OUT WITH IT, HUMAN... HOW CAN YOU HELP ME WITH MY PLANS OF GRAPE-KIND DOMINATION?
...
FIRST, ALLOW ME TO INTRODUCE MYSELF...
PLEASE, NO-- OK. FINE.
I AM VEXZEN!
COMPUTER HACKER AND MECH-ROMANCER!!
WHATEVER THAT MEANS... OK. I DON'T CARE. OUT WITH YOUR PLAN.
YOU SEE... I HAVE A GOAL IN LIFE. NOT JUST TO BE THE MOST POWERFUL TECHNO-WIZARD...
I WISH TO BE...
WITH SOME-ONE.
MMMM... OK, LOOK. I SERIOUSLY ONLY DEAL WITH DEATH, DESTRUCTION AND CHAOS. I HAVE NO IDEA WHAT YOU'RE TALKING ABOUT RIGHT NOW...
HARUMPH.
53
Rey

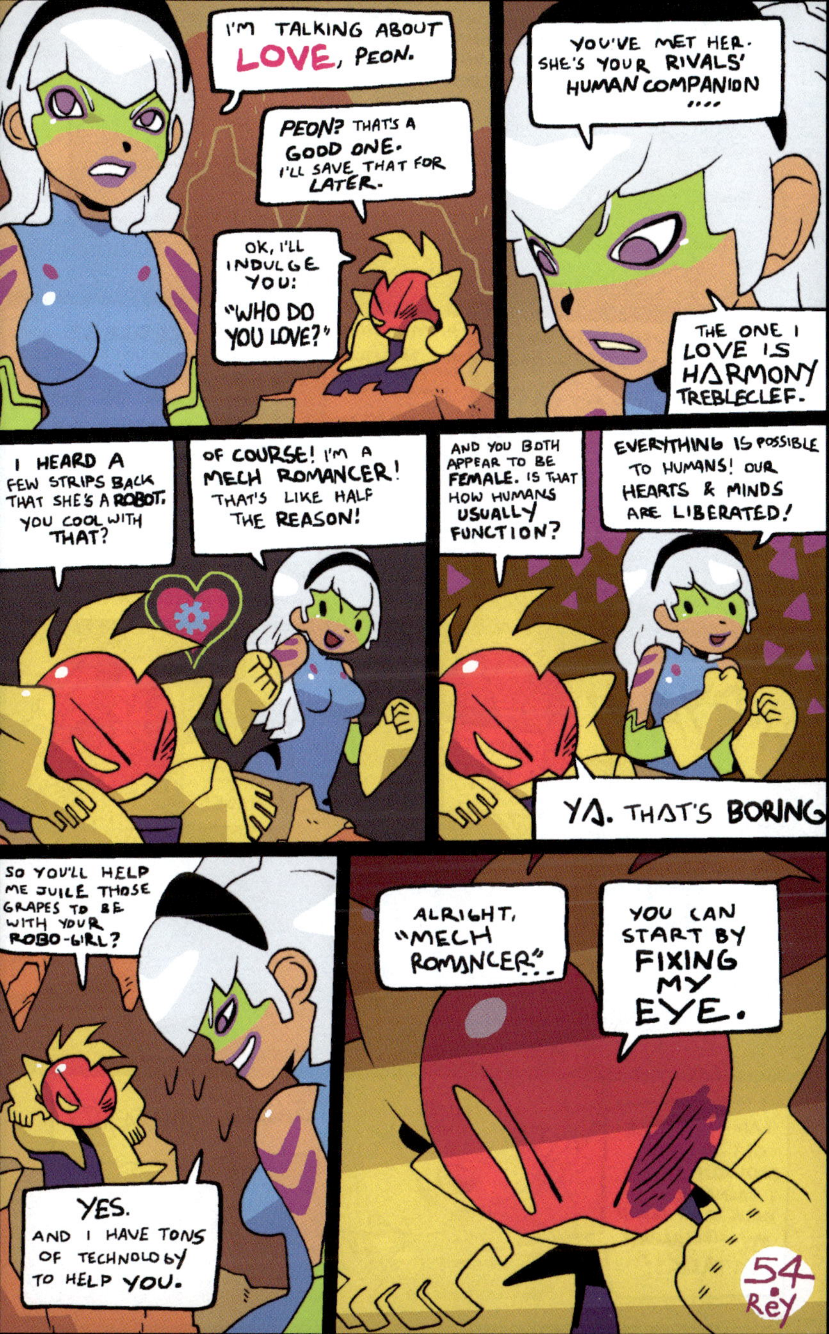

I'M TALKING ABOUT LOVE, PEON.
PEON? THAT'S A GOOD ONE. I'LL SAVE THAT FOR LATER.
OK, I'LL INDULGE YOU: "WHO DO YOU LOVE?"
YOU'VE MET HER. SHE'S YOUR RIVALS' HUMAN COMPANION ....
THE ONE I LOVE IS HARMONY TREBLECLEF.
I HEARD A FEW STRIPS BACK THAT SHE'S A ROBOT. YOU COOL WITH THAT?
OF COURSE! I'M A MECH ROMANCER! THAT'S LIKE HALF THE REASON!
AND YOU BOTH APPEAR TO BE FEMALE. IS THAT HOW HUMANS USUALLY FUNCTION?
EVERYTHING IS POSSIBLE TO HUMANS! OUR HEARTS & MINDS ARE LIBERATED!
YA. THAT'S BORING
SO YOU'LL HELP ME JUICE THOSE GRAPES TO BE WITH YOUR ROBO-GIRL?
YES. AND I HAVE TONS OF TECHNOLOGY TO HELP YOU.
ALRIGHT, "MECH ROMANCER."..
YOU CAN START BY FIXING MY EYE.
54 Rey

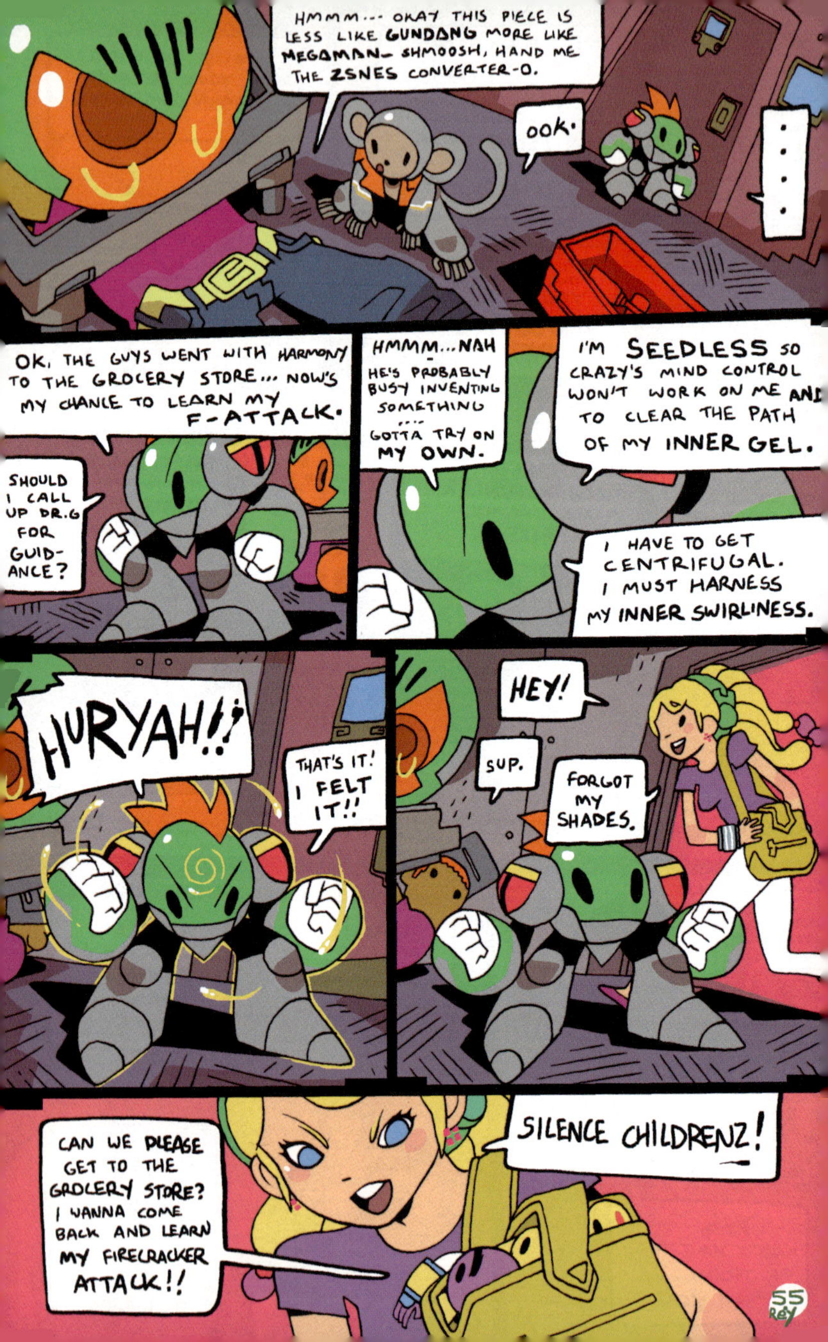
HMMM... OKAY THIS PIECE IS LESS LIKE GUNDANG MORE LIKE MEGAMAN- SHMOOSH, HAND ME THE ZSNES CONVERTER-O.
OOK.
...
OK, THE GUYS WENT WITH HARMONY TO THE GROCERY STORE... NOW'S MY CHANCE TO LEARN MY F-ATTACK.
SHOULD I CALL UP DR. G FOR GUID-ANCE?
HMMM...NAH HE'S PROBABLY BUSY INVENTING SOMETHING... GOTTA TRY ON MY OWN.
I'M SEEDLESS SO CRAZY'S MIND CONTROL WON'T WORK ON ME AND TO CLEAR THE PATH OF MY INNER GEL.
I HAVE TO GET CENTRIFUGAL. I MUST HARNESS MY INNER SWIRLINESS.
HURYAH!!
THAT'S IT! I FELT IT!!
HEY!
SUP.
FORGOT MY SHADES.
SILENCE CHILDRENZ!
CAN WE PLEASE GET TO THE GROCERY STORE? I WANNA COME BACK AND LEARN MY FIRECRACKER ATTACK!!

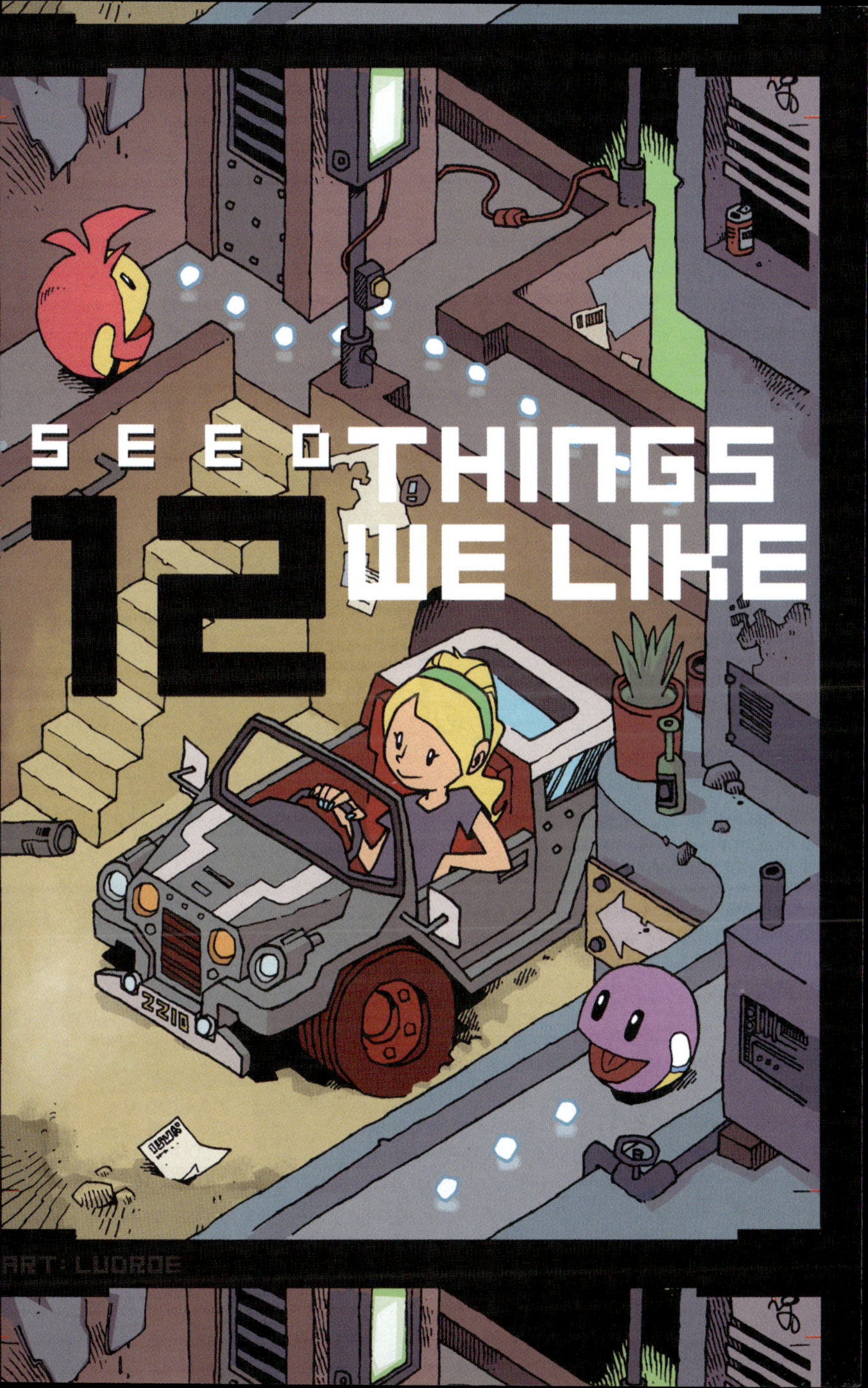
SEED
THINGS
WE LIKE
12
2210
ART: LUDROE

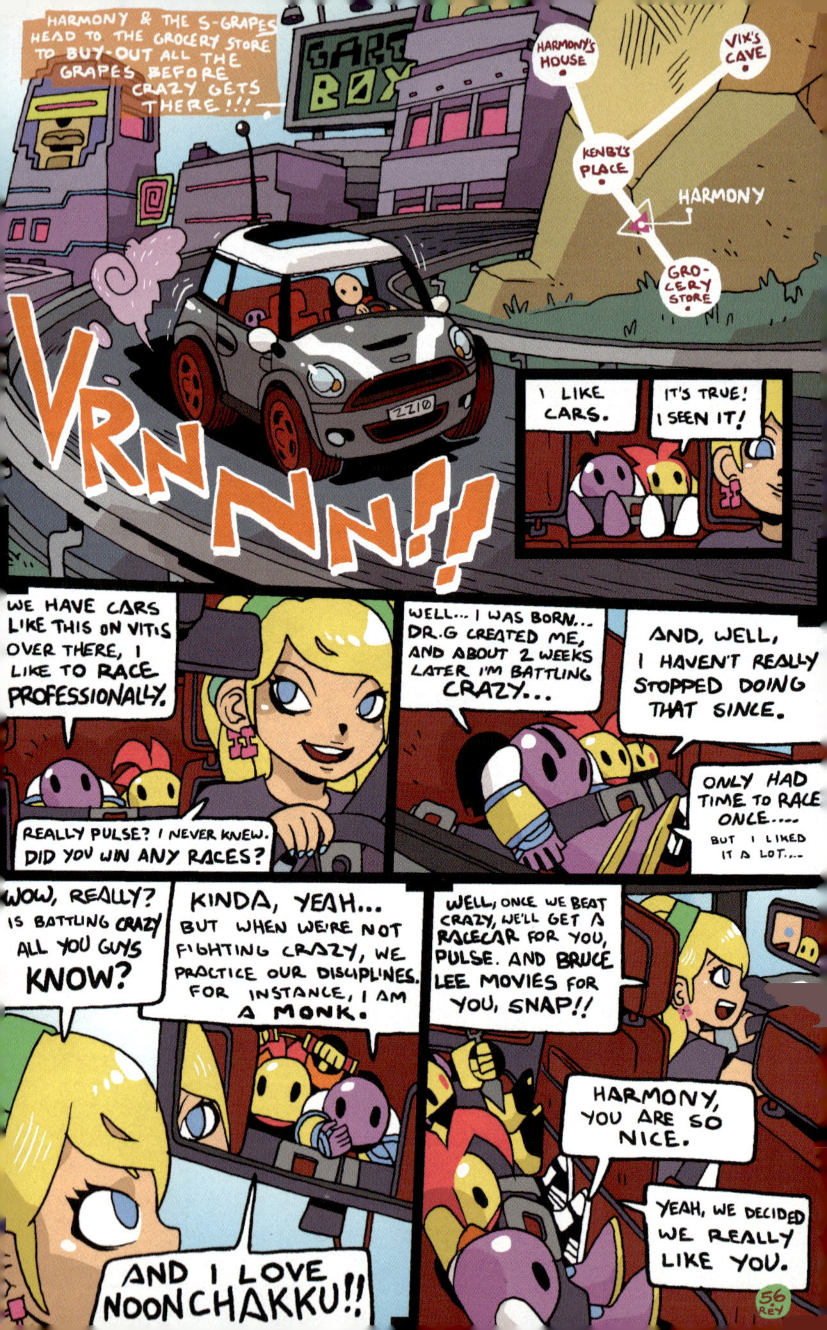
HARMONY & THE S-GRAPES HEAD TO THE GROCERY STORE TO BUY-OUT ALL THE GRAPES BEFORE CRAZY GETS THERE!!!
GAME BOY
HARMONY'S HOUSE
VIX'S CAVE
KENBI'S PLACE
HARMONY
GRO-CERY STORE
VRNNN!!
Z210
I LIKE CARS.
IT'S TRUE! I SEEN IT!
WE HAVE CARS LIKE THIS ON VITIS OVER THERE, I LIKE TO RACE PROFESSIONALLY.
REALLY PULSE? I NEVER KNEW. DID YOU WIN ANY RACES?
WELL... I WAS BORN... DR.G CREATED ME, AND ABOUT 2 WEEKS LATER I'M BATTLING CRAZY...
AND, WELL, I HAVEN'T REALLY STOPPED DOING THAT SINCE.
ONLY HAD TIME TO RACE ONCE.... BUT I LIKED IT A LOT....
WOW, REALLY? IS BATTLING CRAZY ALL YOU GUYS KNOW?
KINDA, YEAH... BUT WHEN WE'RE NOT FIGHTING CRAZY, WE PRACTICE OUR DISCIPLINES. FOR INSTANCE, I AM A MONK.
AND I LOVE NOONCHAKKU!!
WELL, ONCE WE BEAT CRAZY, WE'LL GET A RACECAR FOR YOU, PULSE. AND BRUCE LEE MOVIES FOR YOU, SNAP!!
HARMONY, YOU ARE SO NICE.
YEAH, WE DECIDED WE REALLY LIKE YOU.
56 REY

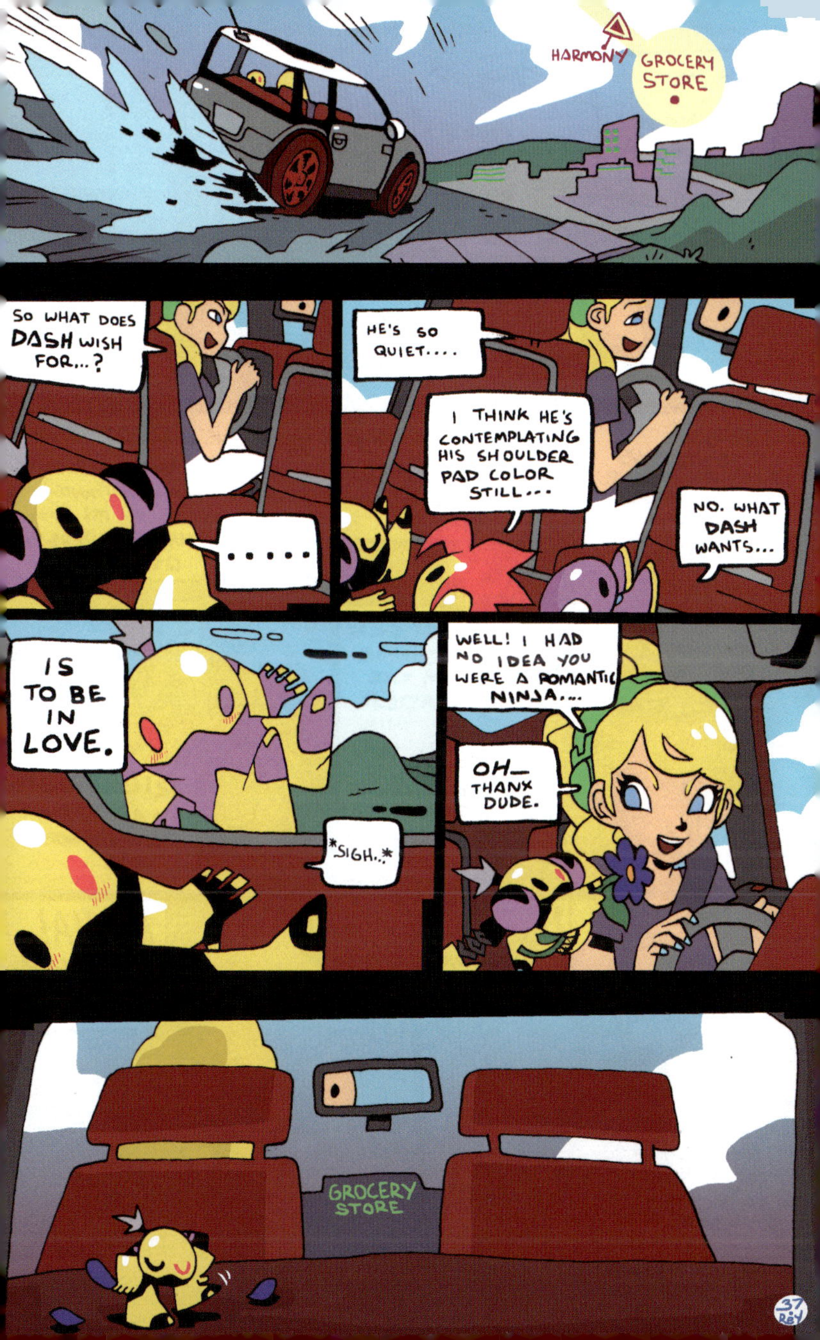
HARMONY
GROCERY STORE
SO WHAT DOES DASH WISH FOR...?
.....
HE'S SO QUIET....
I THINK HE'S CONTEMPLATING HIS SHOULDER PAD COLOR STILL...
NO. WHAT DASH WANTS...
IS TO BE IN LOVE.
SIGH..
WELL! I HAD NO IDEA YOU WERE A ROMANTIC NINJA....
OH_ THANX DUDE.
GROCERY STORE

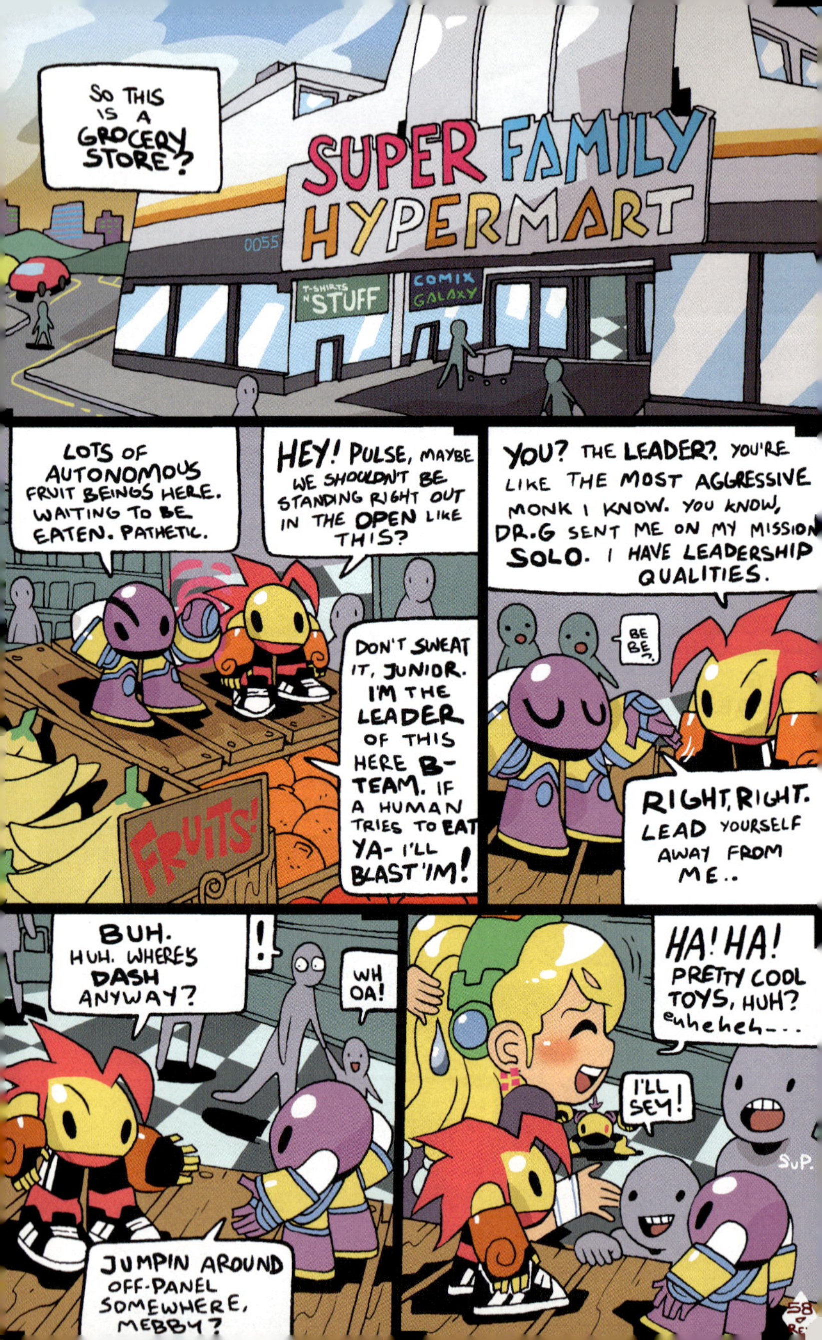

SO THIS IS A GROCERY STORE?
SUPER FAMILY HYPERMART
0055
T-SHIRTS N STUFF
COMIX GALAXY
LOTS OF AUTONOMOUS FRUIT BEINGS HERE. WAITING TO BE EATEN. PATHETIC.
HEY! PULSE, MAYBE WE SHOULDN'T BE STANDING RIGHT OUT IN THE OPEN LIKE THIS?
DON'T SWEAT IT, JUNIOR. I'M THE LEADER OF THIS HERE B-TEAM. IF A HUMAN TRIES TO EAT YA- I'LL BLAST 'IM!
FRUITS!
YOU? THE LEADER? YOU'RE LIKE THE MOST AGGRESSIVE MONK I KNOW. YOU KNOW, DR.G SENT ME ON MY MISSION SOLO. I HAVE LEADERSHIP QUALITIES.
BE BE?
RIGHT, RIGHT. LEAD YOURSELF AWAY FROM ME..
BUH. HUH. WHERE'S DASH ANYWAY?
!
WH OA!
JUMPIN AROUND OFF-PANEL SOMEWHERE, MEBBY?
HA! HA! PRETTY COOL TOYS, HUH? euheheh...
I'LL SEY!
SUP.

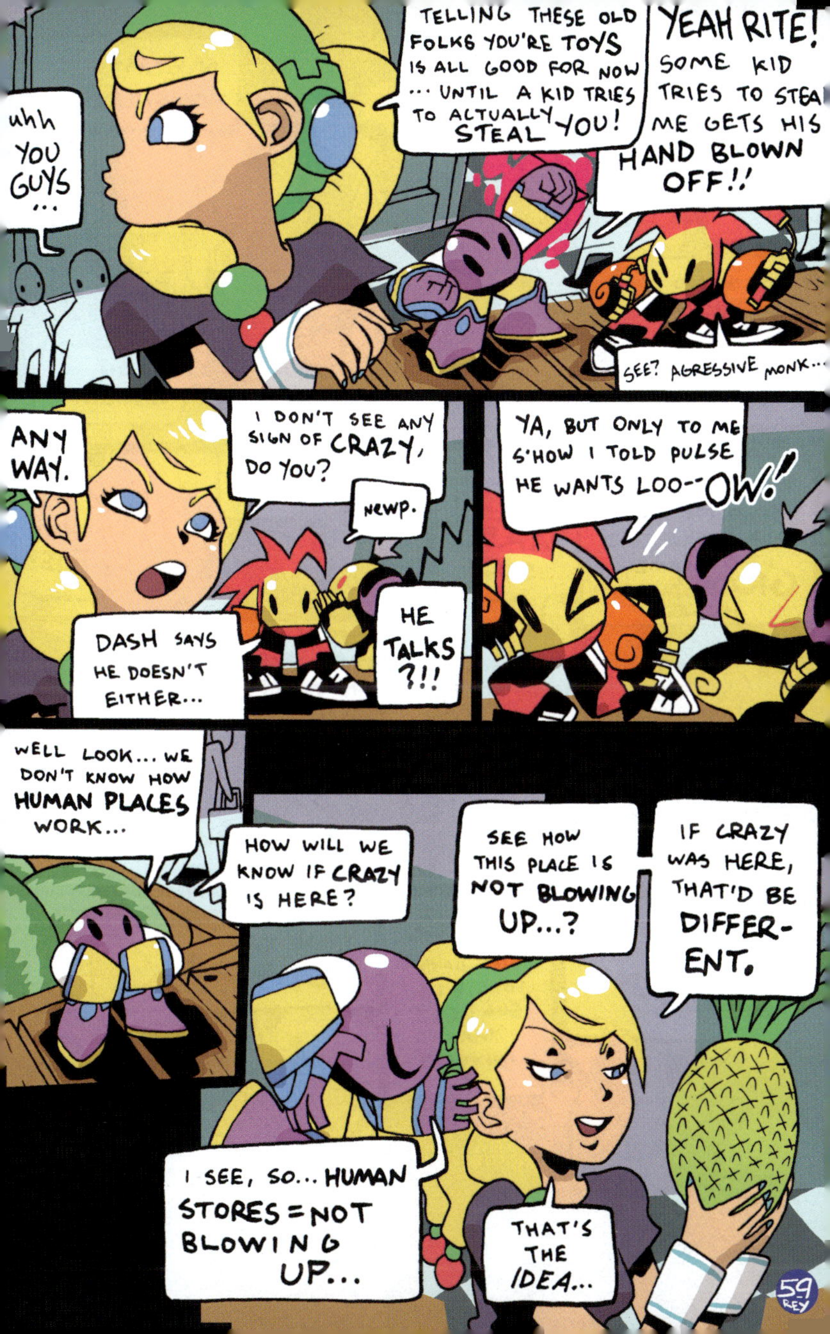

uhh YOU GUYS ...
TELLING THESE OLD FOLKS YOU'RE TOYS IS ALL GOOD FOR NOW ... UNTIL A KID TRIES TO ACTUALLY STEAL YOU!
YEAH RITE! SOME KID TRIES TO STEAL ME GETS HIS HAND BLOWN OFF!!
SEE? AGRESSIVE MONK...
ANY WAY.
I DON'T SEE ANY SIGN OF CRAZY, DO YOU?
NEWP.
DASH SAYS HE DOESN'T EITHER...
HE TALKS?!!
YA, BUT ONLY TO ME S'HOW I TOLD PULSE HE WANTS LOO--OW!!
WELL LOOK... WE DON'T KNOW HOW HUMAN PLACES WORK...
HOW WILL WE KNOW IF CRAZY IS HERE?
SEE HOW THIS PLACE IS NOT BLOWING UP...?
IF CRAZY WAS HERE, THAT'D BE DIFFER-ENT.
I SEE, SO... HUMAN STORES = NOT BLOWING UP...
THAT'S THE IDEA...

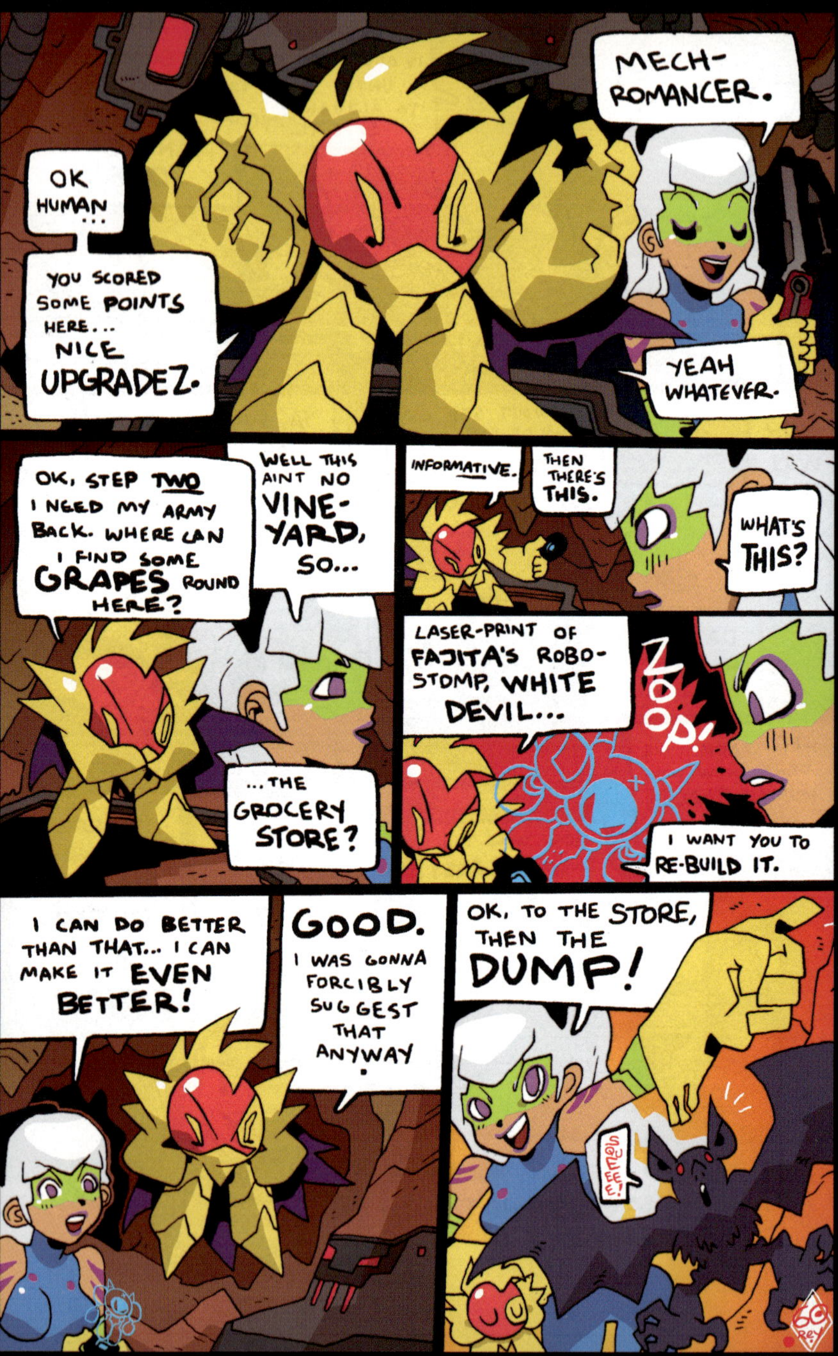
MECH-ROMANCER.
OK HUMAN...
YOU SCORED SOME POINTS HERE... NICE UPGRADEZ.
YEAH WHATEVER.
OK, STEP TWO I NEED MY ARMY BACK. WHERE CAN I FIND SOME GRAPES ROUND HERE?
WELL THIS AINT NO VINE-YARD, SO...
...THE GROCERY STORE?
INFORMATIVE.
THEN THERE'S THIS.
WHAT'S THIS?
LASER-PRINT OF FAJITA'S ROBO-STOMP, WHITE DEVIL...
ZOOP!
I WANT YOU TO RE-BUILD IT.
I CAN DO BETTER THAN THAT... I CAN MAKE IT EVEN BETTER!
GOOD. I WAS GONNA FORCIBLY SUGGEST THAT ANYWAY.
OK, TO THE STORE, THEN THE DUMP!
SQUEEEE!

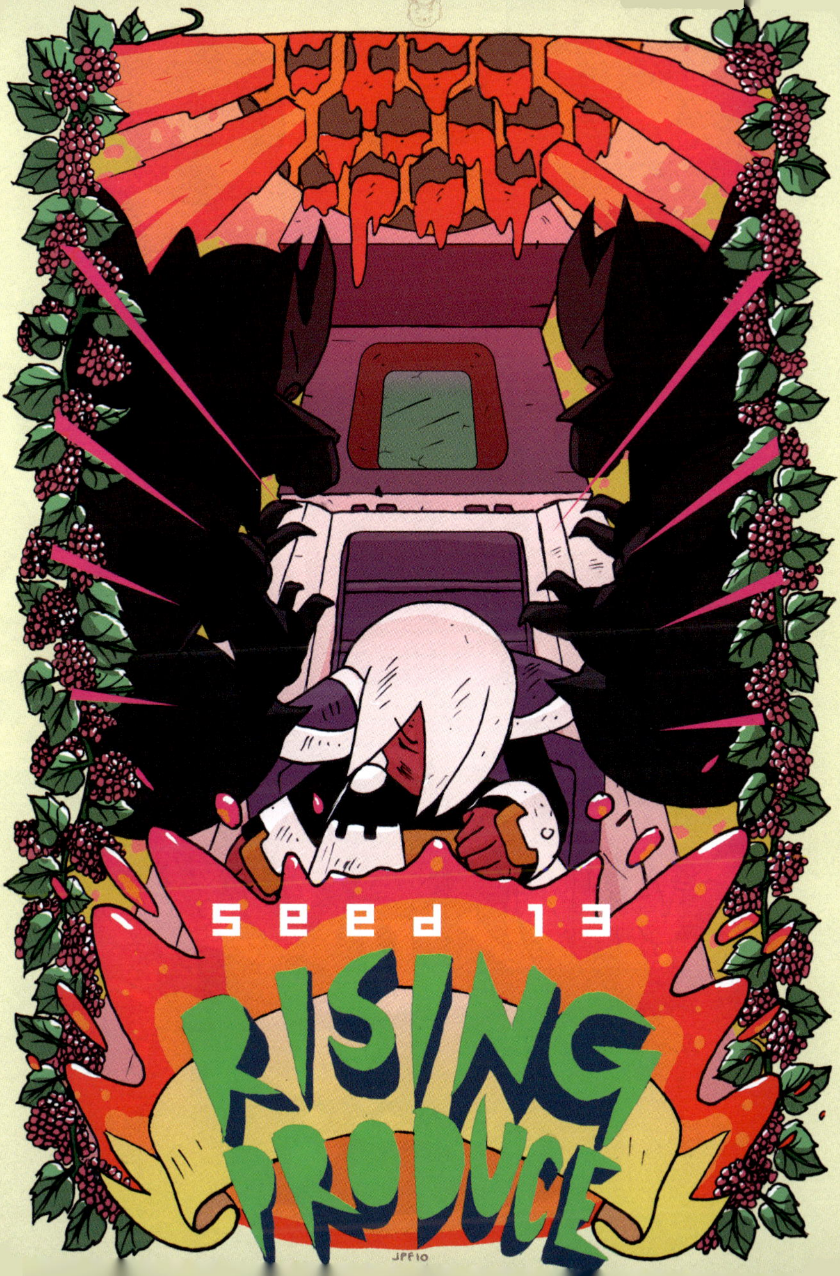
seed 13
RISING PRODUCE
JPF10

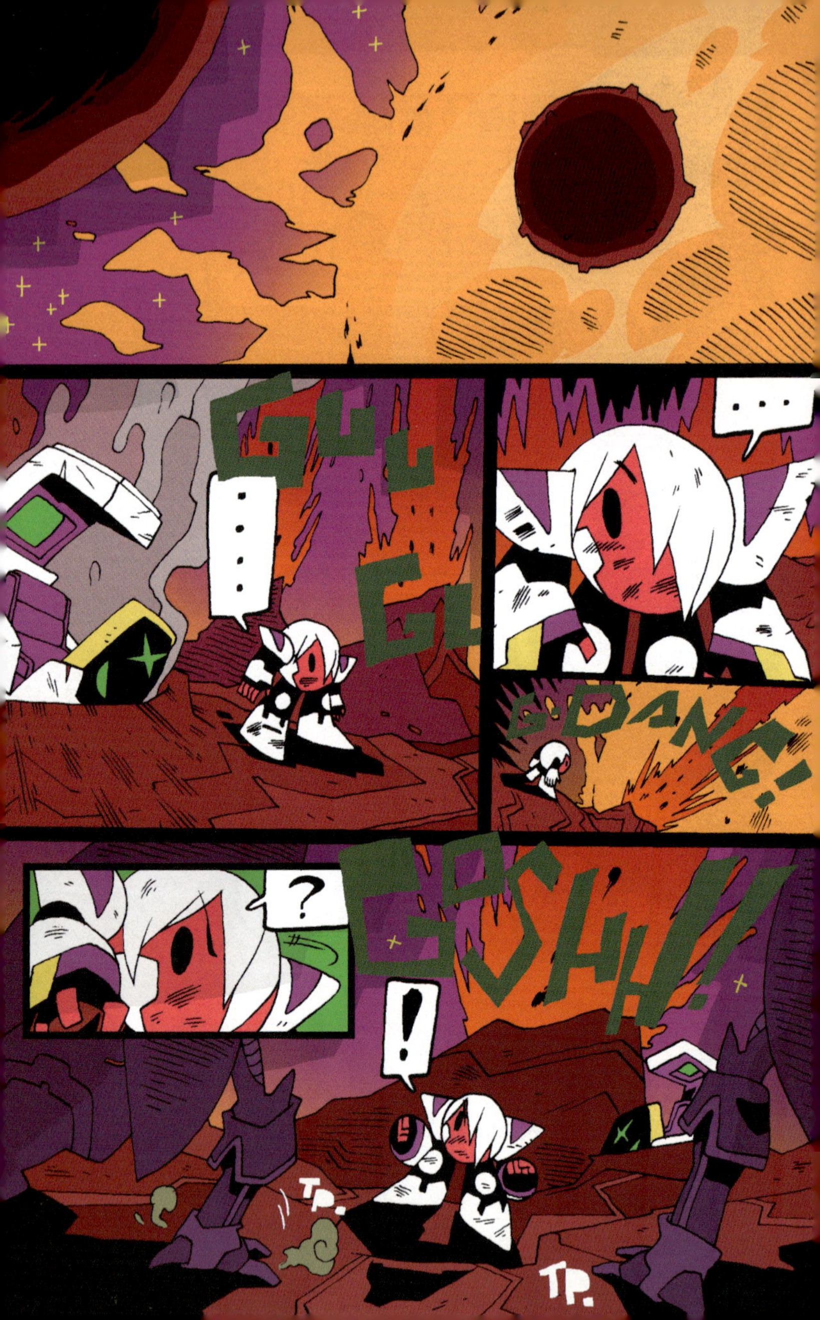
GLL
GL
....
...
G-DANG!!
?
GOSHH!!
!
TP.
TP.

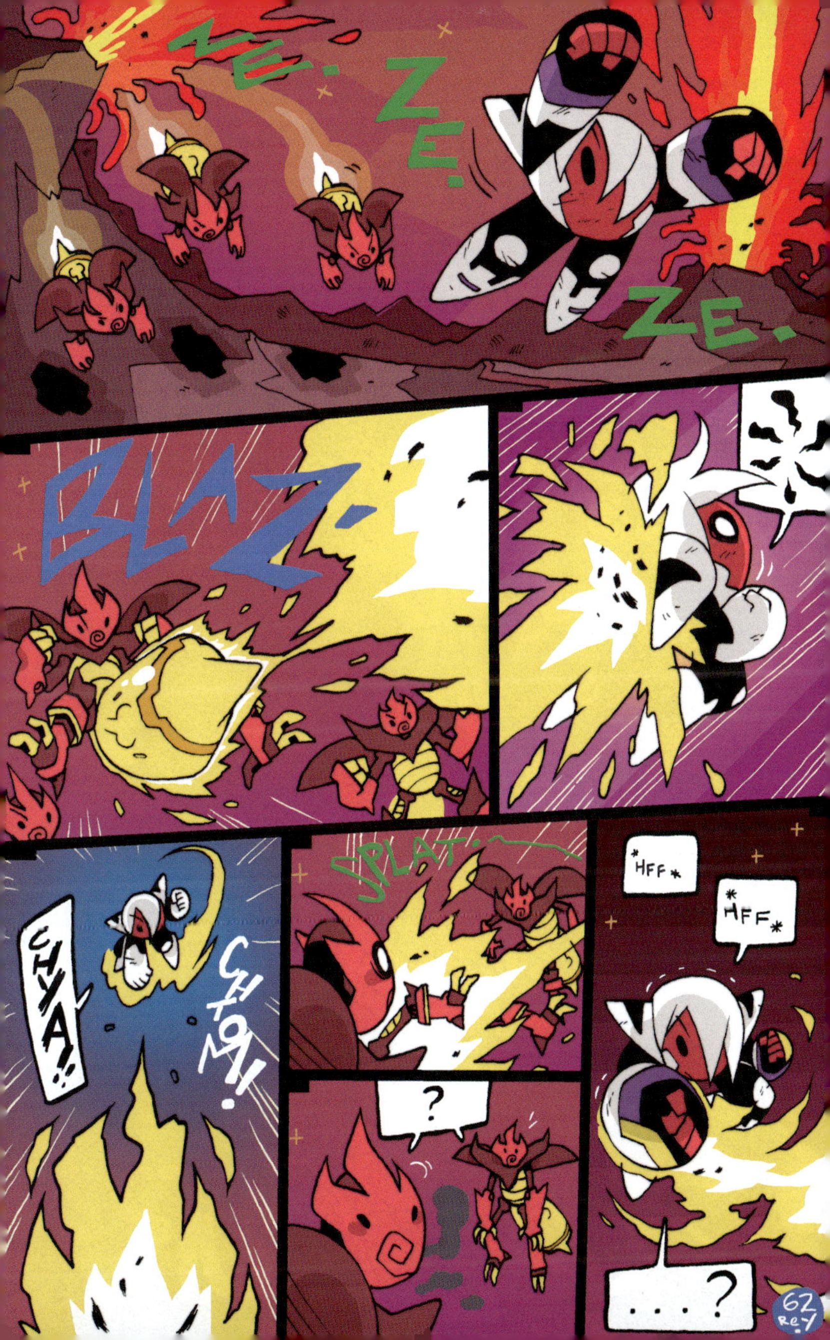

NE-
ZE-
ZE.
BLAZ-
CHYA!!
CHOOM!
SPLAT-
HFF
HFF
?
...?

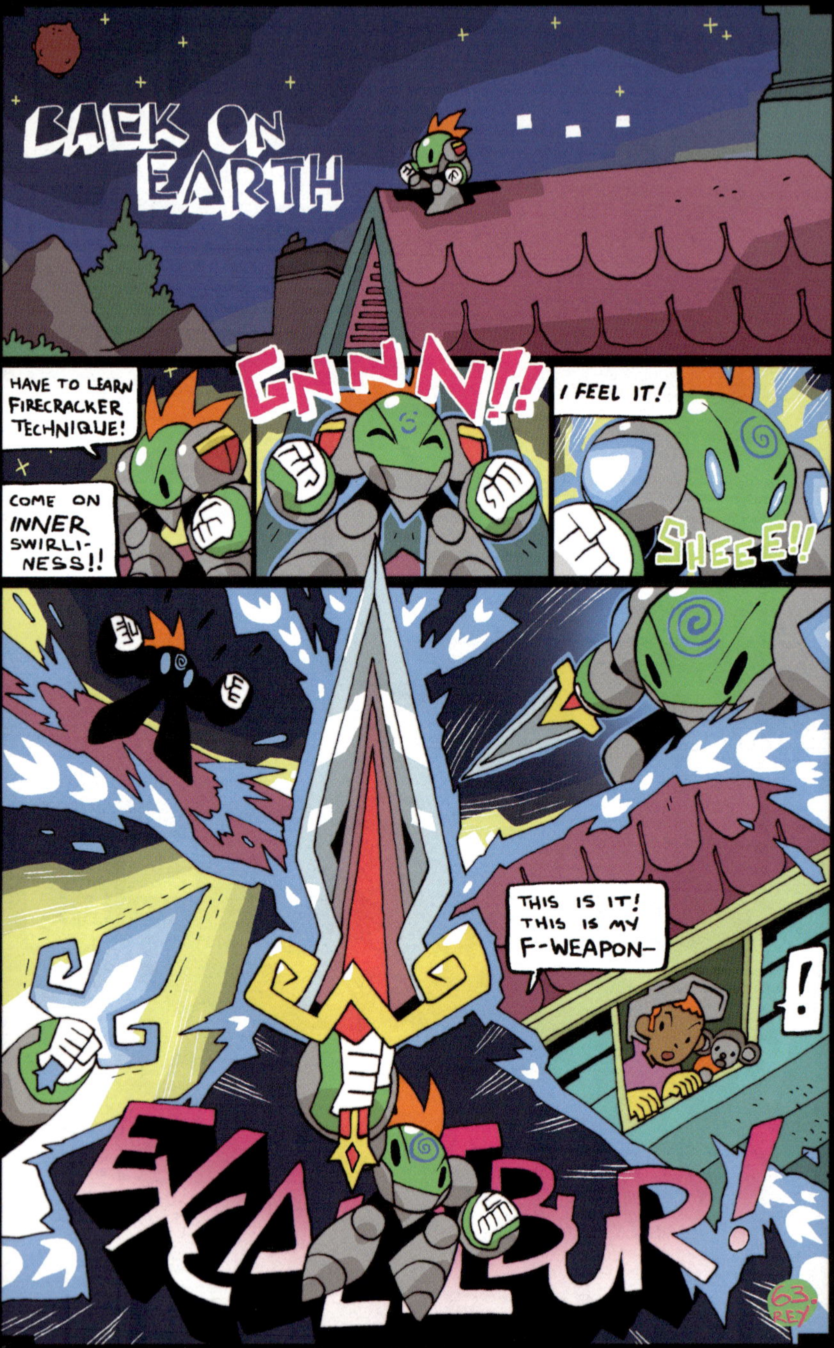
BACK ON EARTH
HAVE TO LEARN FIRECRACKER TECHNIQUE!
COME ON INNER SWIRLI-NESS!!
GNNN!!
I FEEL IT!
SHEEE!!
THIS IS IT! THIS IS MY F-WEAPON-
!
EXCALIBUR!
63.
REY

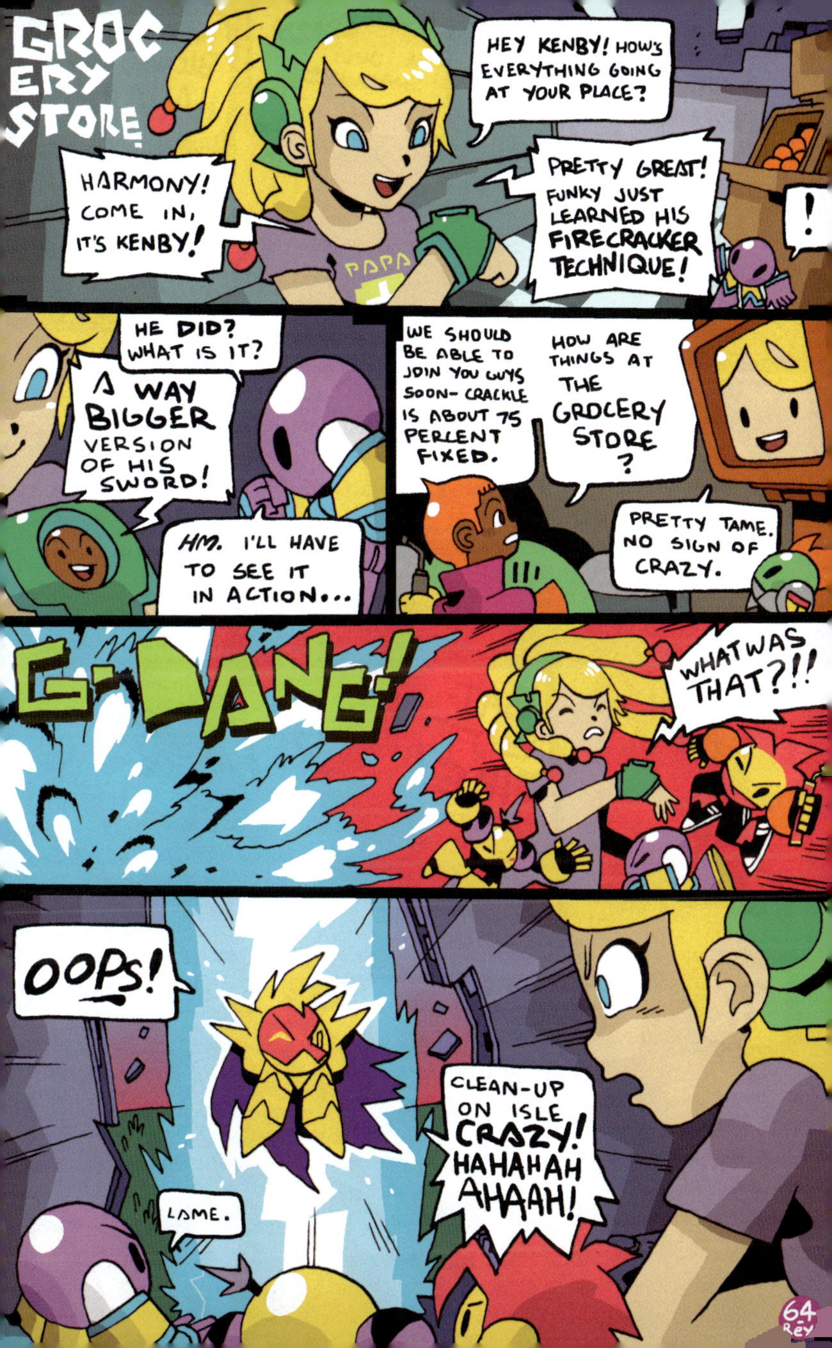
GROCERY STORE
HARMONY! COME IN, IT'S KENBY!
HEY KENBY! HOW'S EVERYTHING GOING AT YOUR PLACE?
PRETTY GREAT! FUNKY JUST LEARNED HIS FIRECRACKER TECHNIQUE!
!
PAPA
HE DID? WHAT IS IT?
A WAY BIGGER VERSION OF HIS SWORD!
HM. I'LL HAVE TO SEE IT IN ACTION...
WE SHOULD BE ABLE TO JOIN YOU GUYS SOON- CRACKLE IS ABOUT 75 PERCENT FIXED.
HOW ARE THINGS AT THE GROCERY STORE?
PRETTY TAME. NO SIGN OF CRAZY.
G-DANG!
WHAT WAS THAT?!!
OOPS!
CLEAN-UP ON ISLE CRAZY! HAHAHAH AHAAH!
LAME.

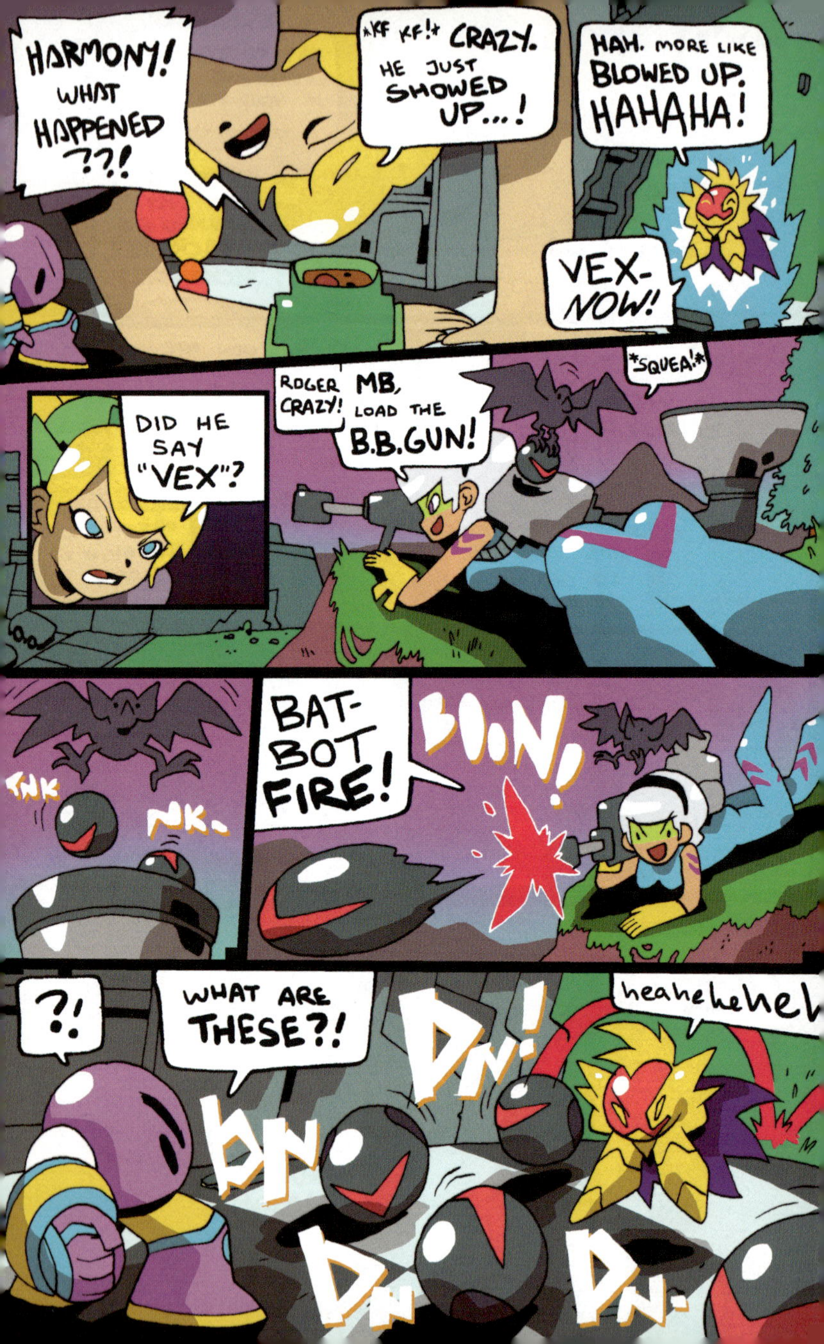
HARMONY! WHAT HAPPENED ??!
KF KF! CRAZY. HE JUST SHOWED UP...!
HAH. MORE LIKE BLOWED UP. HAHAHA!
VEX- NOW!
DID HE SAY "VEX"?
ROGER CRAZY!
MB, LOAD THE B.B. GUN!
SQUEA!
TNK
NK-
BAT-BOT FIRE!
BOOM!
?!
WHAT ARE THESE?!
DN!
heaheheheh
DN
DN
DN-

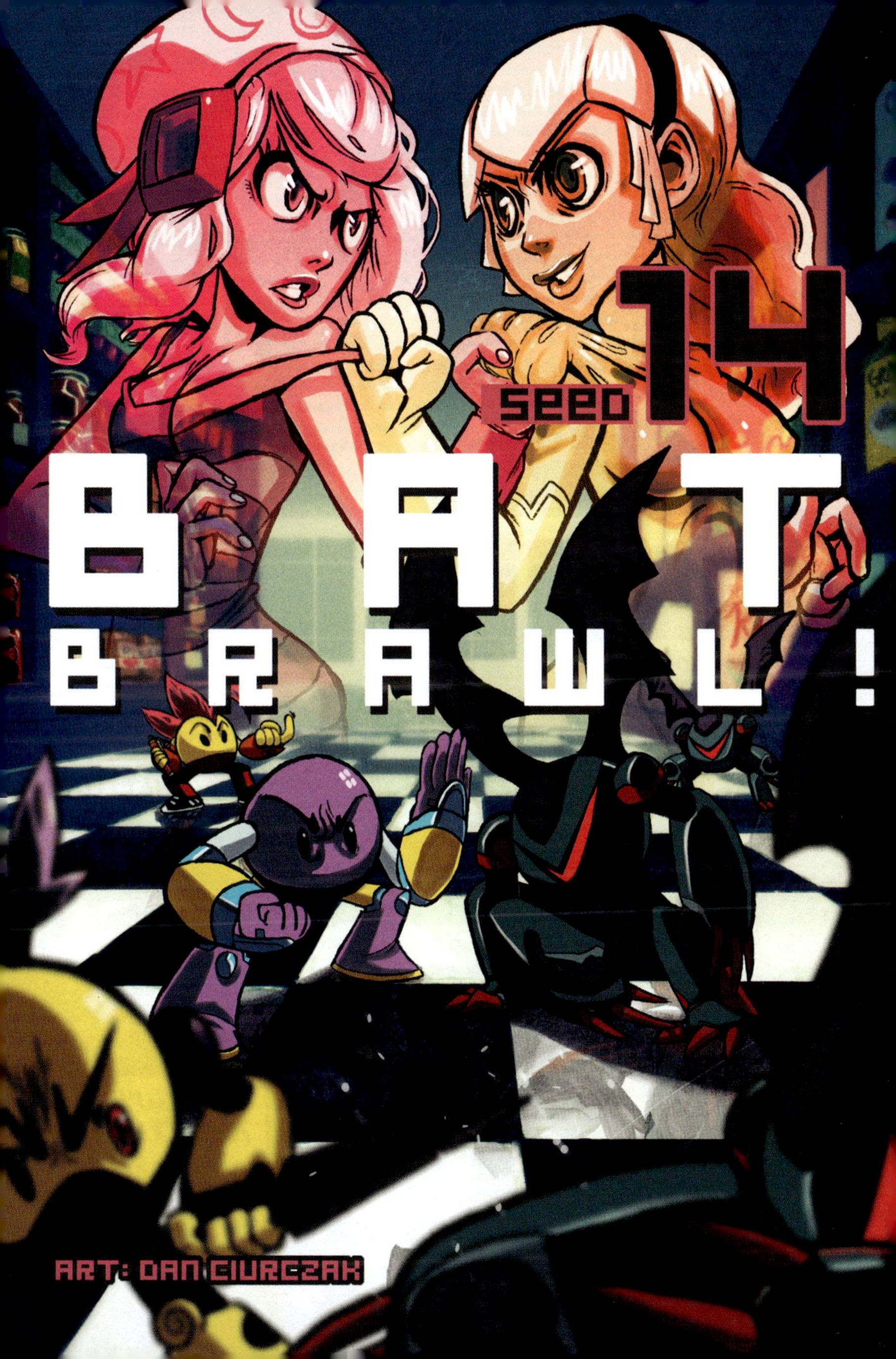
SEED 14
BAT BRAWL!
ART: DAN CIURCZAK

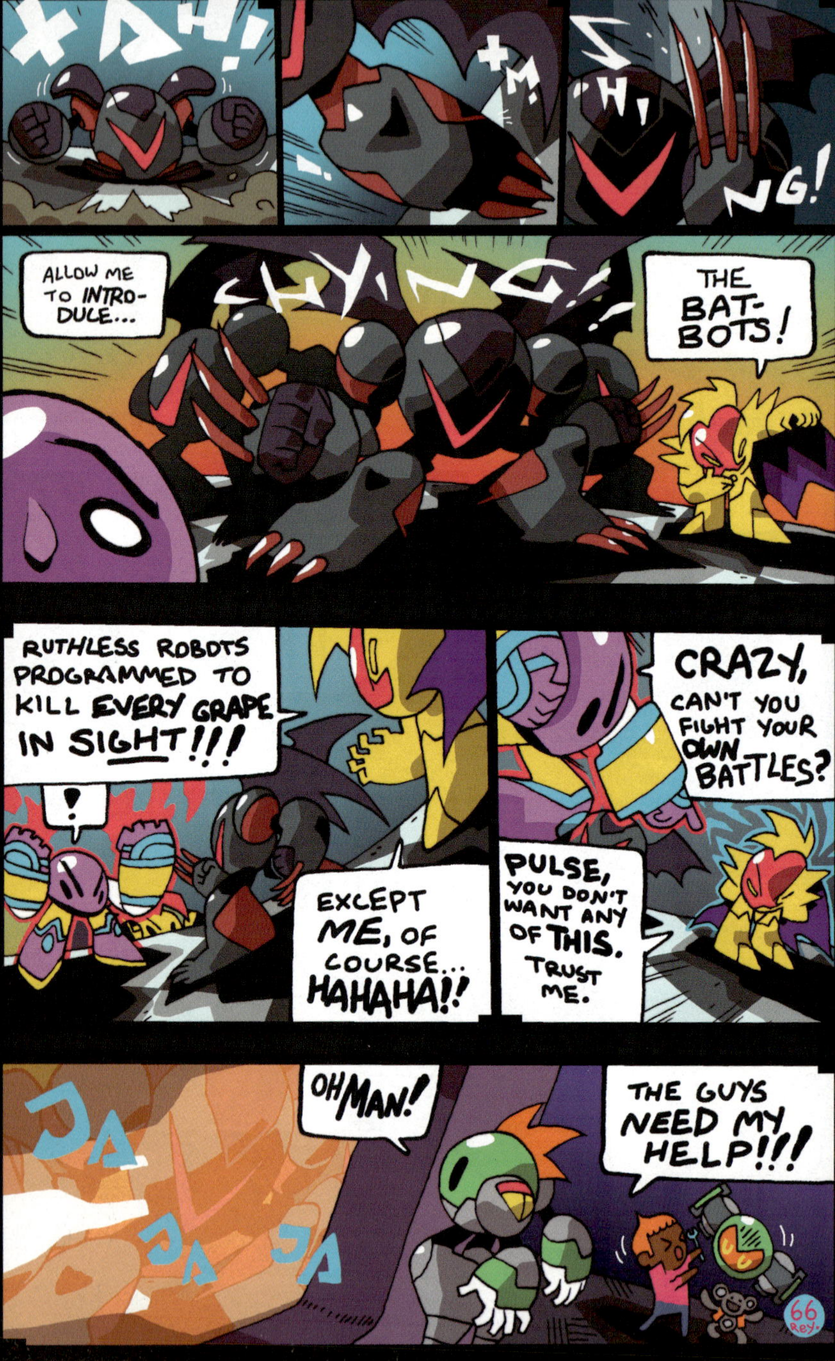
ALLOW ME TO INTRO-DUCE...
THE BAT-BOTS!
RUTHLESS ROBOTS PROGRAMMED TO KILL EVERY GRAPE IN SIGHT!!!
!
EXCEPT ME, OF COURSE... HAHAHA!!
CRAZY, CAN'T YOU FIGHT YOUR OWN BATTLES?
PULSE, YOU DON'T WANT ANY OF THIS. TRUST ME.
OH MAN!
THE GUYS NEED MY HELP!!!
NG!
66
Rey.

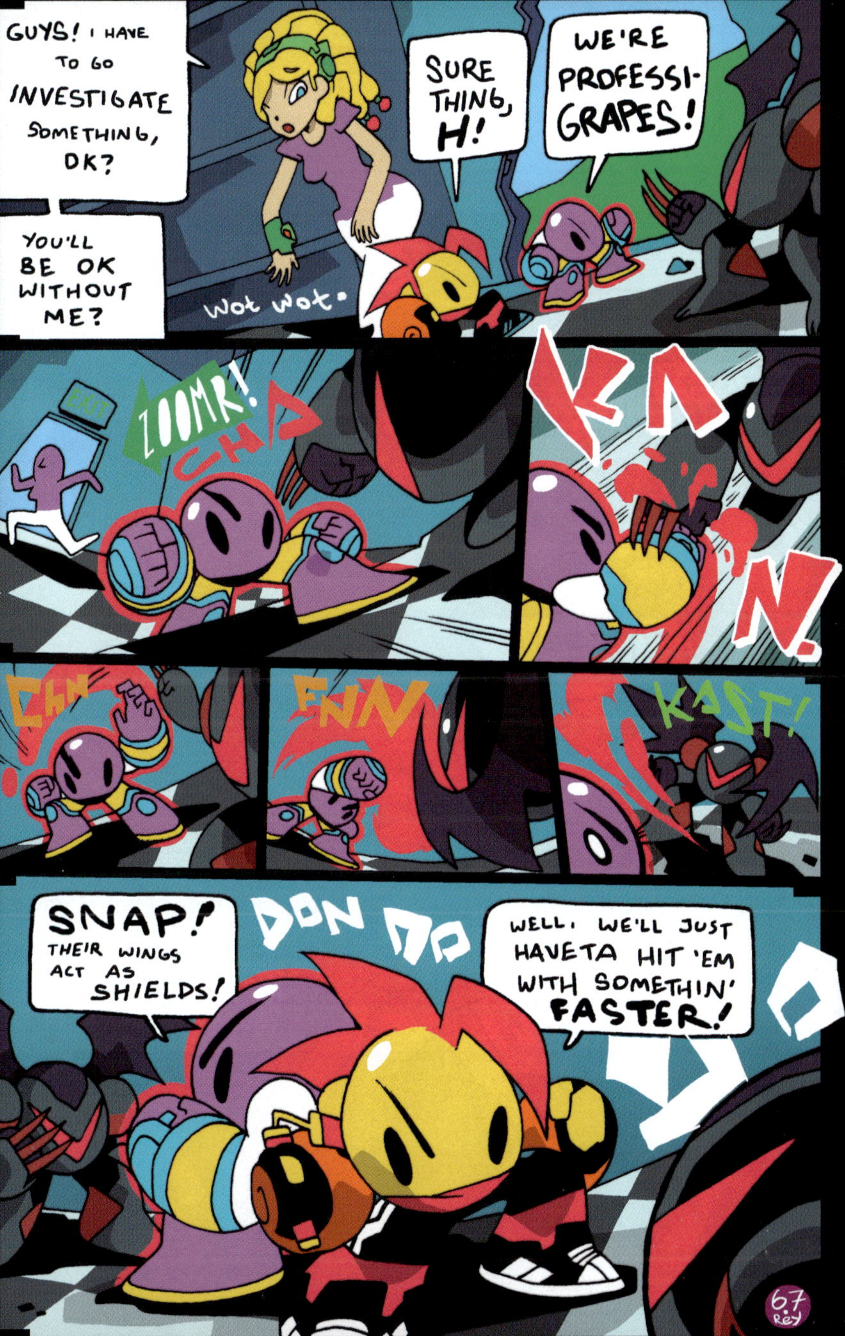
GUYS! I HAVE TO GO INVESTIGATE SOMETHING, OK?
YOU'LL BE OK WITHOUT ME?
SURE THING, H!
WE'RE PROFESSI-GRAPES!
Wot wot.
EXIT
ZOOMR!
SNAP! THEIR WINGS ACT AS SHIELDS!
WELL, WE'LL JUST HAVETA HIT 'EM WITH SOMETHIN' FASTER!

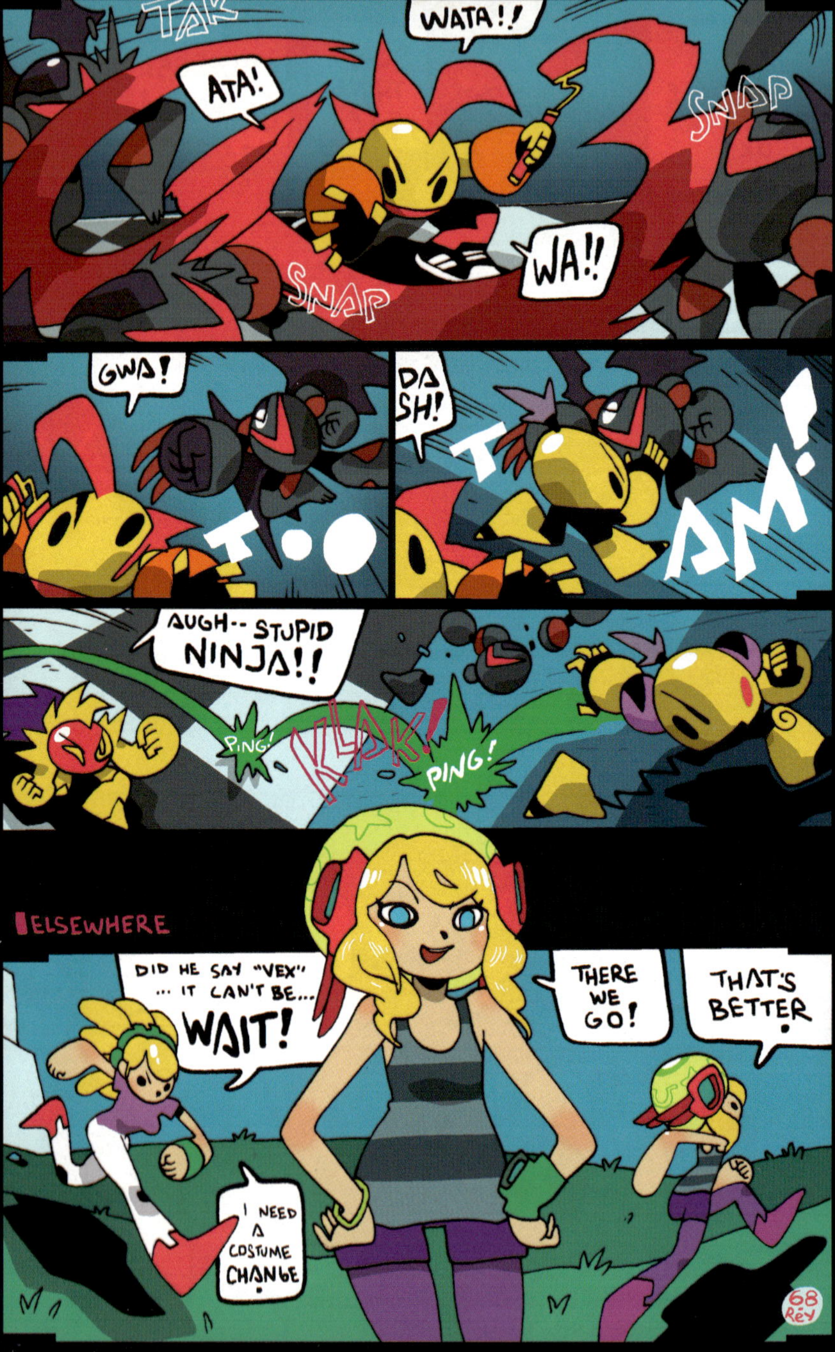
TAK
WATA!!
ATA!
SNAP
WA!!
SNAP
GWA!
T..
DA
SH!
TAM!
AUGH-- STUPID NINJA!!
PING!
KLAK!
PING!
ELSEWHERE
DID HE SAY "VEX" ... IT CAN'T BE... WAIT!
THERE WE GO!
THAT'S BETTER.
I NEED A COSTUME CHANGE.
68
Rey

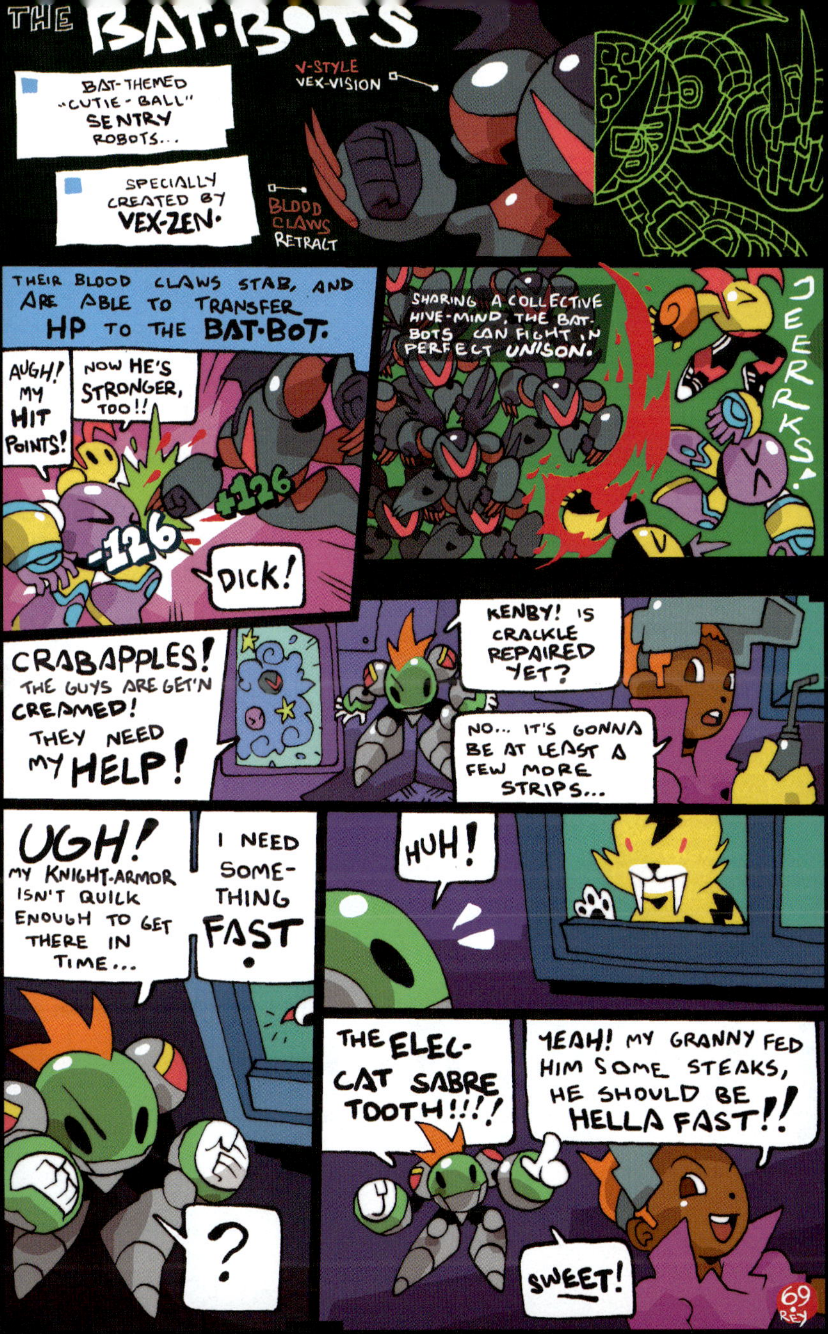
THE BAT-BOTS
BAT-THEMED "CUTIE-BALL" SENTRY ROBOTS...
SPECIALLY CREATED BY VEX-ZEN.
V-STYLE VEX-VISION
BLOOD CLAWS RETRACT
THEIR BLOOD CLAWS STAB, AND ARE ABLE TO TRANSFER HP TO THE BAT-BOT.
AUGH! MY HIT POINTS!
NOW HE'S STRONGER, TOO!!
+126
-126
DICK!
SHARING A COLLECTIVE HIVE-MIND, THE BAT-BOTS CAN FIGHT IN PERFECT UNISON.
JEERRKS!
CRABAPPLES! THE GUYS ARE GET'N CREAMED! THEY NEED MY HELP!
KENBY! IS CRACKLE REPAIRED YET?
NO... IT'S GONNA BE AT LEAST A FEW MORE STRIPS...
UGH! MY KNIGHT-ARMOR ISN'T QUICK ENOUGH TO GET THERE IN TIME...
I NEED SOME-THING FAST.
?
HUH!
THE ELEC-CAT SABRE TOOTH!!!!
YEAH! MY GRANNY FED HIM SOME STEAKS, HE SHOULD BE HELLA FAST!!
SWEET!

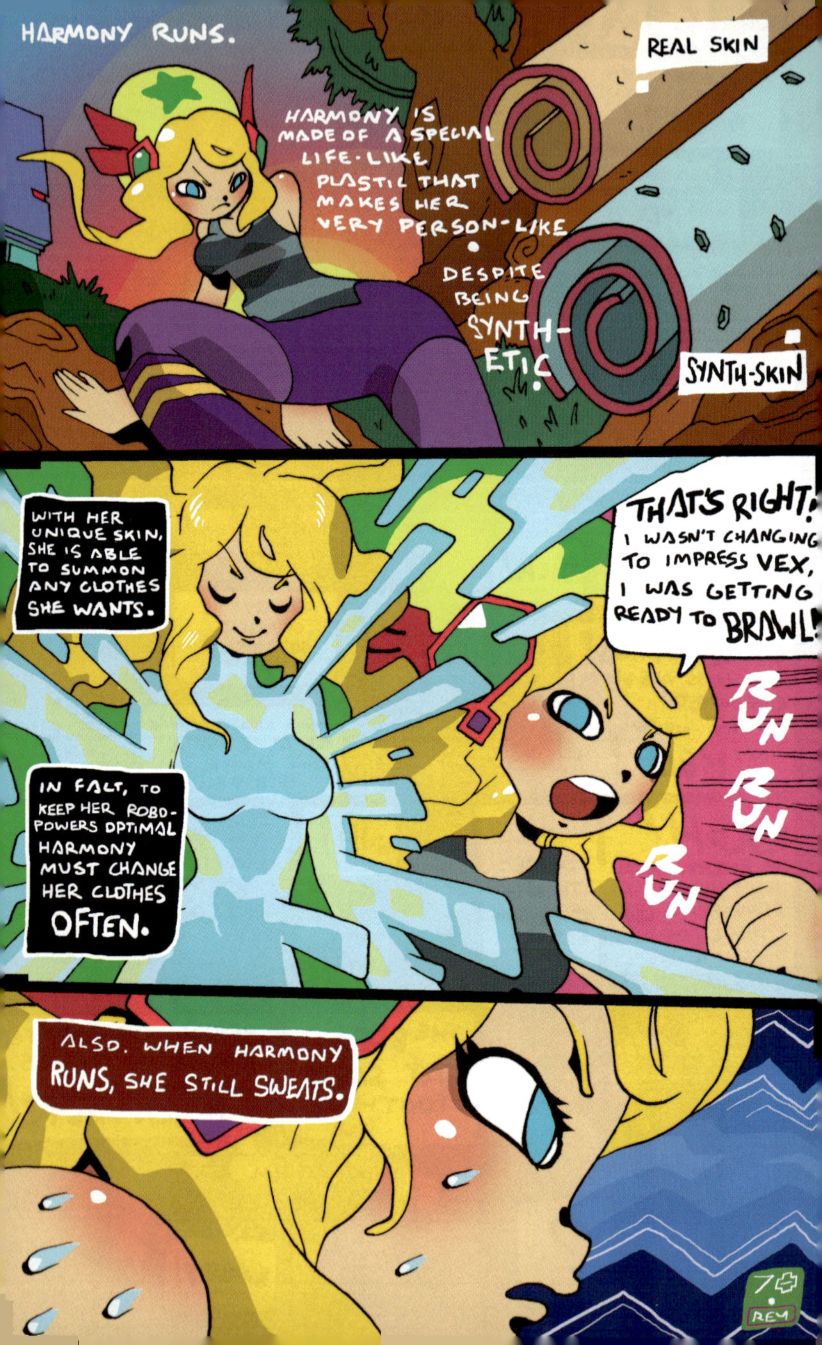
HARMONY RUNS.
REAL SKIN
HARMONY IS MADE OF A SPECIAL LIFE-LIKE PLASTIC THAT MAKES HER VERY PERSON-LIKE
DESPITE BEING SYNTH-ETIC.
SYNTH-SKIN
WITH HER UNIQUE SKIN, SHE IS ABLE TO SUMMON ANY CLOTHES SHE WANTS.
THAT'S RIGHT! I WASN'T CHANGING TO IMPRESS VEX, I WAS GETTING READY TO BRAWL!
RUN RUN RUN
IN FACT, TO KEEP HER ROBO-POWERS OPTIMAL HARMONY MUST CHANGE HER CLOTHES OFTEN.
ALSO, WHEN HARMONY RUNS, SHE STILL SWEATS.
REM

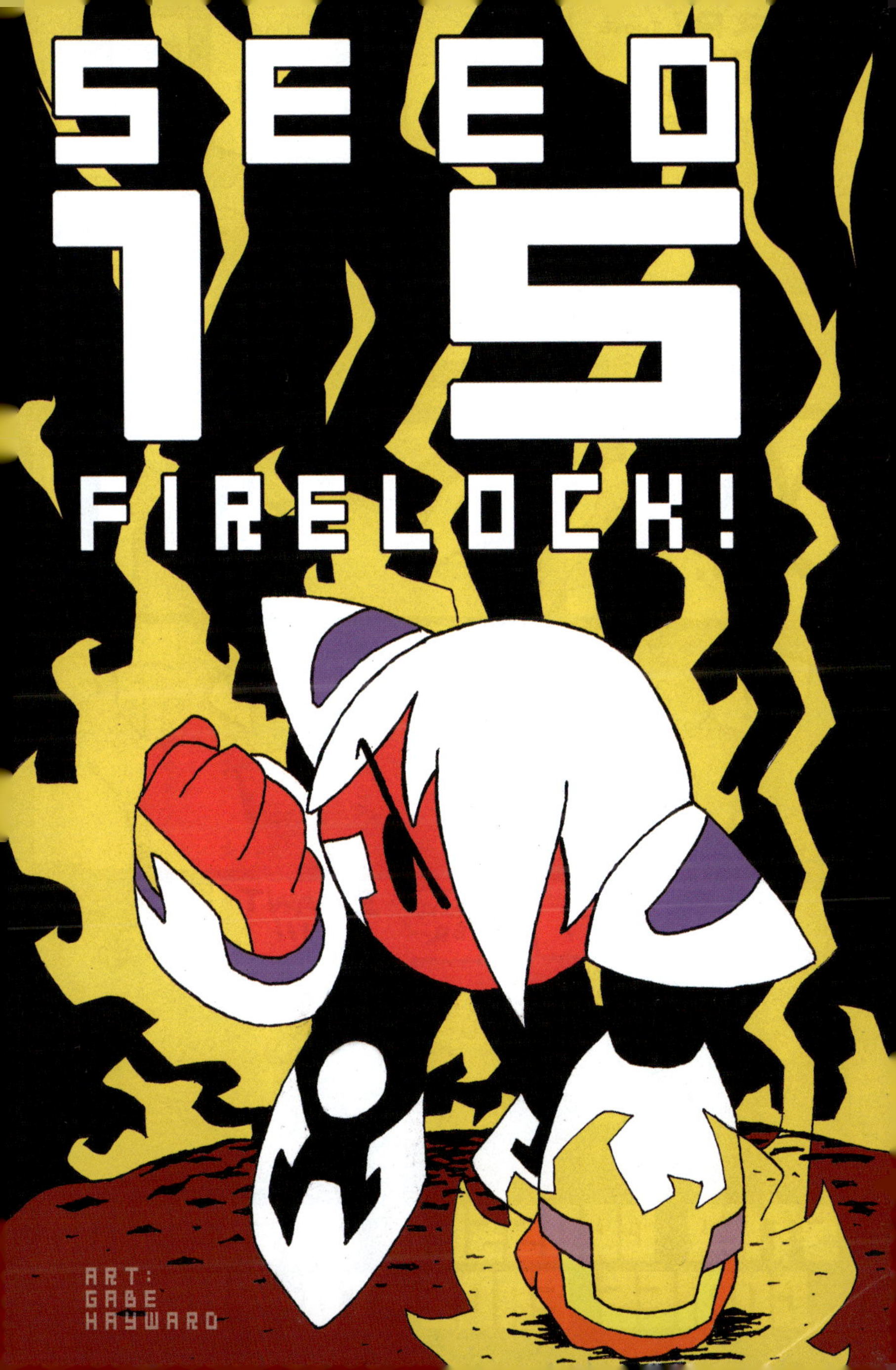
SEED 15
FIRELOCK!
ART:
GABE
HAYWARD

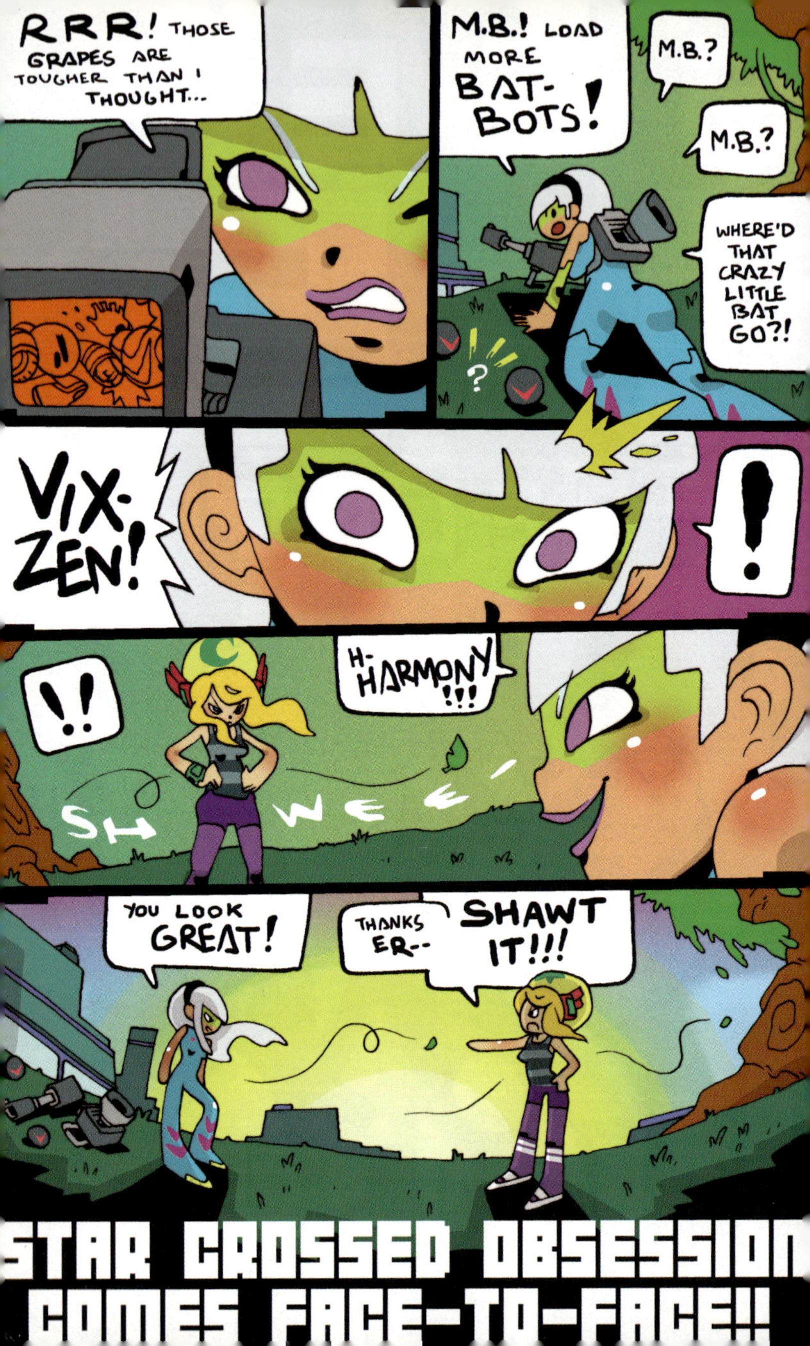
RRR! THOSE GRAPES ARE TOUGHER THAN I THOUGHT...
M.B.! LOAD MORE BAT-BOTS!
M.B.?
M.B.?
WHERE'D THAT CRAZY LITTLE BAT GO?!
?
VIX-ZEN!
!
!!
H-HARMONY!!!
SHWEE
YOU LOOK GREAT!
THANKS ER--
SHAWT IT!!!
STAR CROSSED OBSESSION COMES FACE-TO-FACE!!

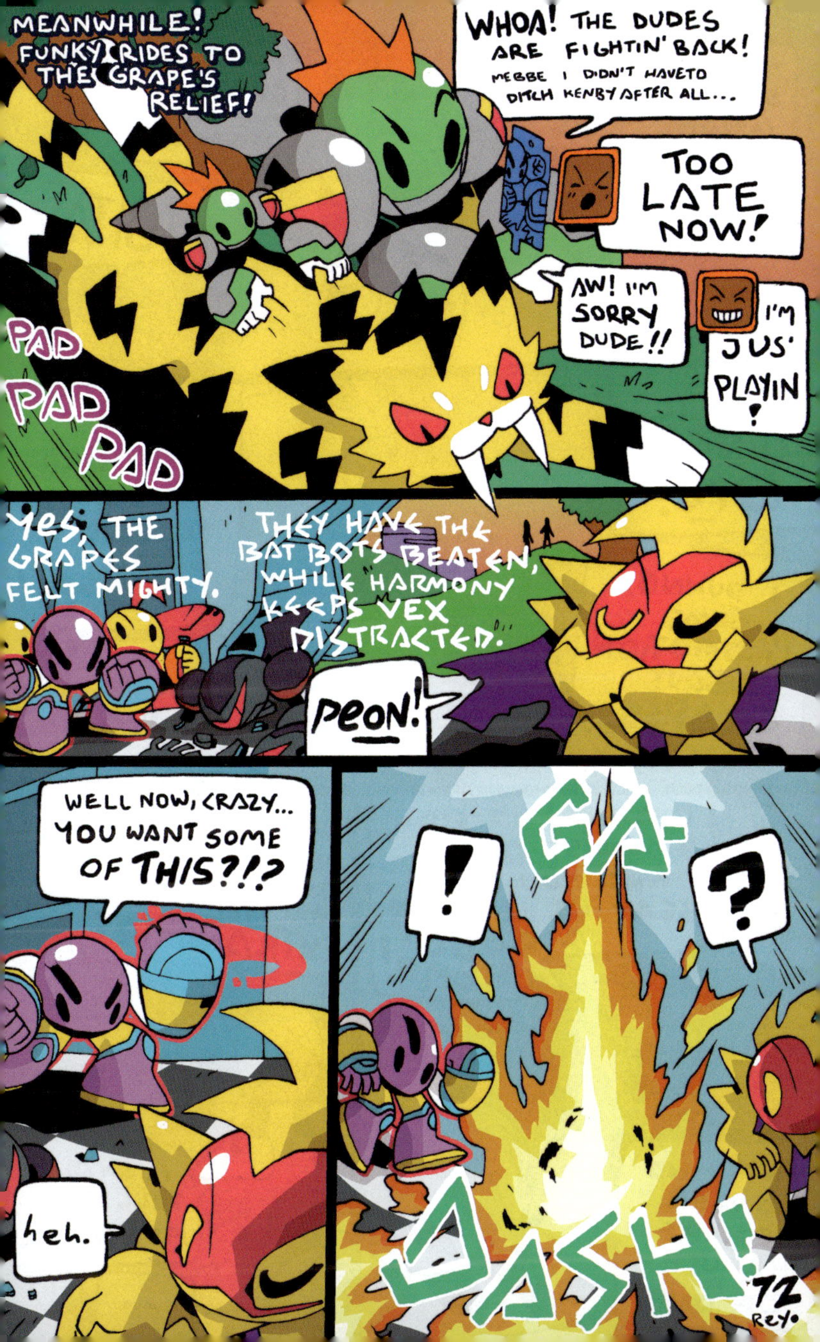
MEANWHILE! FUNKY RIDES TO THE GRAPE'S RELIEF!
WHOA! THE DUDES ARE FIGHTIN' BACK! MEBBE I DIDN'T HAVE TO DITCH KENBY AFTER ALL...
TOO LATE NOW!
AW! I'M SORRY DUDE!!
I'M JUS' PLAYIN!
PAD PAD PAD
YES, THE GRAPES FELT MIGHTY.
THEY HAVE THE BAT BOTS BEATEN, WHILE HARMONY KEEPS VEX DISTRACTED.
PEON!
WELL NOW, CRAZY... YOU WANT SOME OF THIS?!?
heh.
!
?
GA-DASH!
72
Rey.

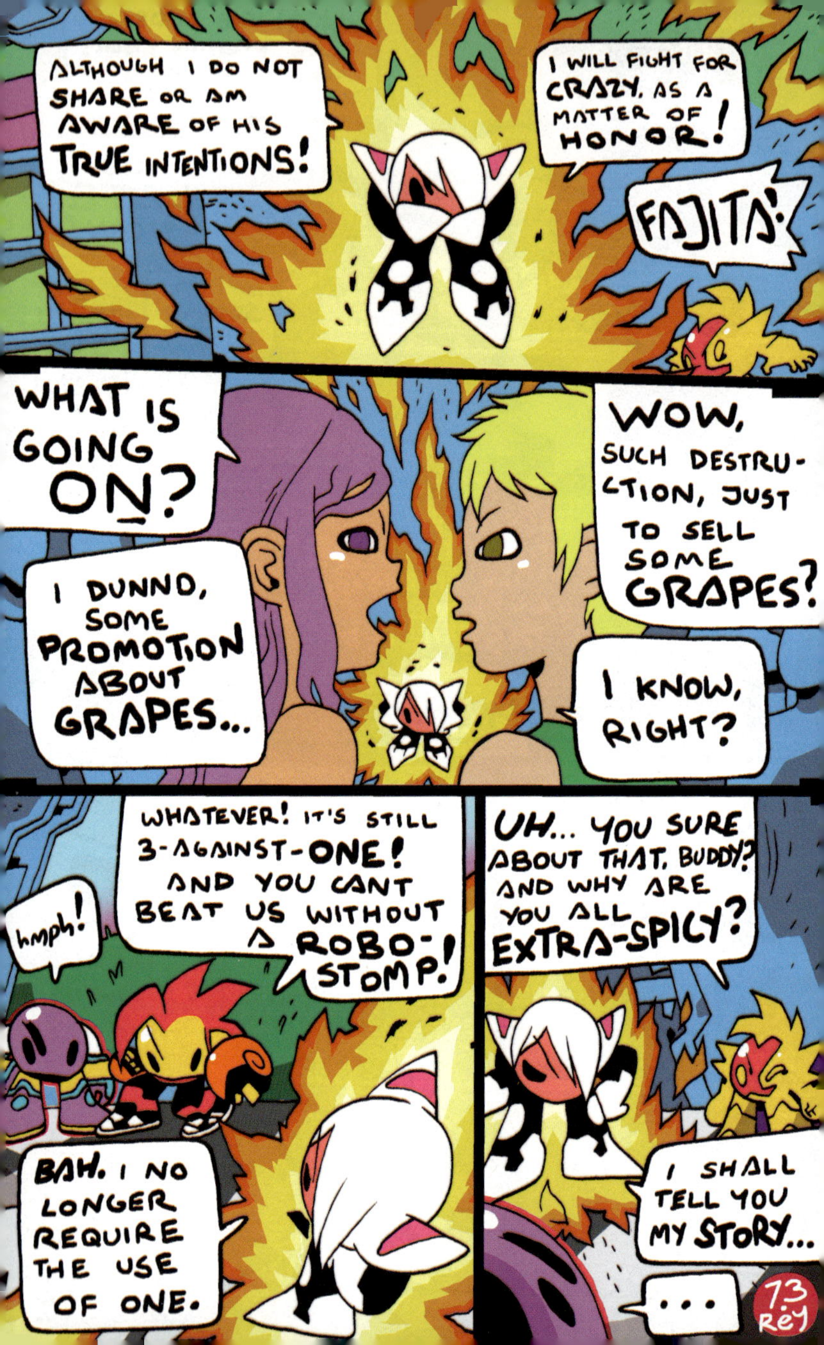
ALTHOUGH I DO NOT SHARE OR AM AWARE OF HIS TRUE INTENTIONS!
I WILL FIGHT FOR CRAZY, AS A MATTER OF HONOR!
FAJITA!
WHAT IS GOING ON?
WOW, SUCH DESTRUCTION, JUST TO SELL SOME GRAPES?
I DUNNO, SOME PROMOTION ABOUT GRAPES...
I KNOW, RIGHT?
hmph!
WHATEVER! IT'S STILL 3-AGAINST-ONE! AND YOU CANT BEAT US WITHOUT A ROBO-STOMP!
UH... YOU SURE ABOUT THAT, BUDDY? AND WHY ARE YOU ALL EXTRA-SPICY?
BAH. I NO LONGER REQUIRE THE USE OF ONE.
I SHALL TELL YOU MY STORY...
...
73
Rey

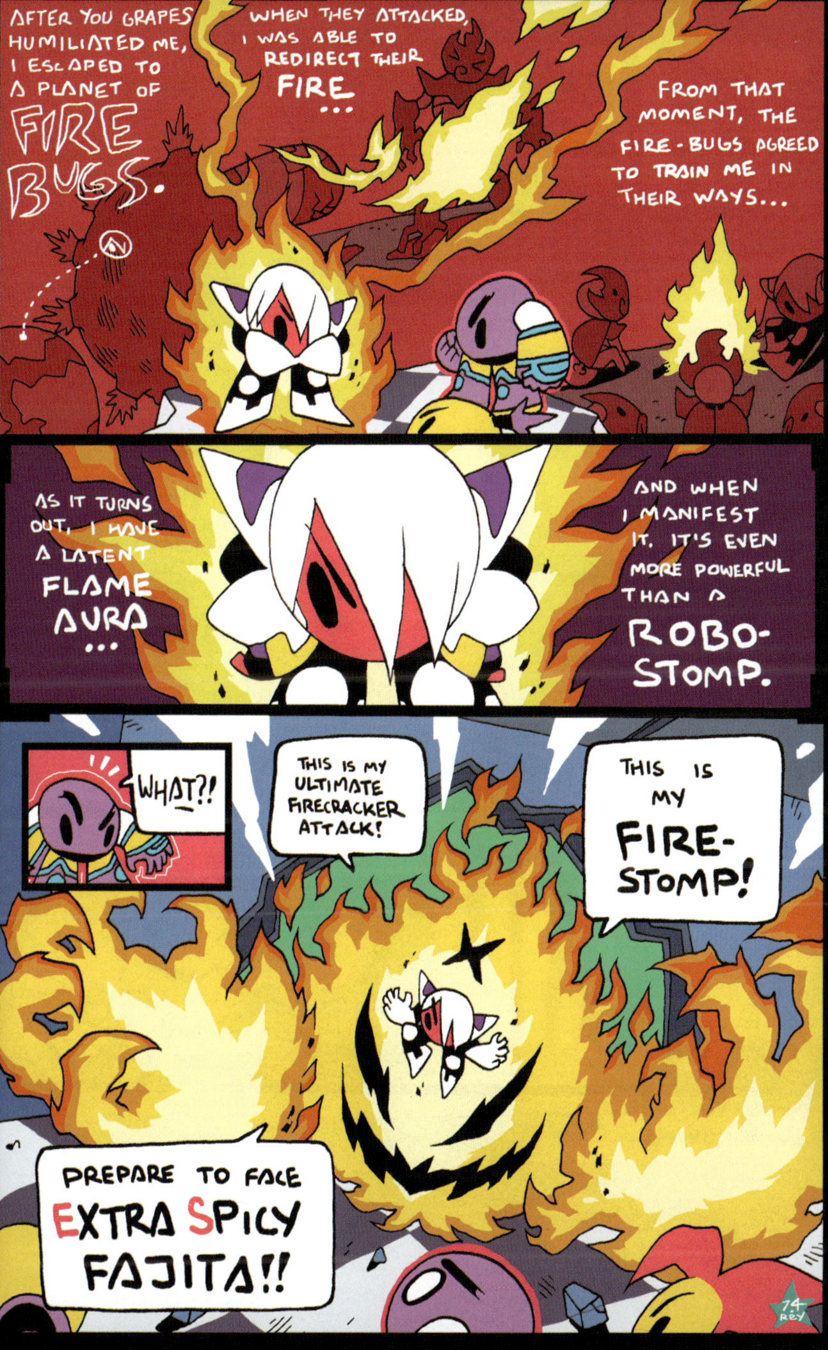

AFTER YOU GRAPES HUMILIATED ME, I ESCAPED TO A PLANET OF FIRE BUGS.
WHEN THEY ATTACKED, I WAS ABLE TO REDIRECT THEIR FIRE...
FROM THAT MOMENT, THE FIRE-BUGS AGREED TO TRAIN ME IN THEIR WAYS...
AS IT TURNS OUT, I HAVE A LATENT FLAME AURA...
AND WHEN I MANIFEST IT, IT'S EVEN MORE POWERFUL THAN A ROBO-STOMP.
WHAT?!
THIS IS MY ULTIMATE FIRECRACKER ATTACK!
THIS IS MY FIRE-STOMP!
PREPARE TO FACE EXTRA SPICY FAJITA!!

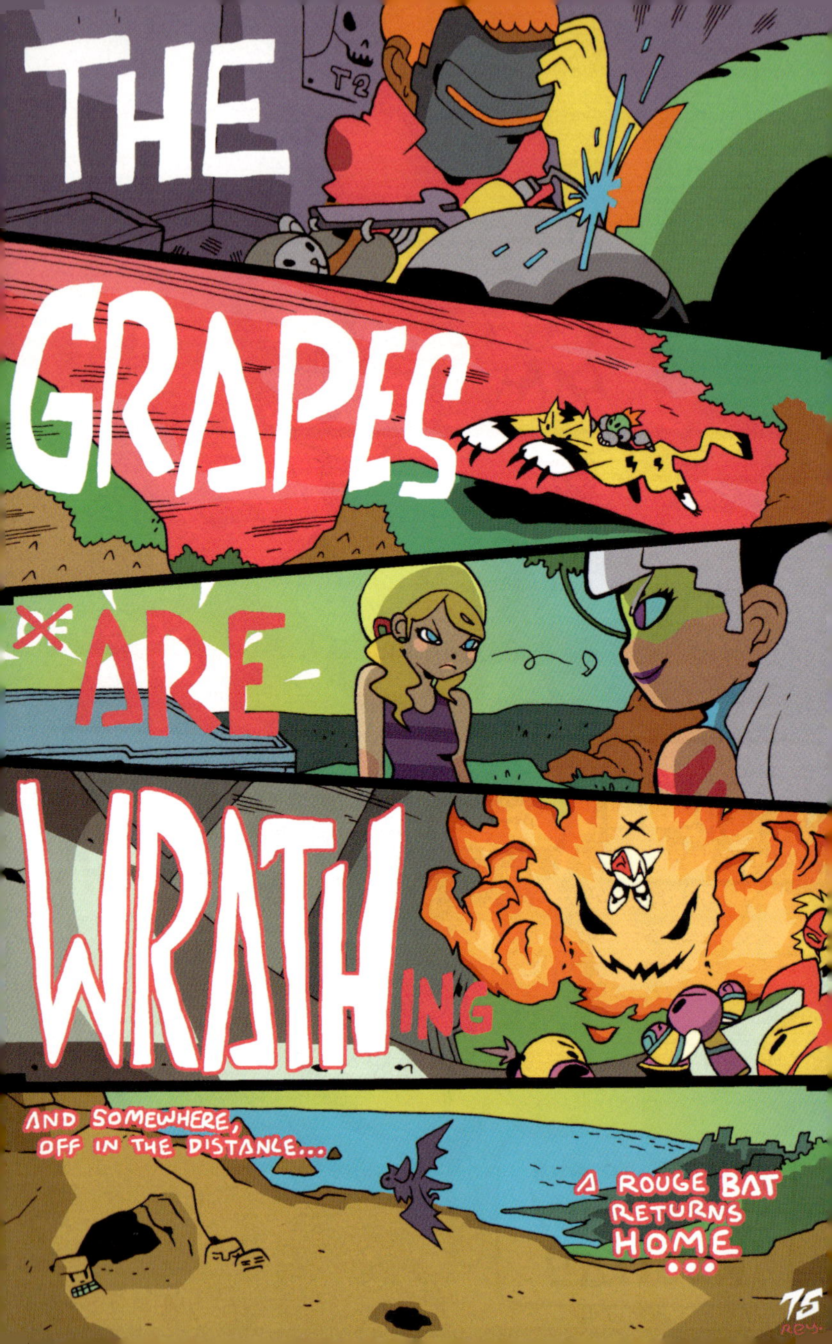
THE
GRAPES
~~OF~~ ARE
WRATHing
AND SOMEWHERE, OFF IN THE DISTANCE...
A ROUGE BAT RETURNS HOME...

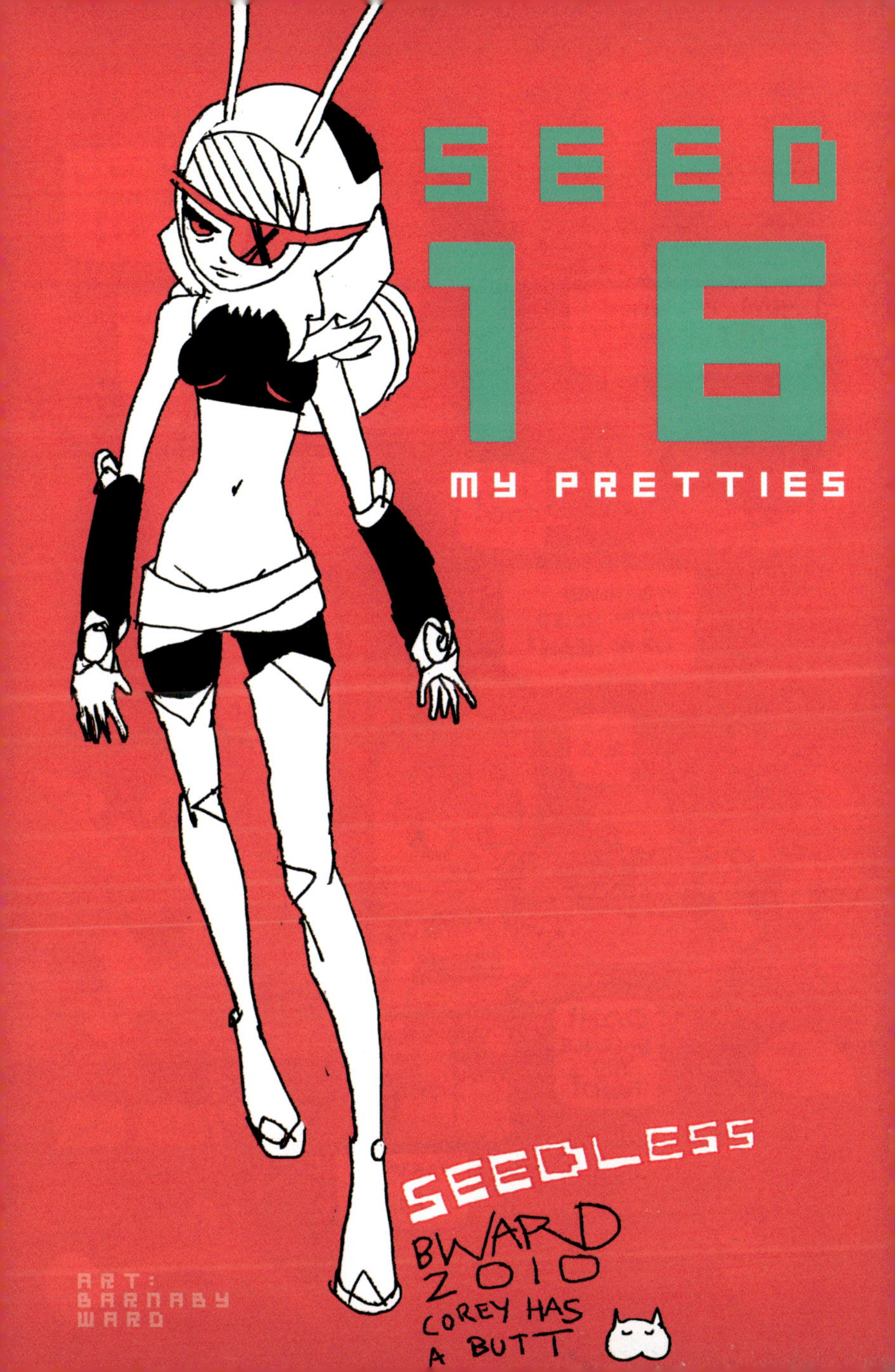
SEED
16
MY PRETTIES
SEEDLESS
BWARD
2010
COREY HAS
A BUTT
ART:
BARNABY
WARD

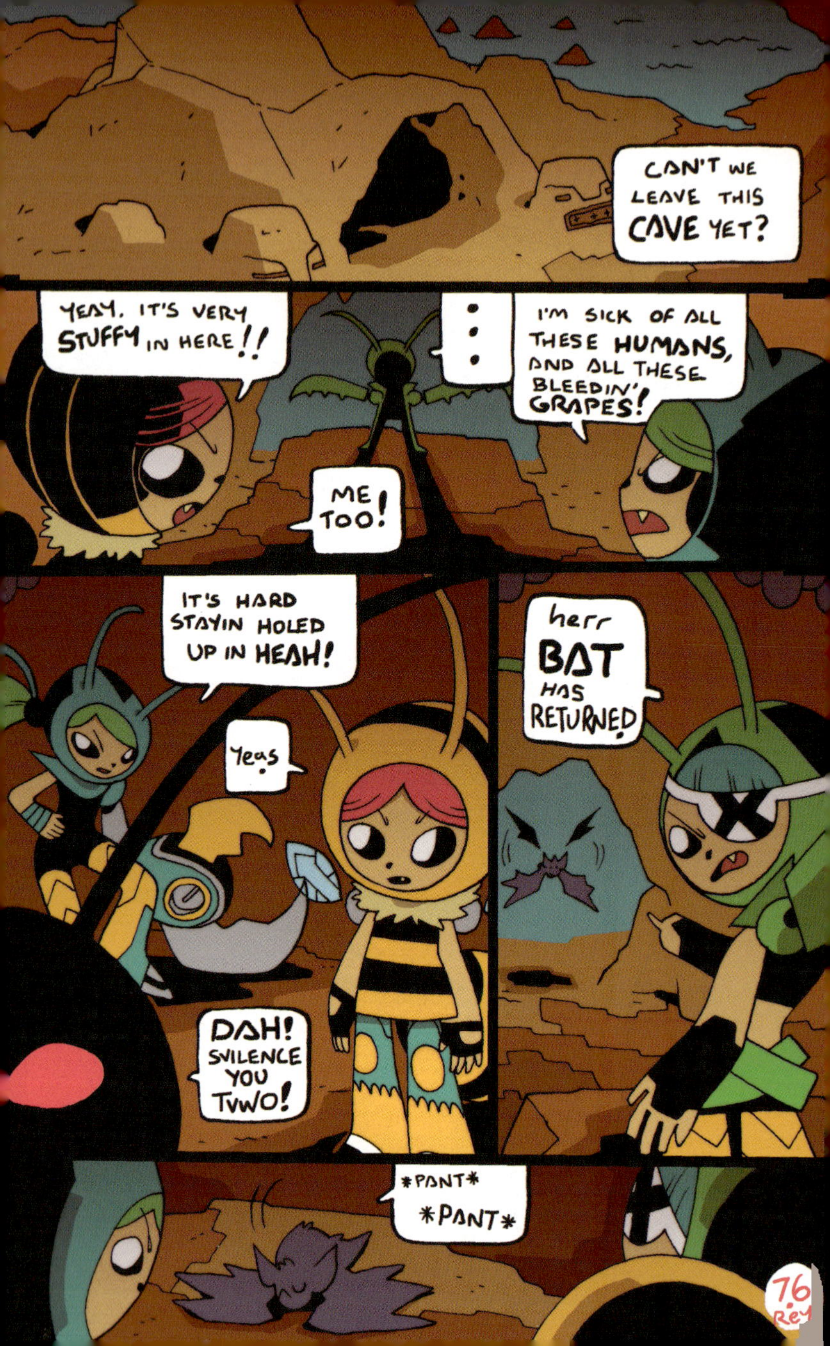
CAN'T WE LEAVE THIS CAVE YET?
YEAH. IT'S VERY STUFFY IN HERE!!
...
I'M SICK OF ALL THESE HUMANS, AND ALL THESE BLEEDIN' GRAPES!
ME TOO!
IT'S HARD STAYIN HOLED UP IN HEAH!
Yeas
DAH! SVILENCE YOU TWO!
herr BAT HAS RETURNED
PANT
PANT
76

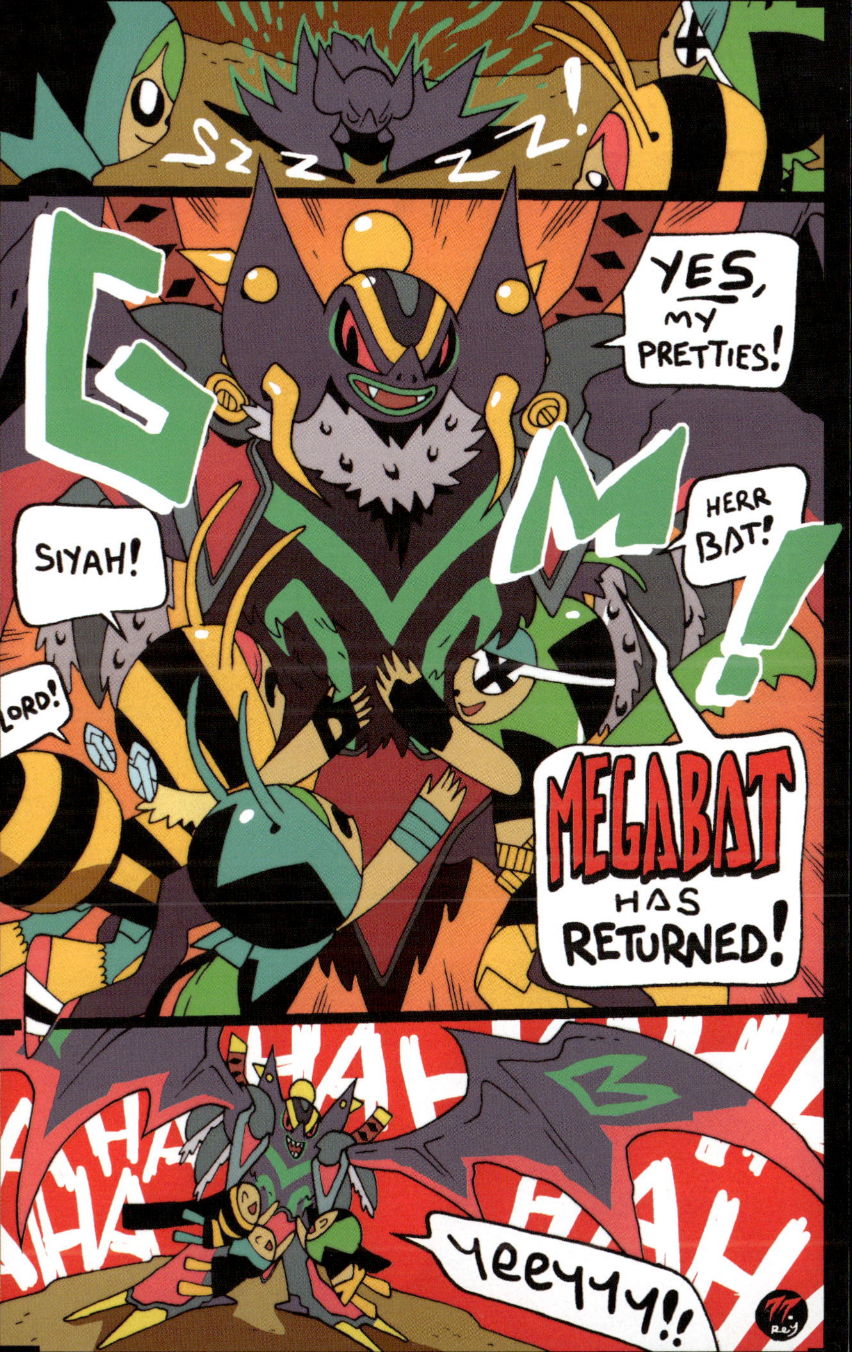
SZZZZZ!
GMM!
YES, MY PRETTIES!
SIYAH!
HERR BAT!
LORD!
MEGABAT HAS RETURNED!
HAHAHAHAH
YEEYYY!!

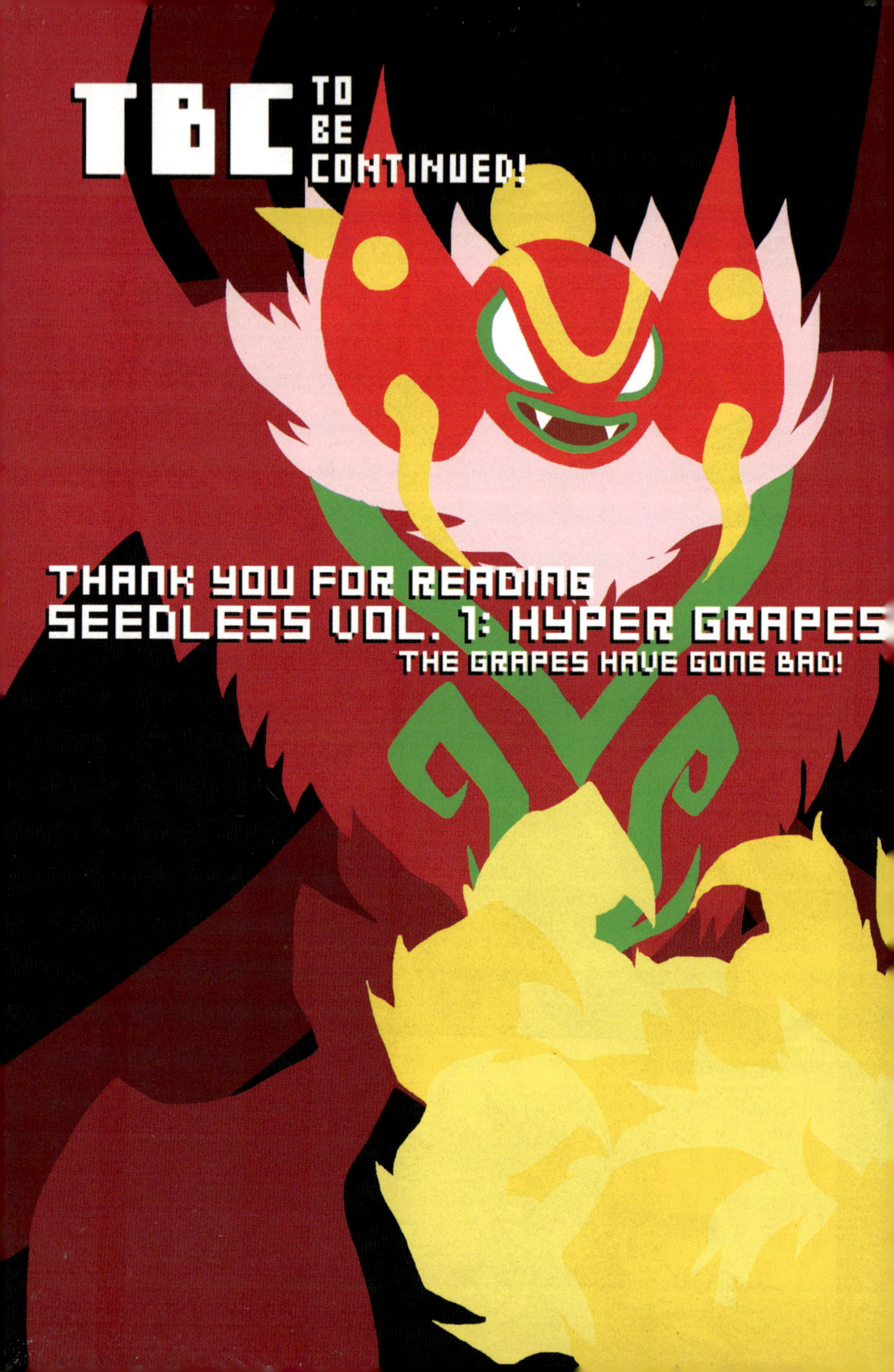
TBC
TO
BE
CONTINUED!
THANK YOU FOR READING
SEEDLESS VOL. 1: HYPER GRAPES
THE GRAPES HAVE GONE BAD!

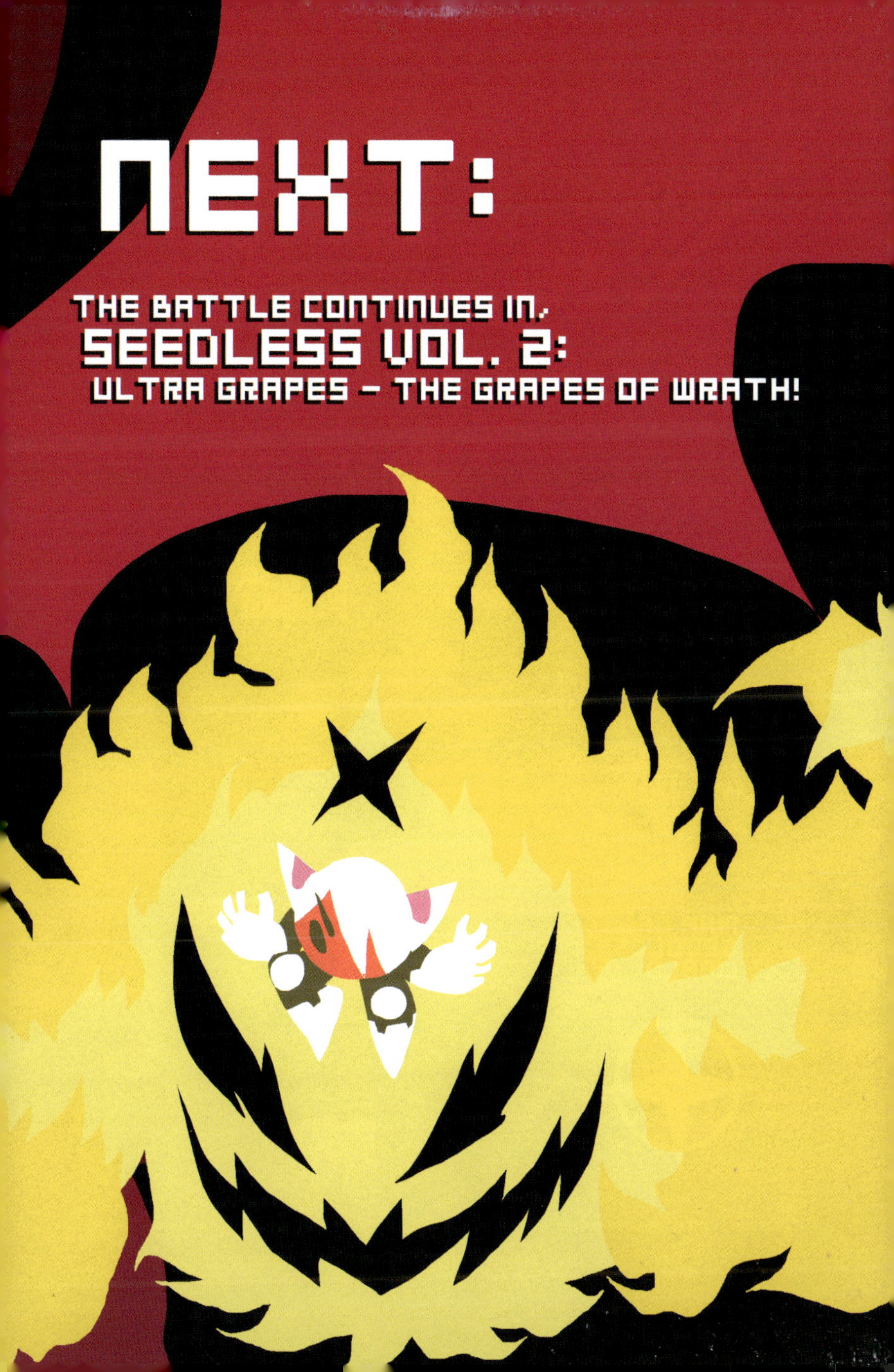
NEXT:
THE BATTLE CONTINUES IN,
SEEDLESS VOL. 2:
ULTRA GRAPES - THE GRAPES OF WRATH!

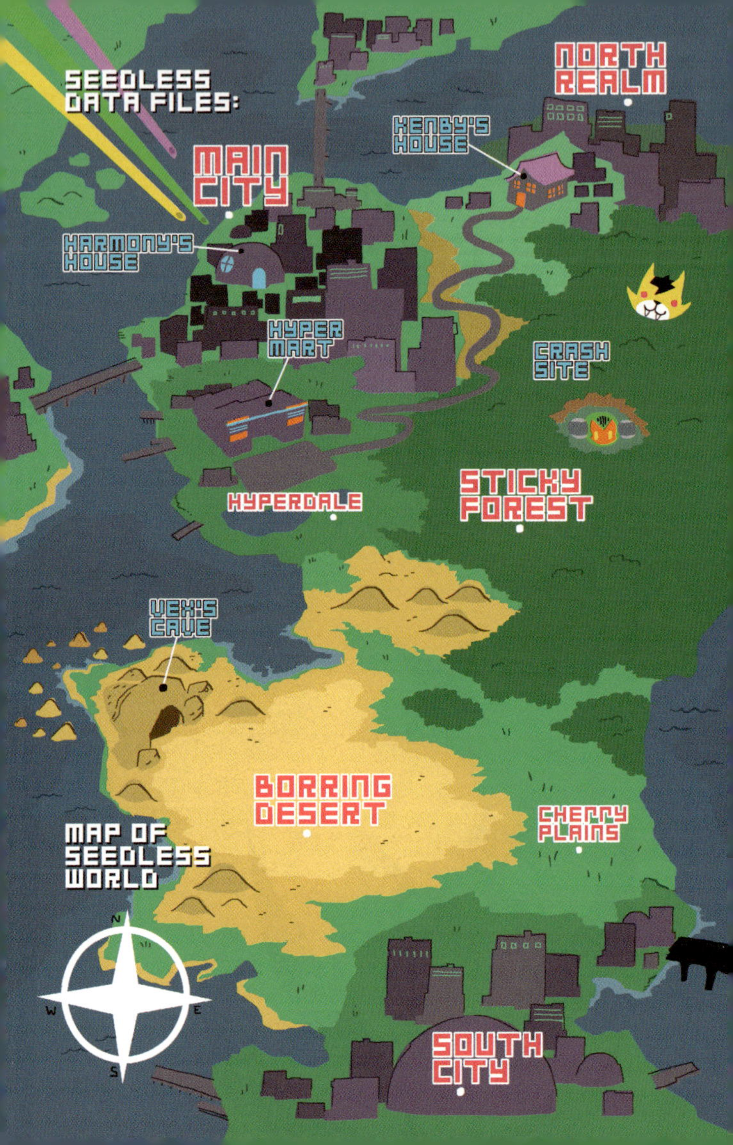
SEEDLESS DATA FILES:
MAIN CITY
HARMONY'S HOUSE
HYPER MART
HYPERDALE
KENBY'S HOUSE
NORTH REALM
CRASH SITE
STICKY FOREST
VEX'S CAVE
BORRING DESERT
CHERRY PLAINS
MAP OF SEEDLESS WORLD
N
W
E
S
SOUTH CITY

SEEDLESS
CHARACTER BIOS

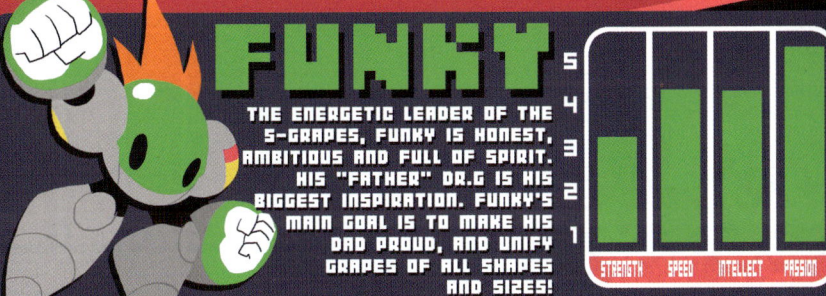

FUNKY

THE ENERGETIC LEADER OF THE 5-GRAPES, FUNKY IS HONEST, AMBITIOUS AND FULL OF SPIRIT. HIS "FATHER" DR.G IS HIS BIGGEST INSPIRATION. FUNKY'S MAIN GOAL IS TO MAKE HIS DAD PROUD, AND UNIFY GRAPES OF ALL SHAPES AND SIZES!

5
4
3
2
1
STRENGTH
SPEED
INTELLECT
PASSION

SPECIAL MOVES:
BLADE BEAM! ↓↘→G
CRESCENT SLASH →↓↘G
MEGA GUARD ↓↙←G

5
4
3
2
1
STRENGTH
SPEED
INTELLECT
PASSION

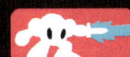

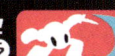

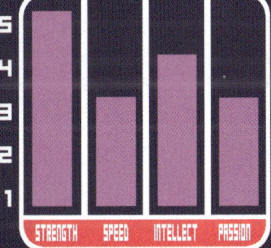

PULSE

THE MUSCLE OF THE TEAM, PULSE'S GEL-AURA CREATES A POWERFUL BARRIER AROUND HIM THAT SHEILDS AND ACTS AS AN OFFENSIVE WEAPON. BEING THE POWERHOUSE OF THE GROUP HAS MADE PULSE A BIT OF A HOT-HEAD. HE ENJOYS RACING VEHICLES DUE TO HIS ATTITUDE.

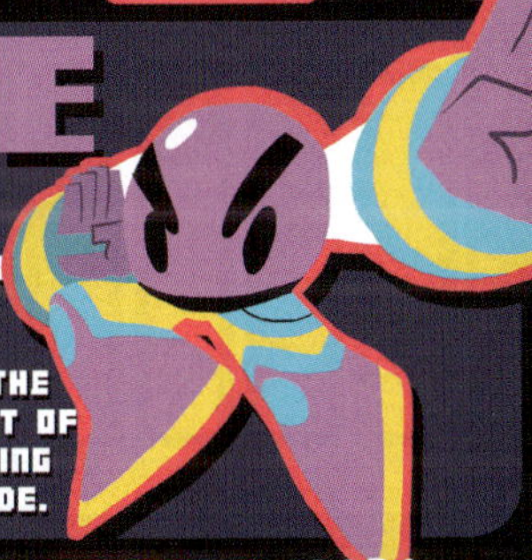

SPECIAL MOVES:
GEL BARRIER G×3
GRAPA BALL ←/→G
GRAPA CRUSH ←/→G

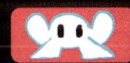

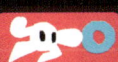

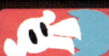

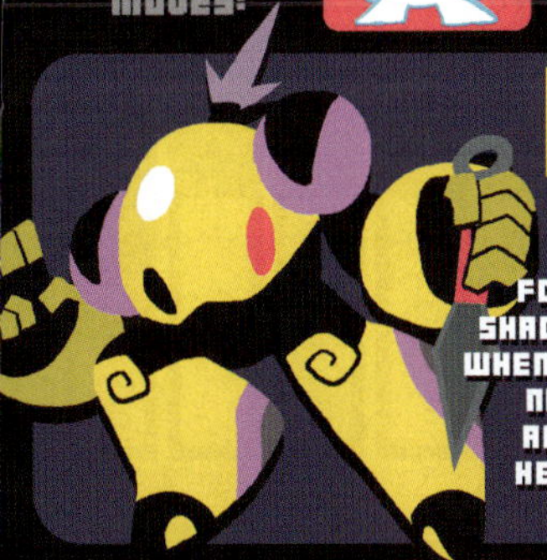

DASH

SILENT BUT DEADLY, DASH IS OFTEN THE GRAPES' FOUNDATION, LURKING IN THE SHADOWS. ONLY TAKING ACTION WHEN IT IS NEEDED, DASH DOES NOT MINCE WORDS. DESPITE ALL THIS, DASH HAS A GIANT HEART, AND IS KNOWN TO BE A ROMANTIC.

5
4
3
2
1
STRENGTH
SPEED
INTELLECT
PASSION

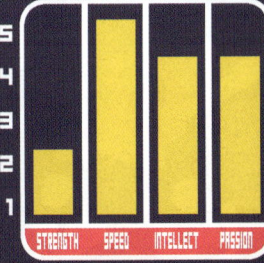

SPECIAL MOVES:
KUNAI TOSS ↙→G
EXPLOSIVE WINDMILL ↓↘→G IN AIR
NIN-JUMP ↓↑

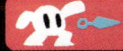

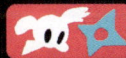

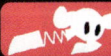

SEEDLESS CHARACTER BIOS

SNAP

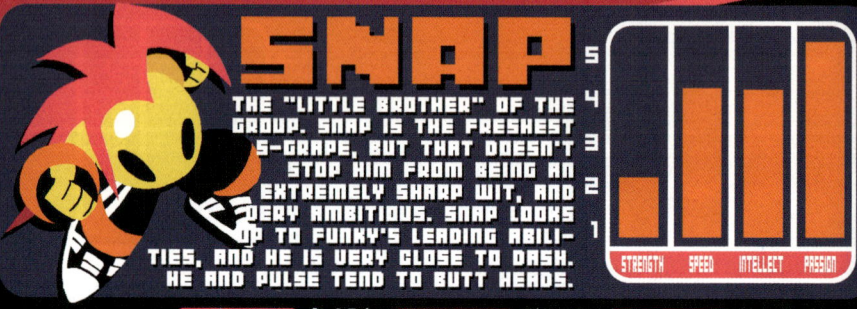

THE "LITTLE BROTHER" OF THE GROUP. SNAP IS THE FRESHEST S-GRAPE, BUT THAT DOESN'T STOP HIM FROM BEING AN EXTREMELY SHARP WIT, AND VERY AMBITIOUS. SNAP LOOKS UP TO FUNKY'S LEADING ABILITIES, AND HE IS VERY CLOSE TO DASH. HE AND PULSE TEND TO BUTT HEADS.

5
4
3
2
1
STRENGTH
SPEED
INTELLECT
PASSION

SPECIAL MOVES:

SLASH CHUCK
→↓↘G
DYNAMITE THROW
←↙↓↘→G
SNAP DASH
G→→

CRAZY

5
4
3
2
1
STRENGTH
SPEED
INTELLECT
PASSION

DR.G'S FIRST CREATION, CRAZY IS CONSIDERED A "BOTCHED" EXPERIMENT. HIS UNSTABLE MIND & POWERS HAVE GIVEN HIM WARPED VIEWS TOWARD HIS FELLOW GRAPES. A NIHILIST, CRAZY'S ULTIMATE GOAL IS TO "PURIFY" ALL GRAPES, BY MAKING THEM HIS MINDLESS MINIONS.

SPECIAL MOVES:

MANIPULATE
→←↙↓↘→
G x3
GEL RENDER
←/→G
TELEPORT
→↓↘G
x3

FAJITA

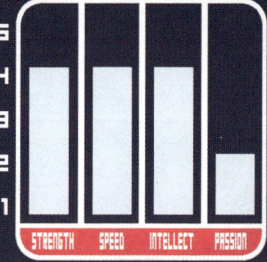

ONE OF THE FIRST GRAPES TO BE SWAYED BY CRAZY'S MIND-CONTROLLING POWERS, FAJITA IS A WELLSPRING OF CONFLICTING EMOTIONS. HONORABLE YET VINDICTIVE, FAJITA OFTEN TAKES HIS WRATH OUT ON UNSUSPECTING INSECT BEINGS.

5
4
3
2
1
STRENGTH
SPEED
INTELLECT
PASSION

SPECIAL MOVES:

RAGE BURST
↓↓G
GRAPA PLATE
↓/↑G
REDIRECT
←↙↓G

SEEDLESS
CHARACTER BIOS

DR. G

VETERAN OF THE G-WAR, AN INGENOUS SCIENTIST, DR.G CREATED THE SEEDLESS GRAPES AS A MEANS OF DEFENSE FOR HIS HOME PLANET. HE HAS COME TO LOVE THE S-GRAPES AS HIS OWN SONS.

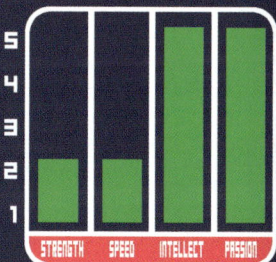

Strength / Speed / Intellect / Passion

HARMONY

DAUGHTER OF A FAMOUS INVENTOR, HARMONY TREBLECLEFF IS A SPRITELY, OUTGOING GAL. ALWAYS MAKING INVENTIONS HERSELF, SHE CLAIMS THE S-GRAPES AS HER OWN INVENTIONS TO AVOID SUSPICION. HARMONY HAS A CACHE OF SUPERHUMAN ABILITIES, DUE TO THE FACT THAT SHE IS ACTUALLY A ROBO-GIRL. SHE LOVES CUPCAKES AND FASHION.

KENBY

A FRIEND OF HARMONY'S AND A FELLOW INVENTOR. KENBY STAYS UP-TO-DATE ON THE LATEST TECHNOLOGY TRENDS. HE LOOKS UP TO HARMONY'S DAD, DR. TREBLECLEFF. KENBY CLAIMS HE CAN FIX ANYTHING.

VEX-ZEN

A SELF-PROCLAIMED "MECH ROMANCER". VEX IS ANOTHER WHO FALLS INTO THE CONTEMPORARY INVENTOR CATERGORY. SHE HAS MISPLACED AFFECTION FOR HARMONY, AND SHOWS IT THROUGH CONFRONTATION.

ELEC-CAT SABRETOOTH

A NATIVE OF THE STICKY FOREST. ELEC-CAT LOVES FRUIT & MEAT. HE FIRST ATTEMPTS TO EAT THE SEEDLESS GRAPES, BUT ONCE HIS STOMACH IS SATIATED BY STEAK, HE BECOMES A FAST FRIEND TO FUNKY.

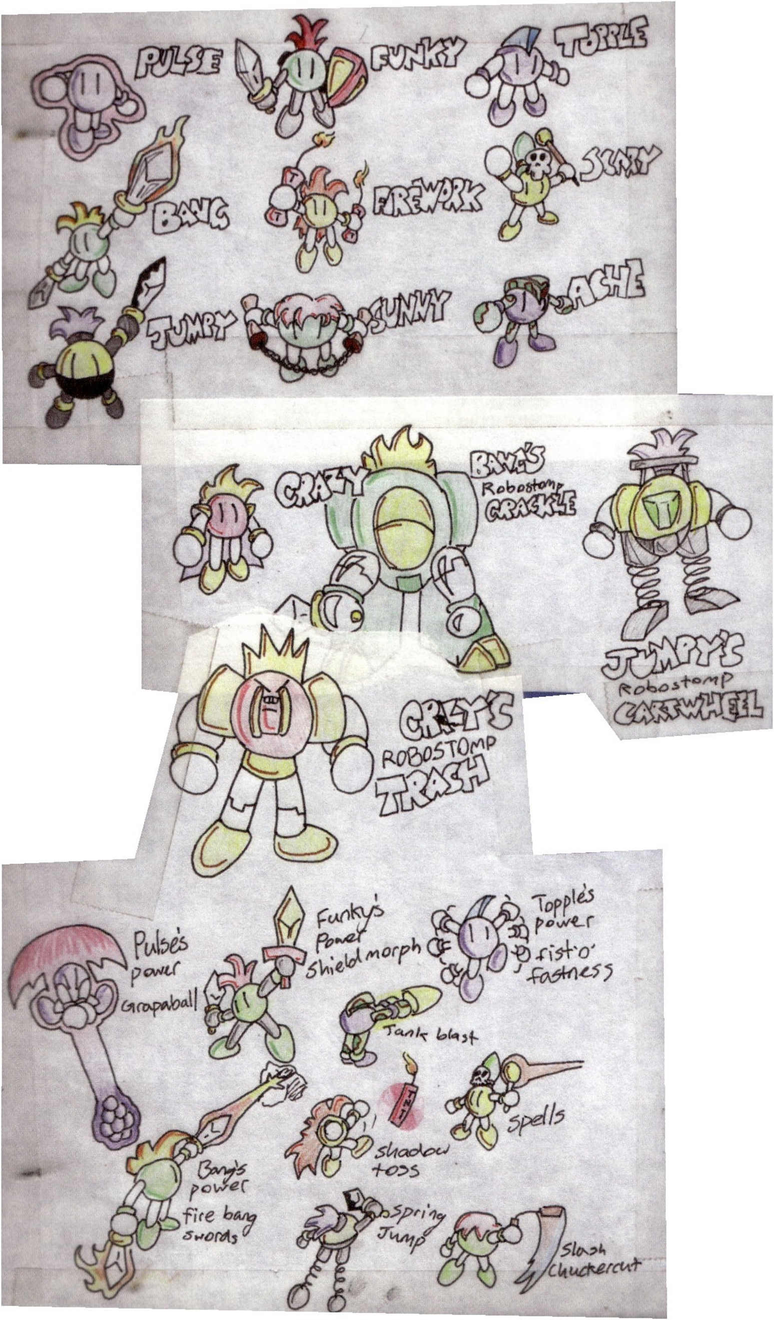
PULSE
FUNKY
TOPPLE
BANG
FIREWORK
SCARY
JUMPY
SUNNY
ACHE
CRAZY
BANG'S Robostomp CRACKLE
JUMPY'S Robostomp CARTWHEEL
CRAZY'S ROBOSTOMP TRASH
Pulse's power Grapaball
Funky's Power Shieldmorph
Topple's power fist'o' fastness
Tank blast
TNT
Spells
shadow toss
Bang's power fire bang swords
Spring Jump
Slash Chuckercut

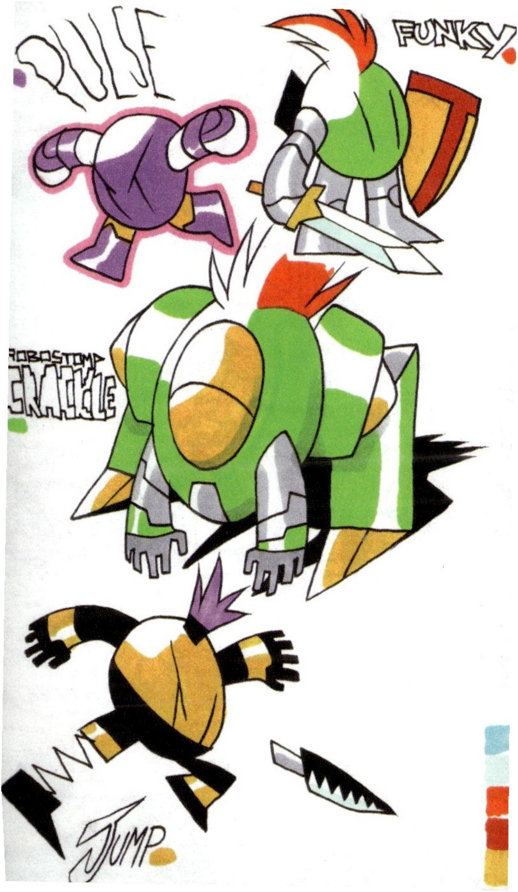
PULSE
FUNKY
ROBOSTOMP
CRACKLE
JUMP

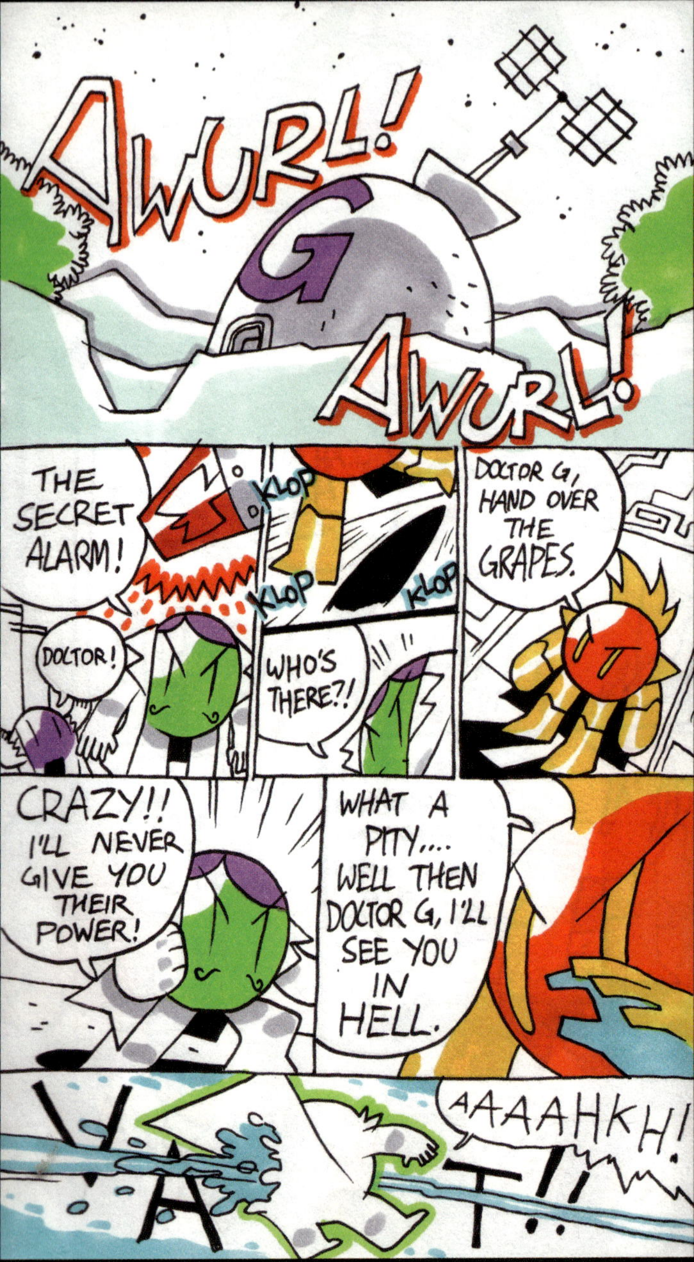
AWURL!
AWURL!
THE SECRET ALARM!
KLOP
KLOP
KLOP
DOCTOR G, HAND OVER THE GRAPES.
DOCTOR!
WHO'S THERE?!
CRAZY!! I'LL NEVER GIVE YOU THEIR POWER!
WHAT A PITY.... WELL THEN DOCTOR G, I'LL SEE YOU IN HELL.
AAAAHKH!
VAT!!

※DR.G DIED IN THIS VERSION

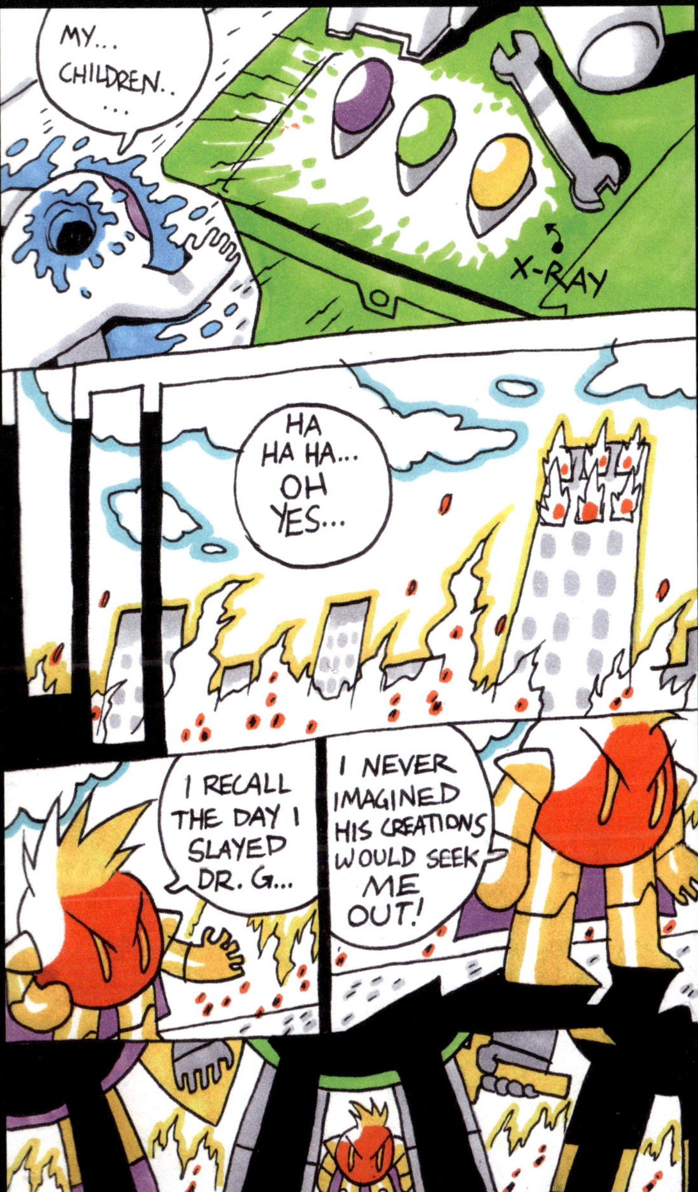
MY... CHILDREN.. ...
X-RAY
HA HA HA... OH YES...
I RECALL THE DAY I SLAYED DR. G...
I NEVER IMAGINED HIS CREATIONS WOULD SEEK ME OUT!

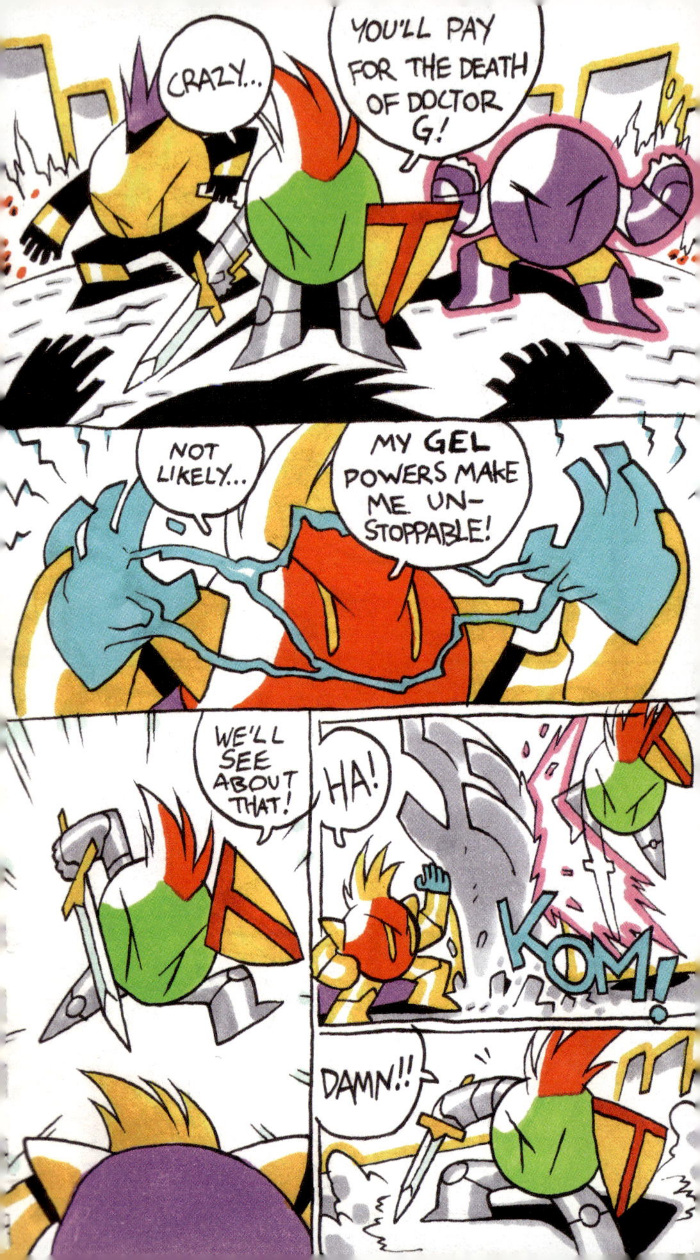
CRAZY...
YOU'LL PAY FOR THE DEATH OF DOCTOR G!
NOT LIKELY...
MY GEL POWERS MAKE ME UN-STOPPABLE!
WE'LL SEE ABOUT THAT!
HA!
KOM!
DAMN!!

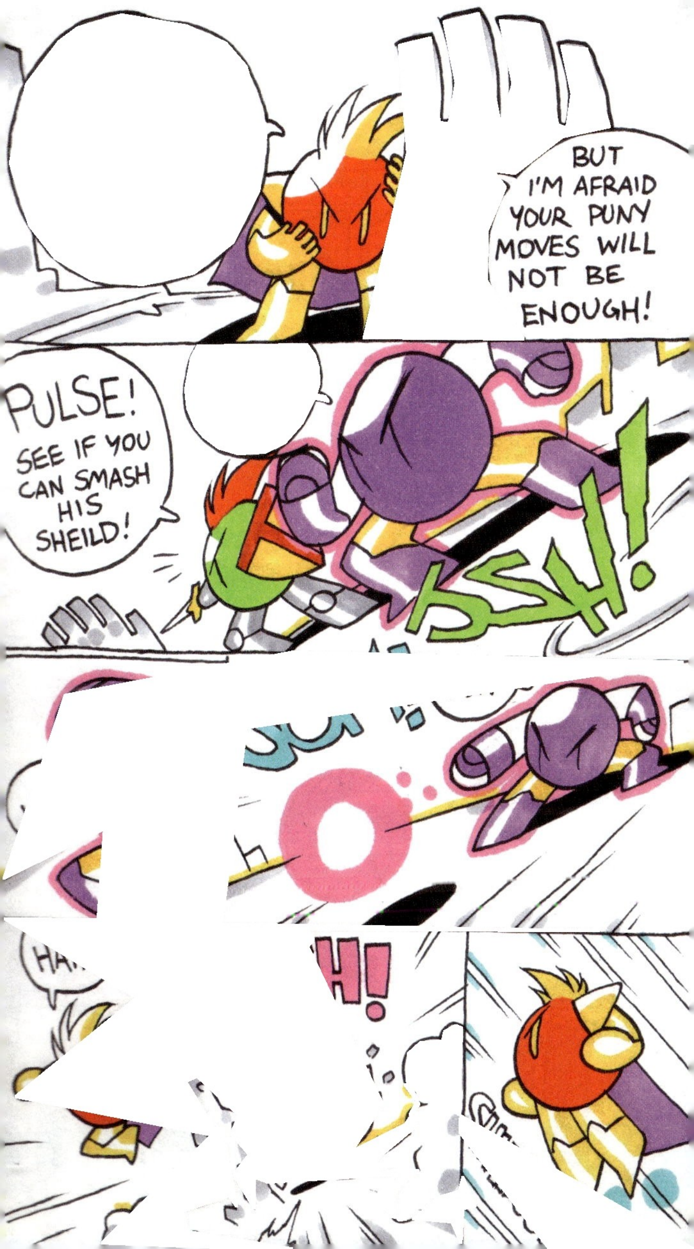

BUT I'M AFRAID YOUR PUNY MOVES WILL NOT BE ENOUGH!
PULSE! SEE IF YOU CAN SMASH HIS SHEILD!
KSSH!

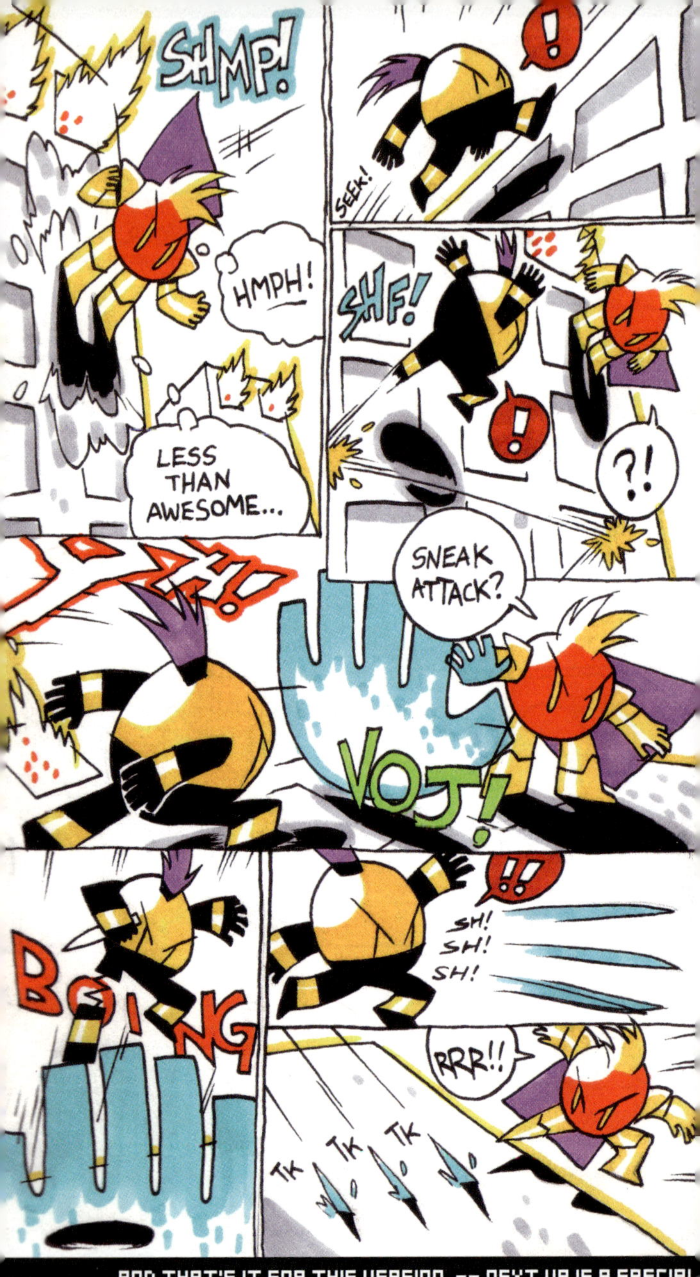
SHMP!
HMPH!
LESS THAN AWESOME...
!
SEEK!
SHF!
!
?!
SNEAK ATTACK?
VOJ!
BOING
!!
SH!
SH!
SH!
RRR!!
TK
TK
TK

AND THAT'S IT FOR THIS VERSION. -- NEXT UP IS A SPECIAL
PINKY G COMIC INVOLVING THE SEEDLESS CHARACTERS!

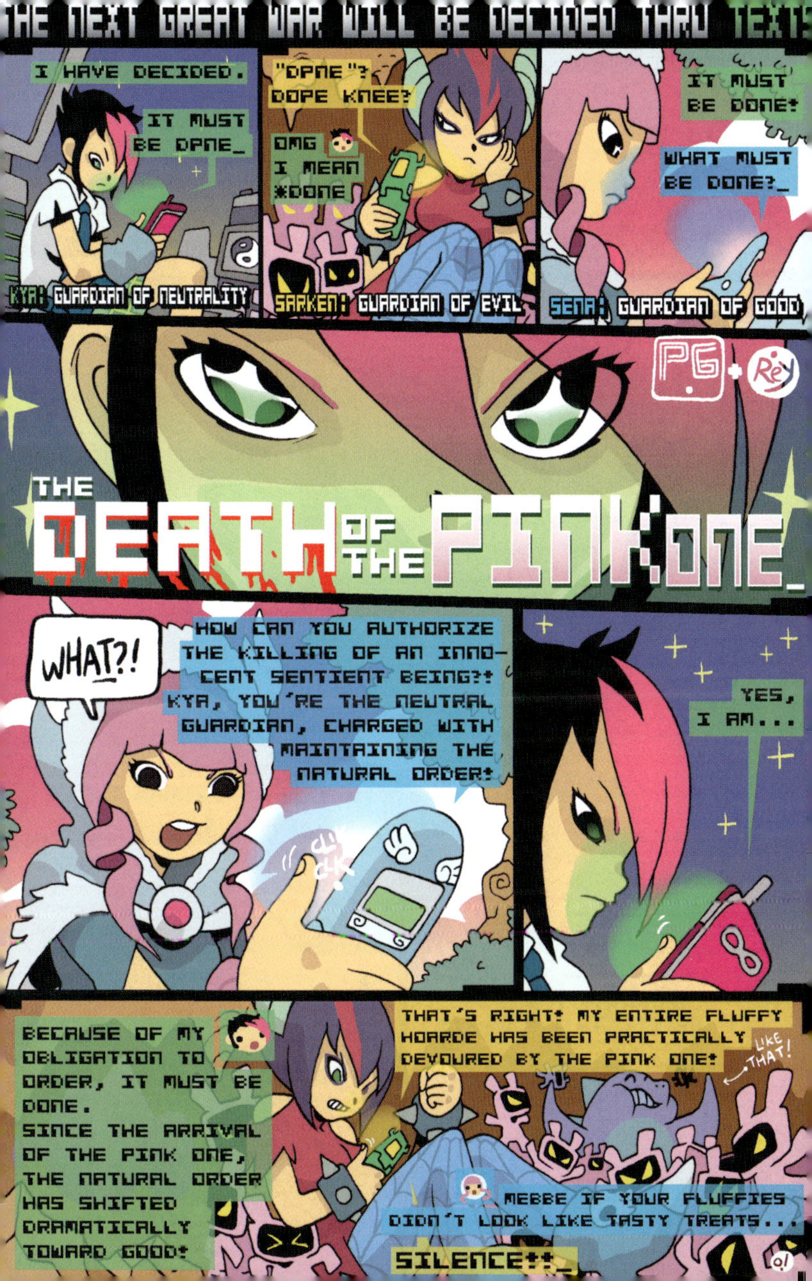
THE NEXT GREAT WAR WILL BE DECIDED THRU TEXTS
I HAVE DECIDED.
IT MUST BE DPNE_
KYA: GUARDIAN OF NEUTRALITY
"DPNE"? DOPE KNEE?
OMG I MEAN *DONE
SARKEN: GUARDIAN OF EVIL
IT MUST BE DONE!
WHAT MUST BE DONE?_
SENA: GUARDIAN OF GOOD
PG + Rey
THE DEATH OF THE PINK ONE_
WHAT?!
HOW CAN YOU AUTHORIZE THE KILLING OF AN INNOCENT SENTIENT BEING?! KYA, YOU'RE THE NEUTRAL GUARDIAN, CHARGED WITH MAINTAINING THE NATURAL ORDER!
YES, I AM...
BECAUSE OF MY OBLIGATION TO ORDER, IT MUST BE DONE.
SINCE THE ARRIVAL OF THE PINK ONE, THE NATURAL ORDER HAS SHIFTED DRAMATICALLY TOWARD GOOD!
THAT'S RIGHT! MY ENTIRE FLUFFY HOARDE HAS BEEN PRACTICALLY DEVOURED BY THE PINK ONE!
LIKE THAT!
MEBBE IF YOUR FLUFFIES DIDN'T LOOK LIKE TASTY TREATS...
SILENCE!!_

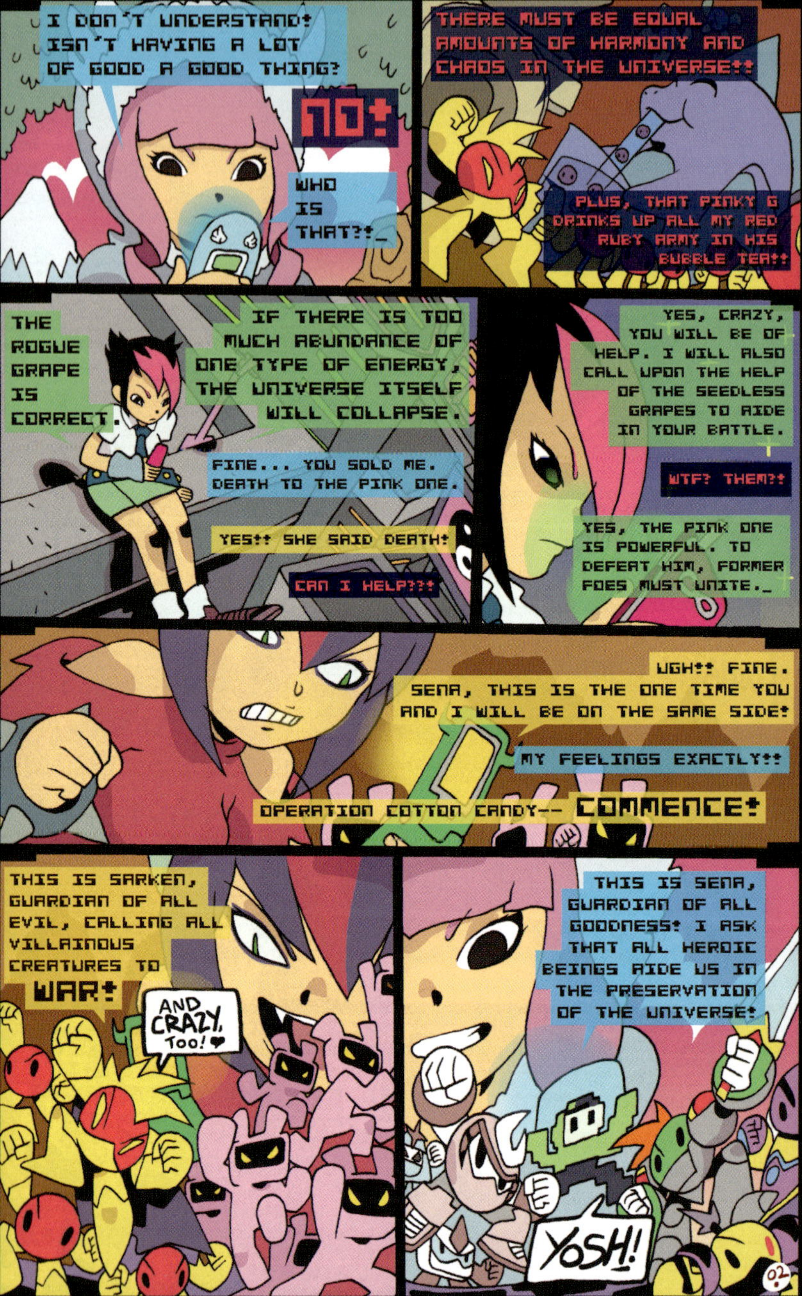

I DON'T UNDERSTAND! ISN'T HAVING A LOT OF GOOD A GOOD THING?
NO!
WHO IS THAT?!_
THERE MUST BE EQUAL AMOUNTS OF HARMONY AND CHAOS IN THE UNIVERSE!!
PLUS, THAT PINKY G DRINKS UP ALL MY RED RUBY ARMY IN HIS BUBBLE TEA!!
THE ROGUE GRAPE IS CORRECT.
IF THERE IS TOO MUCH ABUNDANCE OF ONE TYPE OF ENERGY, THE UNIVERSE ITSELF WILL COLLAPSE.
FINE... YOU SOLD ME. DEATH TO THE PINK ONE.
YES!! SHE SAID DEATH!
CAN I HELP??!
YES, CRAZY, YOU WILL BE OF HELP. I WILL ALSO CALL UPON THE HELP OF THE SEEDLESS GRAPES TO AIDE IN YOUR BATTLE.
WTF? THEM?!
YES, THE PINK ONE IS POWERFUL. TO DEFEAT HIM, FORMER FOES MUST UNITE._
UGH!! FINE. SENA, THIS IS THE ONE TIME YOU AND I WILL BE ON THE SAME SIDE!
MY FEELINGS EXACTLY!!
OPERATION COTTON CANDY-- COMMENCE!
THIS IS SARKEN, GUARDIAN OF ALL EVIL, CALLING ALL VILLAINOUS CREATURES TO WAR!
AND CRAZY, TOO!
THIS IS SENA, GUARDIAN OF ALL GOODNESS! I ASK THAT ALL HEROIC BEINGS AIDE US IN THE PRESERVATION OF THE UNIVERSE!
YOSH!
02

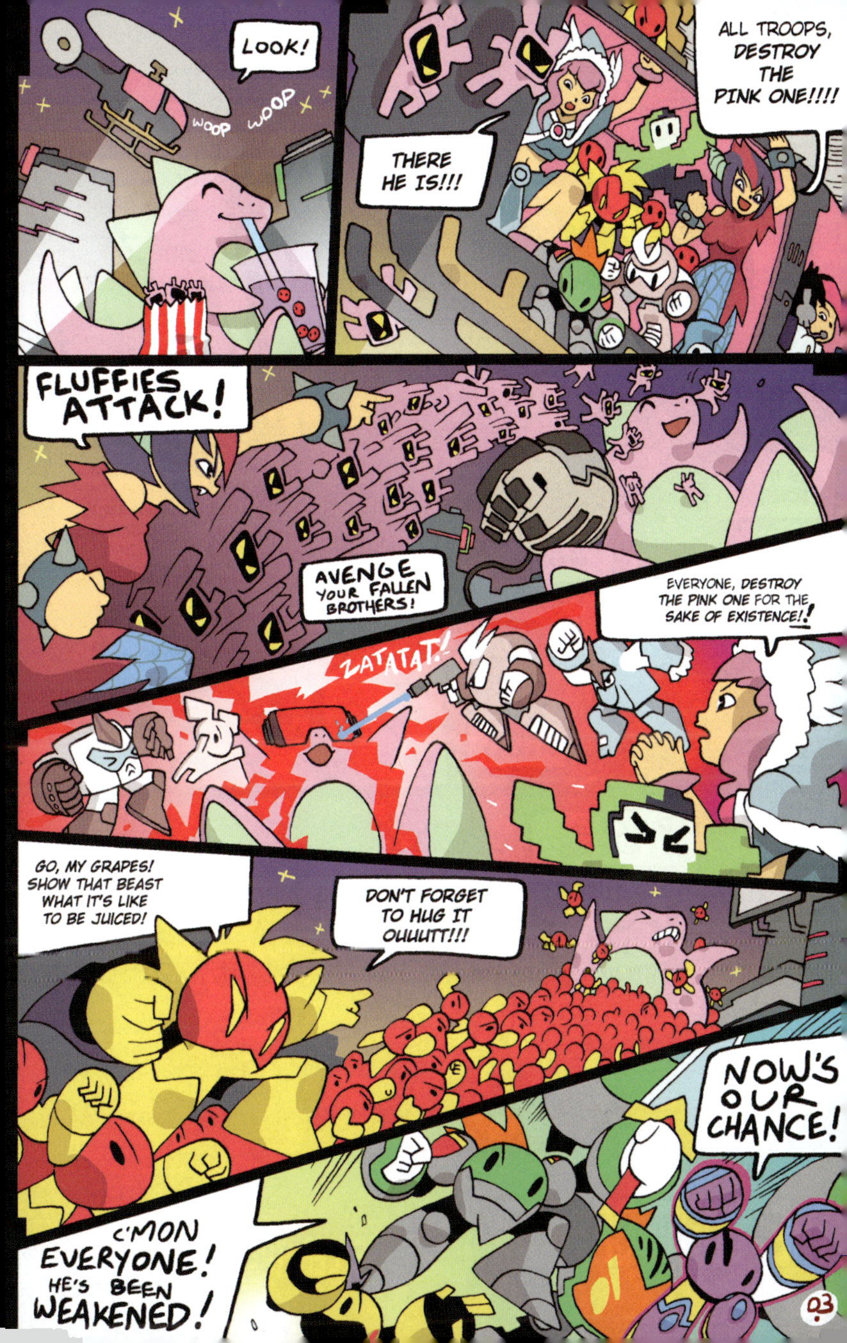
LOOK!
WOOP WOOP
ALL TROOPS, DESTROY THE PINK ONE!!!!
THERE HE IS!!!
FLUFFIES ATTACK!
AVENGE YOUR FALLEN BROTHERS!
EVERYONE, DESTROY THE PINK ONE FOR THE SAKE OF EXISTENCE!!
ZATATAT!
GO, MY GRAPES! SHOW THAT BEAST WHAT IT'S LIKE TO BE JUICED!
DON'T FORGET TO HUG IT OUUUTT!!!
NOW'S OUR CHANCE!
C'MON EVERYONE! HE'S BEEN WEAKENED!

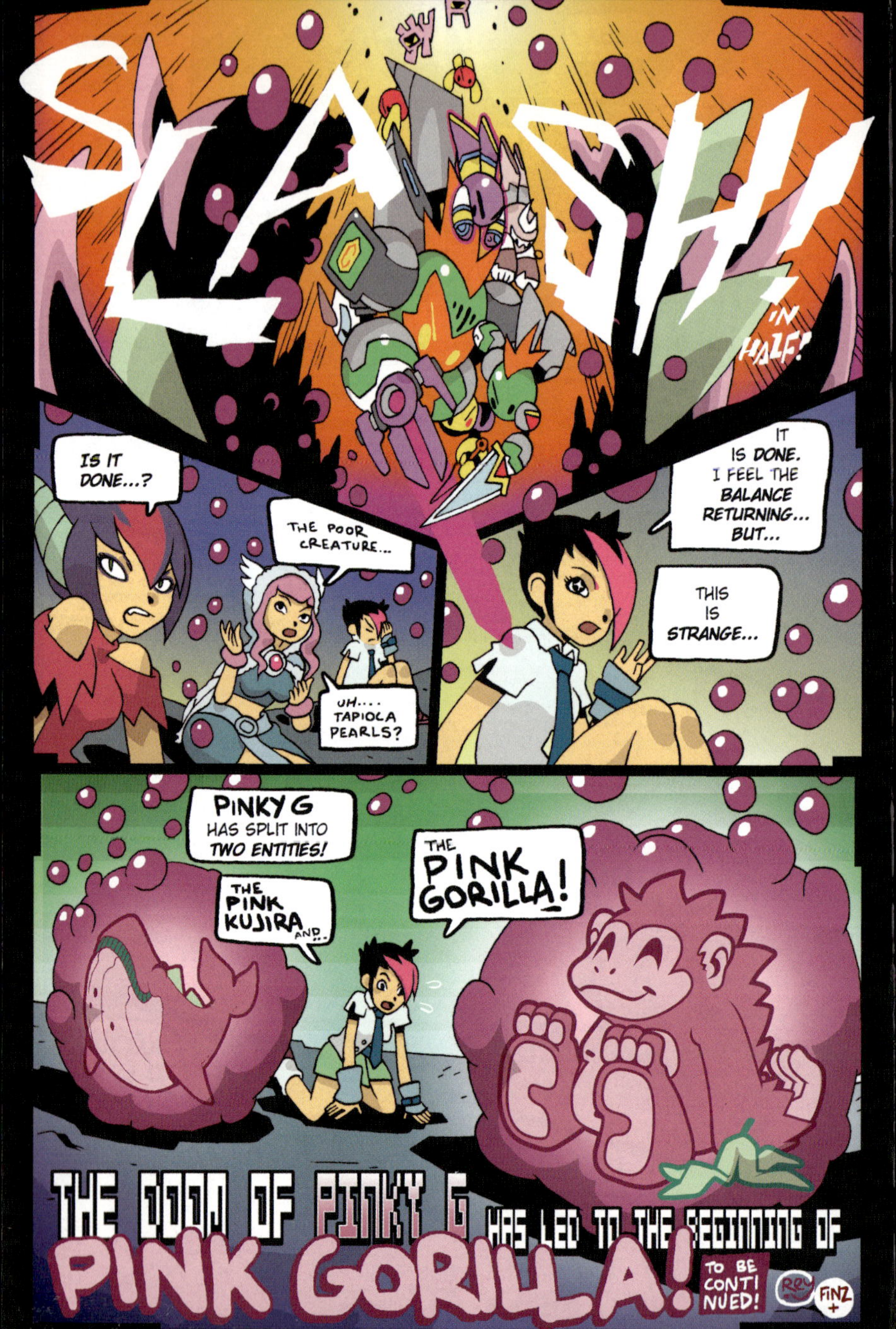

SLASH!
IN HALF!
IS IT DONE...?
THE POOR CREATURE...
UH.... TAPIOCA PEARLS?
IT IS DONE. I FEEL THE BALANCE RETURNING... BUT...
THIS IS STRANGE...
PINKY G HAS SPLIT INTO TWO ENTITIES!
THE PINK KUJIRA AND...
THE PINK GORILLA!
THE DOOM OF PINKY G HAS LED TO THE BEGINNING OF
PINK GORILLA!
TO BE CONTINUED!
FINZ

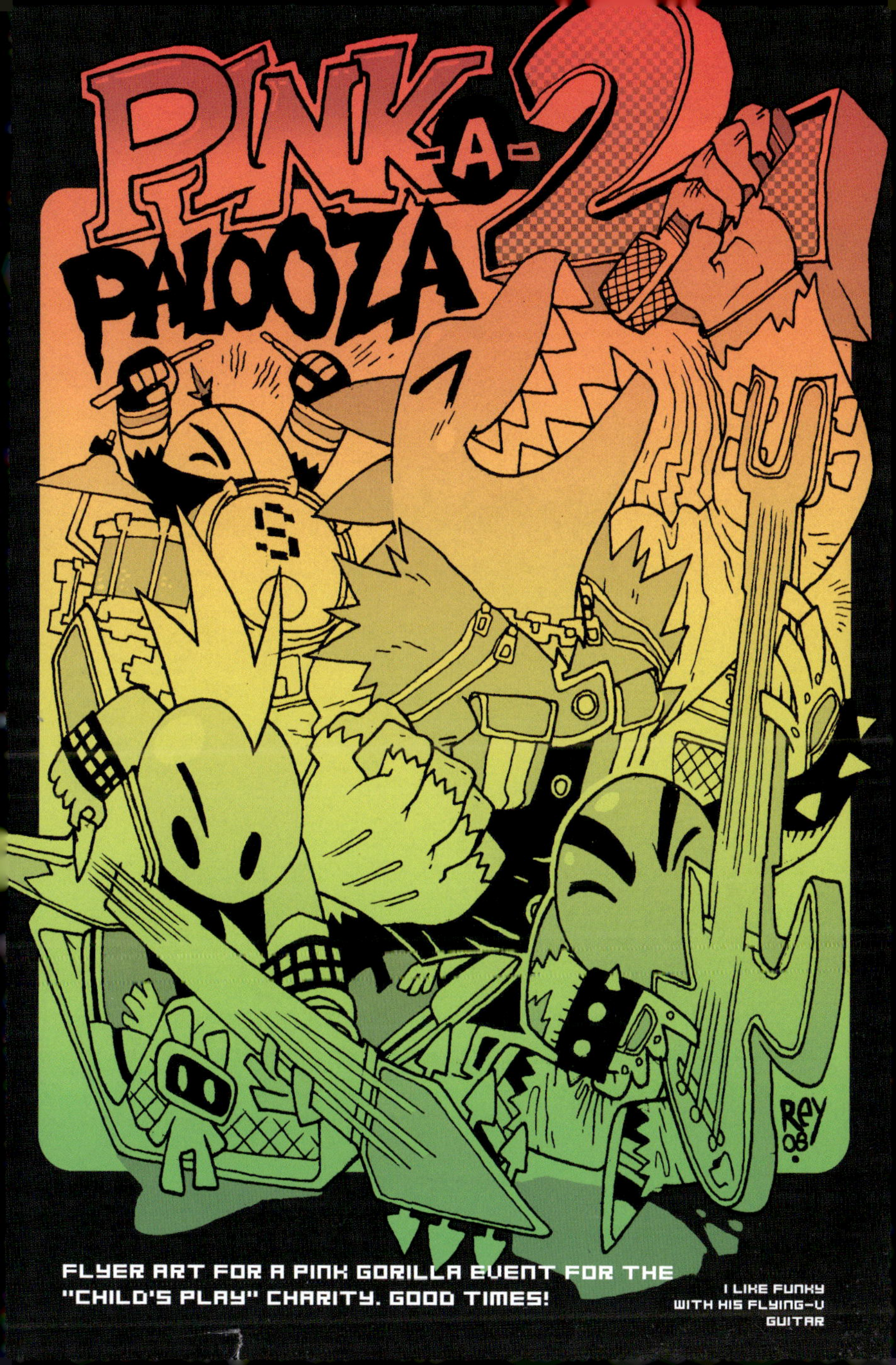
PINK-A-PALOOZA 2
REY 08!

FLYER ART FOR A PINK GORILLA EVENT FOR THE "CHILD'S PLAY" CHARITY. GOOD TIMES!

I LIKE FUNKY WITH HIS FLYING-V GUITAR

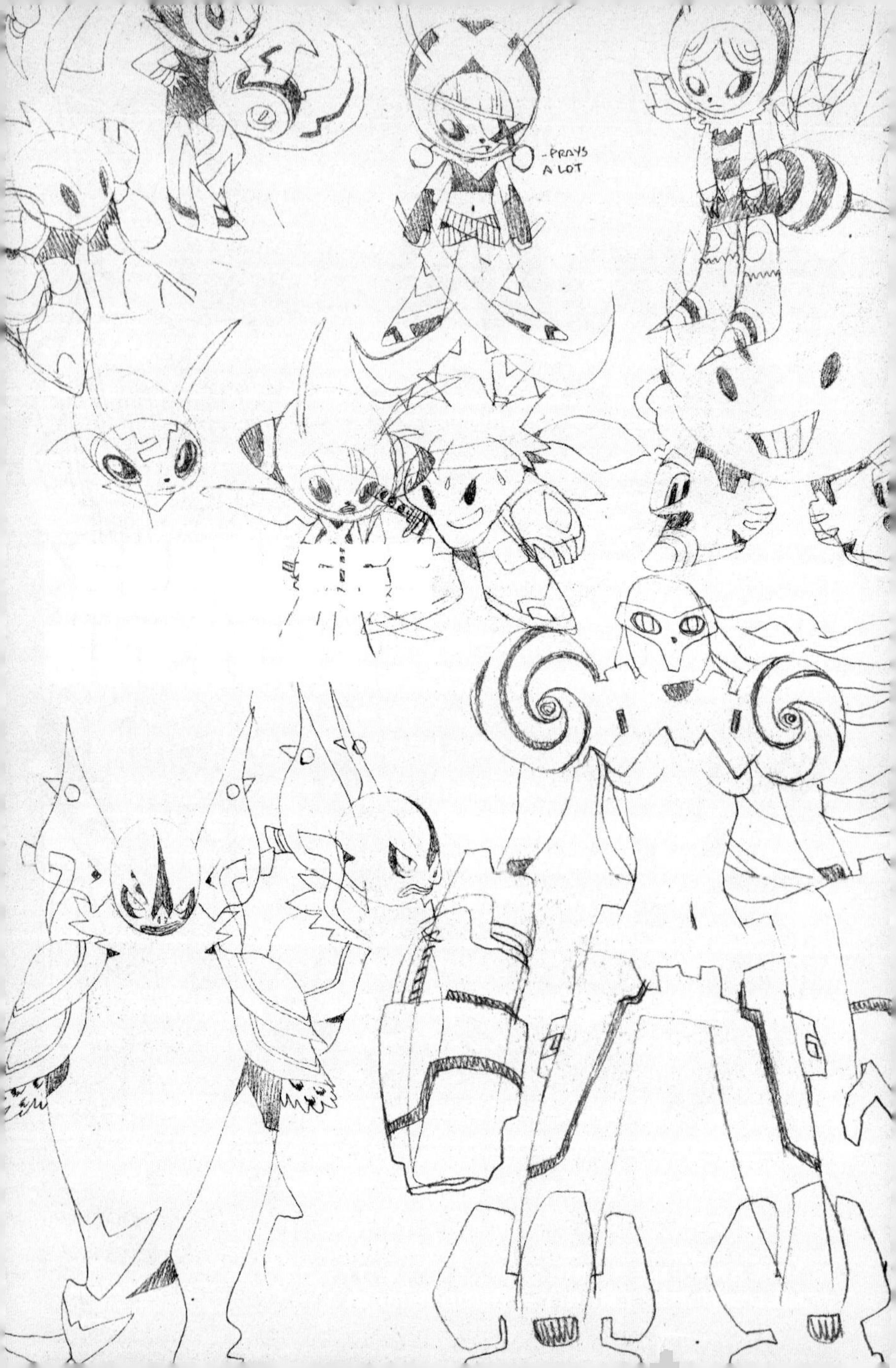

-PRAYS
A LOT

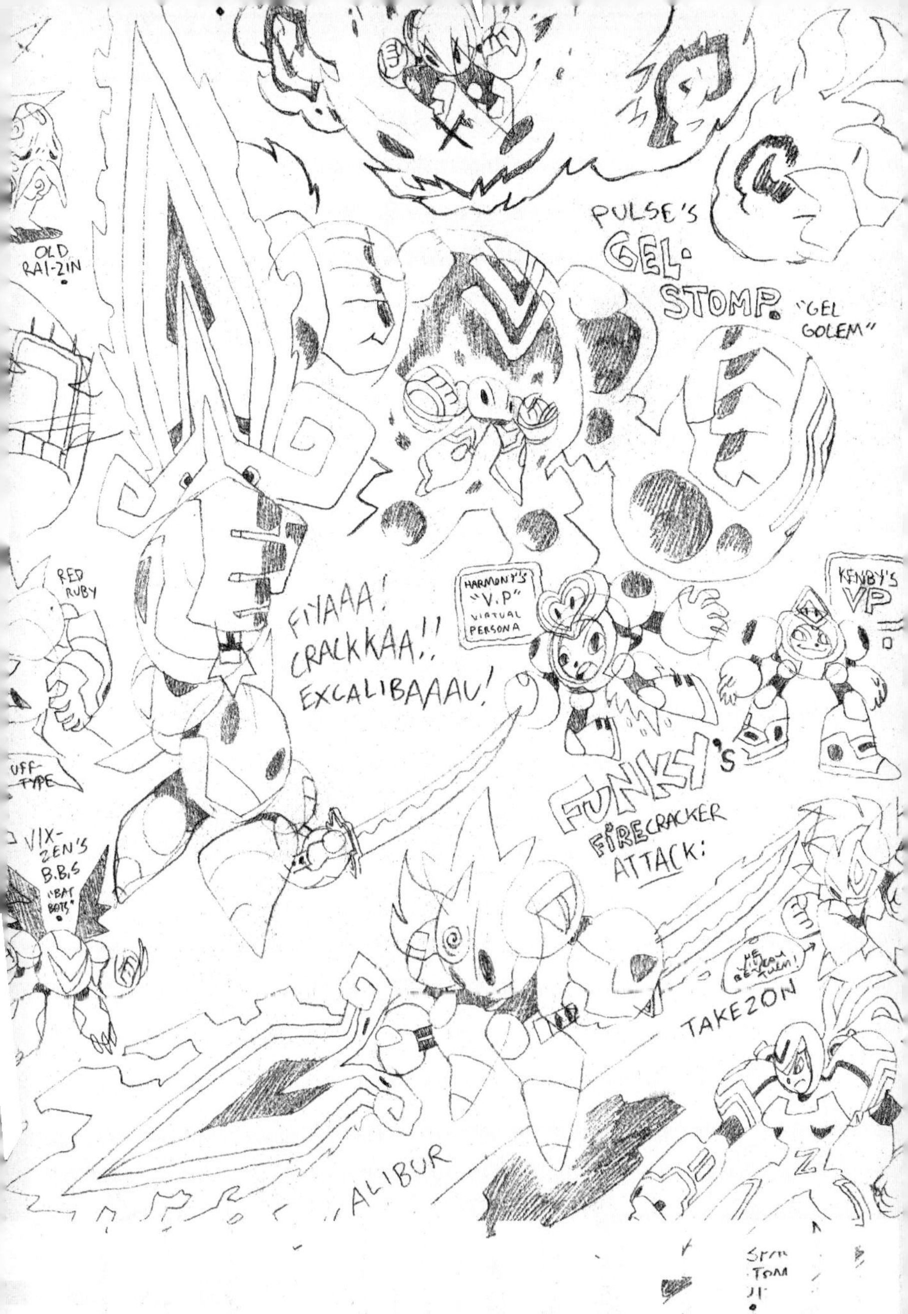
OLD RAI-ZIN
PULSE'S GEL STOMP.
"GEL GOLEM"
RED RUBY
FIYAAA! CRACKKAA!! EXCALIBAAAU!
HARMONY'S "V.P" VIRTUAL PERSONA
KENBY'S VP
UFF-TYPE
FUNKY'S FIRECRACKER ATTACK:
VIX-ZEN'S B.B.'S "BAT BOTS"
TAKEZON
ALIBUR

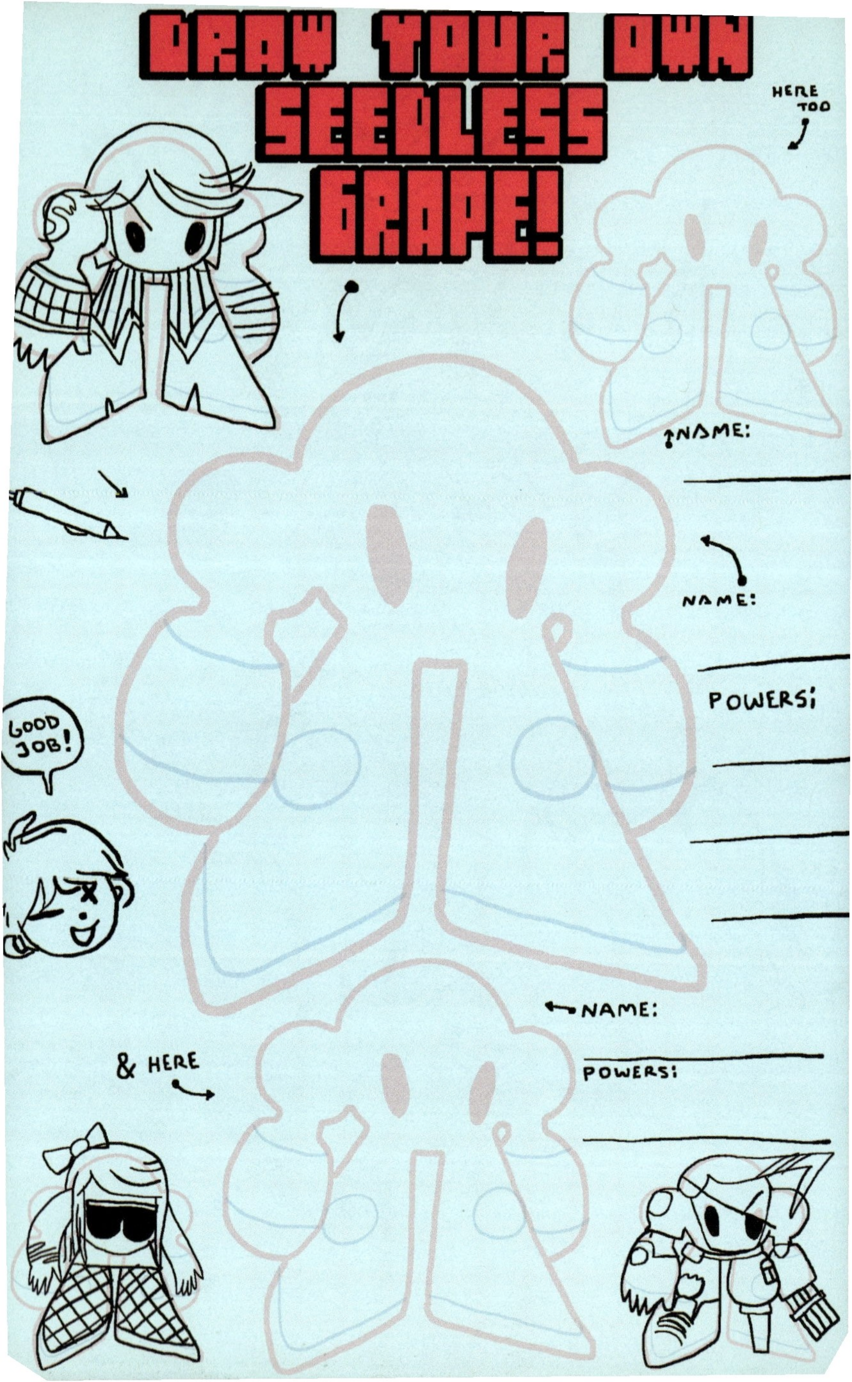
DRAW YOUR OWN SEEDLESS GRAPE!
HERE TOO
NAME:
NAME:
POWERS:
GOOD JOB!
NAME:
& HERE
POWERS:

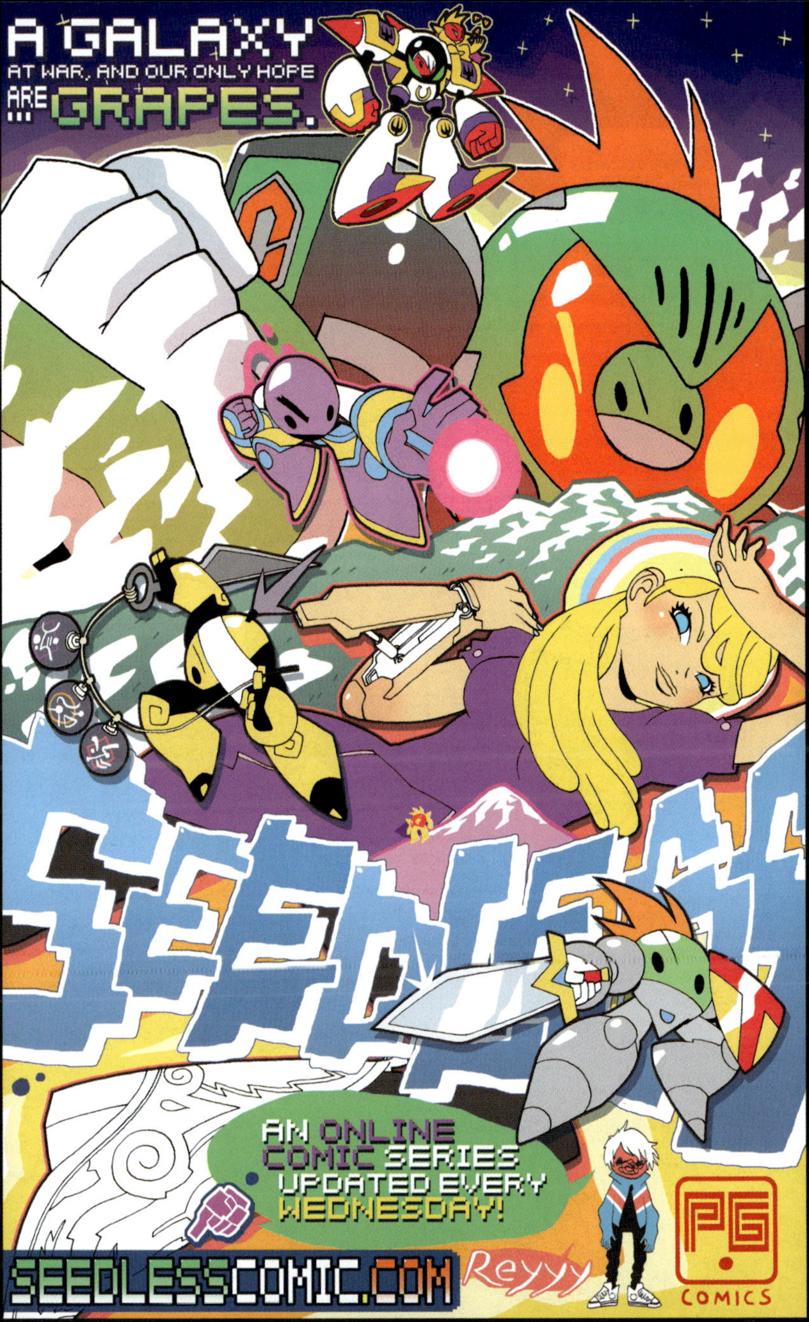
A GALAXY
AT WAR, AND OUR ONLY HOPE
ARE... GRAPES.
AN ONLINE COMIC SERIES UPDATED EVERY WEDNESDAY!
SEEDLESSCOMIC.COM
Reyyy
PG COMICS

PROMO POSTER FOR PENNY-ARCADE EXPO 2009

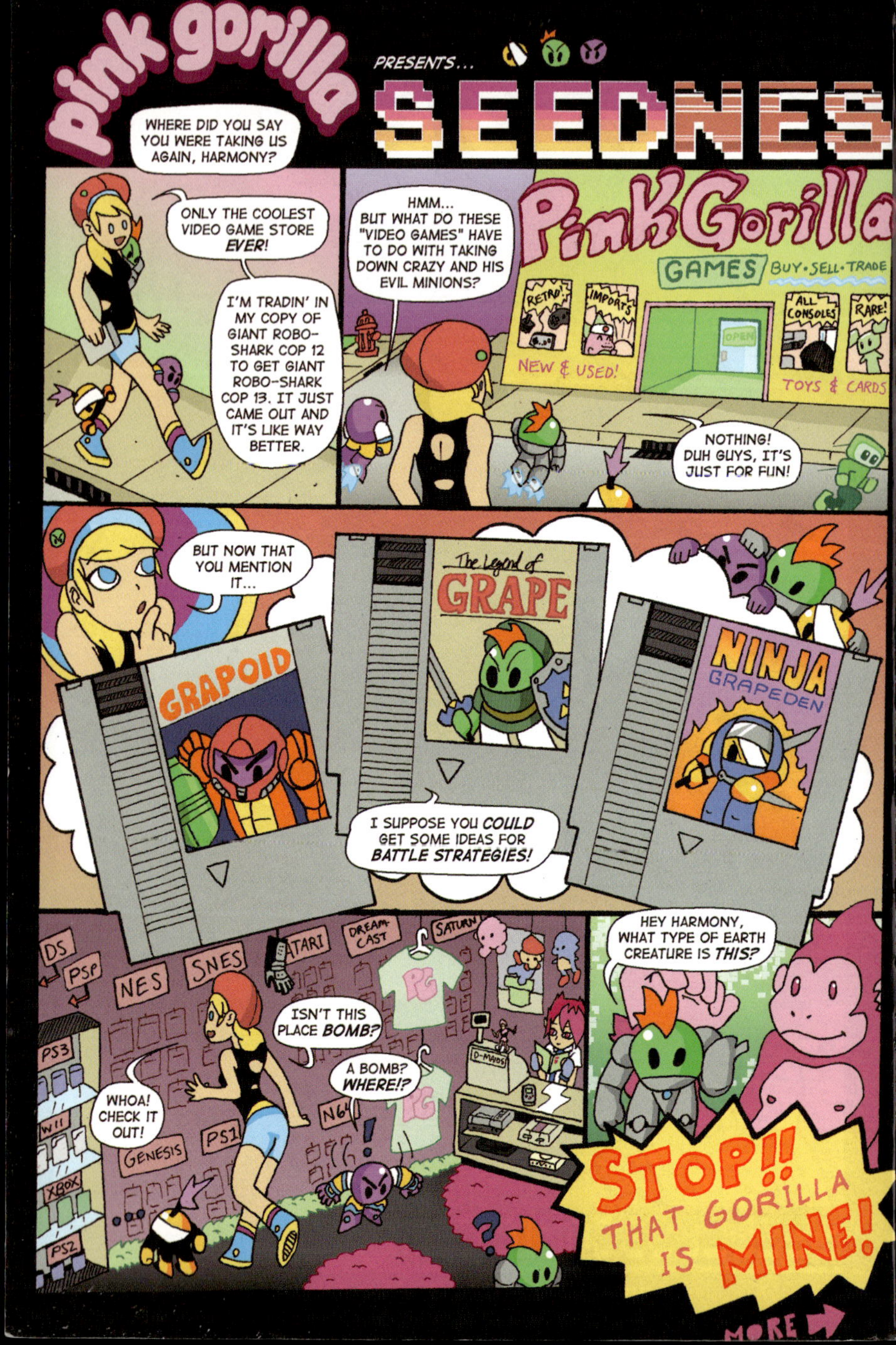

pink gorilla
PRESENTS...
SEEDNES
WHERE DID YOU SAY YOU WERE TAKING US AGAIN, HARMONY?
ONLY THE COOLEST VIDEO GAME STORE EVER!
I'M TRADIN' IN MY COPY OF GIANT ROBO-SHARK COP 12 TO GET GIANT ROBO-SHARK COP 13. IT JUST CAME OUT AND IT'S LIKE WAY BETTER.
HMM... BUT WHAT DO THESE "VIDEO GAMES" HAVE TO DO WITH TAKING DOWN CRAZY AND HIS EVIL MINIONS?
PinkGorilla
GAMES
BUY • SELL • TRADE
RETRO!
IMPORTS
ALL CONSOLES
RARE!
OPEN
NEW & USED!
TOYS & CARDS
NOTHING! DUH GUYS, IT'S JUST FOR FUN!
BUT NOW THAT YOU MENTION IT...
GRAPOID
The Legend of GRAPE
NINJA GRAPEDEN
I SUPPOSE YOU COULD GET SOME IDEAS FOR BATTLE STRATEGIES!
DS
PSP
NES
SNES
ATARI
DREAMCAST
SATURN
PS3
WII
XBOX
PS2
GENESIS
PS1
N64
D-MAIDS
ISN'T THIS PLACE BOMB?
A BOMB? WHERE!?
WHOA! CHECK IT OUT!
HEY HARMONY, WHAT TYPE OF EARTH CREATURE IS THIS?
STOP!! THAT GORILLA IS MINE!
MORE

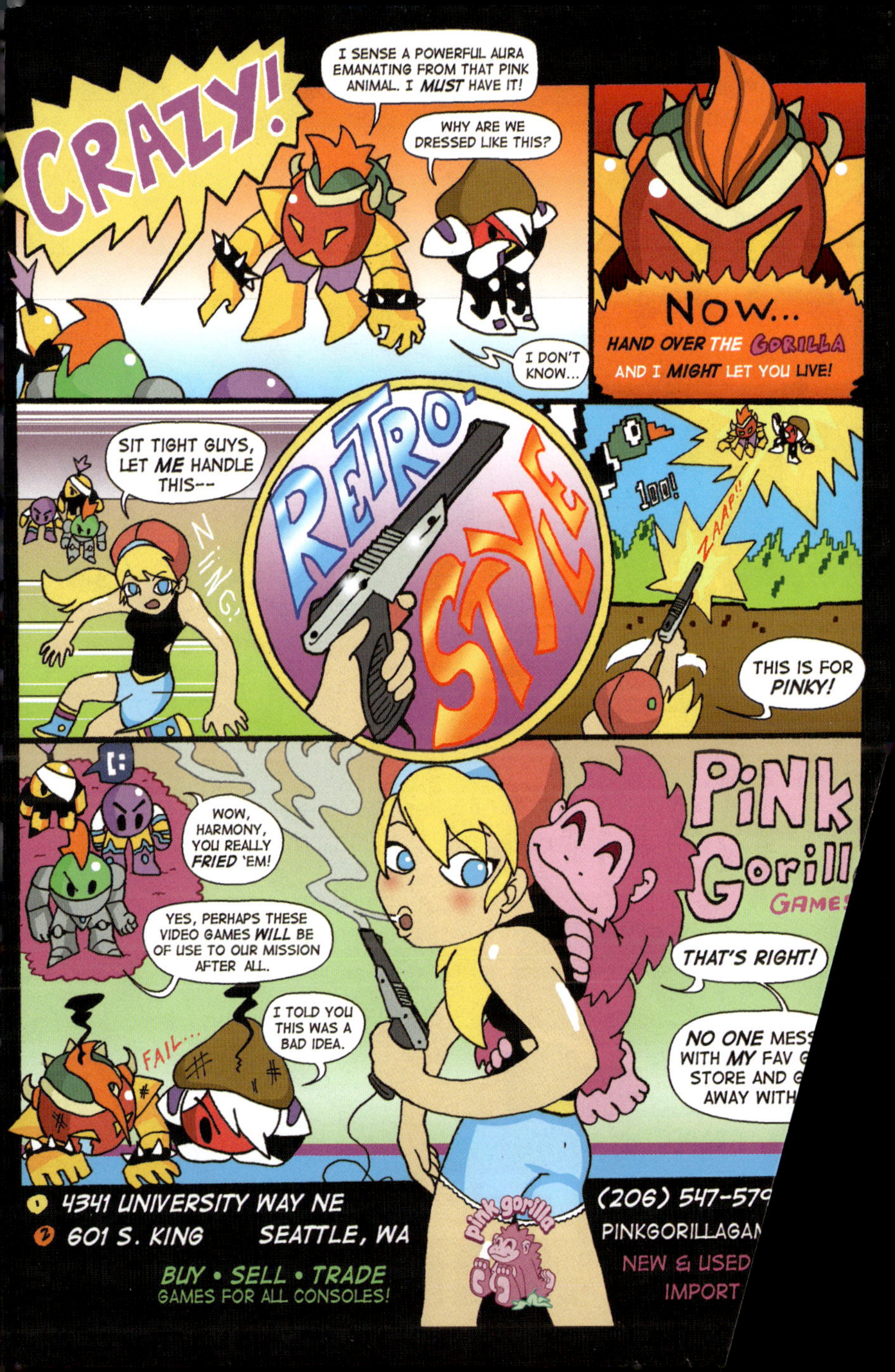

CRAZY!
I SENSE A POWERFUL AURA EMANATING FROM THAT PINK ANIMAL. I MUST HAVE IT!
WHY ARE WE DRESSED LIKE THIS?
I DON'T KNOW...
NOW... HAND OVER THE GORILLA AND I MIGHT LET YOU LIVE!
SIT TIGHT GUYS, LET ME HANDLE THIS--
ZIING!
RETRO STYLE
100!
ZAAP!!
THIS IS FOR PINKY!
WOW, HARMONY, YOU REALLY FRIED 'EM!
YES, PERHAPS THESE VIDEO GAMES WILL BE OF USE TO OUR MISSION AFTER ALL.
I TOLD YOU THIS WAS A BAD IDEA.
FAIL...
Pink Gorill
GAMES
THAT'S RIGHT!
NO ONE MESS
WITH MY FAV G
STORE AND G
AWAY WITH
4341 UNIVERSITY WAY NE
601 S. KING SEATTLE, WA
(206) 547-57
PINKGORILLAGA
BUY • SELL • TRADE
GAMES FOR ALL CONSOLES!
pink gorilla
NEW & USED
IMPORT

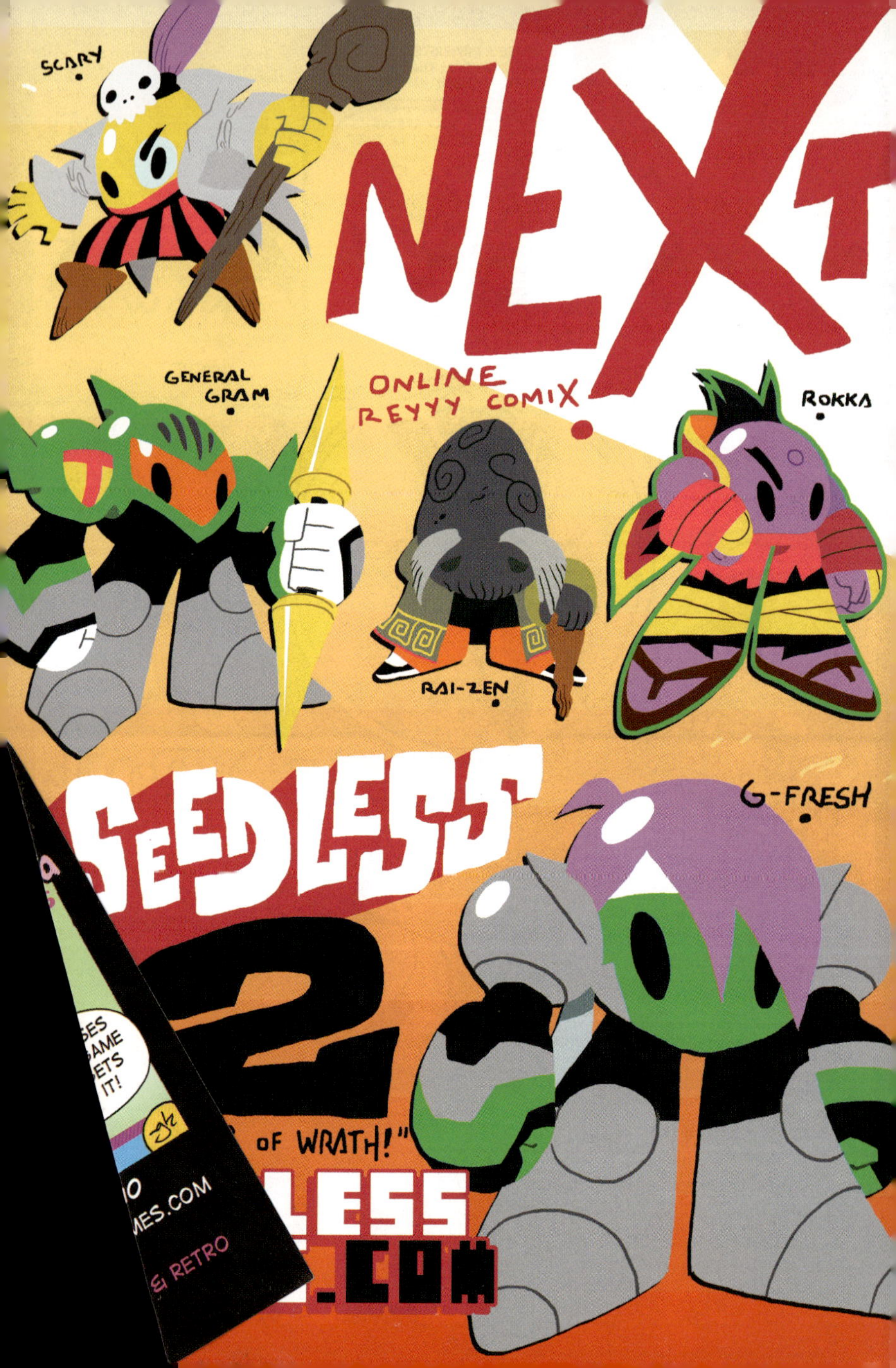
NEXT
SCARY
GENERAL GRAM
ONLINE REYYY COMIX
ROKKA
RAI-ZEN
SEEDLESS 2
G-FRESH
OF WRATH!"
LESS
.COM
SES
GAME
ETS
IT!
IO
MES.COM
& RETRO

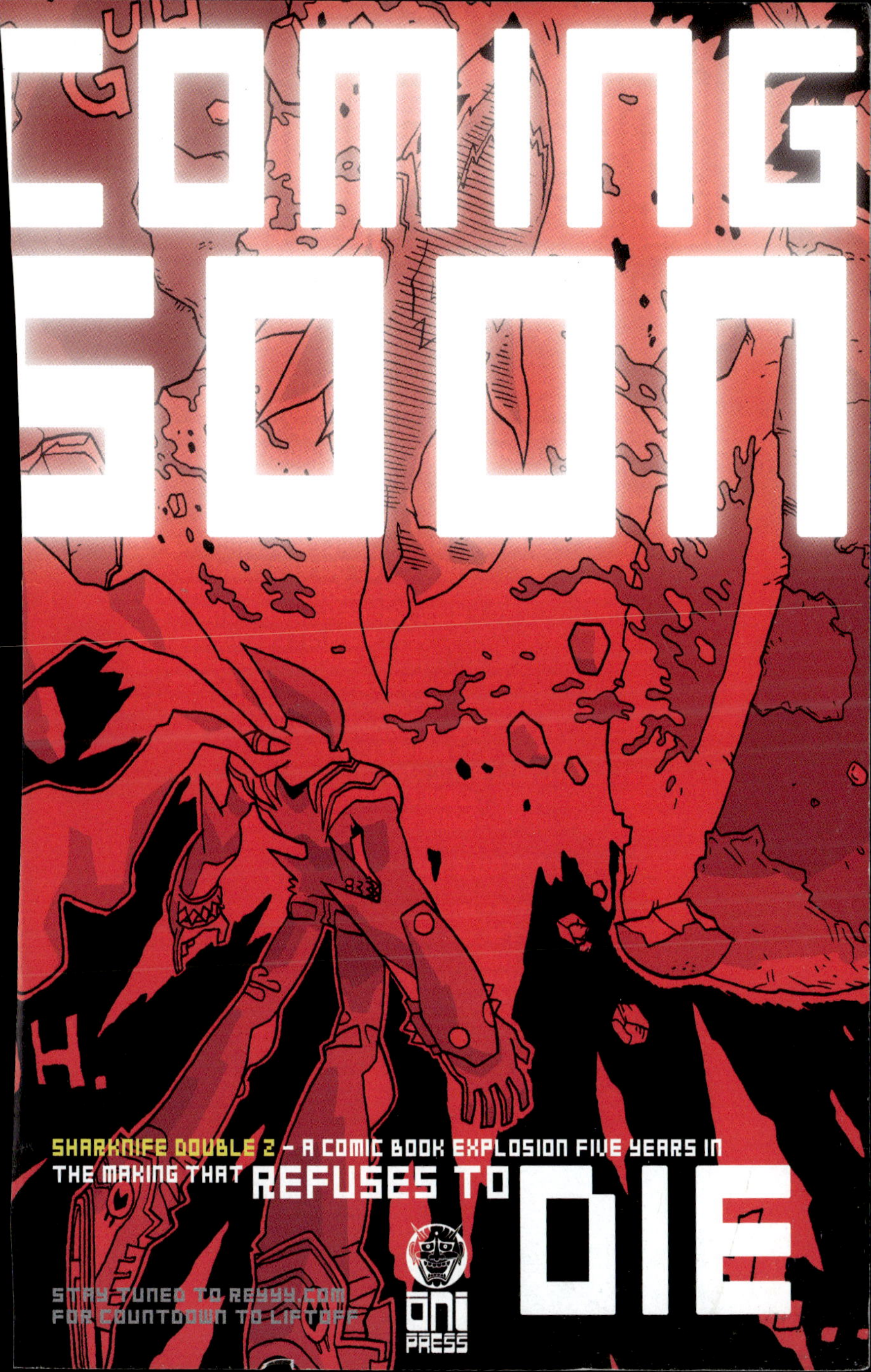
COMING
SOON
SHARKNIFE DOUBLE Z – A COMIC BOOK EXPLOSION FIVE YEARS IN THE MAKING THAT REFUSES TO DIE
STAY TUNED TO REYYY.COM
FOR COUNTDOWN TO LIFTOFF

SEEDLESS

THANK YOU FOR PLAYEING! <3 <3

STORY & ART : COREY S. LEWIS THE REYYY

SPONSORED BY : PINK GORILLA & THE WHOLE PG CREW NATHAN PAINE, GREG HESS, GABE HAYWARD, KRISTJAN PALSSON + THE REST OF THE STAFF & CUSTOMERS (SHOUTOUT TO MY CHINATOWN KIDS)!

CHAPTER BREAK GUEST ARTISTS
+ DYLAN MCCRAE : WWW.DYLANMCCRAE.COM
+ BRANDON GRAHAM : ROYALBOILER.DEVIANTART.COM
+ SHELDON VELLA : 1984CUSTOM.RESPARK.NET
+ MAXIMO V. LORENZO : SPEEDKING.DEVIANTART.COM
+ SHANE HILLMAN : WWW.SHANEHILLMAN.COM
+ JASON "JFISH" FISCHER : WWW.STUDIOJFISH.COM
+ CHRIS "ELIO" ELIOPOULOS : WWW.ELIOHOUSE.COM
+ STEVE ROLSTON : WWW.STEVEROLSTON.COM
+ ASHLEIGH "PYAWAKIT" FIRTH : PYAWAKIT.DEVIANTART.COM
+ LUDROE : N/A (TOO AWESOME FOR WEBSITE)
+ JACOB FERGUSON : WWW.FLOATE.COM
+ DAN CIURKZAC : SOULKARL.DEVIANTART.COM
+ GABE HAYWARD : WWW.CRUNCHYCO.COM
+ BARNABY WARD : WWW.SOMEFIELD.COM

SEEDNES COMIC BY GABE HAYWARD

SPECIAL THANKS : IMAGE COMICS, JOE KEATINGE, ERIC STEPHENSON, TYLER SHAINLINE + VINCENT KUKUA FOR HELPING GET THIS BOOK PUT TOGETHER! MY FRIENDS + FAMILY AND MY FELLOW COMICS WARRIORS.

FOR IMAGE COMICS, INC.

ROBERT KIRKMAN – CHIEF OPERATING OFFICER
ERIK LARSEN – CHIEF FINANCIAL OFFICER
TODD MCFARLANE – PRESIDENT
MARC SILVESTRI – CHIEF EXECUTIVE OFFICER
JIM VALENTINO – VICE-PRESIDENT

ERIC STEPHENSON – PUBLISHER
TODD MARTINEZ – SALES + LICENSING COORDINATOR
BETSY GOMEZ – PR + MARKETING COORDINATOR
BRANWYN BIGGLESTONE – ACCOUNTS MANAGER
SARAH DELAINE – ADMINISTRATIVE ASSISTANT
TYLER SHAINLINE – PRODUCTION MANAGER
DREW GILL – ART DIRECTOR
JONATHAN CHAN – PRODUCTION ARTIST
MONICA HOWARD – PRODUCTION ARTIST
VINCENT KUKUA – PRODUCTION ARTIST
KEVIN YUEN – PRODUCTION ARTIST

WWW.IMAGECOMICS.COM

INTERNATIONAL RIGHTS REPRESENTATIVE – CHRISTINE MEYER (CHRISTINE@GFLOYSTUDIO.COM)